Kaki Warner, 2011 RITA Winner for Best First Book
for *Pieces of Sky*, is
"A truly original new voice in historical fiction."
—Jodi Thomas, *New York Times*
bestselling author

**"Without a doubt, Kaki Warner is a writer to watch,
an author with a promising future. She's definitely
an addition to my must-buy authors list."**
—*All About Romance*

Praise for the Runaway Brides Novels

BRIDE OF THE HIGH COUNTRY

"A smart, resourceful heroine who survives at all costs; a strong, honorable hero who refuses to let her go; and a surfeit of diverse, unforgettable characters combine in a gripping, multilayered story that pulls few punches as it draws readers into the romance and often unvarnished reality of life in nineteenth-century America."
—*Library Journal*

COLORADO DAWN

"Kaki Warner's warm, witty, and lovable characters shine."
—*USA Today*

"Filled with passion, adventure, heartbreak, and humor."
—*The Romance Dish*

"Romance fans will love Kaki Warner's latest book!"
—*Fresh Fiction*

"These runaway brides aren't your typical women, and the men who fall in love with them are just as unique." —*Night Owl Reviews*

continued . . .

"[A] sweet nineteenth-century Western . . . Fans of the series will enjoy another visit to the Wilkins clan, while new readers are sure to admire Warner's vivid descriptions of love and life in the land of enchantment." —*Publishers Weekly*

OPEN COUNTRY

"A thoroughly enjoyable historical romance."
—*Night Owl Reviews* (Top Pick)

"Vivid imagery . . . [A] beautifully spun tale that will leave readers satisfied, yet yearning for Jack's story."
—*The Season* (Top Pick)

"Warner earned readers' respect as a strong Western writer with her debut, the first book in the Blood Rose Trilogy. With the second, she cements that reputation. Her powerful prose, realistic details, and memorable characters all add up to a compelling, emotionally intense read." —*RT Book Reviews*

PIECES OF SKY

"Readers may need a big box of Kleenex while reading this emotionally compelling, subtly nuanced tale of revenge, redemption, and romance, but this flawlessly written book is worth every tear." —*Chicago Tribune*

"Romance, passion, and thrilling adventure fill the pages of this unforgettable saga that sweeps the reader from England to the Old West. Jessy and Brady are truly lovers for the ages!"
—Rosemary Rogers, bestselling author of *Bride for a Night*

"*Pieces of Sky* reminds us why New Mexico is called the land of enchantment."
—Jodi Thomas, *New York Times* bestselling author of *Chance of a Lifetime*

"Generates enough heat to light the old New Mexico sky. A sharp, sweet love story of two opposites, a beautifully observed setting, and voilà—a romance you won't soon forget."
—Sara Donati, author of *The Endless Forest*

Berkley Sensation titles by Kaki Warner

Runaway Brides Novels

HEARTBREAK CREEK
COLORADO DAWN
BRIDE OF THE HIGH COUNTRY

Blood Rose Trilogy

PIECES OF SKY
OPEN COUNTRY
CHASING THE SUN

Bride of the High Country

Kaki Warner

BERKLEY SENSATION, NEW YORK

THE BERKLEY PUBLISHING GROUP
Published by the Penguin Group
Penguin Group (USA) Inc.
375 Hudson Street, New York, New York 10014, USA

USA / Canada / UK / Ireland / Australia / New Zealand / India / South Africa / China

Penguin Books Ltd., Registered Offices: 80 Strand, London WC2R 0RL, England
For more information about the Penguin Group, visit penguin.com.

BRIDE OF THE HIGH COUNTRY

A Berkley Sensation Book / published by arrangement with the author

Berkley Sensation Books are published by The Berkley Publishing Group.
BERKLEY® SENSATION is a registered trademark of Penguin Group (USA) Inc.
The "B" design is a trademark of Penguin Group (USA) Inc.

For information, address: The Berkley Publishing Group,
a division of Penguin Group (USA) Inc.,
375 Hudson Street, New York, New York 10014.

ISBN: 978-0-425-25502-5

PUBLISHING HISTORY
Berkley Sensation trade paperback edition / June 2012
Berkley Sensation mass-market paperback edition / March 2013

PRINTED IN THE UNITED STATES OF AMERICA

10 9 8 7 6 5 4 3 2 1

Cover art by Judy York.
Cover design by Lesley Worrell.
Interior text design by Tiffany Estreicher.

ALWAYS LEARNING   PEARSON

For Joe:
Now and always,
I love you.
—K

Prologue

The first fire wagon raced past Father O'Rourke as he turned onto Mulberry Bend in the wretched Irish district of Five Points. Within minutes, two more rattled by, the horses blowing steam into the chill evening air, the men on the sirens and bells pumping furiously. Quickening his pace, the priest continued toward the reddish glow ahead that was partially obscured by swirls of dark, oily smoke.

The street became more crowded as ragged people came out of the dilapidated tenements, their faces drawn with worry. Father O'Rourke understood the hopeless, helpless fear in their eyes. He had felt it, himself, and had seen it too often over the years in the faces of his fellow countrymen as they had filed off the disease-ridden ships by the tens of thousands only to find the conditions awaiting them in these tenements were as bad as those they had left behind in famine-stricken Ireland.

As he drew closer to the burning structure, Father O'Rourke recognized it as Mrs. Beale's, the building he sought and a well-known brothel that catered to the basest tastes of a dissolute clientele. For the last month, ever since he had heard of the auction of prostitutes, some of whom were still children, he had been on a one-man crusade to have it shut down. Having failed in that, he had come tonight in hopes of appealing to the buyers. Apparently, that wouldn't be necessary now.

Angling through gawking onlookers, he worked his way

toward a fireman shouting orders through a long brass speaking trumpet. Raising his voice over the roar of the fire and the clang of fire bells, he shouted, "Can I help? Is anyone hurt? Did everyone get out?"

"Not sure," the man shouted back. "All we know for certain is it started on one of the upper floors."

In a sudden blast of heat and exploding windows, the roof caved in. Pandemonium broke out as shrieking people fled the shower of shattered glass and flaming timbers, taking Father O'Rourke along with them. It was several doors down before he could escape the shoving throng by ducking into a side alley where a girl stood staring intently at the flaming building.

She was a wee, fragile thing and couldn't have been more than ten or twelve years old. Smudged and dirty, her blond hair falling loose down her thin back, her skimpy dress so sheer her thin legs and naked buttocks showed clearly through the pale muslin. She was shivering so hard he could hear the chatter of her teeth from several feet away.

But even more bizarre was her face. A child's face, but marked with kohl and rouge and lip paint until she looked like a player on a stage—or a depraved man's plaything.

"Child." When the girl didn't respond, O'Rourke reached out and touched her thin shoulder.

With a cry of terror, the girl whirled away. She would have escaped if O'Rourke hadn't been expecting it. Scooping her up, he pinned her flailing body against his chest. She was all bones and flying hair, and she smelled of overly sweet perfume and smoke and kerosene.

"'Tis all right, lass," he murmured over and over into her ear. "You're safe with me. Sure, and I'm a priest and I've come to help you, so I have."

It was several moments before the girl stopped fighting him, more out of exhaustion and defeat than trust. "Can I put you down now, lass? You'll not run away from me?"

The girl didn't answer. But she didn't tense up for another fight, so O'Rourke gently set her back down on her bare feet. Taking off his coat, he draped it over her, then keeping his hands on her shoulders, knelt and looked into her painted face.

No tears. No fear. Nothing. As empty as a battered china doll with a blank, glassy stare.

"I'm Father O'Rourke. Who might you be?"

She didn't answer and continued to stare fixedly past him. He didn't need to turn to see what had captured her attention. The flames were reflected in her sad green eyes, and the distant roar of the flames continued.

"Were you at Mrs. Beale's?"

No response.

"What is your name, child?"

No response.

"Are you hurt, lassie?"

She didn't answer, but he saw her hands flatten against her thin gown. Red hands, with blisters showing on the small fingers. The smell of kerosene wafted up to him again, and a terrible thought arose—one he didn't want to pursue. All that was important right now was getting her away from this place. Finding a safe haven for her. Someplace where she could be a child again.

"Can I wipe that paint off your face?"

No response.

He took out his handkerchief and moistening one corner with spit, began wiping her face. Mostly it smeared, but at least now she just looked dirty rather than whorish. After cleaning her as best he could, he put the kerchief away.

She still hadn't moved or spoken.

"Do you have parents nearby?"

Silence.

"You're an orphan?" There were thousands of them. The conditions here in Five Points were so deplorable most adults didn't last six years. For children it was even worse. Without God's intervention, this one wouldn't have lasted another month.

"Cathleen." It was the merest whisper, barely heard over the shouts of firefighters down the street. Spoken less to him, he suspected, than to herself.

"Your name is Cathleen? Cathleen Donovan?" He had heard of the girl—the wee blond star of tonight's auction. Her body, her sanity, probably even her soul were up for sale to the highest bidder. He closed his eyes against sudden nausea and gave silent thanks to God for sparing this poor, lost child.

He wasn't sure what to do with her. The shelter where he

ministered to the starving and sick would be the first place Mrs. Beale's British henchman, Smythe, would look—assuming he had escaped the fire. The orphanages were little more than workhouses. Then he remembered a man who owed him a debt from years ago, when Father O'Rourke had pulled him from the gutter where footpads had left him to die. The man—a judge—was dead now, but perhaps his widow would find a place in her home for this lost child. He had no other option.

He rose, and letting go of her shoulders, he held out his hand. "Come, Cathleen. Let's leave this place."

The girl finally looked away from the burning building and up at him. Her smudged eyes carried more pain than any child's should. "Am I going to hell, then, Father?"

O'Rourke forced a smile. "No, child. You're leaving it."

One

It had been written and talked about for weeks.

"A fairy-tale romance," the gossip columns called it. "Doyle Kerrigan, dashing railroad mogul, brought to bended knee by Margaret Hamilton, ward of Ida Throckmorton, widow of the late Judge Harold Throckmorton."

Margaret supposed there was a certain make-believe quality to their whirlwind courtship—the penniless nobody plucked from obscurity and thrust into the world of opulence. Who would have guessed that an Irish orphan from Five Points would someday be mistress of a home as grand as Doyle's new townhouse in the most fashionable area of New York?

Hopefully, no one. The only way to protect herself was to ensure that no one ever found out about her Irish immigrant roots. Especially her fiancé. It was a betrayal on every level—not just of Doyle Kerrigan, but of her homeland, her parents, and especially little Cathleen Donovan. But she would do it. She would do anything to stay alive. She had already proven that.

Margaret studied her reflection in the cheval mirror in her third-floor bedroom at Mrs. Throckmorton's Sixty-ninth Street brownstone.

The lilac silk gown Doyle had chosen brought out the green of her eyes. The diamond and amethyst necklace he had given her shimmered against her skin. More gems glittered in the pins securing her blond upsweep. Everything was the finest. Proof of

Doyle's success. At the engagement ball tonight in his lavish new home, when he introduced his unknown but well-connected fiancée to Manhattan's elite, he would be proclaiming to the world that he had reached the highest level of society that money could buy. And she would finally be safe.

A triumph for the Irish in both of them.

Then why did she feel such a sense of loss?

Irritated that she had let her happy mood slip away, and having almost forty minutes to spare before Doyle came to pick her up, Margaret moved restlessly about the room, finally coming to a stop at the tall window that overlooked the street three floors below.

The day was fading. Smoke from thousands of coal stoves hung in sluggish layers in the still air, adding bands of deeper gray to the overcast sky. The distant oasis of the still-unfinished Central Park project seemed less green, as if painted with a muddied brush, and even the sheep dotting the Sheep Meadow looked dingy. She scarcely remembered what stars looked like.

"So you're going through with it," a querulous voice said from the doorway.

Bracing herself for another argument, Margaret turned with a smile. "Yes, ma'am, I am. And you shouldn't be climbing those stairs on your own. I was just about to come down to you."

With the hand not gripping the ivory handle of her cane, Mrs. Throckmorton impatiently waved aside the notion that she would need help. "He's a ruffian and a thug. Do you know the kind of people who will be there tonight?"

Margaret waited, knowing the question didn't require an answer.

"Jay Gould, that's who. And Jim Fisk, and even that Tweed fellow from Tammany Hall. Crooks, all. The judge would never have countenanced an association with such disreputable types. My word, they're Democrats!"

Margaret knew that despite the criticisms, her guardian had only her best interests at heart. But Mrs. Throckmorton would never understand Margaret's driving need for the security this marriage would provide. How could she?

Having been insulated by wealth all of her life, Mrs. Throckmorton had little knowledge of the squalor that prevailed in the Irish tenements of the sixth ward. She could never have imagined the kind of depravity that went on behind the closed doors of the house on Mulberry Bend. Yet when Father O'Rourke had appeared on her doorstep fifteen years ago with a frightened, twelve-year-old Irish orphan, Ida Throckmorton had honored her late husband's debt and taken her in.

But the benign tyrant of this staid brownstone on Sixty-ninth Street had her rules, so she did—the foremost being no Irish tolerated.

From that moment on, Cathleen Donovan had ceased to exist. Margaret Hamilton had taken her place—a distant relative of some twice-removed cousin of the late judge. She had been fed, clothed, and patiently tutored in academics and deportment and elocution until all her rough edges had been buffed away and she was able to pass for one of her guardian's own class.

It hadn't been that difficult. Most of Margaret's Irishness had been beaten out of her by Smythe during the two years she had spent at Mrs. Beale's. And with her blond hair and rosy cheeks, she looked more English than Irish.

But sometimes, in that dark hush just before dawn, when the silence was so heavy it pressed like a weight on Margaret's chest, the ghost of Cathleen Donovan would come calling, bringing with her a confusing mix of good memories and choking terrors that would send Margaret bolting upright in her bed, gasping and clawing at her throat as if Smythe's hand were still there.

Those were bad nights. Hopefully they would plague her less frequently after her marriage.

The thump of the cane heralded Mrs. Throckmorton's progress across the room. "I want you to be taken care of when I'm gone. But not like this. Not in marriage to this upstart Irishman. Perhaps I can break the trust or arrange for—"

"You mustn't," Margaret cut in. "The judge wanted his estate to benefit his charities, and so it shall. Please don't fret. Doyle and I will do well together."

"Unless he finds out you're not the blue blood he thinks you are."

"He won't. You did your work too well. He'll never guess I'm as Irish as he is."

Margaret almost laughed at the irony of it. In transforming an Irish orphan into a proper society miss, Ida Throckmorton had also created exactly the sort of wife Doyle Kerrigan wanted—a non-Irish, impoverished but genteel woman on the fringe of the upper class who was willing to marry an immigrant Irishman in exchange for a life of wealth and privilege. Fate was full of tricks, it seemed.

"I can see you won't listen to reason and are determined to marry the man." Leaning onto her cane with one hand, Mrs. Throckmorton reached into her skirt pocket with the other. "So you might as well have these." She thrust out her hand. Resting in her palm were two diamond pendant eardrops. "Call it my wedding gift, if you must."

Margaret blinked in astonishment. "My goodness, Mrs. Throckmorton. I-I don't know what to say."

"Then you may hug me instead."

Margaret did, noting how frail the small, thin frame felt against her own. "You're too kind to me, ma'am."

"I agree." Pulling back, Mrs. Throckmorton waved her away. "Now stop fussing about and help me to the chair so I can get off this foot. It took me forever to climb those stairs."

As the elderly woman settled into the cushions of the armchair by the coal stove, her gouty foot propped on a damask footstool, Margaret went back to the mirror to put on the diamond drops. She turned to show them off. "They're beautiful. Thank you so much."

"At least when you come to your senses and decamp, you'll have something of value to see you through. Turn. Shoulders back."

Margaret twirled a slow circle, then awaited the verdict.

"Humph. That neckline is too low. It was highly improper of him to pick out your gown, but at least he was right about the color. You look lovely. Too lovely for the likes of that parvenu." With a sniff, she turned her head away. A dab at the long aristocratic nose with the hanky, then a deep, labored sigh. "I suppose because he's Irish, you feel some sort of absurd connection."

Margaret was taken aback. They never spoke of her Irish roots. After fifteen years of silence, all that remained—other than the horrors of Mrs. Beale's and the night terrors—was the memory of endless hunger, living in a dark, windowless room with three other families, and an abiding hatred for the Irish runner who had hastened her father's death. If that was her connection to Doyle, it wasn't a good one.

"He's uncommonly ambitious," Mrs. Throckmorton mused, coming at her from a different direction.

"If so, it has served him well."

"I hear he has a temper."

"Does he? I've never seen it."

"Ask the workers building his railroads. And what kind of man would exploit his own people the way he does?"

"He's not exploiting. He's providing jobs to the Irish when no one else will."

"Stubborn girl." Mrs. Throckmorton's expression soured even more. "I thought you were too intelligent to be so blinded by love."

Love? Hardly that. Although Margaret might want to love her fiancé, she had little expectation of it. Which was certainly not his fault. Blond, hazel eyed, generous—at least with her, less so in business—and so full of life he seemed to draw all the air from a room, Doyle Kerrigan was a man who easily inspired female admiration. But Margaret wasn't sure she was capable of love, or that it would even be wise to open herself to that possibility. If she had learned anything during those first devastating years in this great land of opportunity, it was that love was an illusion and God didn't care and the only thing lower than the immigrant Irish were the despicable runners and procurers who preyed on them.

Another deep sigh caught Margaret's attention and she looked over to see Mrs. Throckmorton dabbing at her eyes. She refrained from snorting. Bribery, condemnation, and now guilt? What ploy would the crafty old woman try next? Full-blown hysteria? Margaret couldn't even imagine such a thing.

"I know why you're doing this." Watery blue eyes looked up at Margaret out of a face that suddenly looked old and defeated. "It's because of what that vile woman did to you, isn't it? You don't think you deserve true happiness, so you're punishing yourself by marrying this man."

Shame rose in a hot flush even as a dark coldness closed around Margaret's heart. How much did Mrs. Throckmorton know about what went on at Mrs. Beale's? And why speak of it now? After avoiding the subject for fifteen years, why did she bring it up on what was supposed to be one of the happiest days of Margaret's life? So angry she couldn't find words to express it, she glared at her guardian, hands fisted at her sides.

"If only I had known—"

"How could you?"

"Your papist priest should have told me."

"It doesn't matter, ma'am." Realizing she had grabbed handfuls of her silk skirts, Margaret forced her fingers to straighten. "It's all in the past."

"I'm so sorry."

Shocked to see real tears roll down those wrinkled cheeks, Margaret let her anger go. Crossing to the chair, she put her arm around the thin shoulders and leaned down to kiss the cool, papery cheek. "Nothing happened, ma'am," she lied. "No one touched me. Father O'Rourke found me before the auction."

"I never thought I'd be grateful to a Catholic priest."

Irish and Catholic were synonymous in the elderly woman's mind, and she had scant liking for either. It still vexed her that Margaret had chosen Father O'Rourke to officiate at the wedding rather than her own Lutheran minister.

A few more tears, then with a pat on Margaret's arm, she gently pushed her away. "Do stop hovering. You know I can't abide it."

Grateful to escape, Margaret went back to the window. To rid herself of the emotions still churning inside, she took several deep breaths, watching the cold glass fog with every exhalation. Closing her eyes, she reached deep into her mind for happier memories—rolling emerald hills, misty dales, waves crashing in frothy disarray against treeless bluffs. Instead of the strident voices of the newsboys hawking the late edition three stories below, she heard the call of terns on a chill north wind, the warble of her father's tin whistle, her mother's soft laughter.

It frightened her how hard she had to work to recall those memories now, and how much they had dimmed over the years. Even Cathleen appeared to her less and less frequently. When those memories faded altogether, would she be more or less whole than she was now?

Pringle suddenly appeared in the doorway. "Mr. Kerrigan's carriage has arrived, madam," he said solemnly, his bushy white brows raised in his usual expression of disdain whenever he mentioned her Irish fiancé's name.

"Very well, Pringle," Mrs. Throckmorton said. "If you are finished eavesdropping in the hallway, you may send a cup of warm milk and a piece of toast to my room."

"Very well, madam."

As the sound of Pringle's slow footsteps receded down the hallway, Mrs. Throckmorton heaved a great sigh. "I should turn him out, the old fool. But he's been in love with me for years, you know, and I haven't the heart to cast him onto the streets like he deserves."

"You're too kind, ma'am." Biting back a smile, Margaret crossed to the mirror. Her mood lifted as excitement gripped her, making it hard to take a full breath against the stays around her ribs. This was it. Her night. "I wish you would change your mind and come with me," she said over her shoulder to the woman watching from the chair. "I wouldn't be so nervous if you were there beside me."

"Nonsense. You will be a stunning success. I have trained you too well for it to be otherwise."

A last look to be sure everything was in order, then Margaret turned to face the woman who had been almost like a mother to her for over half of her life. "Well? How do I look, ma'am?"

The pinched lips thinned in a reluctant smile. "Like a princess."

The carriage ride was short yet seemed to take forever. Margaret would have preferred that Doyle had come for her himself, but she knew he was busy with last-minute preparations for the ball. This was his moment, too, showing off his new home and well-connected fiancée to the very people who had once looked down on him but who now rushed to curry his favor.

There was some justice in that, she supposed.

Doyle and his business partner, Tait Rylander, were standing on the front stoop of Doyle's home, smoking long, thin cigars when Margaret arrived. Flicking his smoke into a brass urn beside the door, Doyle came down the steps to meet her as the driver opened the door.

He looked splendid, his blond handsomeness a perfect foil to the dark severity of his evening attire. She smiled, thinking again how lucky she was.

"Margaret, *a ghra*—my love." He kissed her gloved hand, then her cheek, then gave her that dazzling smile that made women sigh, his hazel eyes alight with anticipation of the evening to come. "You look stunning."

"Thank you. You look quite handsome yourself."

As he escorted her up the wide granite steps, his gaze skimmed over the daring neckline of the dress he had chosen, his expression less one of admiration than satisfaction. "The necklace is perfect with the gown. That color makes her hair gleam like gold, doesn't it, Tait?" he said to the man awaiting them on the top step, one hip perched on the brass handrail.

"It does."

"I'll be the envy of every man here tonight."

"You always are." Straightening, Mr. Rylander dropped his cigar into the urn and gave Margaret a curt bow. "Good evening, Miss Hamilton."

"Mr. Rylander."

In addition to being Doyle's business partner, Tait Rylander was also his friend and legal advisor. They had met during the War of the Rebellion and were of the same age—early thirties— although Mr. Rylander looked older. Perhaps because he lacked Doyle's vibrant animation and ceaseless energy. Or because he favored a scowl rather than a smile. At least around her. They avoided each other whenever possible.

As she relinquished her wrap to the butler in the foyer, Doyle took three champagne flutes from a silver tray held by a waiting footman. He passed one each to Margaret and Mr. Rylander, then raised his high.

"A toast," he announced, smiling at Margaret. "To *mo mhu-irnin ban*—my fair darling. With you beside me, this shanty Irishman can crack elbows with the best of them. May they not soon forget it. *Slainte chugat.*"

"Relax, Doyle," Mr. Rylander reminded him in his odd, hoarse voice. "It's a celebration, not a confrontation."

Doyle threw back his head and laughed, his fine white teeth catching the light of dozens of gaslight flames flickering in the imported crystal chandelier hanging from the intricately plastered ceiling. "You're right, Tait. I'll behave. But it's sweet, so it is, to see them choke on their pride."

Margaret took a sip, savoring the bubbly tartness in her throat as she swallowed. It tasted delicious but did little to settle the butterflies in her stomach.

The few galas she had attended with Mrs. Throckmorton had been smaller, more sedate, and certainly less expensive. Doyle never did anything in half measures, which was why this ball had to be the biggest and the best. It had less to do with proudly introducing his bride-to-be into society than thumbing his nose at the people who had snubbed him before his meteoric rise as a railroad mogul.

She had no illusions that they would be welcomed with open arms. Tolerated, at best. Watched and whispered about, certainly. But always invited. Doyle would make certain of that. In his quest for power and wealth, he had also gained a taste for vengeance—and woe be to anyone who crossed him or tried to cheat him or overlooked him socially. No one would dare not to invite them.

As the tall clock in the hallway chimed the hour, the rattle of approaching carriage wheels sounded through the open door. The guests were arriving.

Doyle set his empty flute on the footman's tray and reached for Margaret's. "All finished, *leannan?*"

"Yes, thank you." Margaret relinquished her goblet, wishing she could ask for another to calm her racing heart.

Doyle placed it on the tray, then turning abruptly, took her face in his hands, and gave her a hard, bruising kiss that pinched her lips against her teeth.

Startled, she drew her head back, aware of Rylander watching. "Doyle!"

"There, *a ghra.*"

She lifted a hand to her throbbing lips and was relieved to see no blood on her gloved fingertips. "There what? Why did you do that?"

"To mark you." He let her go, his eyes gleaming with an emotion she couldn't define. "With your lips swollen from my kiss, no one who sees you tonight will doubt that you're mine."

The next instant, the intensity gave way to a broad grin. He smoothed a hand down the front of his evening coat and straightened his collar. "Smile, lass. Here they come."

Shaken by what he had done, Margaret struggled to regain her composure as the first guests came through the door. For the next two hours she stood at his side in the chilly foyer, receiving the endless stream of guests waiting to wish them well—or wanting to get a first look at the nobody who had captivated the charismatic and flamboyant Doyle Kerrigan. Councilmen, ward bosses, bankers, politicians, judges, and railroad builders—society's finest, all come to honor Doyle Kerrigan and his fiancée.

She hardly remembered a face, much less a name.

Finally, when the muscles holding up her smile began to quiver and she'd lost feeling in her feet, Doyle signaled to Rylander, who was leaning against one of the half-dozen marble pillars that ringed the elegant foyer.

Giving her an apologetic smile, Doyle said, "I must leave you, *leannan*—sweetheart. But only for a short while. Hammond has finally come around and wants to speak to me privately." Unable to restrain his satisfaction, he grinned and leaned closer to add, "I've left the man sweating long enough. Sure, and I'd best sign over the foundry before he collapses." A quick kiss on her cheek, then he handed her over to Rylander. "You left the papers on my desk?"

"I did."

"Excellent. Don't leave her side." Then he was gone, moving with that brisk lightness of step that signaled the chase was on.

Margaret watched him disappear down the hall toward his office with a mixture of relief and irritation. Absently, she lifted a gloved finger to her swollen lip, then remembered the watchdog posted at her side and let her hand drop. She frowned up into a pair of frosty gray eyes. "Oh, do try to smile, Mr. Rylander. People will think you're not overjoyed to be saddled with me rather than that statuesque redhead eyeing you from behind the potted palms."

"I am."

"Overjoyed?"

"Trying to smile."

"My condolences."

It was a moment before he responded, and when he did, it

wasn't what she expected. "You look very nice this evening, Miss Hamilton."

A compliment? How unlike him. And how deflating. Why did the man always bring out the worst in her? "Thank you, Mr. Rylander."

Another long silence. "Would you care to dance, Miss Hamilton?"

"I would not, Mr. Rylander. My feet are numb, my back aches, and this titillating conversation is making me parched. Is there something to drink?"

"Champagne or punch?"

"Whichever is wettest."

Tucking her arm through his, he escorted her out of the foyer, following the music of the orchestra through the receiving and drawing rooms and on toward the ballroom in the back of the house.

Unlike Doyle, Mr. Rylander's fine manners fit him as comfortably as his expensive evening attire. She knew little about him but assumed by the way he dropped his *r*s and dragged out his syllables that his roots were Southern. Perhaps his family had been wealthy, which would account for his social polish and education in the law, although it seemed odd to her that a Southerner would fight for the Union. But then, most everything about Tait Rylander seemed a bit mysterious.

As they moved through the crowded rooms, several people attempted to engage them in conversation, but Rylander deftly steered her on until finally they entered the ballroom. Immediately a liveried footman swooped in with a silver tray of frosty champagne flutes.

Margaret snatched one and tipped it up. As soon as she emptied it and reached for another, she heard Rylander ask the footman to bring a tall glass of cool water.

The press of bodies made this room much warmer than the foyer with its doors opened wide to arriving guests, and despite two glasses of champagne, Margaret was still feeling parched. Crowds always made her uncomfortable, and with the noise and the heat and the nice tingly feeling brought on by the champagne, she felt quite flushed.

When the footman returned with more champagne and the water, she reached for another flute.

Rylander smoothly took it from her grip and replaced it with the glass of water. Dipping his dark head down to hers, he said in his low, hoarse voice, "You've had enough. Drink the water."

Disliking that he felt he could order her about, she opened her mouth to argue, then closed it when she realized he might be right. She was unaccustomed to spirits, and her balance did seem a bit shaky.

In stilted silence they watched dancers waltz by, exchanging nods and smiles with those who looked their way. Between the cloying perfumes scenting the warm air and the swirl of bright dresses, it was like being caught in a spinning garden. She began to feel slightly dizzy.

Beside her, Mr. Rylander emptied his flute and returned it to a footman's tray. As he did, Margaret noted the scarring on his hand. A big, rough hand with enlarged knuckles that robbed his long fingers of any elegance they might once have had. There were other marks of his violent past—a pale scar cutting through his top lip, a thickening along the arc of bone beside his right eye, a slight bump in the ridge of his nose. Small imperfections that gave his chiseled face a dangerous, roughish cast so at odds with his mannered grace. She remembered Doyle saying that Mr. Rylander had fought for money when they had first arrived in New York after the war. "I did the betting and Tait did the fighting," he had boasted. "And many a fat purse he earned us with those big hands, so he did."

Margaret wasn't surprised. Cold, methodical Rylander, calmly slamming his fists into another man's face. It was easy to imagine.

"I am not your enemy, Miss Hamilton."

Startled, she looked up.

He was staring straight ahead, his expression set in its usual austere lines.

"Perhaps not," she allowed. "But you're not my friend, either, are you?"

His gaze dropped to meet hers. She could almost see tiny chips of ice eddying around the dark pupils. "What have I done to make you think that?"

She wondered what to say. *You frown at me? I always feel like you're watching me and waiting for me to do something wrong?* It all sounded so silly. "It's apparent you disapprove of me."

"What reason would I have to disapprove?" He actually looked puzzled.

She knew it would be best to discontinue this conversation. But he had started it, and she was just tipsy enough to say what was on her mind. "I think perhaps you don't want me to marry your friend, thinking I will somehow drive a wedge between you."

The lift of his dark brows signaled disbelief.

Which goaded her into saying more. "Or perhaps you think me frivolous and grasping, just another empty-headed woman drawn to the wealth and power of an ambitious man."

He almost smiled. She saw it in his eyes. The same cold, pale gray-blue of a rainy winter's sky. A fitting complement to his black hair and scowling face, and a stark contrast to Doyle's golden appeal and laughing hazel eyes.

Fire and ice.

She wondered if he had all his teeth. She had never seen him smile.

"I have never considered you empty-headed, Miss Hamilton. Far from it."

"Ah." She acknowledged his omissions with a nod. "But all the rest fits."

He shrugged. "You've worked hard to present yourself as such. I have always wondered why."

"Have you? Then I shall happily enlighten you. Simply put, men distrust intelligence in women. They prefer them helpless and pretty and lacking in meaningful discourse. As do you, it appears, judging by the women with whom you surround yourself." She looked pointedly in the direction of the redheaded woman she had noticed earlier who was watching them again. This time she wasn't smiling.

Impatience flashed across Rylander's stern features, then was quickly masked. "It appears the meeting is over." He nodded toward Doyle, who was coming back into the ballroom with several men Margaret remembered from an earlier gathering. Railroad investors or some such. Doyle looked as smug as a cat with feathers poking out of its mouth.

But when Mr. Rylander took her arm to escort her over, she dug in her heels, suddenly needing to escape all the noise and posturing and inane conversation and find just a few quiet minutes to herself. "Tell him I have to check something with Cook." And before he could argue with her, she pulled free from his grip and walked away.

Once through the doors of the ballroom, she turned down the servant's hall that led to the service entrance beside the kitchen at the back corner of the house. Ignoring the curious looks from the kitchen staff as she walked past, she pushed open the heavy back door and stepped out onto the rear stoop.

Blessed fresh air wafted over her. She took deep breaths, wanting to clear her lungs and fuzzy mind. The chaos stilled. Music dimmed. The clatter of pots and crockery in the kitchen faded.

Gradually, she became aware of other sounds—the call of a nightjar in the shrubbery that lined the back wall. The clop of hooves and jangle of wagon harness on the street around front. A woman crying.

Then a loud male voice rose in the alley. "Go! You're not welcome here!"

Frowning, Margaret cocked her head toward the alley and listened. She caught Doyle's name—something about a foundry—an accident. A baby's cry cut through the night. Then the door in the alley wall burst open and a woman rushed in, carrying a bundle of rags.

Not rags. A child.

"Come back here!" the man shouted. "You're not allowed in there!"

Alarmed, Margaret stepped forward, then stopped when the door behind her opened.

Doyle stepped out, followed by Mr. Rylander and a wide-eyed cook's helper who must have sent for them. "What are you doing out here, Margaret?" Doyle asked.

Before she could answer, the woman veered in their direction as Doyle stepped off the stoop. "Mr. Kerrigan!"

"Stop!" The man from the alley lunged to grab her arm.

"Let her go!" Margaret cried, starting forward again.

A hand clamped on her shoulder.

"Go inside, Miss Hamilton," Rylander said, close to her ear.

"But she—"

"Now." Without waiting to see if she obeyed, he followed Doyle to where the woman stood, clutching the crying baby to her chest. She wore no coat over her faded dress. Her face was so thin her cheekbones rose in stark relief.

"What do you want?" Doyle demanded.

"He's dead," the woman accused in a thick Irish brogue. "Sure, and because of you, Paddy O'Reilly is dead. He told you if the machines weren't repaired, something dire would happen. Well, now it has, and my man is dead. You owe us something for that, so you do."

"I owe you nothing." Doyle stepped closer, making the woman retreat. "Paddy O'Reilly was a lush. And I'll not pay for an accident he caused in a drunken stupor. Carter." He motioned to the man who had followed the woman in from the alley. "Show her off my property."

"Yes, sir." He reached for the woman.

But she dodged his grasp. "Faith, Mr. Kerrigan! Can you spare us nothing? How will I feed our babe and keep a roof over our heads?"

Doyle's fists tightened.

Rylander moved smoothly in front of him. He was taller and broader than her fiancé and easily blocked the woman from Margaret's view. With a pointed glance at Margaret, he said in a calm voice, "I'll handle this, Doyle. Take her away from here."

"What?"

"Miss Hamilton. Take her inside. She doesn't need to see this."

Doyle swung around, saw Margaret watching from the stoop, and confusion gave way to a grimace of anger. "Faith, Margaret! What are you still doing out here? Go inside!"

Margaret rocked back, shocked by the look on his face and the vehemence in his voice. She had heard of Doyle's temper but had never seen it until now.

"Doyle," Rylander warned softly.

Muttering something under his breath, Doyle brushed a hand over his face. When he took it away, his features had slipped back into their normal affable expression. "Love . . . *ta bron orm* . . . I'm sorry."

Without responding, she turned and walked stiffly into the house.

Somehow, she made it through the next two hours. She even convinced herself that Doyle hadn't meant his harsh words. He was probably tired, anxious about the success of the evening. Naturally he wouldn't want a scene that would add fuel to the rumors that always followed in his wake.

"I'm sorry," he told her during one of the few lulls in the evening when they could share a word without eavesdroppers. "I didn't mean to snap at you, love."

"Then why did you? And how did you even know where I was? Do all your servants report back to you on my every movement?"

He looked surprised. "Sure, and you're precious to me, *a ghra*, my love. I would do anything to keep you safe. Even surround you with armed guards every hour of the day if I could. My wealth makes me an easy target. Now you'll be a target as well. I get nervous, so I do, when I don't know where you are."

A sweet sentiment. Yet the thought of having to constantly account for her whereabouts made her vaguely uneasy. "I'll be fine," she assured him. "You needn't hover. I'm more concerned about the O'Reilly woman. You were very rude to her. You should make amends."

"To a beggar?" His expression didn't change, but something cold shifted behind his hazel eyes. She sensed she had touched a nerve. "You're teaching me manners now, are you? You're ashamed of me, then, lass?"

"Not at all. But I'm worried about Mrs. O'Reilly and her baby. Can you do nothing to help her?"

"I can and have. Tait is tending to it now." Then in that capricious way he had of abruptly shifting moods, he grinned and held out his arms. "Now stop frowning, *leannan*, and dance with me so I can show all these fine folks what a beautiful bride I have won."

Two

It was early morning when the last guest departed. Margaret was exhausted but exhilarated. The ball had been a huge success. Because of Mrs. Throckmorton's patronage, she had been easily accepted, even if the glances sent Doyle's way had been less enthusiastic.

Only two things marred an otherwise perfect evening. Three, if one included that rather brutal kiss Doyle had given her just before the guests arrived—which Margaret dismissed as pre-wedding jitters and stress over the evening. That scene with Mrs. O'Reilly behind the house had certainly been disturbing, but the worst was that terrifying moment in the ballroom when she had looked up into a face from her days at Mrs. Beale's.

In the years since she had last seen him, Franklin Horne had aged. But the cold black eyes were the same. And the pointed pink tongue that darted back and forth across his lower lip aroused the same numbing terror as it had when he'd smiled down at little Cathleen Donovan fifteen years earlier.

Luckily, he didn't seem to have as good a memory as she, and passed on by with no more than a lip-licking look at her bosom and a polite nod of disinterest. But it had been several minutes before Margaret's heart had slowed enough that she could take a full breath.

But now the guests had departed, and the servants were

beginning the long process of cleaning up, and Margaret was weary to the bone. Yawning behind her hand, she went in search of Doyle so she could get back to her cozy bed at Mrs. Throckmorton's.

She found him in his study, poring over papers with Mr. Rylander and discussing the business transactions they had finalized between dances. "I hope I'm not interrupting," she said from the doorway.

Doyle looked up with a smile. "Not at all, lass. I was just telling Tait how well the evening went. I negotiated a right-of-way with Bingington, sold a foundry, and arranged financing with Gould for a branch line off the Erie."

"How lovely," she said drily. The man was the consummate businessman. She wondered if he dreamed in deeds and deals.

As the men resumed their discussion, she walked over to one of the armchairs flanking the lit fireplace and sat down with a sigh. Under cover of her skirts, she eased off her slippers, almost groaning with relief when she found her toes could still wiggle.

"A toast is in order." Moving to the array of bottles and glassware on the beverage cart, Doyle poured brandy into three glasses, then passed them around.

"*Saol fada*—long life—to us all. *Slainte.*"

The men drank. Margaret sipped, then hid a shudder and set her glass on the small table beside her chair. She would have to get better at this if Doyle continued to offer brandy toasts all the time. Repressing a yawn, she pulled off her gloves and draped them over the armrest, wondering when he would send for the carriage so she could go back to Mrs. Throckmorton's.

"I'm very proud of you, Margaret."

Proud? Had she passed a test of which she hadn't even been aware? She looked up to find Doyle pouring himself another brandy while Mr. Rylander stared down into his barely touched glass, absently swirling the amber liquid in the crystal tumbler.

"Sure, and you're my greatest asset, lass. The men couldn't take their eyes off of you and the women couldn't stop talking about you."

Margaret wasn't sure if that was a compliment, or not.

Mr. Rylander set his glass down sharply on the mantle, then

bent to toss two small logs onto the fire. In the sudden flare of light, his scowl seemed more pronounced than usual.

"Tait, come look these over." Doyle thumped a finger on a sheaf of papers on his desk. "Gould is a crafty bastard, so he is, and I'd not put anything past him."

While they went over the contract, Margaret tipped her head against the wing of the chair and stared into the fire, lulled by the drone of low voices and the dancing flames. Hiding a wide yawn behind her hand, she closed her eyes.

When next she opened them, the fire was down to glowing coals and the room was quiet. Rubbing a hand over her bleary eyes, she sat up, then froze when she saw Rylander sitting in the chair opposite hers, watching her. He looked relaxed, his left ankle resting atop his bent right knee, both arms stretched along the armrests so that his scarred fingers draped over the edge. Yet there was an intensity in his gray eyes that seemed to cut through her befuddled mind.

"Where's Doyle?" she asked, looking around.

"Having the carriage readied."

To hide her uneasiness at being alone with him, she leaned down to pull on her slippers. Her feet were so swollen it was a tight fit.

"Need help?"

Startled by the impropriety of the offer, she looked up.

He hadn't moved. But his gaze had shifted to the front of her low-cut gown and the fine view she was presenting with her bent posture. She jerked upright. "How long have I been asleep?" she babbled for something to say.

"About an hour."

She sensed hidden amusement in his tone and that irritated her because she didn't know the cause.

"Did you enjoy the ball?" he asked.

"Not particularly." Even as the words left her mouth, she wondered why she would say such a thing to this virtual stranger when she would never admit that sentiment to Doyle for fear of hurting his feelings. Perhaps because she didn't care about Rylander's feelings. Or because she felt no need to lie. Or because if she did, she sensed Rylander would know it immediately. Those watchful eyes didn't miss much.

"You looked like you were enjoying yourself."

"As we assets are wont to do."

His dark brows fell into that scowling line. "You're more than that."

"I am what I need to be, Mr. Rylander, to achieve my aims. Much like yourself, I would guess."

"And what are your aims?"

"Survival. Safety. Security. No matter what grand sentiments or lofty words one couches it in, that's what we all seek. Especially women."

"Not baubles and fine homes and wardrobes filled with expensive gowns?"

Irritated by his condescension, she answered more sharply than she should have. "Imagine if you can, Mr. Rylander, a world in which at least half of the inhabitants are larger and stronger than you and are thus able to force you to their will at any time or any place. That unchangeable fact colors everything in your life—from the route you choose when you walk down the street to what you look for when you enter a room, how you dress, how you smile, how you assess people on first meeting. Friend or foe? Is this person a threat? Will that one do me harm? It's all about survival, Mr. Rylander. Mock a woman's desire for jewels and fine clothes and grand houses if you must, but understand that they are simple manifestations of what she truly desires—survival, safety, security—because those baubles are the things that proclaim to the world that she is of value and, as such, will be protected."

With a flourish, she sat back, crossed her arms over her chest, and awaited his rebuttal. It was a long time in coming, and not at all what she expected.

"You're a frightening woman, Miss Hamilton."

She awoke late the next morning to eight dozen roses and a string of pearls sent by Doyle as an apology for his boorish behavior toward her and Mrs. O'Reilly. Accompanying them was a note saying Tait had arranged for the widow's rent to be paid through the rest of the year, and a big box of groceries had already been delivered, with a standing order for another box to be sent each week until she got back on her feet.

And that was that.

Grateful to put that unpleasantness behind her, Margaret threw herself into frantic preparations for the wedding only days away, which was to be held in the luxurious Fifth Avenue Hotel. The ceremony would take place in the ballroom, which the hotel staff would soon be decorating with tulle and satin and flower garlands, two dozen footed candelabras, a forest of potted cherry trees in full bloom, and dozens of flower arrangements to create a bower around the altar.

Insomuch as Margaret had no male relatives to walk her down the aisle, Doyle had insisted Mr. Rylander do that honor. Once they reached the altar, he would then leave her side and take his place beside Doyle as his best man. A sensible solution, but Margaret would have preferred to go down the aisle alone, rather than on Mr. Rylander's arm. It just seemed wrong, somehow. But she went along, not wanting to cause a fuss.

After the vows, the hundred guests would move into another room for appetizers and wine while the wedding party met with photographers and she and Doyle signed the marriage license, then they would all retire to the elegant dining room for a seated seven-course dinner. Once the meal was completed, they would return to the cleared ballroom for fountains of champagne and dancing well into the night to the strains of a twenty-piece orchestra.

She grew weary just thinking about it. Luckily, Doyle's housekeeper, Mrs. Bradshaw, a rather intense middle-aged woman, was a superb organizer. To Margaret's relief, she took on the task of meeting with the hotel staff in addition to acting as liaison with the florists, musicians, photographers, wine stewards, and society editors representing the various newspapers.

Now, with only two days before the wedding, Margaret's head was a muddle and it seemed her life revolved around endless appointments and ink-smeared lists. As she hurried down the servant's hall in Doyle's sprawling mansion, she studied the latest list—Items for the Ceremony. Only one entry remained. Thinking it might be something Mrs. Bradshaw could handle, she followed the short hall off the kitchen to the housekeeper's office, where she found her going over her own lists.

"I hope I'm not intruding," Margaret said from the open doorway.

Immediately setting down her pen, Mrs. Bradshaw rose. "Not at all, Miss Hamilton. Do please come in. How may I help you?"

Margaret wondered how the slim, straight-backed woman managed all this fuss without a single brownish gray hair slipping from her severe knot. Not even a smudge showed beneath her dark brown eyes. In contrast, Margaret felt as if she'd been dragged behind a carriage.

"I need a drape for the altar," she told the housekeeper. "The one supplied by the hotel is too busy. Perhaps a simple green underskirt with a white topper. That would tie in with the ferns and not fight with the flowers. What do you think?"

Mrs. Bradshaw nodded in approval. "I think that would be lovely. And we may have something suitable on hand. If you don't mind waiting, I'll go now to check the linen closet."

After she left, Margaret pulled a chair around to the end of the long worktable-style desk and sat down, grateful to be off her feet for a while. Careful not to disturb Mrs. Bradshaw's neat stacks of lists and invoices and order sheets, she picked up the pen, dipped it in the inkwell, and read over her own notes.

The smell of baking bread and spices settled around her. Pots and pans clattered. Women's laughter drifted from the kitchen.

An image burst into her mind—a battered ragdoll on the braided rug by the kitchen stove, her mother at the table, sharing tea and laughter with a neighbor. Only a snippet of memory, there and gone in a heartbeat, but it left behind a yearning that brought a gentle ache to Margaret's heart.

Her mother should be here. She should be sharing this special time in her daughter's life. It should be her laughter drifting from the kitchen, instead of that of strangers. If not for that despicable Irish runner, it might have been.

Another image. This one not so cherished: her father, slumped on the curb, shivering with fever and despair, trying to convince her mother he would find a place for them to stay and all would be well.

Voices intruded as two women moved into the short hallway between the kitchen and Mrs. Bradshaw's office, where they began sorting through the tableware needed for the evening meal. Margaret couldn't see them from where she sat, but even though they spoke in whispers, their words carried easily over the clank of silver.

"Hear what happened to that Irish girl who caused the ruckus the other night? O'Reilly, I think her name was."

"The widow lady Mr. Kerrigan sent packing?"

"That's the one. Took a midnight swim in the East River."

Margaret froze, the pen poised halfway between the inkwell and the page.

"No! Did she really?"

"Fished her and her babe out early this morning. The police chief himself came to tell Mr. Kerrigan."

A drop of ink slid off the nib to fall in a fat black splotch on the list. Setting down the pen, Margaret pressed her palms flat against the top of the desk. She shouldn't be listening to this. She should dismiss those vile gossipers on the spot.

"Surely the police don't think Mr. Kerrigan had anything to do with it?"

"Maybe not, but she wouldn't be the first person to cross Mr. Kerrigan and come to a bad end, if you know what I mean."

"Hush, Grace! You want to get us sacked?"

Margaret shot to her feet, almost knocking over her chair. As she stalked toward the door, Mrs. Bradshaw's voice rose in the kitchen.

"Lissy, has the greengrocer brought the blueberries yet?"

"No, ma'am."

"Start on the parfaits anyway. If he hasn't come by four, use peaches."

"Yes, ma'am."

The clack of the housekeeper's heels on the stone floor grew louder as she came into the short hallway between her office and the kitchen. "Finish up with that, you two, then get the potatoes peeled. You're not being paid to chitchat."

"Yes, ma'am," two voices said in unison.

"One moment, please," Margaret said stepping from the office.

Mrs. Bradshaw looked up, her arms loaded with folded lengths of green and white cloth. The two startled maids whipped around. One looked guilty, the other defiant—Grace, the gossiper, Margaret guessed.

She fixed her gaze on that one. Clasping her hands tightly at her waist to hide their shaking, she said in as steady a voice as her anger would allow, "Grace, you disparage the man who gives you employment. That is not acceptable. You are dismissed."

Defiance sagged into shock, then tears. "But, ma'am, I didn't mean—"

Ignoring her, Margaret turned to the housekeeper, who was watching with a mixture of distress and confusion. "Mrs. Bradshaw, please take Grace to her room to pack her things, then have one of the footmen escort her from the premises."

The housekeeper set the cloth aside. "Of course, Miss Hamilton."

After she ushered the protesting Grace away, Margaret turned her attention to the other maid, who stood white-faced and trembling. "Your name?"

"Gretchen, ma'am."

"Those who listen to gossip, Gretchen, are as guilty as those who spread it."

"Y-Yes, ma'am." The stricken woman—little more than a girl, really—covered her face with her hands. Her shoulders shook.

"Tale carrying cannot be tolerated. I'm sure you understand that."

"Yes, ma'am." Her hands muffled her voice but couldn't stop the drip of a tear through her fingers. "I'm s-so sorry."

Margaret looked away, memories of her own fear clutching at her throat. Anger gave way to disgust—disgust with this poor woman for her weakness and shame, with herself for adding to it, and especially with Doyle for inviting such gossip with his suspect behavior. "See that it doesn't happen again." She waved a hand in dismissal. "Attend your duties."

"Oh, thank you, ma'am." The girl fled into the hushed kitchen.

Margaret walked stiffly into the office, the space between her shoulder blades already tingling from the glares of disapproval sure to be headed her way.

Servants talked. That's how they lightened the long hours of toil in the homes of the rich. The only way to prevent it was to gain their loyalty. But now, not only had Margaret ruined any chance of that, she had also added validity to the rumors by overreacting to idle speculation. Now she would have to deal with a resentful staff.

But what if it's true?

She pushed that thought away. Of course it wasn't true. Doyle might be impulsive and somewhat temperamental, but he wasn't a murderer. He would never harm a woman, much less a child. How could she even think such a thing?

But still, the doubt remained.

Mrs. Bradshaw returned with the linens. "I'm so sorry for that, Miss Hamilton," she said, putting the cloth on the table. "Grace knew better. Most of the staff is intensely loyal to Mr. Kerrigan, as well they should be. I will make a point of reiterating our policy regarding such reprehensible behavior."

"Thank you."

The housekeeper stood for a moment, her color high and that worry still showing in her eyes, as if she expected to be dismissed just for hiring Grace. It struck Margaret the control she wielded over the dozens of employees who labored on her behalf. She didn't like that power—didn't want the burden of it. But as mistress of this house, that would be her task.

"Will these do?" Mrs. Bradshaw motioned to the linens.

Margaret forced a smile. "They'll do very well, Mrs. Bradshaw. I'll trust you to attend to it." She needed to get out of this house and away from all these people who fluttered so anxiously about her. She needed room to breathe. "Have the carriage brought around, please," she said, gathering her lists.

"Of course. Will you be coming back later?"

Since the engagement ball, she often joined Doyle for dinner so they could spend time together away from the hectic wedding preparations. The quiet evenings were such a welcome reprieve from Mrs. Throckmorton's pointed comments that Margaret didn't mind if Mr. Rylander often joined them and talk revolved around business. She had a keen interest in such things and learned a great deal from their conversations, even if she wasn't always included in the discussions. "I shall be ready at the usual time."

"Of course, ma'am."

Margaret turned to go, then swung back. "I want to thank you for all your help, Mrs. Bradshaw. And for your support earlier. I hope it doesn't put you in a difficult position with the staff." Then without waiting for a response, she walked from the room.

When the carriage returned at seven that evening and Margaret went downstairs, she saw Mr. Rylander waiting in the foyer rather than her fiancé.

"Good evening, Miss Hamilton."

"Mr. Rylander." Irritated that Doyle had not come for her himself and that she would have to suffer another meal under Mr. Rylander's glowering eye, she swept past him and down the steps.

When they reached the coach, Rylander reached around her to open the door and offered his hand to help her in.

She ignored it and climbed in on her own. "Where's Doyle?" she asked, taking the forward-facing seat.

"Detained." The coach rocked with his weight as he settled against the window corner across from her, his long legs stretched at an angle so they wouldn't crowd her skirts, his right arm resting along the back of the seat. "He hopes to be finished by the time you arrive."

They rode without speaking as the carriage wove slowly through congestion caused by an overturned drayman's wagon. She tolerated his disapproving scowl as long as she could, then finally brought up the subject that had been troubling her since that scene outside Mrs. Bradshaw's office earlier.

"I heard about the O'Reilly woman."

He studied her, his expression betraying nothing. "And what did you hear, Miss Hamilton?"

"That she and her child drowned in the East River."

He nodded but offered no further explanation.

"Well, you must know how that looks, Mr. Rylander, in view of the scene at the house the night of the ball."

His brows rose. "It was ruled a suicide. Are you insinuating it wasn't?"

"Are you so certain it was?"

A long pause. "You think Doyle had something to do with it?"

"I'm sure my fiancé is quite innocent." She put emphasis on "'my fiancé'."

He was too intelligent not to note it. "But you're not as sure about me."

She looked at him in silence, allowing him to draw his own conclusions.

"May I ask what I've done to put that suspicion into your mind?" he asked after a moment.

"A natural curiosity."

He turned his head and looked out the window. Margaret had the sense that he was struggling to contain his temper. When he finally aimed his gaze back at her, his dark brows formed a scowling ridge over his deep-set eyes, and his hoarse voice vibrated with indignation.

"I assure you, Miss Hamilton, I had nothing to do with the deaths of Mrs. O'Reilly and her child. The woman was obviously despondent over her husband's death." The words were short and clipped, his Southern accent stronger than usual.

"So it would appear." Margaret shifted under that furious glare but refused to look away. "Yet it seems strange to me that despite a promise of free rent for a year and a weekly delivery of groceries, she was still so distraught she decided death was her only recourse. Doesn't that seem odd to you, Mr. Rylander?"

"Tragically so. But then I have always been amazed by how the female mind works. By what logic does a woman make the decisions she does? Or are her conclusions based solely on emotion? What is your opinion, Miss Hamilton?"

It was Miss Hamilton's opinion that he was no longer talking about Mrs. O'Reilly. Uneasy with the turn in the conversation, she deflected it with an offhand gesture. "I think it is beyond male understanding to grasp the nuances of female thinking, so men shouldn't even bother to try. There has been talk among the servants."

He didn't respond.

"They're saying Mrs. O'Reilly hasn't been the only one to cross Doyle and come to a bad end." She felt foolish voicing such a thing aloud, but it needed to be said and she needed to see his reaction when she did. "Naturally, I dismissed the kitchen maid who said that. But—"

"But now you're wondering if it's true." He watched her, those cold gray eyes boring into her, his long, big-knuckled fingers drumming softly on the back of his seat. She sensed dark currents running through his mind but couldn't fathom where they would lead his thoughts next.

"I have known Doyle Kerrigan for over five years, Miss Hamilton. He can be unforgiving, hot-tempered, even ruthless. But he's not a cold killer."

"Are you?" Shocked that she had spoken that fear aloud, she pressed back against the cushions, expecting an explosion of anger.

Instead, the corners of his eyes narrowed in amusement. "No, Miss Hamilton, I'm not." He punctuated that with the first full smile she had ever seen on his stern face. "Not yet, anyway."

The man definitely had all his teeth.

Dinner was a quiet affair in the grand dining room. Normally Margaret would have preferred a more intimate setting for a group of three, rather than clustered at one end of the thirty-foot-long table under the watchful eyes of footmen standing in the shadows. But this evening she was not in a particularly talkative mood, her mind preoccupied with wedding details and that awkward scene earlier with the gossipers and the even more awkward scene with Mr. Rylander in the carriage. She didn't know why she let the man distress her so. Like now. Even though he had been utterly polite throughout the meal, she could feel the weight of his gaze across the table, and it made her extremely uncomfortable. To make him aware of it, she narrowed her eyes at him in warning.

He narrowed his back, although that crinkle at the corners of his eyes hinted at amusement rather than ire. Horrid man.

Even Doyle seemed subdued throughout the meal. Perhaps he had heard the talk about Mrs. O'Reilly, too. Or perhaps a business proposition had gone sour. Or his shoes were too tight. With Doyle, she never knew, his moods were so difficult to gauge and he shared so little of himself with her. It was a bit sad that they didn't know each other better, considering they would be spending the rest of their lives together.

"Hammond came to see me today," Rylander said as footmen served peaches and cream in tall crystal parfait glasses. "Seemed upset."

"He knew what he was getting into."

Margaret took a small bite, found it too sweet, and set her spoon aside. "Is this the same Hammond who bought the foundry?"

Doyle didn't answer.

"Some of the workers have walked off," Rylander continued to Doyle as if she hadn't spoken.

Determined not to be ignored, Margaret tried again. "Is this the place where the accident occurred and Mr. O'Reilly was killed? Is that what they're upset about?"

Doyle took a long sip of wine, then returned the goblet to the table. He watched her, twirling the delicate stem in blunt fingers, his mouth tight.

Realizing she would get little information from her fiancé, Margaret turned to Mr. Rylander. "Perhaps if they knew about the generous compensation Doyle offered Mrs. O'Reilly, they would be less angry."

"It's not about that. It's about the machinery."

"It's unsafe?"

"Faith, Margaret!" Doyle slapped his open palm onto the table so hard the parfaits rattled on their serving plates. "This doesn't concern you. Sure, and you should be fretting over doilies and flowers and some such, rather than involving yourself in business matters."

Margaret felt heat rise into her face. Did he take her for an imbecile?

"Yes, it's an issue of safety," Mr. Rylander cut in smoothly, his calm tone belied by the barbed look he shot at Doyle. "Hammond was aware of the accident and the cause. He had ample time to make further inquiries and assessments."

"It was Hammond who pressed for a quick sale, not me." Doyle tossed his napkin beside his plate and rose with a smile to show his good humor was restored. "Shall we retire to the drawing room?"

As a footman stepped forward to pull back Margaret's chair, Rylander rose and buttoned his dark frock coat. "I'd best go talk to Hammond."

"Why?"

"It's good business, Doyle. The man has influence."

"You're pandering to a fool."

Rylander rounded on him. "It's not pandering. It's rebuilding trust. Something I wouldn't have to do if you thought with your head instead of that chip on your shoulder. These dodgy deals harm your credibility."

Margaret blinked at him in surprise. She had always thought of Rylander as Doyle's flunky, seeing his natural reserve as weakness. Now, she wasn't so sure.

Doyle spread his arms to indicate his grand home. "Sure, and those dodgy deals have also made me rich, so they have."

"For now. But I can't cover for you forever."

Her fiancé laughed. *"Pog mo thoin."*

A bit shocked, Margaret glanced at Rylander, wondering if he knew his friend had just told him to kiss his backside in Irish Gaelic.

The taller man sighed. Turning to Margaret, he gave a slight bow. "Miss Hamilton, always a pleasure. Doyle, I'll let you know how it goes with Hammond."

After he left, Doyle led Margaret to the sitting room, where a fire crackled in the fireplace and a frosty bottle of champagne stood beside his usual decanter of fine French brandy. While he poured, Margaret went to stand at the hearth, feeling a bit chilled from their walk through the cool hallway.

"Drink, *a ghra*," he whispered in her ear as he reached from behind to press the tall flute into her hand. "Let the bubbles trap your worries and carry them away on a sigh." His lips brushed the side of her neck.

She could feel the heat of him against her back, the whisper of warm brandy-scented breath flowing past her shoulder and down her chest to the lace edge of her low square-cut gown. Tipping her head back, she took a sip of champagne, knowing it opened her bosom to more of his gaze.

She hadn't been touched intimately by a man in a dozen years, ever since she was fifteen and had attempted to use the greengrocer's son to dispel the shame and horror that had been—and still was—Smythe's legacy. It hadn't worked. Their furtive fumblings had been just another degrading, painful memory to add to the others from Mrs. Beale's. Hopefully with Doyle it would be better.

Champagne bubbles burst on her tongue, sent warmth down her throat to pool low in her belly. She took a deep breath, let it out, heard his breathing change, and felt her own excitement build with his.

Perhaps tonight. She had denied them both all these months, partly because of concern about pregnancy, partly to keep his interest peaked, but also partly from fear. What if this attempt was a failure, too? Not for Doyle, of course. She knew what the marriage bed entailed—she had lived two years at a brothel, after all, and had seen more than most women could even imagine. She understood the mechanics of the thing and that men derived enjoyment from it even if the woman didn't. But what of her own hopes—that abandonment and emotional loss of self that put one utterly in the power of another person? Would that happen this time? Did she trust Doyle enough to allow it to happen?

Perhaps tonight. Perhaps if she shared that intimacy with the man she was about to marry, all the little fears and niggling doubts would go away, and she would know she was doing the right thing. Perhaps then she would be able to love him as she should.

She took another swallow of champagne, then Doyle reached around to lift it from her hand. Even his hands were beautiful—no scarring or enlarged knuckles beneath the faint dusting of golden hair. She imagined them moving over her body and shivered as something went liquid deep inside.

"Are you cold, lass?" The words rustled in her ear. She watched his hand set the goblet on the mantle, then come back to stroke the flushed skin below her throat, those beautiful, unmarked fingers just long enough to slip below the lace-edged neckline of her gown. "Shall I warm you like this?"

His hand sipped lower. Flesh to flesh. Kisses along her neck.

"You are so soft, *leannan*. Except here." He tweaked her nipple.

She sagged back against him, her eyes drifting closed.

Think only of Doyle. Let the past go.

Before she was hardly aware of it, he had both cap sleeves of her gown pulled down, trapping her arms at her sides and exposing her breasts to his gaze and the heat rising from the fire.

A tingling weakness enveloped her as he continued to leisurely stroke her while he whispered in her ear how beautiful she was, how smooth her skin felt, how much he wanted her. Her legs were starting to tremble when his other hand came around to caress her throat.

She jumped, startled, and the next instant her mind was spiraling back in time and other fingers were tightening around her neck and Smythe was laughing, squeezing—

A cry pressed against her clenched teeth. But before it passed her lips, a distant door slammed.

Doyle froze. Voices rose in the foyer.

With a curse, he jerked up the sleeves of her gown so that she was covered again, then stepped away from her as purposeful steps approached the sitting room. A perfunctory knock sounded on the door just before it swung open.

"Doyle—"

"Don't you knock?"

Stopping abruptly, Rylander looked from Margaret to Doyle, then covered his surprise with a curt nod. "My apologies."

Margaret hoped those sharp eyes would think her flush was from the heat of the fire, rather than acute embarrassment.

"What are you doing back here?" Doyle snapped.

"There's been an explosion at the foundry."

"The one I just sold to Hammond?"

Rylander nodded.

"What's that got to do with me?"

"I thought you should know."

"Why? It's Hammond's foundry now. Let him handle it."

"Hell, Doyle, show some concern."

Margaret stepped forward. "Was anyone hurt?"

It was apparent from Doyle's expression that he hadn't considered that. "Surely no one was there at this hour?"

"A night watchman. He wasn't harmed."

"Well, then."

Rylander's brows shot up. "'Well, then?' That's it?"

"Faith, man! What do you want me to do? I had nothing to do with this. It's not my foundry anymore."

"You can give Hammond your support."

"For what? His own stupidity?" Running fingers through his blond hair, Doyle went to the beverage cart and poured himself another brandy. He tossed it back in one swallow, then returned the glass to the tray with a loud clink. "He knew the risks."

"Perhaps to ease the situation," Margaret said, glancing from one scowling face to the other, "you could offer a no-interest loan to replace the damaged machinery. It would cost you little and might buy back his good will."

Both men turned to look at her—her fiancé's expression showed impatience. Rylander's was harder for her to read.

Then he stunned her by saying, "She's right, Doyle. And it would deflect some of the suspicion that's sure to be headed your way."

"Suspicion about what? I didn't do anything." He was starting to sound like a little boy caught with an empty jar and cookie crumbs on his face.

"Maybe not. But you'll do this." Spinning on his heel, Rylander walked toward the door. "Hurry," he called back from the hall. "We can drop Miss Hamilton off on the way."

"Bossy bastard." With an apologetic smile, Doyle offered his arm to Margaret. "Tomorrow, *a ghra*," he whispered in her ear as they left the office and turned toward the foyer. "You'll stay with me. You'll let me love you all night long, so you will."

She glanced up at him, saw the hunger in his beautiful hazel eyes, and felt that shivery, shimmery feeling run through her again. "I promised to spend the evening with Mrs. Throckmorton."

"Then come after."

"She's helping me pack." More like supervising, and no doubt making several last-minute attempts to talk her out of this marriage. But it would be their last night together and Margaret didn't want to miss it. The cranky old dear was the closest thing she had to family, and Margaret cared deeply for her. "Besides, we'll be married in two days."

He put on a pained expression and groaned. "I can't wait that long."

"You'd better."

His laugh echoed through the foyer, bringing Rylander's head around from where he stood by the front door, issuing instructions to Doyle's footman. For a moment, before he masked it, Margaret glimpsed the oddest expression in his slate gray eyes. Something fleeting and unexpected and utterly confusing—a flash of anger so intense it felt like a slap. But directed at Doyle, not her.

Three

The morning of the wedding dawned clear and sunny with the faintest touch of spring in the crisp breeze. Margaret tried to sleep in, but excitement had her climbing out of bed not long after dawn, her mind churning with last-minute details. Padding barefoot to her desk, she looked over her lists.

Everything had been checked off her to-do list. Her dress had been delivered to the hotel suite assigned to her and Mrs. Throckmorton, their bags were packed, and anything of hers that remained in this room would be sent directly to Doyle's townhome after she and Mrs. Throckmorton left for the hotel. Mrs. Bradshaw was handling everything else.

Which left her wedding day list, starting with the carriage taking her and Mrs. Throckmorton to the hotel later this morning. There, she would suffer through a final dress fitting and meet with Mrs. Bradshaw and Father O'Rourke. After a light luncheon, she would bathe, sit for the hairdresser, take a last tea with Mrs. Throckmorton, dress, and just before six, Rylander would come to escort them down to the ballroom. Then the ceremony, the signing of the marriage certificate, more photographs, the reception line, dinner, toasts, dancing, and finally— if she could stay awake for it—her wedding night. All that on four hours of restless sleep.

A knock on her door heralded the arrival of breakfast.

And her wedding day began.

Most of it passed in a haze. She couldn't have managed without Mrs. Bradshaw and the efficient staff of the Fifth Avenue Hotel. The only worrisome moment came when Mrs. Throckmorton had a brief fainting spell while Margaret was absent at her meeting with Father O'Rourke. She was quite recovered by the time Margaret returned to the suite, but as a precaution throughout the rest of the afternoon, she lay in regal repose on the settee in the sitting area of the suite, happily supervising the final preparations.

Margaret might have suspected her guardian of making another sly attempt to delay the marriage if not for the paleness of her face and the dark smudges beneath the faded eyes. But with sniffs and dramatic sighs, the elderly woman waved away Margaret's concerns, insisting she would "see the wretched thing through as a show of support even though it was all a ghastly mistake and would no doubt bring endless despair and regret to both of their lives."

Quite the thespian, Mrs. Throckmorton. No wonder she so favored the Shakespearean tragedies.

By the time everyone but Mrs. Throckmorton had left and Margaret stood bathed and coiffed and weighted down by her elaborate wedding gown, waiting for Mr. Rylander to come escort them down to the ballroom, all those second thoughts her guardian had warned her about came rushing into her mind.

"Let it stay in the past," Father O'Rourke had advised when she'd asked if she should tell Doyle about her Irish roots and those sordid years at Mrs. Beale's. "Cathleen Donovan is dead and buried. Let her rest, poor mite."

She's hardly resting, Margaret thought. In fact, since Margaret had come face-to-face with Franklin Horne at the engagement ball, poor Cathleen had been even more active than usual, plaguing her with appearances every night since.

"I saw Franklin Horne at the engagement ball," she had told the priest earlier that afternoon. "I don't think he recognized me."

"Sure, and why should he, lass?" A look of disgust had crossed Father O'Rourke's lined face. "He prefers children, so he does. He'll not be a threat to a beautiful grown woman like yourself."

Now as Margaret regarded herself in the mirror of the suite

several hours later, she fervently hoped that was true. The burden of having to guard all these secrets was preying on her, and the thought of having to watch over her shoulder for the rest of her life left a bitter taste in her mouth.

"There's still time to decamp," Mrs. Throckmorton said from her settee beside the hearth. She was dressed in her finery as well—a deep purple gown, strings of pearls around her thin neck, and an elaborate ostrich plumed chapeau atop her tight gray curls. Queen Victoria couldn't have done better. "You could slip down the servant's stair and be out in the back alley in a trice. No one would even notice."

"Except for my wedding dress."

"Don't be pert. You could borrow my funeral gown. I take it everywhere I go, just in case, and I have a lovely hat with a heavy black lace veil. You would look quite mysterious. And old."

To combat her impatience with the waiting, Margaret played along. "And where would I go, ma'am? Would I sail back to Ireland? Travel up into the frozen north? Cross the bridge to New Jersey?"

"West." The watery blue eyes took on a distant look. "There's a vast country beyond our little island, my dear. Mountains so tall they brush the clouds. Deserts of painted rocks and prickly plants. Endless rolling plains covered with thousands upon thousands of those big hairy buffaloes. Were I younger, I would drag you there myself."

"Why, Mrs. Throckmorton." Margaret smiled in fond surprise. "I never knew you had such an adventurous spirit."

The older woman waved a blue-veined hand in dismissal. "We've made a mess of this place. Factories spewing smoke and soot into the air, starving children working for a pittance in mines and foundries, too many people in too little space. The constant noise makes me grateful my hearing is failing. But west . . . now there's a grand place to make a fresh start."

Margaret wondered if such a thing were possible. How did one escape one's own past?

Mrs. Throckmorton must have guessed her thoughts. Leaning forward, she whispered urgently, "Do it, dear. Make your own destiny rather than trying to fit into a mold made by another. Take a chance—"

A knock sounded on the door.

The lovely images in Margaret's mind faded.

Mrs. Throckmorton sank back with a deep sigh.

The floor maid announced herself and opened the door. A figure loomed in the hallway behind her and Margaret wondered if she had been saved—or doomed—by Mr. Rylander's arrival. He filled the opening, tall and elegant and very dark, the crisp whiteness of his starched shirt and cravat a blinding contrast to his glossy black hair and severely formal black tails. Then he looked up and saw Margaret.

His lips parted. She could almost feel the sharp intake of breath, then the slow release, and she wondered how she had ever thought those gray eyes cold.

But the next instant, as if a shutter had slammed closed, all expression left his face. With a curt nod, he stepped into the room. "Miss Hamilton, you look lovely. As do you, Mrs. Throckmorton. If you're ready, ladies, I'll escort you down now."

"I won't take that screw thing," Mrs. Throckmorton announced as the maid helped her from the chair. "It could blow up and kill us all."

When she saw Mr. Rylander's frown of confusion, Margaret explained. "The vertical screw railway that moves between floors."

"It could catch on my skirts and grind me up like blood sausage."

While Margaret struggled to block that grisly image, Rylander stepped smoothly in. "It's protected by a screen, ma'am. And the steam engine is in the basement where it's constantly monitored so it won't explode. You would be quite safe. But if you prefer, I'll be glad to carry you down, myself."

Down three flights of stairs? Was he jesting? Margaret wished Mrs. Throckmorton would accept the offer just to watch him try to weasel out of it.

Instead her guardian batted him away with her fan. "You'll do no such thing, you upstart. I shall go down on my own or not at all. But you may offer me your arm."

He did and, with grave solemnity, ushered the elderly matron from the room.

"Don't dawdle," Mrs. Throckmorton called back to Margaret, who followed behind them. "And you," she added with a wave at the maid, "bring her veil and see that her train doesn't catch. Come along."

It was slow going, but eventually they made the ground floor, where Mrs. Bradshaw was waiting to sweep the bride into a small alcove beside the ballroom. There Margaret would wait, unseen, until Mr. Rylander seated her guardian, then returned to escort her down the aisle.

Margaret's nerves were so frazzled her skin felt prickly and hot. Her tight stays made it difficult to take a full breath, which threw her into a mild panic she had to struggle to keep under control. She dreaded the ordeal ahead, having all eyes turned on her. It reminded her of those awful evenings at Mrs. Beale's when Smythe would parade her through the downstairs gaming rooms and men would look at her in pity or disgust or with that grinning, slack-faced hunger that made her feel dirty and nauseated.

"You're a beautiful bride," Mrs. Bradshaw said, reaching up to pin Margaret's veil to the tiara already anchored in her upsweep. "I'm sorry the staff at the townhouse couldn't be here to see you."

"Please don't," Margaret said when the housekeeper tried to pull the veil over her face. "Not yet. It makes me feel . . . smothered."

"Would you like some champagne? That might settle your nerves."

"Water would be nice." No use adding lightheaded and tipsy to her list of ailments.

"Of course. I'll send for some with ice."

After Mrs. Bradshaw left, Margaret took a few moments to gather her thoughts and settle her breathing. This was supposed to be her grand day. She didn't want to be so addled she couldn't even remember it.

Late guests were still arriving, their voices carrying from the hallway as they waited outside the ballroom to be ushered to their seats. Gradually, the voices faded until only two remained. Margaret stiffened when she recognized one from her past.

"I swear she's Irish," Franklin Horne said. "I don't care who her guardian is, the bitch has the look of the Irish in her. It's those green eyes."

Fearing to be seen, Margaret ducked against the wall by the arched opening.

"I doubt it," said another man, whose voice Margaret didn't recognize. "No decent Irish woman would marry him."

Horne snickered, and the sound of it made Margaret clap a gloved hand over her mouth to keep from retching. She remembered that laugh. Those black eyes. The fat, white fingers reaching out—

His voice cut through her terror. "She may not be as decent as we think. There's something about her . . ."

"She can't be Irish," the other man insisted. "The Irish hate him because he was a runner. One of McGinty's best. Helped him make a fortune fleecing the dumb bastards before they even cleared the gangplanks."

A runner? Margaret sagged against the wall, one hand still pressed over her mouth, the other clutching her churning stomach. Doyle was a runner?

Horne snickered again. "I didn't know that. Useful information to have."

Lights danced behind her eyes, and something cold spread through her chest. *Da . . . oh, Da . . .*

"McGinty?" Horne went on. "Wasn't he killed by an Irish mob?"

Run! Her father's voice echoed through her memory. *Run, Cathleen!*

The stranger's voice dropped to a low whisper. "There's some say Kerrigan was part of it and joined up with the Irish Brigade when the war broke out just to escape the law. But don't spread that about. The man's got a long reach."

"I'm not afraid of that Irish bastard."

"Maybe you should be," the other man warned. "If not him, then Rylander. Some say he's the real power. He's certainly the brains. Quiet, here he comes."

Footfalls approached. Margaret looked frantically for escape when Rylander suddenly appeared in the archway, Mrs. Bradshaw at his side with a frosty glass of water in her hand.

"Miss Hamilton," he said gravely. "They're ready for you."

Margaret struggled to catch her breath. "I . . . ah . . ."

Frowning, he stepped closer, causing her to shrink back. "Are you all right?"

"Here, ma'am. Drink this." Mrs. Bradshaw put the glass in her hands.

Margaret tried to drink but was shaking so hard water spilled down her skirt. "I can't—"

"Thank you, Mrs. Bradshaw," Rylander cut in, taking the glass from Margaret's grip. "Tell the orchestra to wait until we're at the door. We'll be there momentarily."

Bracing one hand against the wall, Margaret closed her eyes and tried to slow the spinning. She heard the housekeeper leave but knew Rylander was still there. She could feel him, hear him breathing. She wanted to scream at him to go away.

A runner. Dear God . . . I'm marrying a runner. Acid burned in her throat and she almost gagged as she swallowed it back. Her knees started to wobble. *Da . . . help me.*

"Margaret, what's wrong?" A hand touched her shoulder.

She flinched. "Go away."

"Are you ill?"

She willed her legs to carry her weight. To carry her from this place.

"Take a breath. Slow and easy. Now another."

She did and gradually the dizziness faded. Slowly, her head cleared. When the shaking eased, she pushed away from the wall and looked up into worried gray eyes. Rage shot through her. "Did you know Doyle was a runner?"

The dark brows rose. "A what?"

"A runner. How could you not know?"

"What are you talking about? What's a runner?"

Oh, God. How could this be?

"Miss Hamilton—Margaret—what's wrong? Talk to me."

A figure moved into the opening. "The orchestra is waiting," Mrs. Bradshaw said in a worried voice. "Mr. Kerrigan is getting impatient."

"We're coming," Rylander said curtly. "Tell them we're on our way." After the housekeeper left, he turned back to Margaret. "Are you ready?"

"No."

"Of course you are." Ignoring her weak protests, Rylander pulled the veil over her face and, with awkward clumsiness, tried to smooth the draped folds. "There." Stepping back, he offered his arm. "Shall we?"

She didn't move.

"Margaret. It's time. Take my arm."

She blinked up at him through the lacy design. "I—I can't do this."

"Yes, you can. Just take my arm. I'll get you through it."

When she still didn't move, he lifted her hand and tucked it under his arm, pinning it hard against his side.

He felt solid and real and warm against her chilled arm. "I can't do this," she said again as he forced her to step forward.

"Yes, you can. This is what you want, remember? Safety and security. Doyle can give you all of that and more. He'll protect you."

His soft, hoarse voice went on and on, crooning, cajoling, forcing her to take just one more step. Then another.

Perhaps the man with Horne was wrong. Perhaps it was just evil gossip. Doyle was an easy target and no doubt had made enemies along the way. Perhaps this was just a base rumor started by some small-minded person who was envious of his success. She looked up into Rylander's worried gaze. "You didn't know?"

He smiled. Or tried to. But it didn't reach his eyes, and she knew he was still confused. "I don't even know what a runner is, Margaret. But if he had been one, surely I would have known, don't you think?"

Yes. That made sense. Of course, Rylander would have known. Those watchful eyes saw everything. Unless Doyle was too ashamed to admit it, even to his friend. Certainly he wouldn't want his employees to know. No true Irishman would ever willingly work for a runner.

"This is just nerves, Margaret. Come along. Doyle is waiting. Just lean into my shoulder and step with me."

As they neared the ballroom, music started. The wedding march. Beyond the white screen of her veil, Margaret saw dark figures rising. She felt them watching her, heard them murmur. Digging her gloved fingers into Rylander's hard forearm, she moved numbly forward, one foot in front of the other.

Toward Doyle. Toward a future she wanted. Needed.

The music swelled. Doyle came forward to take her hand.

Rylander passed her off, then stepped to the side as Father O'Rourke began to speak.

But what if it's true?

"Now you." Grinning, Doyle set the pen down on the table and motioned her forward. "Mrs. Kerrigan."

Margaret looked bleakly down at the document in front of her.

After the ceremony, the wedding party had come directly to this small office down the hall from the ballroom. The wedding guests had been herded in the opposite direction into a large meeting room where they would be served wine and punch and appetizers while the bride and groom attended to their first task as man and wife.

The signing of the marriage certificate.

Father O'Rourke picked up the pen, dipped it in the inkwell, and held it out. "Go ahead, lass. They're waiting."

Margaret took the pen in nerveless fingers. As she did, her gaze fell on the gold wedding band Doyle had slipped over her gloved finger. A manacle. Another brand that marked her as belonging to Doyle Kerrigan. A runner.

She started to shake. Letters swam before her eyes. She should talk to Doyle. She should ask him if what Horne said was true. She should find out the truth before she penned her name on this document.

And if it was true, then what? An annulment?

He would never stand for that.

She was vaguely aware of people milling around her— Rylander and Mrs. Throckmorton waiting to sign as witnesses, Doyle lifting a goblet from a footman's silver tray, Mrs. Bradshaw hovering in the doorway with several photographers, while behind them, other people she didn't know scribbled on small note tablets.

How was she to sign? Margaret Hamilton? Cathleen Donovan? Margaret Kerrigan? She didn't know who she was anymore. Tears stinging her eyes, she looked up at the priest who knew her as all three. "What do I write?"

"Your full name, lass. Margaret Hamilton Kerrigan." His kindly eyes held pity, and perhaps a hint of sadness. The rope of lies that bound them together felt like a noose tightening around her neck. But if she broke her silence now, might she bring harm to both him and Mrs. Throckmorton? Doyle was a vengeful man.

Do it. You'll be safe. They'll be safe. No one will ever be able to touch you.

She signed.

As soon as she slipped the pen back into the holder, Doyle thrust a goblet into her hand. Grinning, he raised his high, offering Gaelic and English toasts to wealth and health and happiness.

Margaret forced herself to drink. Over the rim of the glass she saw Rylander studying her with those unreadable, slate-colored eyes, and felt a renewed surge of fear. Had she betrayed herself by asking him about Doyle? Would Rylander realize she knew more about the Irish than she should, and tell her husband? Seeing the goblet wobble in her hand, she carefully set it back on the tray.

"I have a gift for you, *leannan*." Doyle dropped a thick folder onto the table beside their marriage certificate and kissed her cheek. "A token of my love, *a ghra*, and to mark our wedding day. Open it."

With shaky fingers, Margaret lifted the cover. Inside were stock certificates issued by the Hudson and Erie Railroad to Margaret Hamilton Kerrigan. Each certificate was worth twenty shares, and there must have been two dozen certificates. "I don't understand. What does this mean?"

Doyle laughed. "It means you're part owner of a railroad. I know security is important to you. I wanted you to have something of your own."

Looking past Doyle's shoulder at Rylander, she wondered if he had shared with her husband their conversation of two days ago after the engagement ball.

But he was staring hard at Doyle's back, speculation in his gaze.

"Th-thank you." She looked back at her husband. "What am I to do with them?"

"Hold on to them for now, lass. We'll go to Tait's office tomorrow to sign the proxy papers, then to the bank to put them directly into the vault so they'll be safe."

"Proxy for what?"

"So I can cast your vote for you." Leaning down, he gave her a quick kiss to distract her. "It's just business, *a ghra*. Don't worry your pretty head about it. Mrs. Bradshaw," he called, swinging toward the doorway. "As soon as Tait and Mrs. Throckmorton sign, you can let in the reporters and photographers."

"I don't . . . feel . . . well," a halting voice said.

Margaret turned to see Mrs. Throckmorton slumped in the chair, one hand clasped to her chest. Her face was flushed and wispy curls stuck to her damp forehead. She was breathing heavily. "Ma'am? Are you ill?"

Everyone turned to stare. The old lady groaned.

Heart thudding, Margaret looked around in panic, saw the papers and folder on the table, and snatched them up. Rushing to her guardian's side, she began fanning her flushed face. "Ma'am, what's wrong? Are you overheated?"

"Can't . . . breathe . . ."

Margaret fanned harder.

Rylander loomed at her shoulder. Mrs. Bradshaw stooped beside him to loosen Mrs. Throckmorton's collar while Doyle herded the photographers and reporters away from the doorway.

Rylander told Mrs. Bradshaw to get water and a doctor. "Now."

Margaret stared up at him in terror.

"It's probably nothing," he said in his calm way. "Too much excitement."

As Mrs. Bradshaw rushed away, Father O'Rourke took her place at Mrs. Throckmorton's side, his rosary in his hand. His lips moved in a silent prayer.

"She's Lutheran," Margaret said stupidly, grasping at anything to block the fear churning inside.

"The Lord will forgive her."

"Take . . . me . . . to my . . . room," Mrs. Throckmorton said weakly.

"Let's wait for the doctor, dearest." Still fanning, Margaret smoothed her free hand over her guardian's brow. It felt cold even through her thin glove. "He'll be here soon. Then we'll get you up to your bed. You've overdone, I'm afraid. I shouldn't have forced you to come."

"Didn't . . . force . . ." The words trailed off. Her eyes closed.

"Ma'am?" When there was no answer, Margaret looked up at Rylander. "Do something," she cried, her nerves starting to unravel. Mrs. Throckmorton was all she had. The thought of losing her was too unbearable to contemplate.

Rylander's big hand patted her shoulder. "Keep fanning. She'll be fine."

A middle-aged man with a black satchel shoved through the crowded doorway. "I'm the hotel doctor. Where's the patient?"

"Over here." Rylander moved to make room for him.

"She fainted earlier today," Margaret told him as the doctor bent over the slumped woman. "But she's been fine since. She's quite hearty for her age."

"Who are you?"

"Her ward. What's wrong with her? Will she be all right?"

Mrs. Throckmorton moaned piteously.

The doctor listened through his stethoscope, looked into each of the faded blue eyes, poked and prodded until the elderly woman shoved his hands away. Leaning close to her ear, he shouted, "Can you hear me, madam?"

Mrs. Throckmorton flinched. "I'm faint. Not deaf. Nitwit."

He pursed his lips. "She can hear and speak and move," he told Margaret. "So I doubt she's suffered an apoplectic seizure. Heartbeat strong. Lungs clear. Dyspepsia, perhaps. Or nervous prostration. A phlebotomy might help." He reached into his satchel.

Mrs. Throckmorton's fingers tightened on Margaret's.

"You mean a bloodletting?" Rylander's expression of disgust made it clear what he thought of the practice.

The doctor frowned at the interruption. "It's often quite helpful in draining poisonous humors from the body."

"No," Rylander said.

Margaret looked at him in surprise. Not because he was averse to a practice that she, too, thought barbaric, but because he seemed genuinely concerned about an old woman he didn't even know. And where was Doyle through all of this? Seeing the doctor was about to argue, she quickly broke in. "I agree. Don't open her veins. Not unless she worsens. Can she be moved?"

With a huff, the doctor closed his satchel. "She'll have to be carried."

"I'll have one of the bellmen take her to her room," Doyle said, finally having cleared the doorway.

Rylander stepped forward. "I'll do it."

Clutching the folder to her chest, Margaret stepped aside as he scooped up the frail body as if it weighed no more than a sack of grain.

"No screw thing," Mrs. Throckmorton said weakly against his shoulder as he carried her to the door.

Mrs. Bradshaw and Margaret started to follow when Doyle's hand on her shoulder brought Margaret to a stop. "Where are you going, lass? Sure, and the photographers and reporters are waiting."

She frowned, taken aback by the suggestion that she abandon her guardian to appease a pack of gossip columnists. "She needs me, Doyle."

"I need you."

"But—"

"You'll stay, *leannan*. We have guests."

Anger flashed. She wrenched her shoulder from his grip. "I must make certain she's all right. I'll be back as soon as I can."

Without giving him a chance to argue, she swept through the door and raced to catch up with Rylander and Mrs. Bradshaw.

Mr. Rylander was huffing by the time they reached the third-floor suite. Mrs. Bradshaw went ahead into the bedroom to pull back the coverlet, and as soon as Rylander gently laid Mrs. Throckmorton down, Mrs. Bradshaw began unbuttoning her sensible high-topped shoes.

Tossing the folder on top of the bureau, Margaret went to help loosen the elderly woman's clothing. "We'll have you tucked in in no time, ma'am."

"Not . . . in front . . . of them." Turning toward Margaret, the stricken woman lifted a trembling hand. "Please . . . Margaret. Make them . . . go."

Margaret hesitated, fearing to be all alone if something else happened. Just knowing Rylander was nearby to manage things was a comfort.

"Please . . . Margaret."

Promising she would send word by the floor maid if her guardian worsened, Margaret ushered Rylander and Mrs. Bradshaw out.

After she closed the door behind them, she turned to see her guardian bolt upright.

"I thought they would never leave," the old woman said, swinging her feet to the floor. "Get my valise. There, by the wardrobe."

Margaret gaped. "Y-You're all right?"

"Of course I am. But it's apparent you're not. You've been in a state of nerves ever since you came downstairs. Hurry, we haven't much time."

"You big faker!" Caught between hysterical relief and sputtering outrage, Margaret snatched the valise from the floor and almost threw it in the old biddy's face. "I was sick with worry. Why would you do such a thing?"

"So you can decamp." As she spoke, the elderly woman rummaged through the bag. "I could tell you'd finally come to your senses the minute you stumbled into the ballroom on that nice Mr. Rylander's arm. You moved like you were headed to your own hanging. Put this on." She held up a wrinkled black dress. "And this." She tossed out a fur wrap. "I know you dislike wearing dead animals with the heads and tails intact, but it will give you presence. Where's my hatbox?"

Margaret stared blankly, her mind in such turmoil she couldn't think.

Mrs. Throckmorton stopped rummaging and glared impatiently at her. "You do want to decamp, don't you?"

"I . . . I . . ."

"Good. I'll tell you what to do while you dress. They'll be coming soon."

Buffeted along like a leaf in a gale, Margaret did as she was told. "He was a runner," she said as she slipped out of her wedding gown and into Mrs. Throckmorton's funeral dress. "You remember I told you how they met the ships as they came in, full of promises of food and places to stay and a doctor's care. Lies. All of it. They stole everything we had. Even Da's tin whistle and my mother's rosary. And Da so sick, he couldn't even fight back."

She didn't realize she was crying until she felt Mrs. Throckmorton's thin arm slide around her shoulder. Looking into those gentle blue eyes, Margaret felt the pain of betrayal harden into a fury so profound she shook with it. "There was no doctor. No food. No place to stay. My father died in the gutter, trying to protect us from the procurers. Because of men like Doyle."

"How did you find out he was a runner?"

Margaret blotted her tears but still more came. "I overheard two men talking outside the ballroom. I recognized Franklin Horne's voice. He and Smythe were cut from the same cloth. They did things . . . terrible things." She repressed a shudder of revulsion. "I didn't want to believe it. But . . ." She gave her guardian an imploring look. "What if it's just gossip? What if I'm wrong about Doyle?"

The old woman sighed. "You're not, dearest. I had Mr. Quincy at the bank make inquiries. The poor man has been in love with me for years, you know."

"Inquiries about Doyle? What did he find out?"

"That your fiancé had a foul reputation even among the Irish. Now we know why. Quincy didn't mention that he had been a runner, but I don't doubt it."

Oh, God. "Why didn't you warn me?"

"I tried. You wouldn't listen. Now stop sniveling, we haven't time for it. And fetch my hat. The one with the veil. You can drop your wedding dress in the waste chute on your way. That will delay them a bit."

Numbly Margaret followed orders. Within minutes the transformation from white to black was complete, including hat, gloves, and slippers—hers, since Mrs. Throckmorton wore a larger size. Staring through the heavy black veil into the mirror, she saw a small woman in a baggy black dress and fur wrap, wearing a droopy hat that covered her scarfed head. She hardly recognized herself. "Where will I go?"

Mrs. Throckmorton finished packing Margaret's valise and buckled the strap. "West. As fast and as far as you can. I've packed two changes of clothes, your jewelry, the stock folder, and my ready money. I wish there was more, but my income is limited to the trust allowance and we haven't time to get an advance."

"The stock folder? With Doyle's railroad shares? Why did you pack that?"

"They're not his shares. They're yours."

"Mine?"

"He gave them to you, didn't he? What other source of money do you have?"

"But . . ."

"Just take them." Her guardian thrust the handle of the valise into Margaret's gloved hand. "You can decide what to do with them later. You should be able to reach Philadelphia before you have to sell anything. Once you do, don your own clothes and change your name. That should throw them off."

New tears flooded Margaret's eyes. "How can I leave you?"

"You'd rather stay with that Irish runner?"

"No, but—"

"Then hurry. The waste chute is just down the hall." She pressed the wadded wedding dress into Margaret's other hand and marched her toward the door. "Don't try to contact me directly. Kerrigan is too devious not to find out."

A new fear gripped Margaret. "Will you be safe?"

"Me?" She laughed, despite the tears glistening in her eyes. "A confused old woman who suffers fainting spells? I'll run rings around that cad."

Margaret stood helplessly, her hands full, tears dropping down onto the once beautiful wedding dress crushed in her arms. "Oh, ma'am, I don't want to leave you. What if I never see you again?"

"Hush that foolishness. Perhaps I'll come visit you out west once all this blows over. Meanwhile, if you need money, write to me through Cyrus Quincy at the Merchant's Bank. I've left his direction in your bag. I'll do what I can." She poked her head out to check the hallway, then pushed Margaret through the door. "Go, dearest."

Margaret looked back, trying to memorize the beloved face. Unspoken words she had guarded for too many years rose in her throat. "I love you, ma'am."

"I love you, too, daughter. Now run. My spirit will be with you every step of the way." Then she slammed the door in Margaret's face.

After stuffing her wedding attire into the refuse chute, Margaret took the screw railway down, hoping if Doyle came looking for her, he would be too impatient for its slow progress and would take the stairs, instead.

On the second floor the car stopped and several men entered. Shuffling restlessly, they continued their descent in a tight knot—both awed and wary of Otis's railway contraption.

Margaret was perspiring under her fur wrap by the time they reached the ground floor. Exiting the car with the others, she almost collided with Mr. Rylander, who was rushing by with Mrs. Bradshaw. They both looked worried. At the far end of the hall, wedding guests milled and whispered among themselves, ignoring the footmen trying to herd them into the dining room.

Keeping her head down, Margaret kept pace with the men until they veered off toward the smoking room, then she continued alone across the lobby. It seemed to stretch an endless distance toward the giant double front doors.

She heard a familiar voice behind her. Daring a glance over her shoulder, she saw Rylander speaking urgently to the concierge. Battling panic, she forced herself to keep her steps measured and slow, as befitted a woman of advanced years, her entire being focused on passing through the lobby without fainting or breaking into a run.

It seemed forever before she reached the entrance. Her heart was pounding so hard she could hear nothing above the thud of it, and her grip on the valise was slippery with perspiration despite her cotton gloves.

The liveried doorman opened the massive doors. "Good day to you, madam. May I summon transportation for you?"

Margaret tried to answer, couldn't, and nodded instead.

Waving up a hansom cab from the long line of buggies parked along Fifth Avenue, he waited until it stopped at the curb, then opened the door with a flourish. "Where may I direct the coachman to take you, madam?"

She gave an address on Cortland Street, then refusing to let him take the valise from her hand, she climbed in on wobbly legs. As she settled back, movement caught her eye.

Rylander strode through the double doors. He stopped, coat pushed back and hands on hips as he scanned the street. His scowling gaze swept past Margaret, then jerked back.

She froze, unable to look away, certain he recognized her even with the veil.

The coachman snapped the whip and the cab started forward.

As it pulled away from the hotel, she looked back through the small oval window to see Rylander still standing there, staring after her.

Four

"What do you mean, you can't find her?" Doyle demanded. Mrs. Bradshaw clasped and unclasped her hands at her waist. She looked frightened, her dark brown eyes refusing to meet his. "She's not in the suite, sir. Or in the staircase, or the vertical railway between floors. I-I can't find her."

Doyle could see she was on the verge of tears. He had no patience for it. They had already delayed serving the first dinner course and the guests were getting restless. "Have you asked the concierge? Or Father O'Rourke? She may have come down unnoticed."

Tait walked up, tension evident in the stern lines around his mouth. "They haven't seen her. I checked."

Damn woman. He told her they had guests waiting and not to leave. He would have to put a stop to such disobedience. "Where the hell is she?"

Realizing his voice had drawn the notice of several guests standing outside the dining room doorway, Doyle struggled to hide his irritation behind a bland smile. "What did the old lady say?" he asked his housekeeper.

"I-I didn't speak directly to her. She was resting."

"Faith! I'll go talk to her myself." He spun away.

Tait fell in behind him, calling back orders as he followed Doyle toward the stairwell. "Mrs. Bradshaw, check the ladies' retiring rooms and the ballroom, then serve the first course. If anyone asks, tell them Mrs. Throckmorton is unwell and Doyle and Margaret are checking on her."

Doyle sprinted up the stairs, Tait close behind him. "Where could she be?"

"Calm down, Doyle. We'll find her."

Doyle wasn't convinced. He had a bad feeling about this. Margaret had been acting strange and unsettled even before her guardian took sick. Was she sick, too? Had someone said something?

When they stepped onto the third floor, he saw the floor maid at her post in the hallway. "Come along," he snapped, marching ahead to Mrs. Throckmorton's suite. He knocked.

No response.

Whirling, he glared at the wide-eyed maid. "Have you seen anyone leave this room?"

"N-No, sir."

"Have you left your post in the last half hour?"

"Only when I took fresh pillows to room three thirteen."

"Do you have a key?"

"Yes, sir."

"Open the door."

"But I'm not allowed—"

"*Damnu ort!* Mrs. Throckmorton isn't feeling well. Now open the door or look for another position!"

The maid opened the door.

Doyle pushed inside, calling for Margaret. A weak answer came from the bedroom on the right, but it wasn't Margaret's voice. Waving the maid forward, he instructed her to tell Mrs. Throckmorton he needed to speak with her.

The maid slipped inside the bedroom. A moment later, she came back out. "S-She says she's not up to visitors, sir."

"Jasus!" Shoving the stupid woman aside, he charged into Mrs. Throckmorton's bedroom. "Where is she?"

The old woman frowned up at him. She was fully dressed, stretched atop a settee beside the glowing coal stove, her legs covered by a cotton throw. The room was stifling. "Where is who?" she asked.

"My wife!" Doyle crossed to the wardrobe, flung it open but saw no one hiding, then went to the window and swept aside the drapes. Nothing. Not that he expected it. Margaret wasn't some cringing violet.

Pain pounded against his temples, and he knew if he didn't get himself in hand, he'd start yelling at the old crone. Striving for a reasonable tone, he walked back to the settee. "My wife is missing. Do you know where she is?"

"M-Missing?" Faded blue eyes darted from Doyle to Tait, who stood at his shoulder. "Margaret is missing? What have you done to her?"

Rankled by the accusation, Doyle stepped forward, not sure what he intended to do. Mrs. Throckmorton had been a bane to him since the first with her sly jabs and honey-coated criticisms. But now that Margaret was safely under his care, he had no intention of allowing this interfering biddy's influence to continue. "She came up here with you but never returned. So where is she?"

"I d-don't know." The old woman cringed as if he'd shouted it. "Stay away from me, you bounder! H-Help! Somebody help me."

Doyle blinked, confused. He glanced at Tait, saw the same bewilderment mirrored on his face. But before he could calm the crazy woman down, the maid rushed in from the sitting room.

"Ma'am, what is it?"

Mrs. Throckmorton lifted a fluttering hand. "H-Help me," she quavered. "This devil is threatening me."

"*Bi ciuin!* I did no such thing!"

"See? He's yelling in tongues." The old lady cowered against the cushions, her frail hand clutching at her chest. "Don't leave me, Rachel."

The maid looked fearfully up at Doyle and Tait. "I won't, ma'am."

Doyle wanted to hit them both.

Tait stepped forward. Speaking in that irritatingly reasonable voice he used whenever he was trying to calm down a situation, he said, "We're sorry to disturb you, Mrs. Throckmorton. I'm sure Mr. Kerrigan meant no harm. He's just worried about Margaret. But the guests are waiting and we need to find her. You have no idea where she might be?"

Ignoring Doyle, she spoke directly to Tait. "No, I don't. She sat with me for a minute, then said she needed to freshen up before going downstairs. That's the last I saw of her." Tears welled in her eyes. "You don't suppose something has happened to her, do you?"

"Not at all. We probably crossed paths when we came up. I'm sorry we troubled you, ma'am." He turned to the maid. "Find us if you see Mrs. Kerrigan."

"Yes, sir."

Grabbing Doyle's arm, Tait marched him back out the door. As soon as they were in the hall, Doyle jerked free. "She knows something."

"Maybe. But yelling at her won't get answers."

"So what am I supposed to do? Christ." Doyle dragged a hand through his hair. Where was his wife? What was going on? "Sure, and I've got a hundred people waiting to toast the bride and groom. What do I tell them?"

"That she's still with her guardian and will be down as soon as she can. Meanwhile, I'll get some of the hotel staff and keep looking. We'll find her."

"You'd better." Doyle stomped down the hall. "Check every room. She's got to be here somewhere. She can't have just disappeared." A terrible thought brought him to an abrupt halt. He whirled, making Tait sidestep to keep from crashing into him. "You don't suppose someone took her, do you? Or has done her harm to get at me?"

"Of course not."

"Then where the hell is she?"

"I don't know, but we'll find her. Just calm down."

"Feis ort." Spinning on his heel, Doyle continued down the hall.

This couldn't be happening. Not on his wedding day. Not to him.

The lamplighter was starting his rounds when the cab drove off into the lowering sun, leaving Margaret standing on the walk outside a closed dress shop. She looked around, half expecting to see Rylander bearing down on her.

But the street was empty except for the lamplighter and a

dozing beggar huddled in a doorway, the yellow stripe down the empty leg of his tattered Confederate uniform barely discernible in the dwindling daylight. Resisting the urge to push back the heavy black veil so she could see better, Margaret shifted the valise to her other hand and started walking.

She wondered if they realized yet that she was missing. Judging by Rylander's scowl when he'd stepped out onto the walk in front of the hotel, they did. Had they approached Mrs. Throckmorton yet? Would they be rough with her? Remembering the way Doyle had treated Mrs. O'Reilly, she wasn't reassured.

She should go back. Face Doyle with the rumors. If they were true, she could demand that they dissolve the marriage.

On what grounds? That he had lied to her about his past? But hadn't she done the same thing to him? And what about the railroad shares? Even though Doyle had given them to her as a gift, what if they thought her disappearance was part of an elaborate deception to abscond with them? And if they found out she wasn't who she and Mrs. Throckmorton and Father O'Rourke said she was, wouldn't that open them all up to charges of fraud or theft?

Even worse, she had seen Doyle's temper. He was not a man who would take such a betrayal lightly.

No, she couldn't go back. Not now. Not ever.

She trudged on. Dusk crept closer. After several minutes, she heard the clatter of hooves, and turned to see a horsecar coming down the street. After flagging the driver down, she climbed aboard, paid her coin, and took a seat, the valise clutched tightly in her lap. Two blocks farther, she exited at the Regal Hotel, where two hansom cabs stood at the curb. The coachmen were leaning against the elevated dash of the first buggy, smoking and talking. When they saw her coming down the walk, they turned to study her.

Margaret studied them, too, wondering which might be the more trustworthy. The older one—a squat, gray-haired man with untrimmed sideburns—smiled, showing gaps in his teeth. He had kind eyes, so Margaret addressed her inquiries to him. "Are you available?"

"Yes, ma'am." Pinching off the end of his smoke, he slipped the butt into his vest pocket, then reached for her valise.

Margaret stepped back. "I'll take care of it." She didn't dare let the bag out of her hands. It contained her entire future. After setting it on the passenger seat, she climbed in after it.

The coachman took his position in the raised driver's box and unwound the reins from the brake lever. "Where to, ma'am?" he called back over his shoulder.

"The Paulus Hook ferry. Have we time to make the last one?"

"If we hurry. Hold on."

Twenty minutes later, she was steaming across the Hudson River toward New Jersey, the lamplights of Manhattan just beginning to show in the darkening sky behind her. If Doyle or Rylander came after her, they would either have to wait for the morning ferry or go all the way around to the bridge. That would give her somewhat of a head start. Now all she had to do was find a train leaving tonight, and she would be on her way.

Luck continued to smile on her; the evening train to Philadelphia had been delayed and was just boarding when she arrived at the Pennsylvania Railroad terminal. She hadn't enough money for a Pullman sleeping car but was too nervous to sleep anyway. The other travelers took no notice of her as she bought her ticket and moved at a stately pace across the platform toward the train.

She settled in a forward-facing window seat on the depot side, the valise tucked between the back of her calves and the front of the bench seat. Hands clasped tightly in her lap, she scanned the platform as the rest of the passengers filed in and took their seats, but she saw no familiar faces.

The door closed. The conductor moved down the aisle, calling out the next stops on their route as he punched vouchers. The train didn't move.

She sat sweating beneath her fur wrap, her gaze pinned to the station doors, expecting to see Doyle and Rylander burst out and try to stop the train.

They didn't.

Minutes ticked by.

After what seemed an interminable wait, the train jerked, then rolled forward.

Margaret almost wept in relief.

Moving at a snail's pace, the train left the station and crawled past loading docks behind unlit warehouses and factories.

Hurry, Margaret urged silently, counting every clack of the wheels over the joints in the track. Slowly they picked up speed. There was still enough light as they crossed the Hackensack River for her to see the fishing boats returning home, but by the time they crossed the new bridge over the Passaic, it was too dark to see anything but the faint glitter of lights on the far shore. Once past the river, buildings gave way to moonlit fields and the train settled into a swaying rhythm.

Slumping back, Margaret heaved a great sigh. Her heart pounded so hard she felt dizzy and breathless. The palms of her black cotton gloves were damp with sweat, and she felt weak from the unrelenting tension. But it was done.

The first part of her escape was over.

With a trembling hand, she pulled her watch from her reticule.

Eight forty-one. Less than three hours had passed since she had gone upstairs with Mrs. Throckmorton. If the day had proceeded as planned, the wedding guests would now be enjoying the baked meringue puffs with bourbon raspberry sauce she had so carefully picked out.

Instead, Doyle would be looking in earnest now. His initial anger that she had left him to tend her guardian would have faded into puzzlement over why she was taking so long. He would send someone—Mrs. Bradshaw or Rylander—to hurry her along. When they reported they couldn't find her, the first doubts would form. He would wonder if something sinister had happened. He had enemies. She suspected he took pride in that, seeing it as proof of his power. The thought might come to him that one of them could have spirited her away.

At that point he would demand the hotel staff check every floor and room, the exits, the kitchens, the pantries and linen closets, the basement and roof. When she still couldn't be found, he would call in the police.

First, they would question Mrs. Throckmorton, the floor maid, and Mrs. Bradshaw. Then they would question the guests. Even now, men might be searching the hotel suite, going through her private things. They would find the dresses she'd left behind in the wardrobe. Her coat. They would see her extra brush on the vanity, her robe on the hook in the water closet, and her slippers beside the bed.

But they wouldn't find her wedding gown. Or her jewelry. Or her valise. They wouldn't find the folder containing the railroad shares. And when they reported that to Doyle, he would know.

Then God help her.

Doyle swirled his cup and watched the dark liquid rise up the sides, exposing a thick sludge of coffee grounds in the bottom. He needed something stronger. Something to calm his nerves. Take the edge off the anger and worry. His gaze shifted to the decanter of brandy on the table beside the bookcases in his office.

Just one drink. That's all. Surely Tait wouldn't begrudge him that.

Instead, he shoved the cup aside. Rising, he walked to the window overlooking the street that ran in front of his house. The tall streetlamps cast pools of light on the cobbled street, flashing briefly off the badges of uniformed men clustered around a closed police wagon. More men moved through his house—he heard them cross the floor overhead, tromp up and down the stairs, slam shut doors on cabinets and wardrobes.

He hated this invasion of his privacy. But after they'd found nothing at the Fifth Avenue, he'd had no choice but to call in the police. Within half an hour, they were swarming the hotel like blue-backed ants. Wasting their time, searching the same places Tait had already checked, and badgering the guests with the same questions he'd already asked. They even went to Mrs. Throckmorton's house to search Margaret's room there. And now they were here in his home, doing another useless search rather than combing the streets for his wife. When he'd seen them digging through the luggage Margaret had sent over earlier, putting their hands on her underthings and intimate items, he'd been so filled with frustration and disgust he'd had to walk away.

Five hours ago he'd been anticipating his wedding night. He thought he finally had everything he wanted within his reach. Now he was watching strange men paw through his wife's personal belongings.

Where was she?

Cursing under his breath, he walked back to his desk and sank into the chair.

Jasus, what a mess. Dealing with the wedding guests had been humiliating. He had put it off as long as he could, but when Tait insisted he call in the police, he'd had no choice but to inform them that his wife was missing.

Shock. Concern. Sly smirks. He could guess the thoughts behind those knowing looks—that they knew all along no decent woman would marry an uneducated Irish immigrant no matter how rich and powerful he was. No surprise to them that she would leave him the first chance she got.

But Margaret wasn't like that. Despite her lofty ways, she seemed to understand and accept him. And once he explained what he expected of her, she would have made the perfect wife and hostess and mother for his children. She would understand her role as his bridge from the past to the future—from what he had been to what he wanted to be. She would help him build a dynasty.

Assuming he found her. Faith, where could she be? What happened?

With a sigh, he rested his elbows on the desk and threaded his fingers through the hair at his temples. Staring blindly at the wood grain of his walnut desk, he tried to come up with a logical explanation for her disappearance.

He could draw only two conclusions, neither of which made sense.

His wife had been taken, either for ransom—but then where was the demand for money?—or by someone who wanted to harm him—but who?

Or she had left him. Why? For what reason? Two days ago she had been more affectionate toward him than she'd ever been. They were fine.

And yet, she was gone. He couldn't escape that.

Gone on purpose? Or under duress?

A knock on the door brought his head around. News, at last. He was desperate for something, good or bad. He couldn't take the not knowing much longer. "Enter."

Tait walked in. Doyle knew it wasn't good news when he saw his friend's face. Then he noticed the wad of cloth under his arm. Stained white silk. Torn lace and tiny crushed pearls. Margaret's wedding dress.

The air left him.

"It was caught on a nail in a garbage chute, halfway between the second and third floors." Tait dropped the ruined gown over the back of one of the chairs in front of Doyle's desk, then slumped in the other, weariness evident in the deep lines bracketing his wide mouth. "There was no blood on it, thank God."

Doyle stared stupidly at the crumpled dress, remembering the last time he'd seen it hours earlier. Margaret had looked so beautiful coming down the aisle toward him. His bride. Slim. Petite.

Trembling. Why?

Nerves? Or something else?

"We also found this. Wrapped up inside the veil." Tait pulled an item from his pocket and set it on the desk.

Smooth and golden. Small enough to fit his little finger. The wedding band he had given his bride.

It took a moment for it to sink in. Then rage arced through his chest. A red haze formed behind his eyes. He started to shake.

Goddamn her.

His fury built with every heartbeat, hammered through his head. He had trusted her. Given her wealth, the promise of an easy life, a position as one of the most powerful hostesses in New York. And this is how she repaid him?

"Goddamn her to hell!"

Tait straightened in the chair. "You're blaming Margaret? For what? We don't even know yet what happened."

"She left me. That's what happened." The realization exploded in Doyle's mind, loosening a maelstrom of other thoughts that swirled and circled and bounced back at him from a dozen directions. "The bitch played me for a fool."

"How do you figure that?"

"By this." With shaking fingers, Doyle held up the ring. The words he'd had engraved on the inside of the band caught the light. *Ta gra agam duit*—I love you. Faith, he was such an idiot. "If she'd been taken for ransom, they would have sent this back to me as proof that they had her. Or if it was someone who intended to harm her or threaten me, they would have sent it back still on her finger. No, boyo." He let the band drop back to the desk, where it landed with a clink and spun to a stop. "This ring wasn't stolen or lost. It was thrown away. Like garbage."

Like me.

She would pay for that, may the devil take her soul. And for making a fool of him in front of all those people. By God, she would pay.

"Margaret wouldn't do such a thing," Tait said flatly. "There was no reason for it."

"Oh, there was reason." Another burst of anger almost sent Doyle from his chair. "She had plenty of reasons. Twenty-five of them. And each worth twenty shares in the Hudson and Erie Railroad."

Tait slumped back. Doyle could see him working it through in his logical way. His friend had a brilliant mind but a soft nature. He was too easily swayed by sentiment. He lacked the ruthlessness, the kind of ambition and drive it took to claw out a handhold in the highest reaches of the business world. He was a man of such high-minded principle he had fought for the Union even though he knew the defeat of the South would destroy the home he loved.

Fortunately, Doyle wasn't burdened with that kind of self-defeating weakness. He had no time for blind loyalty or faltering excuses. He knew the baseness of people—he'd seen it—lived it. Principles never stoked a fire or filled a belly, and Doyle was determined he would never be cold or hungry again.

He would find her. She couldn't run far enough to evade his reach. And then she would pay for this humiliation.

"That doesn't wash," Tait said, apparently still trying to find an acceptable reason for Margaret's defection. "She stood to gain more as your wife than as a thief on the run. Besides, she didn't even know about the stock certificates until you gave them to her. And even if she had, how did she plan to sell them? No bank would buy them without wiring for verification of the serial numbers, and as members of the board of the Hudson and Erie, we would know immediately." He shook his head. "More to the point, Margaret wouldn't do it. She's not a devious woman. I don't believe it."

Doyle didn't want to believe it, either. He wasn't often deceived, especially by women. He wouldn't have thought his wife smart enough to conceive such a plan, much less execute it all on her own. And he knew she didn't have help. The men he'd had watching over her up until this morning had kept him apprised of every contact in her life.

Unless he'd been wrong about that, too.

Angry all over again, he yanked open the center drawer and swept the ring inside. Slamming it closed, he sat forward, arms folded on the desk. "Start over. Figure out how she left the hotel, then track her from there. If she's running, she'll go by train since that's the fastest. But not to a small town where she would be easy to find. She'll go to a city, someplace big enough to get lost in. North is Albany. I'll wire a man I know up there and have him watch the stations. If she's headed west, she'll have to go south, then across to Philadelphia. That's where I want you, Tait. Meanwhile, I'll get some boys to start looking closer by. If she's still on this island, we'll find her."

Abruptly, Tait rose and walked to the window. He stood for a moment, looking out, then turned. Doyle recognized the mulish look. "And then what, Doyle? When you find her, what do you intend to do?"

Doyle didn't answer because he didn't know what he would do once he caught up with his runaway bride. Divorce her? Such a public scandal would be impossible to live down.

A quiet annulment? On what grounds—desertion? The smirks would never end, then.

Take her back? He could do that, pretend everything was a simple misunderstanding. Sure, and he would have to keep a watch on her, but once she provided the children he needed, he could send her into a quiet retirement in a carefully chosen institution. Not a particularly pleasant idea, but doable.

Forcing a smile, he sat back. "Don't you worry about that, boyo. Just find her. I'll take care of the rest."

Margaret dozed on and off throughout the night, awakening to bright morning sunlight as they clattered over the bridge across the Delaware River on their approach into Philadelphia. She felt wretched, every muscle stiff from fighting the bounce and sway of the passenger car, and so weary she was numb.

Several minutes later the train shuddered to a stop at the

Thirtieth Street Station. She studied the figures on the platform. She didn't expect to see Doyle or Rylander, knowing they couldn't have gotten here ahead of her even if they'd known which route she would take. But a telegram could cover the hundred miles from New York to Philadelphia in a matter of minutes. Doyle could have wired ahead to the authorities. Sheriffs, marshals, tellers, detectives, even hotel keepers within several hundred miles of Manhattan could all be looking for her now.

But no one meeting the arriving passengers stood out as being overly watchful. Just to be sure, she waited for a family of four to pass down the aisle toward the exit, then slipped in behind them. Making appropriate cooing noises at the infant peering at her over her father's shoulder, she struck up a conversation with the mother, a sweet-faced woman with a quick smile. Chatting amiably in what she hoped was an old woman's voice, she accompanied them into the depot before bidding them good-bye and ducking into the ladies' washroom.

Ten minutes later, she emerged as fresh as a woman could be after spending the night on a hard bench on a moving train. Seeing no one lurking suspiciously about, she went to check the schedule. There was a train bound for Pittsburgh leaving late that afternoon. Hopefully that would give her ample time to complete her business, and by then she would have enough money to purchase a sleeping berth. She couldn't take another night without sleep.

After reserving a private compartment on the afternoon westbound, she picked up her valise and walked out onto the street. Approaching the first hansom cab in the line awaiting fares, she asked him to take her to the Girard Bank.

While the coachman negotiated the narrow cobbled streets, Margaret took her jewelry case out of her valise. Selecting to impress, rather than for style, she quickly put on the amethyst and diamond necklace Doyle had given her and the diamond earbobs from Mrs. Throckmorton. Then she covered herself once again with the heavy veil and fur wrap and sat back, her mind racing.

During the long hours of the night, she had come up with a plan to get her through the next phase of her escape. She went over the details one more time, but her thoughts kept tangling up and she couldn't seem to concentrate. Exhaustion was setting in. She felt it in aching muscles and in the numbness of her mind after all the hours of fear and tension. But she couldn't relax yet. She had to set this next part of her plan in motion and get out as quickly as possible. Then she could rest.

The sun arced higher, shining through the window behind her seat. The nasty fur Mrs. Throckmorton had insisted she wear had been welcome in the coolness of the night. But now, as it warmed in the sun, it gave off a faint musty animal odor.

She wondered how Mrs. Throckmorton was doing, and if Doyle had been harsh with her. She knew he was capable of it. She wasn't sure about Tait Rylander. He had surprised her with his kind treatment of her guardian and his defense of the widow O'Reilly. Hopefully, he had been there to curb Doyle's temper when he had questioned Mrs. Throckmorton.

Weariness sapped her spirit, opened her mind to regret and doubt. But determined not to let weakness overcome her, she concentrated instead on exactly what she would say when she met with the banker.

That was the key. The most dangerous step. If she could get through the next few hours and escape Philadelphia before Doyle found her, she would finally be free.

Five

Leaning a shoulder against the window frame by his seat, Tait Rylander tried to doze despite the constant motion of the passenger car and the glare of morning sunlight shining into his face. He'd been awake and on the move all night. But even though his body was worn out, his mind wouldn't slow.

Thoughts of her kept circling in his head—the stricken look on her face when he'd led her toward the altar; the tremble in the gloved hand on his arm; the short, rapid breaths that had sent a quiver through the white bridal veil; the way she smelled.

Had it been nerves? Fear? An act? The woman had him so confused he didn't know what to think.

The woman.

The clever and enigmatic Margaret.

His business partner's wife.

Giving up on sleep, Tait straightened. As he rubbed the stiffness from his neck, he looked around. The car was almost full. Mostly businessmen. A few farmers. A couple of families. The New York to Philadelphia route was one of the busiest. The PRR ran four trains a day, which was lucky for him, because that would give him his best chance of catching up with her.

She must be exhausted by now—he sure as hell was—and she had to sleep sometime. Philadelphia was a big city, a good place to hole up, get some rest, and reorganize. That's what he would do if he were on the run.

But she'd surprised him several times already, and she might again. The lady was damned clever.

An image flashed through his mind of a frail woman dressed all in black from her heavy mourning veil to her dark shoes, making halting progress across the Fifth Avenue lobby. But instead of the plain half boots favored by most elderly women, she wore stylish black slippers with low heels. And her progress might have been slow, but her spine had been straight and her shoulders level, despite the weight of the valise she carried.

He had seen all that in a glance but had discounted it without a thought; he had been looking for a bride, not a widow. And a few minutes later, when he'd walked outside and had seen her look back at him through the rear window as the hansom cab had rolled away, that sudden shock of . . . something he couldn't define . . . had halted him in his tracks. But even then, it still hadn't registered that she might have been Margaret.

Then they'd found her wedding dress. And the ring. And as his mind had scanned back through all the events of that afternoon, the image of that darkly clad woman with her stylish shoes and youthful posture and firm grip on a vaguely familiar valise had come back to plague him.

He knew that slim figure. It had haunted his thoughts for a year.

But why would she do this? Had it all been a ruse? An elaborate scheme to steal a valise full of railroad shares she couldn't even sell?

And yet she was gone, along with her jewelry and the stock certificates.

He still didn't want to believe it. He didn't like the idea of being so easily fooled by a pretty face. There was a mystery beneath that careful smile, and harsh experience behind those watchful green eyes, and that presented a challenge he couldn't resist. He would find out the truth about the elusive Margaret Hamilton. He would track her down and learn all her secrets, then he would return her to her lawful husband. And finally, maybe he would be able to forget her.

But first, he had to find her.

Beyond the window, the scattered farms and towns of central New Jersey rolled by, dotted here and there with hardwoods and a few stands of pine. Far to the northwest, the shadowed silhouette of the Allegheny range of the northern Appalachians left a smudge across the horizon, while to the southeast, the distant horizon sank into the Atlantic Ocean.

He remembered this place.

Even though the towns had grown, and the fields were now bisected by new fences and roads, there was a familiar feel to the humid air and the faint salty tang in the breeze. Almost seven years ago, he had marched through here on his way to meet Lee's army at Gettysburg—an untested, twenty-seven-year-old who thought being a lawyer also made him wise. Fueled by patriotism, dazzled by idealism, and blinded by the certainty of youth, he had rushed headlong into the fray, only to stagger back out three days later, bloodied, horrified, and changed forever. Ironically, a day after victory, having survived the deadliest battle of the Civil War, he might have died anyway, if not for Doyle Kerrigan.

He wondered how much longer he would have to pay on that debt.

With a weary sigh, he tipped back his head and closed his eyes.

This was it, he decided. Once he returned Doyle's errant wife to him, he would put an end to this partnership that grew more burdensome every day.

But first, he had to find her. Hopefully, in Philadelphia he would, because if she made it to Columbus, Ohio, he could lose her for good. That was where she would either go up to Chicago or west to St. Louis, and if he guessed wrong, he might never find her again. He would definitely have to be more careful this time, he reminded himself. She had already thrown him off track more than once.

He smiled, admiring her ingenuity despite the trouble she had caused him. But once he'd realized she was using the disguise of an elderly widow lady, it had simply been a case of staying on her trail.

He had finally picked it up late last night when he'd questioned the coachmen still on duty outside the Fifth Avenue Hotel. After learning one of them had taken an old lady to Cortland Street earlier in the evening, Tait had hired him to return to the exact spot where he had left her.

An odd place to stop, he'd thought as the cab drove away.

No houses, or hotels, or eateries. Why here? To visit the printer's shop? That haberdashery across the street? As he'd puzzled over that, a cough had drawn his attention, and he'd looked over to see a one-legged man in a tattered Confederate uniform slouched in the recessed entry of a closed shop.

"Spare a coin?" the man asked.

Tait reached into his pocket and pulled out several. Hunkering before the old soldier, he handed one over. "I'm looking for a woman," he said. "An old widow lady wearing all black and carrying a valise."

"Younger one would be livelier." Pleased with his quip, the Reb snickered, then doubled over with a wheezy cough.

Tait waited for the spasm to end, then continued. "Came by hansom cab several hours ago. You notice anyone like that?"

"Widow lady? Carrying a traveling bag? Around dusk? Yep."

"You see where she went?"

"Hmm . . . let me think."

Tait held out another coin.

Dirty fingers snatched it from his grip and pointed down the street. "That a way."

Tait gave him two more coins, then headed in the direction the Reb had indicated, checking each doorway as he walked past. It was night, so none of the shops and office buildings were open. Nor, he realized, would any have been open earlier when Margaret had come by. Confused, he stopped and looked around, wondering again why she would come here if everything was closed for the night.

Then he saw the rails in the street and nodded in grudging respect.

Clever lady. Trying to throw him off her trail by switching from hansom cab to horsecar. Walking briskly, he followed the rails to the next stop at the Regal Hotel. Pushing open the door, he went inside.

The Regal wasn't as fancy as the Fifth Avenue with its twenty-four-hour concierge, but it did have a desk clerk napping in his chair. Tait thumped the counter to wake him, then made his inquiries.

"No, no widows have checked in," the old man said around a yawn as he ran a gnarly finger down the short list of guests that had arrived since six o'clock the previous evening. "Did someone let her off here?"

"I'm not sure."

"Did you check with the coachmen out front?"

"Didn't see any."

"They should be coming back on duty soon. Best ask them."

Tait did, got the information he sought, and an hour later, just as the first rays of dawn cast an orange sheen across the sluggish waters of the Hudson River, he was steaming toward Paulus Hook, New Jersey, on the first crossing of the day. He figured he was less than ten hours behind his quarry.

From the ferry dock it was only a short walk to the Pennsylvania Railroad station. Hoping Doyle was right about where his wife might be headed, Tait purchased a seat on the next train to Philadelphia, departing in twenty-three minutes and arriving at two seventeen at the Thirtieth Street Station—"give or take an hour." Then he queried the stationmaster and ticket agents about his "widowed aunt" who might have taken the westbound late yesterday.

The stationmaster had been at dinner during the time in question, and neither of the two agents had been working the late shift the previous evening.

"Normally, that last train departs at six forty-five, give or take," a talkative fellow in a Pennsy cap told him. "But yesterday it was running late. She might have made it. If so, she should be arriving in Philadelphia at about nine this morning. Give or take an hour or so."

"And from there to Pittsburgh?" Assuming she continued west, that would be her next major stop.

There were two daily; one leaving Philadelphia at eight in the morning—which she would miss because of the delay—and the evening run at six.

That was the one.

Feeling like he was finally closing in on her, Tait thanked the agent and settled on a bench in the lobby to await the boarding call for the seven twenty-eight to Philadelphia. Give or take.

That was five hours ago. And here he sat with two more hours to go—low on money, hungry, unshaven, wearing the same clothes he'd put on after hurriedly changing out of his wedding garb hours ago, and so tired he could hardly think.

All because of a woman who was married to another man. He had to be the stupidest man alive.

Margaret had decided to maintain her widow's disguise until after she finished at the Girard Bank. It would add a bit of urgency to her request and hopefully create sympathy. She would have to use her real name, of course, just as it appeared on the certificates. But once the transaction was completed, she could discard the dress and nasty fur, and become herself again. But with a new name.

The Girard Bank of Philadelphia was an imposing structure with an elaborate marble façade that sported six huge fluted columns and a tall arched doorway. She had heard Doyle mention this bank in his business discussions with Rylander, and hoped to make use of that connection. Her heart pounding against her ribs, she walked stiffly up the seven steps to the marble-framed doorway.

As she neared the entrance, a uniformed man pulled the door open from inside. "Good morning, ma'am. How may I direct you?" he asked with a half bow.

"The bank manager, please."

"Mr. Bigelow is not in today, ma'am. May I direct you to someone else?"

"Oh, dear. He specifically said to come by on Monday. When will he return?"

"Today is Tuesday, ma'am. And he'll be away for the rest of the week."

"He's out of town? Oh, dear. He didn't go to New York, did he?"

"Baltimore. I'm sorry you missed him. Perhaps you would care to set up another appointment with his secretary?" He pointed a white-gloved finger toward the back, where a bespectacled man not much older than she sat at a desk positioned between two closed doors.

"Yes, thank you. You've been most helpful. I shall commend you to Mr. Bigelow when next I see him."

"Thank you, ma'am. May I help you with your bag?"

"Heavens, no. My husband said it wasn't to leave my hand until it was in the vault."

"Of course, ma'am."

Her footfalls echoed up to the high ceilings as she crossed the buffed marble floor toward the secretary's desk. There was a feeling of reverence in the hushed voices of the tellers, and the tang of floor polish and furniture wax hung in the still air. She could almost hear the clink of coin and smell the money shuffling through the teller's hands. Ignoring the racing of her pulse, she kept her head high and her steps unhurried, as if she had every right to be in this grand place.

"Is he in?" she asked, stopping before the desk, the valise clasped in both hands against the front of her skirts.

The man looked up, his brown eyes barely discernible behind the smudged lenses. "What?"

"Mr. Bigelow. Is he in? It's imperative that I see him straight away."

"I'm sorry, but Mr. Bigelow will be away for the rest of the week."

"Oh, dear. He hasn't left for Baltimore already, has he? This is most vexing." Margaret sniffed, made a show of looking around, then said with strained patience, "The assistant manager, then. Is he available?"

"Mr. Lufkin?"

"Of course, Mr. Lufkin."

"May I ask why you wish to see him?"

"I have need of the vault." She nodded down at the valise. "And to establish a line of credit. Tell him Mrs. Kerrigan is here to see him. From New York. Manhattan, to be precise."

More blinking.

"Honestly, must I find another bank to take my money?"

That brought him to life. "I'll tell Mr. Lufkin you're here." He disappeared into the right-hand office, the door of which bore the nameplate HORACE LUFKIN. A minute later, he emerged, a nervous smile on his face, and ushered her into a darkly paneled room with a tall window on one wall, bookcases on another, and a huge walnut desk facing the door. Behind it sat another bespectacled man. This one was middle-aged, better dressed, and—judging from the way he looked down his long nose at her—very proud of his position.

Rising from his leather chair, he indicated the wooden chair beside his desk. "Please . . . Mrs. Kerrigan, is it?"

"Yes. Mrs. Doyle Kerrigan. Of Manhattan."

The banker showed no recognition of the name. A bit of a setback, but she couldn't falter now.

While Margaret took her seat, the valise tucked beside her leg, Lufkin returned to his chair. Leaning back, he propped his elbows on the armrests and regarded her over his steepled fingers. "How may I help you, Mrs. Kerrigan?"

"I'm sure Mr. Bigelow explained the purpose of my visit."

"I'm afraid he didn't, madam. Perhaps you could enlighten me."

"Oh? Well, I suppose Doyle asked for discretion. He's like that, you know."

As she spoke, Margaret pushed aside the fur wrap so that it hung over the back of her chair, allowing him a fine view of the diamond and amethyst necklace and the rounded bosom on which it lay. Then lifting her arms, she pushed the heavy black veil over the top of her hat and gave him a broad smile—the one that best showed off her straight white teeth and the dimple in her left cheek.

It was obvious by his expression that he had expected a much older woman to be hiding beneath the widow's hat.

"I was supposed to meet with Mr. Bigelow on Monday," she went on, "but I got my days all mixed up. You know how it is when one is traveling. And with my recent loss . . ." She paused to press splayed fingers against her bodice just above her bejeweled breasts. "It's been most difficult."

Lufkin stared at her hand. "My condolences, madam."

"And secretive," she added in a breathy voice.

When he said no more, he pulled his gaze up to meet hers. "Secretive?"

"Mr. Kerrigan. Something about railroad shares and such like. And then there's our recent wedding, and now my father's death, and . . . oh, it's just so involved." She sighed and plucked at the top button of her dress, drawing his attention back to her bosom. It was one of her best features, judging by the attention Doyle gave it. And Rylander, too, when he thought she didn't notice. "Are you hot? I am. It gets so stuffy under that heavy veil." She made a fluttery motion just over her right breast. The bigger of the two, but not by enough that one would notice.

Lufkin cleared his throat. Balling his steepled fingers into fists, he lowered his hands to his lap. "Perhaps a glass of water?"

"That would be lovely."

There must have been a bell button beneath his desk, because within moments the door opened and the secretary whisked inside.

"Water," Lufkin barked in a strained voice.

"Of course."

Margaret fluttered and fanned until the secretary returned to set a tray with a pitcher and two glasses on the edge of the desk. He poured, passed a glass to Margaret, then hastily retreated.

Margaret drank slowly, then carefully licked the last droplets from her lips, all under Mr. Lufkin's rapt gaze. Setting the glass back onto the tray, she sighed wearily. "Now where were we? Oh, yes. The railroad shares." Reaching down, she pulled the folder of certificates from the valise and set it on the desk. "My husband was most specific that I not sell them . . . something to do with retaining ownership for a shareholder vote, I think." She paused to shoot him another dimpled smile. "Such business matters are far over my head, I fear. But I understand he had instructed Mr. Bigelow to set up a line of credit, whatever that is, using these shares as collateral. Does that make sense?"

"It does. May I?" Lufkin motioned to the folder.

"Of course." Margaret pushed it across the desk and sat back as he thumbed through the certificates.

"These represent quite a substantial sum," he said after a moment. "Did you intend to put all of them up as surety?"

"Heavens, no. Certainly no more than four or five. Hopefully that should be enough."

"Enough for what, if I may ask?"

Margaret pulled a hanky from her sleeve and dabbed at her eyes. "This is so embarrassing. But what else can I do, Mr. Lufkin? He was my father, after all. It's only right that I honor his debts, don't you think?"

"Your father?"

"Died. He didn't even make it to the wedding. It was so sad." She took a moment to regain her composure before continuing. "And now my husband wants to set up offices here and has sent me ahead to find a suitable dwelling for us, and settle my father's debts, and hire servants, and who knows what all." Reaching across the desk, she rested a hand on the banker's arm. "If it weren't for the kindness of men like you, Mr. Lufkin, I don't know how I would manage." A gentle squeeze, a quivering smile, then she sat back. "Which would be a suitable neighborhood, do you think? I'm thinking something moderate that would require no more than a couple dozen servants. And a garden. I find gardens so restful, don't you?"

"That would be expensive."

"Oh, my husband is most generous. He has extensive investments—railroads, iron works, foundries—he and Jay are always into something."

"Jay? Jay Gould?" His small blue eyes lit up like twin flames. To be privy to the inside investments of a financial mogul like Jay Gould could be worth a fortune to a discerning investor. Margaret was banking on Mr. Lufkin recognizing the opportunity. Judging by his expression, he did.

"Oh, dear," she said regretfully. "I wasn't supposed to mention that. I'm making a muddle of everything." With a disheartened sigh, she reached for the papers. "Perhaps I should wait for my husband—"

He slapped a palm on the folder, anchoring it to the middle of the desk. "That won't be necessary, Mrs. Kerrigan. He requires us to tend these matters, and so we shall."

"Thank you, Mr. Lufkin. I'm sure he will be most grateful. And loyal."

"How much do you think you might need?"

Margaret gave it some thought, her fingers idly playing over the buttons between her breasts. "He said I should put up no more than five certificates as collateral, which would be a hundred shares. How much could I borrow against that?"

He named a figure. Margaret refrained from gasping. "I suppose that will be sufficient to get me started," she murmured once she caught her breath. "But I would need it right away." She motioned to the valise. "As you can see I have only just arrived and will need to find a suitable hotel and make arrangements for my father's funeral and tend his affairs and . . . oh, it exhausts me just to think about it. Is there a hotel close by you could recommend? Someplace where my things would be secure?" She gently thumped the necklace against her chest.

He swallowed. "If you're worried about your valuables or the other certificates, we could set up a safe deposit box for you here in the bank."

"Oh, would you?" Another arm squeeze. "You've been such a help, Mr. Lufkin. Doyle will be so pleased to learn how well you've taken care of me."

A moment later, the secretary magically appeared in the doorway.

Lufkin listed the forms he required and wrote down a sum on a piece of paper with instructions to have the funds brought directly to him once the forms were filled out. The secretary whisked away again. As the door closed behind him, the banker aimed a honeyed smile at Margaret's breasts. "You say your husband will be arriving in a few days?"

"Two weeks at most. Perhaps a month. He's involved in some sort of secret negotiations over a branch line up north somewhere." She fluttered fingers in airy dismissal. "It's always something. I can scarcely keep up with him."

"I'm leery of you traveling about with that much cash on your person, Mrs. Kerrigan," Lufkin said with a frown. "Perhaps you should open an account here at the bank."

Margaret gently rubbed a fingertip back and forth along her lower lip as she thought it over. Then with a sigh, said, "I'd best wait for my husband, I think. But I can certainly put the greater portion of it in your safe deposit box, and the rest in the hotel safe."

"Of course."

The secretary returned with the completed paperwork, a stack of bank notes, and a drooping canvas bag that clinked when he set it in Mr. Lufkin's pale, pudgy hands.

As the banker carefully studied the papers, Margaret checked the clock on the wall. Almost noon. She should have ample time once she finished here to purchase a few items, dine, and arrive back at the station to board the six o'clock train to Pittsburgh.

Six more hours and she would be free. The thought almost made her giddy.

"And now, if you don't mind, Mrs. Kerrigan," Mr. Lufkin said, having completed his inspection of the loan papers, "I'll need to see some identification. Purely as a formality, of course."

Margaret's heartbeat faltered. "Identification?"

"Just something to show you're who you say you are. For the forms."

Margaret stared at him, her thoughts so scattered, she couldn't think of a response.

His smile faded into an expression of consternation. "A letter addressed to you, perhaps? A bill? A receipt? Anything with your name on it, besides these certificates." As he spoke, he thumbed through the papers in the folder, then stopped. "What's this?"

Margaret looked across the desk and felt a jolt of surprise. "My marriage certificate." Not having looked in the folder since leaving the Fifth Avenue, she hadn't been aware that she had inadvertently picked it up, too.

"What's it doing in here?"

"I-I'm not sure." Margaret remembered scooping up the stock folder to fan Mrs. Throckmorton. Had she accidentally grabbed the certificate along with it? Or had her guardian slipped it in with the stocks when she'd packed her valise?

"Dear lady, it hasn't been witnessed or registered. Look, there's no stamp on it." He pointed to a blank space near the bottom of the document.

"E-Everything was so rushed, I guess it got pushed into the folder by mistake. We only married yesterday. Then news this morning of my father's death . . ." This time she didn't have to fake the tears. Panic was making her voice wobble and her eyes burn. "Oh, dear. What does this mean?"

Something in her tone must have made him panicky, too. "There, there, Mrs. Kerrigan," he said hastily. "A marriage certificate is sufficient for identification. But as soon as your husband arrives, you must have him register it with the proper authorities. Until it is, your marriage isn't really considered legal."

"It isn't?"

"I'm afraid not."

The words were slow to penetrate. When they did, panic gave way to mind-churning euphoria. She wasn't truly married? Even if he found her, Doyle couldn't force her to go back? Ever?

She was scarcely aware when the banker rose and came around to assist her from her chair. "Let's see to that safe deposit box now, shall we, Mrs. Kerrigan?"

In a daze, Margaret followed him down the hall and through a heavy metal door that opened into a windowless room, the walls of which were lined with small, locked doors similar to those in a mausoleum.

Lufkin unlocked one of the doors, extracted a long metal box, and set it on the table in the center of the room. "I shall leave you in privacy, Mrs. Kerrigan," he said gravely, and bowed himself out.

Margaret quickly removed her necklace and earbobs, but instead of putting them into the box, she slipped them back into her valise, along with most of the money, which she stuffed into her toiletries case. The rest—five medium denomination bank notes and several each of half eagles, eagles, and double eagles—she put into her reticule. When she returned the deposit box to its slot on the wall of locked compartments, all it contained was her copy of the paperwork she had signed.

Ten minutes later, she was climbing into the back of a hansom cab, so frazzled by what she had done she was shaking like the palsied old woman she was pretending to be.

"Where can I take you, ma'am?" the coachman asked.

Margaret thought for a moment, then grinned. "What's the finest and most exclusive women's clothier in the city?"

"That would be Hillman's on Broad."

"Then take me to Hillman's."

With a snap of the whip, the cab lurched forward.

Margaret sank back, one trembling hand pressed over her mouth to stifle giggles of pure relief.

She had done it.

She was free.

And not married.

And rich.

Mrs. Throckmorton would be so proud.

Six

As Tait waited in the ticket line at Philadelphia's Thirtieth Street Station, he scanned the faces of the travelers shuffling through, hoping he'd chosen the right stop.

It was the closest to the heart of the city. He doubted she would pick one of the rural stations where there would be fewer people to blend in with and less opportunity to disappear. Plus, if she planned to go on west to Pittsburgh or south to Baltimore, she would have to come through here. According to the schedule, there was an afternoon train to Baltimore, and another departing for Pittsburgh at six o'clock. He would have to watch both.

He yawned and scratched his stubbled chin. He was so tired his eyes felt coated with sand. His suit looked like he'd slept in it—which he wished he'd been able to do—and his teeth hadn't been cleaned since yesterday.

When he'd left Doyle's office the previous night to begin backtracking Margaret's movements, he hadn't expected to be on his way to Philadelphia only a few hours later. He hadn't even stopped to pack spare clothes or pick up traveling money. His credit was good; any big bank within two hundred miles would extend him funds on his signature alone. It was finding the time to go by one that was the problem.

As soon as he verified the train schedule and questioned the ticket agent, he would attend to that. If the Baltimore run was delayed, he would have time to go by a bank and purchase the necessaries. Maybe a suit if he could find a ready-made big enough, then a bath and a shave and something to eat. His stomach was so empty it felt like it was rubbing against his backbone.

He almost hoped the woman had slipped past him. He wasn't sure what he might say if he caught up to her in his present frame of mind.

"Help you, sir?"

Realizing his turn had come, Tait stepped up to the counter where a pinch-faced man wearing a visor bearing the PRR emblem sat on a high stool. "The Baltimore train on time?"

"So far. Arrives in an hour. Departs in two. Give or take."

That wouldn't allow him time to tend his errands and get back to see who boarded. Which left Pittsburgh. "The six o'clock to Pittsburgh still on time?"

"More or less."

That was probably the one she would take—assuming she wasn't stopping permanently in Philadelphia and planned to continue west rather than south, and that she hadn't gotten off at an earlier stop. Lots of assumptions. Tait didn't like assumptions, but at this point, he had no choice. "How much for a Pullman sleeping compartment to Pittsburgh?"

When the agent told him, Tait checked his cash and saw he didn't have enough. "Can I reserve one now and pay for it before I board?"

"You could, sir. If one was available."

Hell. Another sleepless night. "Do you have a list of passengers who have already reserved or bought Pullman tickets to either Pittsburgh or Baltimore?"

The lips pinched even tighter. Tait wondered how the fellow could even speak. "As I explained to the other gentleman, sir, we're not allowed to—"

"Look!" Tait slapped a palm down on the counter, making the man flinch and his eyes widen. "This is a family emergency. I need to locate my aunt. Widow lady. Dressed in black. Hat with a veil. One bag. Has anyone by that description bought or reserved a Pullman sleeper berth on either the Pittsburgh or Baltimore train departing this evening? Sir?"

"N-Not from me. But I just came on an hour ago."

With a curse, Tait turned and left the station. There were several hansom cabs parked outside. He walked to the first in line, hoping they made regular runs to and from the station.

None had picked up a passenger meeting Margaret's description.

Which left Tait a choice: Either go to the bank and do his shopping—which he had time to do if she was taking the later train to Pittsburgh. Or stay here in case she took the earlier train to Baltimore, instead.

Muttering, he stomped back inside.

The first thing she did after alighting from the buggy was to toss the veiled hat into a trash bin in an alley. The second was to drop the fur wrap into the grateful hands of an elderly woman wearing a thin worsted coat and clutching a tattered bundle as she trudged down Broad Street. The third was to sweep into Hillman's and announce to the saleswoman hovering inside the door that she was done with widow's weeds and required several new ensembles.

Three hours later, she exited the shop carrying her valise, four ribbon-tied parcels, and wearing one of her altered-to-fit dresses—a heavy silk in a soft lilac that boasted the new narrow sleeves and elliptical overskirt, which was looped up to reveal a ruffled ivory underskirt. Over that she wore a knee-length heavy-weight wool traveling cape in a dark green, and she completed the ensemble with dainty kid half boots and a matching green Marie Stuart bonnet with a shirred ivory under-brim and two sets of ribbons—one tied under the chin, and the other trailing off the back. The parcels contained a heavy robe, sleeping attire, a square ivory shawl of the softest wool, a simple traveling dress in a lovely shade of yellow, and another in a delicate rose.

It had all cost her a fortune. But she had a fortune, so why not?

A thorough wash would have been nice, too, but that would have to wait until she boarded the train and made use of the washroom that was—as stated on the window advertisement at the depot—"the standard of excellence on the newest and most luxurious Pullman sleeping cars the Pennsylvania Railroad has to offer."

She ardently hoped that was true.

From Broad she walked past City Hall to Eleventh Street. Finding a shop that offered leather goods, she stepped in to buy another valise, which she filled with her recent purchases. Then carrying both valises, she walked two doors down to an over-priced restaurant in an expensive hotel. It was certainly nice—but not as elegant as the Fifth Avenue Hotel had been. Taking a seat by the window, she happily ordered more food than she could possibly eat.

She enjoyed it immensely, but by the time she set her napkin aside, the sleepless hours had begun to catch up with her. After settling her bill—and leaving a generous gratuity—she allowed the doorman to help her into a cab and headed back up to the train station. By the watch pinned inside her reticule, she calculated she had ample time to return to the depot, pay for the compartment she had reserved, and board the train to Pittsburgh. Then her new life could begin.

As she watched the city buildings roll by, she wondered what she should call herself now. Chloe? Lucretia? No, Lucinda. She'd always liked that name. It had a fresh, happy ring to it. Lucinda Hathaway. That would do nicely.

Tait jerked upright, not sure where he was or what had alerted him. Groggily, he looked around.

People sat on benches, luggage at their feet. Children whined. Somewhere nearby, a locomotive exhaled panting breaths like a blown horse.

Philadelphia. The Thirtieth Street Station. He must have dozed off.

Yawning, he reached for his hat, couldn't find it, and realized someone had relieved him of it while he slept. His pocket watch was gone, too. With a curse, he felt his other pockets and was relieved that what money he had was still there.

He checked the clock on the wall. Twenty minutes past six.

Twenty minutes past six?

He lurched to his feet, almost staggering on legs that were

still half asleep. Outside, a man called "all aboard" to people hurrying across the platform to a waiting train.

His train?

He rushed to the ticket window. The same pinch-faced man in the PRR visor stared back at him. "Is that the train to Pittsburgh?" Tait asked, pointing at the cars lined up at the platform. Earlier he'd checked the train to Baltimore but hadn't seen her board. She had to be taking this one.

"It is."

Son of a bitch. He scanned the figures crowding the steps at the end of the two Pullman cars. Had she boarded already? Had he missed her? Not seeing the trim, familiar figure, he turned back to the agent. "Did you see the widow lady board? The one I asked about earlier?"

"I don't know."

"You don't know?"

"I-I mean I saw no widow. But then, I just came back from break. You might check with the other agent. I believe he was talking to a man about a woman wearing black. He might know."

Tait itched to grab the man's throat, but the conductor was shouting, "Last call to Pittsburgh," and he knew he was running out of time. All he could do was board and check every car. If he didn't find her, he could get off at the next stop and start backtracking again. He reached into his pocket. "Just give me a ticket."

"To Pittsburgh?"

Tait slammed a handful of money on the counter. "Of course to Pittsburgh!"

A minute later, he was sprinting across the platform.

"I'm looking for my aunt," he told the conductor as the portly man stowed the steps and closed the gate. "A widow lady. Traveling alone. Wearing black. Maybe this tall." He raised a flattened palm level with the top button on his waistcoat. "And slim. Could be staying in one of the sleeper cars."

The conductor thought it over, lips pursed to one side as he tugged on the corner of his mustache, which was only slightly less bushy than his eyebrows. "Nope. No widows up here. But you might check with the Pullman porters."

"Thanks." Tait started down the aisle of the passenger car.

"That's where I sent the other fellow."

Stopping abruptly, Tait swung back. "Other fellow?"

"Looking for his sister, he said. Sounds like your aunt."

Someone else was tracking Margaret? "What did he look like?"

The conductor gave it more thought. "English. Stocky. Bent nose. Dark hair like yours, but turning gray." He gave a smug smile. "Got an eye for faces, people tell me. Part of my job, I guess. Tell a lot from a man's face. Hands, too. You were a bare-knuckle fighter, I'm guessing. I'd peg the other fellow as a dock worker, considering his build and that he was missing two fingers on his left hand."

Tait thanked him and hurried down to the next car, almost losing his balance when the train lurched forward.

Had Doyle sent another tracker after his wife? Or was it someone else entirely? But who? And why would someone else be following Margaret?

The porter in the first sleeper was a gray-haired ex-slave wearing the standard pressed white jacket and visored Pullman cap. He also carried the standard name of "George" in deference to his employer, George Pullman. He said there were no unattended elderly widow ladies in any of the four sleeping compartments on his car, although he recollected that there might be a woman traveling alone in the second Pullman car.

"But she warn't no old lady, naw,' suh," he added, shaking his head.

"Why do you say that?"

"Too young. Dressed fancy and not in black. Real pretty little blonde." He chuckled, showing pink gums and missing teeth. "Popular lady, that one."

"Was someone else asking about her? A man? Stocky? English accent?"

Something in Tait's voice put him off. The old man looked away and began refolding a stack of linens. "Don' know 'bout that. Best check with George in the next car. He'll know. You ask George."

Realizing he would get no more out of the skittish fellow, Tait tipped him with one of his few remaining coins, then moved on to the second Pullman.

His nerves were humming now—with both excitement and alarm. He knew he was getting close. He could feel it. Feel her.

But he could feel someone else getting close, too. And he didn't know why.

He found the second George carrying a bucket and rags down to one of the forward compartments. A noxious odor and the wails of a crying child came through the open doorway, and Tait could only guess what catastrophe awaited the harried fellow. Stopping the porter before he ducked inside, he quickly asked about the blond woman traveling alone.

"Miss Hathaway," the young Negro man said, clearly distracted by the distasteful task awaiting him. "Room three. But she stepped out to the ladies lavatory. You want, you can wait in the gentleman's smoking room at the end of this car, or in the Parlor Car at the end of the train. That's where I sent her brother. Now if you'll excuse me."

Tait debated going to the smoking room, then realized if the man posing as Margaret's brother had followed her from New York, he might have seen Tait following her, too, and would recognize him. That would put the follower at an advantage, since Tait had never seen him and had only a secondhand description of what he looked like. Better the man not know Tait was on board.

After checking that there was no one coming down the narrow aisle behind him and that the porter was still in the forward compartment, Tait hurried down to room three. Hoping Margaret hadn't locked the door, he tested the brass knob.

It turned.

He opened the door and slipped inside.

Three flickering candles in polished brass fixtures bolted to the walls lit the empty compartment. A sleeping berth was folded up against the ceiling on one side of the narrow room. Opposite it, a second berth had already been lowered and was ready for use. Below each bed was a couch, and on the exterior wall a framed mirror separated two windows trimmed in black walnut with elaborate inlays. The deep pile carpet and French plush upholstery on the couches gave the small room the ostentatious elegance of the fancier saloons and gambling halls on the steam riverboats. Tait wasn't surprised that these newer sleepers were referred to as Pullman Palace Cars.

He studied the room for anything he might recognize as belonging to Margaret. Several dresses and a shawl hung from hooks on the wall beside the door. A green cape lay over the arm of the couch, a matching bonnet on the seat. The valise on the floor looked new. It was open and empty.

It could be any woman's room.

But he recognized a faint scent in the air. Distinctive. Flowery. Exotic. Something he had only ever noticed when he was near Margaret.

That surge of energy coursed through him again. He'd found her. Finally. Smiling grimly, he braced a shoulder against the wall for balance and crossed his arms. Now all he had to do was wait for her to come back.

Beyond the window, fewer lights showed as the train rolled out of the city and into open countryside. They would have to stop every twenty miles or so to put water in the tenders, but he would wait until they reached a major town before he pulled her off the train. Bigger place, more resources. Harrisburg, maybe. But that wouldn't be until late tomorrow morning. Which meant he had to get through the next few hours in a private compartment with a woman who had haunted his thoughts for months— and who also happened to be another man's wife.

It promised to be a long night.

Margaret—Lucinda now, she had decided for certain—finished her wash and repacked her toiletries into the valise. She felt immeasurably better but so exhausted she could scarcely think. The euphoria that had carried her through the afternoon had faded, leaving her hollow with fatigue. As soon as she got back to her compartment, she would climb into her berth and sleep until Pittsburgh. Or at least for the next twelve hours.

With her new dress draped over one arm, the valise of railroad shares gripped in her other hand, and wearing her new sleeping gown under her new hooded robe—a soft, luxurious velvet that was so generously cut it completely obscured her figure—she left the washroom and lurched down the narrow, walkway of the rocking Pullman car.

Thankfully she reached her compartment without being seen in her casual state of undress. Glad she had left the door unlocked—everything of value was in the valise that never left her side, so why bother?—she pushed open the door and stepped inside, then almost screamed when she sensed movement behind her.

Before she could turn, a big hand clamped over her mouth and an arm grabbed her around the waist and pulled her back against a solid body. "Shh."

Her legs went weak. The valise and the dress hit the floor.

"You're a hard woman to find, Miss Hamilton," a familiar husky voice said in her ear.

Rylander! Her heart seemed to stop, then come pounding back with a fury. In wild panic, she twisted, kicked, clawed at the hand over her mouth.

But the arm holding her didn't loosen even when her heel caught his shin.

"Stop this, Margaret! You know I won't hurt you."

She knew no such thing but could see struggling was getting her nowhere. Breathing hard through her nose, she stopped fighting but kept her fingers dug into the hand over her mouth.

"If I let you go, you'll behave?"

"Id owa na roo!"

"Does that mean yes?"

She tried to stomp his foot and missed.

Apparently taking that as a "yes," he released her and took his hand away, but she saw it hovering at the edge of her vision and knew he would clamp it back over her mouth if she tried to scream.

Instead she whirled and slapped him in the face. "Get out of my room!"

He jerked back, then grabbed her wrist when she tried to strike him again. He gave it a shake. "Stop it, Margaret. Now!"

A new fear gripped her. She glanced fearfully around. "Is Doyle here?"

"No."

Twisting free, she snatched her dress from the floor. "So why are you?"

"We need to talk." He took the garment from her hands, hung it on the last hook, then swept a hand toward the couches. "Sit, please."

"I will not." To hide the shaking of her limbs, she crossed her arms over her uncorseted torso and hiked her chin. "I prefer Lucinda now—and if you don't leave immediately, I'll scream."

"I'd suggest you not do that."

"You would further manhandle me?"

"I would silence you. One way or another. Please." Feet braced as the train rolled into a curve, he nodded toward the couch behind her and smiled. Not pleasantly. "Or we could tussle a bit more. Up to you."

In defiance, she chose the other couch under the ready berth, knowing it hung too low for him to duck beneath easily. Plopping back onto the cushions, she once more crossed her arms atop her heavy robe. "Why are you here?"

"Doyle asked me to find you."

"Still doing his dirty work, I see."

His eyes darkened from smoky blue to an ominous gray, the way clouds did just before a storm broke. But his voice remained calm. "He was worried about you. We both were. We thought you might have been abducted."

"Abducted? By whom?" She made an impatient gesture to show how little credence she gave that notion, then saw the way her hand trembled and hurriedly lowered it. "I wasn't abducted. I left."

"Why, Margaret?"

"Lucinda. And I'll not discuss it with you."

"Where are you going? Do you even have a destination?"

She glared at him in stony silence, wondering how he had found her and what she had to do to escape him a second time. The man was relentless. She should have bought a gun in Philadelphia. No one would have blamed her for shooting a man who broke into her sleeping compartment. She smiled, picturing his shock when she fired.

With a sigh, he braced his arms on top of the bed above her and rested his weight on one leg. The action spread his frock coat wide and lifted the bottom edge of his silk vest, and she saw that his wrinkled shirt had slipped partially free of his rumpled trousers. For such a fastidious man, he was a mess. She took comfort in knowing she was probably the cause of it.

He rubbed a hand over his unshaven face, muttered something, then dropped his arm back on the bed. "A man has been asking about you. He followed you onto the train and even now might be somewhere on this car. Why?"

Two men had been following her? And she had seen neither

one? On reflex, she looked around, half expecting to see a shadowed figure lurking in a dark corner. "Who? What does he look like?"

"I haven't seen him, but the porter described him as being stocky and having gray hair. He said he was British and his nose was bent, which probably means it had been broken in the past, and he was missing two fingers on his left hand."

"Oh, God." She pressed a palm to her chest, trying to staunch the sudden terror flooding through her. *Smythe!*

"You know him?"

Why is Smythe here? How did he find me? She struggled to suck air into her constricted lungs. How had he even survived?

"Margaret?"

She almost cried out when Rylander touched her. Hooking his bent forefinger beneath her chin, he tilted her head up, forcing her to look at him. "You're safe with me. Whoever he is, I won't let him hurt you."

How? If fire hadn't stopped Smythe, nothing would. She started to jump up, but her legs were so wobbly she couldn't rise, and Rylander was in the way. "The door. Make sure it's locked. And close the drapes. He's here? You're sure of it?" Her skin crawled as if his hands were on her. Bile churned in her throat.

Rylander checked the door and closed the drapes, then came back to where she sat shivering against the cushions. The wood frame groaned when he sat down beside her. He tried to keep a space between them, but the couch was small and he was a big man. "Who is it? Tell me who he is so I can protect you."

Protect her how? No one could protect her. The man could rise from the dead. "All these years . . . I-I thought it was over." She took a deep shaky breath and tried to calm her breathing. But her heart continued its erratic beat. "How did he even find me?"

"If I could, he could. But the question is why?"

Horne.

Horne had known Smythe. They had shared the same proclivities. The same children. She shuddered. If Horne had recognized her at the engagement party, he might have told Smythe, especially if they were still up to their same disgusting habits. But why would he care about an adult woman? It was children they both preferred.

Fingers closed over hers. Squeezed hard. "His name, Margaret."

She stared down at his hand—big, capable—the knuckles enlarged from hitting other men's faces. Rylander had been a fighter. He was bigger and younger than Smythe. He might be able to protect her. But why would he? She was nothing to him but his partner's runaway bride.

She looked up and met his calm, stone gray eyes. She had always sensed that behind them was a decent—if irritating— man. She thought of the times Rylander had tried to curb Doyle's cruelty. He had stood up for Widow O'Reilly and Mrs. Throckmorton, hadn't he? Maybe he would do so for her.

It was a risk she had to take. She had no other choice.

"I only know him as Smythe. The last time I saw him was fifteen years ago in a burning building. I thought he had died in the fire."

"In Manhattan?"

She could feel his mind probing hers, could see by the fierce concentration of his gaze that he was carefully analyzing every bit of information she gave up.

Tait Rylander had been both the brains and the brawn of the Rylander-Kerrigan partnership. Doyle had provided charm and the ruthless ambition of a born survivor, as well as a delight in twisting an adversary's weaknesses to his own advantage. That's how it had worked with her, she now realized. Sensing her need for security, he had wrapped her in jewels and luxury to give the illusion of protection, then had begun to bend her to his will.

Rylander was much more direct. He didn't manipulate—he ordered. She liked it no better, but at least there was honesty in it.

So she would be as honest as she dared in return. "In Five Points."

"Five Points?" His dark brows lifted in surprise. "You're Irish?"

"I was. Until it was beaten out of me."

"By Smythe?"

She nodded but didn't mention Mrs. Throckmorton. Her guardian had only sought to improve her life, to elevate her to a better, safer place. Unlike Smythe, with his carefully placed blows designed to break the spirit but not the skin.

She shuddered, remembering the way he breathed while he did it—like a rutting animal—a raspy, wheezing sound coming out of his open, wet mouth every time his hand came down. Even years later, when she was walking down the wealthy streets of Manhattan and the wind swirled through the awnings and past the narrow alleys, it would make that same high-pitched whistling noise, and it was all she could do not to break into a run.

But she wouldn't tell Rylander that. To do so would open herself to questions about her past and expose the fear that pressed against the edges of her mind. She sensed once she gave up her secrets, he would tell Doyle and her almost husband would know exactly how to control her.

"Does Doyle know you're Irish?"

"No. He wouldn't have married me had he known."

"So you lied to him."

"I didn't have to. He never asked."

Abruptly Tait rose and paced the small room, his steps uneven as he fought the rocking of the car, the tips of his tousled black hair almost brushing the low ceiling. "So you married him strictly for his money." He stopped pacing and glared at her. "How does a woman as intelligent and capable and beautiful as you sell herself like that?"

Was he truly that naïve? Had he no idea the horrors that awaited the Irish when they walked off the immigrant "coffin" ships? Or how vulnerable a woman all on her own with no money, no prospects, no protection was? She sighed, feeling even emptier now that the rush of fear was past. "As I told you before. The most important things to me are security and safety. Money provides that."

"Safety from men like Smythe?"

"And from cold and hunger and fear."

That sharp gray gaze was so intrusive she had to look away. "Who are you really, Margaret?"

This was a mistake. The cost of his help was too high—he

would demand to know everything about her and she couldn't bear that.

Gripping the armrest for balance, she rose. Every breath was an effort. Her head ached, her stomach hurt, and her thoughts were so sluggish she could scarcely put together a sentence. "I'm Lucinda Hathaway. And I wish to retire. Please leave."

He continued to stand there, taking up most of the narrow space, studying her as if she were some sort of exotic, vaguely dangerous insect he wasn't sure what to do with.

"I'm very tired." She glanced pointedly at the door.

"You won't be safe here alone."

Surely he didn't expect to stay in the compartment with her? The notion was both terrifying and oddly comforting. "I'll be perfectly fine."

"What about Smythe?"

"I'll lock the door."

He smiled in that unpleasant way again. "He's gone to a lot of trouble to find you. Now that he has, do you think a locked door will stop him?"

A coil of fear tightened in her chest. Would Smythe really try to break in? On a crowded train? He would never get away with it . . . unless he came in the middle of the night . . . when everyone was asleep, and the sound of the moving train muffled noise, and she was too weary to stay alert. He would be on her before she even knew he was there. "I'll push something against the door."

"What? Everything is bolted down."

"Then what do you suggest?" She wanted him to say it. If she asked him to stay, that would acknowledge that she needed him and she refused to do that.

He smiled again. But this time it was a sad half smile that carried neither threat nor malice. It softened his features and made him seem almost handsome in a sharp-angled, hard-eyed sort of way. "I mean you no harm, Margaret."

"No? You came all this way to bid me a safe journey, did you?" Fearing she might burst into tears, she turned her back on him to reach up onto the bed where the porter said the ladder was. "And it's Lucinda now," she added, patting the bedding over her head. Where was the cursed ladder?

"I just want the truth."

"The truth?" Suddenly it was too much. So furious and frightened and exhausted she wanted to scream, she whipped toward him. "Well, here's a truth for you, Mr. Rylander. Life is hard and cruel and will drag you down at every turn if you let it. But not me. You know why? Because I've seen the worst it has to offer and I've survived it. Just as I'll survive this, and anything else you or Doyle or Smythe can throw at me. There's your truth! Now leave."

He looked taken aback by her outburst. Reaching into his pocket, he pulled out a folded handkerchief and thrust it toward her. "I didn't intend to upset you."

"Oh? Since when?"

"There's no need to cry. We'll figure this out."

"I'm not crying."

"Then your eyes are leaking."

Through a wet blur, she saw him take a step toward her. She lurched back, knocking her head against the bed frame. If he touched her, she would scream. Shatter into a thousand sharp pieces. Lose the last of her strength.

"I'm sorry—"

"I don't want your pity."

"Margaret—"

"Just leave. Now."

"But I—"

"Get the hell out of my room!"

She expected him to be shocked by her coarse language. She certainly was. But he simply stood there, frowning and looking every bit as tired and confused as she was. With a deep sigh, he put the handkerchief into the inside pocket of his rumpled frock coat, then let his hand fall back to his side. "No," he said. "I can't leave you here unprotected."

A wave of utter hopelessness swept over her. Feeling the sting of more tears, she pressed a shaking hand over her eyes. *God, You win. Take me now. I can't bear more of this.*

She heard him move past, then the door closing. When she took her hand away, the room was empty and he was gone. She blinked. Had he truly left her? Relief gave way to astonishment—then indignation. With Smythe out there?

That lying cad.

Furious all over again, she was stomping over to lock the door when it swung open in her face. "What do you want?" she demanded as he stepped inside, not sure whether to be relieved or angry that he had returned.

"Money. Just until I can wire my banker. I left right after the wedding and didn't have time to pack or go by the bank." He glanced at the valise sitting on the floor where she'd dropped it. "I know you have money in there with all the stock certificates."

"Now you're stealing from me?"

He gave her a look. "A brief loan. I'll pay you back."

Muttering every Irish insult she remembered from her days in Five Points, she yanked her reticule from the valise, counted out three double eagles and several half eagles, and slapped them into his hand. "You certainly will repay me," she said nastily, enjoying even this inconsequential power over him. "With interest."

"So . . ." He showed his fine teeth in a broad grin. A weary imitation of that startling transformation that had caught her off guard that day in the carriage. "You're asking me to come back, then?"

"With my money."

"Your husband's money."

She started to argue the point, but he had turned away to open the door. "Lock up behind me," he ordered, checking the hall. "I'll just be down the way, talking to the porter. Don't open the door for anyone but me." He took a step, hesitated, then without looking at her added, "And by the way. In case anyone asks, we're eloping."

Eloping? Before she could respond to that absurdity, he slipped into the hallway and closed the door in her face.

Seven

Tait found George sorting through extra bedding in a small alcove at the front of the car. "That man you mentioned earlier—Miss Hathaway's brother—is he still in the smoking compartment?"

"I don't believe so, sir. I saw him move earlier to the Parlor Car at the end of the train."

"When's the next stop?" Perhaps that's where Smythe would make his move. Tait hoped so. And once he dealt with that threat, he could safely get Margaret—Lucinda—off the train in the morning.

The porter studied the clock on the wall. "Just over an hour, sir. Water stop in Cardwell's Crossing."

"A big town?"

The Negro shook his head. "Maybe two streets. Nice place, though. Friendly folk."

"How long will we be there? I need to pick up a few things if they have a store." He motioned vaguely at his rumpled attire. "I left in a bit of a rush."

It was apparent by his expression that the question confused the porter. People rarely left the train at a water stop, Tait guessed. Especially at night.

"Twenty minutes at most, sir. Just long enough to fill the tender. But I'm afraid the store will be closed. In fact, the whole town will be shut for the night. Perhaps you'd best wait until we arrive in Harrisburg tomorrow morning. We'll be there for almost an hour to load coal."

That's where Smythe would strike, then. Bigger place. More resources. *Damn*. Tait wanted this over. Now.

In a voice carefully devoid of emotion, George said, "Shall I lower the other berth in Miss Hathaway's compartment, sir? The bed is already prepared."

Tait hesitated. He saw honesty and a willingness to help in the curious brown eyes, but also a growing suspicion. No dimwit, this George. Well spoken, educated, a bright future ahead of him. Tait decided to take a chance.

"Here's the thing, George. Miss Ham—Hathaway—is my wife. Or soon will be. We're eloping. And her brother, the man in the Parlor Car, is against the union. So rather than cause a ruckus, I'd prefer he not know I'm on the train. Or Miss Hathaway, either."

"But I already told him a lady by her description was on board."

"Tell him you were mistaken."

George frowned.

Seeing the deception didn't sit well with him, Tait tried to make it more palatable. "As you probably guessed, I didn't pay for a private sleeping compartment." He pulled several coins from his pocket. "I figure it's a lot more expensive than seats in the coach cars, and I don't want you getting into trouble because of that. I hope this will cover the difference in the fares and any inconvenience to you." He handed over two twenty-dollar gold pieces—at least twice the amount required.

George stared at the double eagles in his pink palm, probably more money than he'd ever held at one time. "Well . . . I . . ."

"Thanks, George. I appreciate it." Continuing before the fellow could refuse, Tait quickly added, "I haven't eaten all day. Since I'd prefer not to run into Miss Hathaway's brother in the dining room, I was hoping you could bring me a plate. Or two. Whatever's available." He held out a five-dollar half eagle. "I'd be most grateful."

This time George nodded. Slipping the money into his pocket, he looked up with a broad smile. "Yes, sir, I'll tend to it straight away. Shall I bring it directly to your room?"

"Good man. One last thing." He gave a hopeful grin. "You don't happen to keep a supply of toiletries on board, do you?"

Happily, George did. A packet containing a comb, a tiny cube of soap, a little folding brush for his teeth, and a small tin of tooth powder. No razor. Delighted, Tait gave George a friendly clap on the shoulder and headed back down the swaying hallway to the men's lavatory.

Ten minutes later, he returned to the compartment, combed, washed, and smelling like peppermint tooth powder. A vast improvement.

Margaret—or Lucinda—as she now called herself, actually looked relieved to see him when she opened the door. Maybe having Smythe around was a good thing. At least it would give Tait an excuse to stay close to her.

"Did you see him?" she asked as he locked the door.

"George?"

"Smythe."

"No. But I wasn't looking." He moved to the couch across from hers and sat down with a yawn. He was so weary he almost didn't care that he'd be sleeping in his clothes again. Or that a beautiful, desirable woman who was strictly off-limits would be sleeping only a few feet away from him.

He watched her pace the small room, admiring the way the candlelight brought out the gold in her blond hair and cast a lively sparkle to her green eyes. Doyle had no appreciation for what he'd lost.

A remarkable woman, this chameleon. He doubted he'd even begun to scratch the surface of the layers she hid behind. Maybe tomorrow, while they waited for the train to reach Harrisburg, he would get answers to the questions plaguing him.

"I didn't have time to pack before I left Manhattan." He rubbed a palm over his bristly cheek, then looked down at his wrinkled clothing. "This is all I have to wear. When we stop in Harrisburg tomorrow morning, I'd like to purchase extra garments. And a hat. I want you to go with me." He would much prefer luring her off the train with the ruse of a shopping excursion than dragging her off kicking and screaming. And if Smythe followed them and made his move, so much the better. Tait had no doubt he could handle an older man with a shorter reach. He'd made money proving it every week for almost two years.

"You don't know how to purchase your own clothing?"

"I don't like leaving you here alone with Smythe lurking about."

She stopped pacing. Her pretty eyes widened. "Lurking about?"

An ingenious phrase. Guaranteed to strike fear in any woman's heart. Even this formidable female. "I'll watch over you, Margaret. You'll be safe."

"Lucinda. Safer with you than on a crowded train with the porter nearby?"

"Most of the passengers will step off to stretch their legs, and George will be busy cleaning the compartments. He won't have time to keep an eye on you."

"But—"

"Just trust me, will you?" *Jesus.* The woman would argue with the devil, himself. Where did she get the energy?

She started to say something more—something he probably didn't want to hear, judging by her mulish expression—when a knock on the door sent her spinning around with such a look of pure terror Tait wondered again what the fellow, Smythe, might have done to her.

"It's all right," he said, rising from the couch. "That's George with my supper." But as a precaution, he motioned her out of the way in case it wasn't George, then asked who it was before he unlocked the door.

It was George, bearing a tray loaded with two napkin-covered plates, two glasses, and a pitcher of water. Tait didn't know how he kept it all balanced with the constant motion of the train.

"Wasn't sure which you would prefer, sir, so I brought one each of the chicken and roast beef. Shall I put it on the table by the windows?"

Aware of Margaret's—Lucinda's—probable embarrassment at being seen alone in a private sleeping compartment with a man who wasn't her husband, Tait took the tray, smiled his thanks, and sent George on his way.

"You hungry?" he asked, setting the tray on the table.

"No."

Delighted to hear it, he carried one plate back to the couch, sat, and dug in.

She puttered around a bit, moving the valise to the end of her bed—did she expect him to dip into it?—and fluffing the dresses hanging on the hooks. Then she sat on the couch opposite his, crossed her arms in that combative way she had, and watched him eat.

He prayed for silence, and got it. But not for long.

"You and Doyle are very different," she observed when he started on the second plate.

He picked up a glass and took a sip of water, almost spilling it down his vest when the car gave a sudden lurch. "How?"

"You certainly eat more."

"I'm hungry."

"How did you meet?"

"At the battle of Gettysburg," he said between bites. "He saved my life."

"You were wounded?"

He nodded curtly, not wanting to talk about that morning Doyle had ridden out of the cannon smoke to cut him down. Even now, the memory of it made that suffocating panic grip his throat.

"So now you feel you owe him a debt. That explains a great deal."

He studied her as he chewed. That thoughtful look didn't bode well. He didn't feel up to a cross-examination, and a woman as smart as Margaret—Lucinda—wouldn't settle for half answers. So to keep her from plaguing him with more questions, he posed one of his own.

"What's a runner?"

She looked away. Crossing one knee over the other—crossed arms, crossed legs, fully shutting him out—she began to swing her slippered foot, sending ripples of motion through the heavy fabric of her robe. Her foot looked narrow and delicate and unexpectedly fragile on such a forceful woman. His shin remembered it well.

"Doyle didn't tell you?" she finally asked.

"I didn't know to ask."

Her foot swung harder. Agitation crackled around her like a building storm front. "They met the immigrant boats when they docked. They pretended to help, offering places to stay, food, the names of doctors willing to treat the poor sick fools who stumbled down the gangplank thinking they were saved and had finally arrived in the land of plenty."

Abruptly she turned her head and looked directly into his eyes. What he saw there took him aback—fury, grief, a pain so deep it burst out of her like a scream.

"Instead, they were stripped of everything," she went on. "Belongings, hope, pride. But even worse, the men who dealt that final, humiliating, unforgiveable blow were their own Irish countrymen. Like Doyle. That's what he did."

"To you?"

"To those like me." Blinking hard, she looked away again. "Good Irish families."

He toyed with another bite of chicken, but appetite gone, he set his fork back onto the plate. He knew what Doyle was capable of. He had seen his cruelty often enough and didn't want to think of it being directed toward this woman. "What happened to yours?" he asked.

"My father died trying to protect me and my mother."

"And your mother?"

"Eventually, she died, too." She pressed her lips in a thin, red line that reminded him of a barely healed scar.

"You must have been very young. What happened after they died?"

"I survived."

Those two words carried such a wealth of despair Tait had to wonder exactly what she had done to stay alive, and what horrors she had been forced to endure at the hands of men like Smythe. But maybe that was a secret he would be better off not knowing. "I'm glad you did."

"Are you?"

How could she doubt it? Was she that blind? Rising, he stacked his dirty plates and utensils on the tray, then leaving the pitcher and glasses on the table, carried the tray to the doorway. "I'll be stepping down the hall for a moment. Lock the door behind me."

"I always do."

He stepped into the hall, waited for the click of the door lock, then carried the tray to George's alcove and continued on to the men's lavatory.

Doyle had never told him about being a runner. Was he ashamed of preying on his own countrymen? If so, that might mean there was still a conscience beneath the charm. Tait had his doubts. And those doubts were making him wonder if he was doing the right thing taking Margaret—Lucinda—back to her husband. Which was a clear indication that his own conscience was faltering.

As he washed his hands, he wondered if he should confront Smythe now, despite being so tired he was almost staggering. If he waited until Harrisburg and something went wrong, that would leave Margaret—Lucinda—unprotected. But if he let Smythe know tonight that Margaret was under his protection and any interference would be dealt with harshly, the man might back off.

Or he could skip that, and simply toss the bastard off the train tonight. He liked that solution better. Which told him how skewed his thinking had become if he was contemplating murdering a man he had never met, solely on the woman's word that he was a threat.

The woman.

Lucinda.

The new name helped. Made him feel like what was going through his mind wasn't a betrayal of Doyle.

Although, of course, it was.

Damnit. Bracing his hands on the counter, he stared at his reflection in the lavatory mirror and there in his eyes saw the truth he'd been avoiding from the first.

He didn't want to take her back. He didn't want Doyle to have her. He could guess what a life with a man like him would do to a spirited, intelligent woman like her. She deserved better.

Furious with his own weakness where Lucinda was concerned, he dried his hands and returned to the compartment, both appalled and ashamed at how much he was looking forward to spending the night in the company of another man's wife.

* * *

Lucinda let him in, then locked the door behind him. He looked angry, and she wondered what she had done now.

Finding it easier to sit than stand in the rocking car, she returned to her couch while he lowered the other berth and straightened the bedding. Once he had set it to rights and had propped the ladders against the ends of both beds, he ducked his head and slid into the couch opposite hers. They sat facing each other in silence while his gaze roamed the room, looking anywhere but at her.

She sensed he was hiding something from her. Something he didn't want her to know.

"Tomorrow when we're in Harrisburg," he said, ending the long silence, "I don't want you to leave my side. I'm hoping Smythe will show himself. Then we can find out what he wants and why he's following you."

"Then what? You'll take me back to Doyle?"

An odd look crossed his face. "Margaret, I—"

"Lucinda," she cut in sharply. "And the threat won't stop with Smythe, you know. The real danger is from the man who sent him." The ring leader in all their horrid games. But why? What could Horne possibly want with her now?

"Do you know who that is?" he asked.

She debated telling him. But the thought of dredging up that pain and putting words to that horror made her stomach cramp. It was too humiliating. Desperate to change the subject, she asked if he had spoken to Mrs. Throckmorton before he left New York. "She's very dear to me. I hope she's recovered."

A knowing smirk tugged at Rylander's wide mouth. "Remarkably so," he said. "In fact, I'd say her recovery was just short of miraculous."

"You knew," she guessed.

"Not at first. But later, when we went to her house."

She sat up, almost hitting her head on the bed frame above the couch. "You went to her house?"

"We were concerned. We didn't know what had happened to you."

"You weren't rude to her, were you? She's just a helpless old—"

His snort cut her off. "Helpless? Hardly. She even had Doyle intimidated."

"Good." As she sank back, a sudden longing clogged her throat. What she wouldn't give for one of her guardian's brusque hugs right now.

"I still don't know why you ran, Lucinda. If you didn't want to marry Doyle, why didn't you just tell him?"

"It was a sudden decision. A combination of many things." All coming together in that single awful moment in the alcove outside the ballroom at the Fifth Avenue. Horne's voice. Finding out Doyle was a runner. The panic and confusion and utter devastation she had felt when everything she had believed—every cherished hope and dream—had all come tumbling down around her in an instant. "He never would have let me go willingly. And you know his temper and how he can be when things don't go his way."

"He wouldn't have harmed you."

She thought of Mrs. O'Reilly. "How can you be sure?"

"I wouldn't have let him."

She looked at him in surprise. "You'd have gone against him on my behalf?"

He didn't respond, but the answer was there in his eyes.

It shocked her, sent her mind whirling. It made no sense, and she was too weary to deal with it right then. Rising, she crossed to the candle on the wall beside the mirror and blew it out. "I'm going to bed," she announced without looking at him. "Good night."

She felt his gaze follow her as she made her way to the ladder at the foot of her bed. It was difficult to climb wearing the long, heavy robe, but she wasn't about to take it off and let him see her clad only in her sleeping gown. Once she made it onto the bed, she dropped her slippers over the side, then struggled to pull the covers over the bunched robe without banging her head on the ceiling. But when she was finally settled, she saw that the candle bolted to the wall beside her couch was still burning.

Muttering under her breath, she sat up.

"I'll get it." Rylander rose and came over to blow it out, throwing the room into shadow, except for the one candle left burning beside his couch. He went to the window closest to his berth, shoved aside the drape and opened it.

Immediately, the smell of coal smoke from the locomotive wafted into the compartment.

She was about to remonstrate with him when he picked up the pitcher from the table and tossed what water remained out the window. He emptied the glasses, as well. Then he shut the window, pulled the drape closed, and carried the empty pitcher and glasses to the door.

Curious to see what he was up to, she leaned up on one elbow and watched him set the pitcher upside down against the door, then stack the glasses on top of it. They clinked gently against each other with the motion of the train. When he was satisfied they were balanced just so, he straightened to find her watching him.

"If the door opens, we'll hear it," he explained, walking back to his couch.

"And then what?" She hadn't noticed if he was wearing a gun.

"Then I'll take care of it." Leaning over, he blew out the candle beside his berth. Instantly the compartment was plunged into darkness.

She lay back down. The inky blackness seemed to magnify every sound, as if her sense of hearing was compensating for her lack of sight. Over the rhythmic clatter of the wheels, she tried to listen for movement so she would know where he was and what he was doing. She heard the rustle of cloth—was he undressing? Then a soft thump followed by another—his shoes? More rustling. Was the man stripping off *everything*? Unwelcome and shocking images filled her mind. She had seen naked men before. But she had never imagined Tait Rylander in that state. Yet now she couldn't not picture his tall form and long limbs—

A series of creaks from the ladder jerked her out of those lurid imaginings. Then a heavy whumping sound, followed by more groans and creaks, rustling and thumps. A heavy sigh, then silence.

Sleep forgotten, she stared blankly up at where she imagined the ceiling to be. It felt more than strange to be lying in utter darkness, hearing another person—a male person—toss and turn not ten feet away. Intimate. Disturbing. She would never be able to—

"You can take off your robe now, Miss Hamilton."

"W-What?"

"I promise I won't look."

She heard the amused condescension in his tone and it made her snappish. "I'm perfectly fine, thank you. And it's Hathaway now."

"Very well. I bid you good night, then."

"Good night."

It was absurd. Ridiculous. Mrs. Throckmorton would faint if she knew.

She stared up into the inky blackness, her thoughts giving way to fear as it often did when darkness closed around her.

"Mr. Rylander?" she called after a moment.

A sigh. "What, Miss Hathaway."

"Please don't take me back."

He didn't respond.

"I'll pay you."

"With Doyle's money. Ironic, don't you think?"

"It's not his money. It's mine. He gave it to me." And she couldn't survive without it. Hearing the edge of desperation in her voice, she fought for control before she humiliated herself by begging or bursting into tears.

His stillness added weight to the blackness, made it hard to breathe. "He doesn't care about me," she said after a while. "He never really has. You know that."

Silence.

"He would be much happier with someone else."

"Are you ever going to sleep?"

"Please, Mr. Rylander." This time she couldn't keep the wobble from her voice. "Let me go."

The silence seemed to last forever before it finally ended on a deep sigh. He sounded weary. Defeated almost. "All right. After this thing with Smythe is settled, I'll let you go."

She sat up, then flinched when her head bumped the ceiling. "Truly? You won't take me back?"

"Truly. Now go to sleep."

Tears clogged her throat. It was a moment before she could speak. "Thank you, Mr. Rylander."

"You're welcome, Miss Hamilton. Good night."

"Hathaway. It's Hathaway now, remember?"

"Fine."

"But I'd rather you not tell Doyle—"

"For the love of God, woman—"

"Of course. You're tired. We'll talk more tomorrow." Slumping back to the mattress, she smiled tearfully up at the ceiling. "Good night, Mr. Rylander."

"Jesus."

The train made several brief water stops during the night. Each time, the absence of motion pulled her out of deep sleep, and she would awaken with a gasp, surrounded by a suffocating press of dark, silent nothingness, and for one terrifying moment she would think she was back in the closet at Mrs. Beale's.

Then she would hear the slow, steady breaths of the man in the other berth, and her throat would relax, and her heart would cease its furious rhythm, and she would lie back to wait for the train to start moving again.

But finally the cycle ended when she awoke to open drapes and bright sunlight. Relieved that the interminable night was over, she looked around.

Rylander was gone, his bed latched back up against the ceiling, no sign of him left in the room. Hurrying in case he returned, she climbed out of her berth and straightened her twisted robe. She was brushing the tangles from her hair when she heard his voice outside in the hall.

After making certain she was presentable and covered, she opened the door.

He stepped past, holding a tray with two steaming cups and two napkin-covered plates. "We missed breakfast, but this should tide us over until we reach Harrisburg. After we tend our errands, I promise to take you to lunch. You prefer coffee, I believe?"

Good morning to you, too. "Correct," she answered, a bit surprised that he remembered. Moving to the tray he had set on the table by the window, she studied the selection of fruit and pastries, wondering how much of her money had been spent on the delicacies. "How late is it?" she asked, carrying her cup and a scone to the couch under her berth.

"After ten. We're due in Harrisburg in about an hour and a half. Give or take." Picking up a piece of toast and his cup of black coffee, he took them to his own couch, where he sprawled with a sigh, legs outstretched and crossed at the ankles. His dusty shoes almost reached to her couch.

She studied him as she ate. It was apparent he hadn't had as restless a night as she had. The bristles were longer—had it truly been less than thirty-six hours since she had walked with him into the ballroom at the Fifth Avenue? Yet he looked much less haggard and rumpled this morning, although his shirt, from what she could see of it beneath the vest and coat, still looked as if he'd slept in it, which she fervently hoped he had.

"I'm confused," she said, brushing scone crumbs from her lap.

"About what?"

"I thought you were letting me go. Now you're offering to take me to lunch."

He looked at her across the narrow room, his expression betraying nothing, his brow creased in a scowl—which she now recognized as thoughtful concentration, rather than anger. "Is there any chance you could reconcile with Doyle?" he asked.

"None whatsoever."

He finished his toast, wiped his mouth, then said, "What about the railroad certificates? Do you intend to return them?"

"Why? He gave them to me."

"He gave them to his wife."

Irritation mingled with guilt and made her voice sharp. "What do you suggest? That I send them back with you and flee penniless into the night?"

"Sounds rather dramatic. And hardly penniless. Mrs. Throckmorton is—"

"Her wealth is in trust. None of it will ever come to me." She made an impatient gesture. "Just tell him you couldn't find me. Tell him I'm dead."

"And when you try to sell the certificates?" He let the sentence hang.

Setting the empty coffee cup on the ledge beside her couch, she crossed her arms over her chest and stared out the window.

They were heading into the Appalachians now—or Alleghenies, as some called them—and fields were giving way to rolling hills dotted with stands of elm and alder and pine. The train had slowed as the locomotive pulled the grades, and she could tell by the difference in sound whenever they crossed over a culvert or trestle. She had never been this far west before, and at any other time would have enjoyed the scenery.

It was several minutes before he spoke again. "Both Doyle and I are on the board of the Hudson and Erie. We would know immediately of a sale when the bank wired to confirm authenticity of the serial numbers on the certificates."

She knew that. Which was why she wasn't selling the stocks, but borrowing against them . . . and at less than face value. That way, when she didn't repay the loans, the banks could sell the certificates she had given them as surety at their true value and thus recover their money . . . assuming the market didn't weaken. And by the time Doyle traced the serial numbers back to the banks, she would be miles away, using a new name, and completely untraceable. Did Rylander think she was as ignorant as Doyle seemed to?

Apparently not. "But you're too smart to leave a trail like that, aren't you, Miss Hathaway?" He actually smiled as he said that. Like he was impressed.

The man confused her at every turn.

"So if you didn't sell them," he went on, "you must have taken out a loan using the certificates as collateral."

"Actually it was a line of credit."

"Ah. Thus buying yourself extra time. Clever. Which bank?"

"That's none of your business."

His dark brows rose. "He'll still find out. What then?"

"Hopefully I'll be long gone. Like you promised." She gave him a look, daring him to contradict her.

He didn't. But he didn't confirm that, either. "The lack of ethics doesn't bother you?" he asked.

Of course it bothered her. But the alternatives of being married to a runner or starving in the streets bothered her a great deal more. "Suppose I gave him back half the certificates?" she offered, just to get him to leave her alone. That would still leave her enough to make a new start.

He shook his head. "That won't work. He has to maintain possession of all the shares to control the vote."

"What vote?"

"He's hoping to take over the board of the Hudson and Erie by voting out the current chairman and putting himself in his place. Then he can push for a merger with his own line. But to get enough votes to accomplish that, he needs your shares and his."

"So he was hiding ownership by putting them in my name."

"Well . . . technically, I suppose—"

"And giving the certificates to me," she cut in as it all started to make sense, "was less a gift than an attempt to defraud the railroad."

She saw by his expression that she had caught him off guard. Surprise, a sudden wariness, perhaps even a spark of admiration showed in his face.

Or perhaps not. The man was devilishly hard to read.

"Not defraud," he argued. "It might seem murky, but it's not illegal. In fact, it happens all the time in business."

"Does it?" She smiled sweetly, feeling a lessening of the guilt that had been nagging at her. "And doesn't *that* lack of ethics bother you, Mr. Rylander?"

He had no answer for that.

Now that she knew for certain Doyle had simply intended to use her and thought her too stupid to realize it, she felt immeasurably better about taking the certificates. "If giving me the certificates was not illegal," she went on, "then my keeping them should not be illegal, either. He signed them over to me, after all. In front of witnesses. You may remind him of that when you return to New York without me." She almost laughed at his expression.

"Now if you will excuse me, Mr. Rylander." Keeping a grip on the armrest—although when the train was climbing, as it was now, the rocking wasn't nearly as pronounced—she rose from the couch. "I would like to get dressed. You're taking me to lunch, I believe, as a good-bye treat."

He blinked up at her with an expression of such consternation it was hard to keep her face straight. "What about Smythe?" he asked.

"A problem, to be sure. Which is why, when we're in Harrisburg, I'd like for you to advise me on the purchase of a firearm."

"Good God."

"Does that mean you won't?"

"Have you ever fired a gun?"

"No. Have you?"

"Of course I have."

"Then how hard can it be?"

Instead of being insulted by the barbed remark, he burst into laughter.

It shocked her, that unguarded response. And seeing the change it brought to his normally somber face made her smile back. How much more she might have liked this man had he revealed this approachable side of his nature sooner.

"You're a remarkable woman, Miss Hathaway."

Thinking the same thing about him but not about to admit it, she motioned toward the door. "If you don't mind . . ."

Still grinning, he rose. "Be quick about it. We'll only be in Harrisburg an hour or so, and we have a lot to do."

Eight

"Place hasn't changed much," Rylander observed as he helped Lucinda step from the train, his attention on the other departing passengers.

She turned to follow his gaze, fear making it hard to breathe. But she saw no one who resembled Smythe, even though it had been fifteen years since she'd last seen him. Relieved, she stepped onto the platform. "You've been to Harrisburg before?"

"In sixty-three. The town may have crept a little deeper into the corn fields in the last seven years, or stretched farther up and down the banks of the Susquehanna, and there's definitely more smoke in the air from the foundries and gas works, but it's still a pretty town."

Lucinda had to agree. Red brick buildings, lofty church spires, busy streets. Like many Pennsylvania towns, especially those with huge stores of coal nearby to fuel industry, it seemed to have prospered with the growth of the railroads.

"Seems there will be a slight delay before departure," Rylander told her as they walked toward the station. "George says we have at least two hours. Shall we walk? Or would you rather take a horsecar?"

After being forced to stay in that small compartment to avoid Smythe, the idea of stretching her legs sounded heavenly to Lucinda. "Walk." But as soon as the word left her mouth, she caught her toe on a nail protruding through the rough boards and she stumbled forward.

Before she could fall, he dropped her valise—which she had refused to leave behind—and caught her shoulders. "Are you all right?"

"I think so." Laughing and embarrassed, she straightened, feeling clumsy and rather breathless for some reason. "Although I may have to learn to walk on solid ground again after battling the constant motion of a railcar for so long."

He tucked her arm through his, picked up her valise, and continued into the station. "Until you do, I'll be here to catch you."

She looked up at him, thinking what a sweet thing that was to say. But he was looking back over his shoulder, his studied gaze taking in every passenger on the platform.

Her playful mood evaporated. "Do you see him?"

Those gray eyes swung to meet hers. Something in them, in his face—an expression she didn't recognize—made odd things happen inside her chest. "No. And you're not to worry about it, Lucinda. I'll keep you safe." The look lasted a second longer before he turned away. "We'll go left," he said as they exited the station. "As I recall, there were several decent eateries in the downtown area close to the state capitol. It's not far."

She matched her pace to his. It was a beautiful spring morning with a cool breeze and a warm sun. Perfect for a walk. "Did you live here long?"

"Only as a soldier. First, in training at Camp Curtin, and later, to recuperate after Gettysburg."

"You were wounded?"

He nodded. "Leg. Luckily I didn't lose it to the surgeons and it healed fairly quickly. But a sergeant is expected to issue orders, and I couldn't." He met her questioning look with a wry smile. "I'd been hanged and couldn't speak."

Hanged? In her shock, she almost stumbled again.

He seemed not to notice. "Until the swelling went down and I could talk loudly enough to issue orders on a battlefield, I was stuck on administrative duty. I hated that."

Hanging would certainly explain the huskiness in his voice. "Why were you hanged?" She still couldn't fathom such a thing. Was he a criminal? A spy?

He shrugged. She felt the flex of it all down his arm. Despite his height, Rylander had never struck her as possessing a particularly imposing figure—not like a dock worker or laborer who used his strength to earn a wage. Granted, he was bigger and broader than Doyle, but he was always so impeccably dressed and carried himself with such grace and elegance she often forgot his size or that he had once fought for money. But feeling the hard strength of the arm beneath her hand, she realized that hidden under the fine clothes and polished manners was a very powerful man. It was a bit shocking to think of Tait Rylander that way. He could hurt her if he so chose, and she could do little to stop him.

"Simple revenge," he said in answer to the question she had forgotten she'd asked.

"For what?"

"Winning. The Battle of Gettysburg was over. The South was in retreat. Three Rebs ran by, saw me under a tree trying to stop the bleeding in my leg, and decided to rid the Union of one more soldier before they fled the field."

"So they hanged you?"

"It seems they were out of bullets."

Lucinda was now even more confused. "But you were a Southerner, too."

"I still am. But at the time, I was wearing a Union uniform."

"Why?" It had always been a mystery to her why a Southerner would fight against his own. "Were you an abolitionist?"

Again, that shrug. "My family were merchants. We never owned slaves, and even though we were opposed to the practice, that issue didn't impact us in a personal way. But secession would damage everyone and leave us open to foreign influence. I thought the nation would be stronger undivided. History will decide if I was right."

Not wanting to be dragged into a political discussion of a moot point, she returned to the original issue. "So they left you hanging?"

"Until Doyle rode up and cut me down."

"And you've been friends since?"

He nodded but said nothing. Lucinda sensed his friendship with her controversial Irish almost-husband wasn't altogether comfortable for a man as strict in his thinking as Rylander.

Which was probably why he spent so much of his time cleaning up behind his friend and putting out the fires Doyle started with his impulsiveness and hot temper.

"First, we'll stop at a bank," he said as they waited for a buggy to rattle by. No boardwalks here, but brick or stone walk-ways on either side of the cobblestone road, crowded with pur-poseful people. "I'll obtain funds to repay your loan"—he sent her a chiding look—"with interest, of course. Then, if it's all right with you, I'd like to stop at a haberdashery." He looked down in distaste at his frock coat. "I doubt I'll be able to find a coat in my size, but hopefully I can have this one brushed. If not, George says Pittsburgh will be a much longer stop and I should have ample time to get it cleaned."

Pittsburgh? She thought they would be parting company here in Harrisburg. Why did he insist on staying? "You're going on to Pittsburgh?"

He continued walking, his gaze fixed straight ahead. "I told you I wouldn't leave you unprotected until the issue of Smythe is resolved."

"What if it's not Smythe? Neither of us has seen him. The porter could be mistaken."

"Then I guess you're stuck with me until we reach your des-tination." He sent her a speculative look. "Where might that be, exactly?"

She looked away. "I haven't decided."

"I'd advise you to do so before you reach Columbus. That is, if you're intending to go on up to Chicago."

"As I said, I haven't decided." The man was utterly relentless.

"Here we are." He nodded toward the building they were approaching that bore the brass nameplate of Harris Bank and Trust. "This shouldn't take long. Was that interest to be simple or compounded?" he asked as he released her arm to swing open the door with the hand not gripping her valise.

"For you, Mr. Rylander? Compounded." She smiled sweetly. "Daily."

"I would expect no less, Miss Hamilton."

"Hathaway."

"Of course."

"Well," Lucinda huffed ten minutes later when Rylander— now many times richer than when he went in, judging by the thickness of the inside pocket on his frock coat—led her out of the bank. "That was certainly disheartening. You didn't even have to flaunt your breasts."

He stumbled, almost missing the step. "My what?"

"Breasts. Even with a valise full of railroad shares, and these"—she made an offhand gesture at her chest, which drew his eye, she noticed, then sent a blush blossoming across his cheeks—"I had much more trouble securing funds than you did on your signature alone. It hardly seems fair, does it?"

"Miss Hathaway." He made a helpless gesture. "I don't know what to say."

"Then don't speak. And stop looking at my breasts."

A startled laugh burst out of him. "You let everyone else. Why can't I?"

"It's unseemly. Look." She pointed up the walk. "There's a gunsmith. Shall we pop in and get my weapon? Nothing too cumbersome. Something that will fit handily into my reticule. Do come along."

Almost two hours later, they were hurrying back to the train, Lucinda's little Christian Sharps four-barrel pepperbox pistol and a box of cartridges tucked inside her reticule, and Mr. Rylander in his smart new bowler and freshly brushed frock coat, carrying her old valise in one hand and his new one in the other, which was now bulging with his new clothing purchases and apothecary items.

It had been a lovely morning, although Lucinda was a bit surprised at the growing ease between Mr. Rylander and herself. They might no longer be enemies in the strictest sense, but they were certainly still at cross purposes. Yet the hours had flown by. She even forgot about Smythe for a while.

But not so, Mr. Rylander. He seemed ever vigilant, studying each face they passed, scanning the street behind them whenever she stopped to admire something in a display window, pausing for a moment inside the door whenever they entered a shop. His alertness allowed her to relax her own, and it almost felt like they were on holiday.

They had been so busy with errands they hadn't even taken time for a noon meal, nor had she had an opportunity to send a wire to Mrs. Throckmorton. Even now, as they rushed through the depot, the conductor was making his last call for passengers.

Lucinda studied the faces watching from the passenger car windows and the other people crowded at the boarding steps. But again, she didn't see Smythe. Perhaps they were mistaken about him being there. Perhaps Smythe had died in the fire as she'd hoped all these years. Perhaps Horne wasn't a threat at all.

"Is the dining car still open for lunch?" Rylander asked George when they stepped through the door of their sleeper car.

The porter nodded. "For at least another hour, sir. Shall I take those valises down to your room?"

"I'll take them. What's the next big stop, and how long will we be there?"

"Altoona, sir, scheduled to arrive at seven fifteen this evening. Since we'll be heading into the mountains, we'll have to add another locomotive and tender, so we won't be departing there until nine twenty."

"Excellent." He grinned down at Lucinda, crowded beside him in the narrow aisleway. "I promised you a meal here in Harrisburg. Instead, we'll have it in Altoona. If that suits?"

Lucinda couldn't help but smile back. "It does."

But it occurred to her as she swept past him down to their compartment that she was beginning to enjoy Tait Rylander's company much more than was wise.

A while later, Tait headed back to the compartment, clean and shaved, wearing his new attire and feeling almost human again.

Lucinda seemed to agree. As she let him into the room, she gave him a quick inspection. "You look quite elegant, Mr. Rylander."

Oddly pleased by the compliment, he hid a smile as he set his valise on the floor beside his couch. "I can't believe I let you talk me into a purple waistcoat."

"Vest. And it's mauve."

"It's purple."

"It quite becomes your dark coloring."

To cover the discomfiture her approval gave him, he pulled several bank notes and coins from his pocket. "Here is the money I owe you, Miss Hathaway." He counted it out and set it on the table between the windows. "With interest, compounded daily." Out of concern for how it might appear to others, he hadn't given it to her earlier in the bank, or later, out on the street. Although, insomuch as they were sharing a sleeping compartment, it might be a bit late to worry about her reputation.

"Thank you, Mr. Rylander."

He watched her slip the money into her valise and thought again what an odd, contradictory woman she was. Brazen, beautiful in a serene, almost cold sort of way, and far too intelligent for her own good, she had captured his attention from the moment he had first seen her on Doyle's arm at the Wallingford garden party the previous year. He should have made his move then, he realized now. But how could he have competed with Doyle's easy Irish charm and blond good looks?

Unless it wasn't Doyle's charm that had won her, but his money. Which Tait had in abundance, as well.

But if he had to guess, based on what he now knew about this resourceful and independent woman, she would probably prefer using her wits to earn her own money rather than having it doled out in payment for her beauty and social connections. It was apparent both he and Doyle had greatly underestimated the demure Miss Hamilton.

And how pretty she would look in that fine yellow dress, despite a near sleepless night.

Picking up her valise, which he knew she would insist on taking even though they would be only two cars away, he motioned to the door. "Shall we?"

"What about Smythe? What if he sees us?"

"I'm hoping he will. If he makes a move, I'll deal with it. If not, at least I'll see who and what I'm up against. At the very least, we'll enjoy a hot meal."

"So you're using me for bait?"

He smiled. "You'll be safe, Miss Hathaway. My word on it."

Lunch was a continuation of the easy companionship they had enjoyed throughout the morning in Harrisburg. As they chatted amiably over bowls of salad and soup and tall glasses of lemonade, the threat of Smythe faded into the background drone of other voices, the clink of tableware, the constant clack of the wheels beneath their feet. Insulated by the noise around them, they talked freely of many subjects, from her life with Mrs. Throckmorton to his upbringing in a small North Carolina town and their shared fascination with business matters. She was witty and charming and so quick-minded he often found himself struggling to keep up with her. A novel occurrence, as far as his experience with women went.

Then he blundered by asking her about Smythe.

Immediately she slipped behind the serene façade. Instead of answering, she put on a smile as impersonal as it was cool, and asked his opinion about the instability of the bank note with all the counterfeiting since the war, and whether he thought President Grant had been instrumental in the Black Friday scandal and collapse of the gold market the previous year.

Not a conversation Tait had ever expected to have with a woman over a plate of ham slices and cucumber sandwiches. But recognizing it as his punishment for prying into her personal life, he allowed himself to be drawn into a rather dull discussion, if only to keep her from retreating further.

They were like dancers in a verbal waltz—skirting around controversial subjects, saying the proper things, and keeping the proper space between them, as careful with their words as dancers were with their steps.

Or perhaps with Lucinda, it was more like a fencing match. Thrust, parry, retreat, attack. The woman definitely kept him on his toes.

But just when he thought he'd dodged the worst of it, she slipped under his guard with a jab of her own.

"Doyle told me you once fought for money," she said, catching him with a mouth full of lettuce. "Explain that if you will."

Touché. But being no coward, Tait finished chewing, set down his fork, and answered as best he could while telling her as little as possible, not only because it wasn't a suitable topic for dinner conversation, especially with a woman, but because he didn't enjoy brutality—given or received—and had worked hard to put behind him that unsavory period in his life.

"It was a difficult time for returning soldiers after the war. Especially an Irish hustler with more ambition than skill, and a struggling Southern lawyer with no clients. The quickest way to build a stake was for me to win fights and for Doyle to increase the earnings with well-placed bets."

"So Doyle took the money and you took the beating."

A harsh view but unfortunately correct. "It was the best use of our talents at the time. Doyle has always had a genius for turning a dollar. He could triple a bet twice over while I was still plodding along, mulling the risks."

"You? A plodder? I think not."

"Perhaps a dog with a bone, then," he amended, toying with his fork to hide his discomfiture at having to dredge up unpleasant memories. Tait hated talking about those years. Hated even thinking about them. "I fear I have an obsessive nature when something interests me or I'm confronted with a puzzle. I can't seem to let it rest until I have it figured out." He shot her a pointed look.

"As you've so readily demonstrated," she fired back. "Repeatedly." Yet, some of the combativeness left her eyes as she studied him.

He could almost feel her mind probing his—assessing, weighing, peeking into every dark corner. He allowed it because he had nothing to hide, and because doing so might gain her trust, and because he was a man and what man didn't enjoy being scrutinized by a beautiful woman. But this reversal of role was difficult for him, and he had to flatten his palm against the table to keep from fidgeting with impatience.

"I appreciate that you're wise enough to consider the risks, Mr. Rylander," she finally said. "Not all men are. And that you had the courage to fight when it was necessary, and the wisdom to stop when it wasn't."

He shook his head, uneasy with the sentiment. "I'm afraid it had less to do with courage and wisdom, Miss Hathaway, and more to do with the ache of empty stomachs. I take no pride in what I did. But one does what one must."

She gave a sad smile. "Yes. One does."

He sensed currents running between them. Not sure what they meant, but unwilling to disrupt them, he sat motionless as she reached across the table. With great care, as if fearful of causing pain, she brushed a fingertip over the cracked knuckles that rose like swollen bee stings on the back of his battered right hand.

A simple touch, yet he felt it all through his body, like a bolt of energy racing along his nerves to lodge in his heart.

"Do they hurt?"

He cleared his throat. "Sometimes. In winter. Not bad."

"I'm sorry for that."

He had to fight to keep from grabbing her hand when she pulled it away.

Sitting back in her chair, she cocked her head to one side and smiled at him in a way that took away his breath. "Are we friends again, then, Mr. Rylander?"

Feeling as if a weight had been lifted off his chest, he smiled back. "Always, Miss Hathaway."

They resumed eating. Tait hardly tasted it but went through the motions to give himself something to do other than stare at her. He tried not to be obvious about it, but everything about her fascinated him, and he found himself searching each movement and expression for a clue to the mystery that was Lucinda.

Was the way she glanced around the car after each sip of her lemonade a sign of boredom? Curiosity? Or was she assessing danger?

Did those pursed lips indicate pique? Or an attempt to suppress a smile?

Was she betraying nervousness or impatience when she fussed with her napkin or smoothed a fold in her skirt or lifted a hand to check her hair?

Tiny tells that left him with more questions than answers, yet challenged him to keep trying until he could fit all the pieces together.

Who was she? How did she get that tiny scar on her wrist? What were the night terrors that had brought her out of deep sleep whenever the train stopped last night?

He had known women who were more beautiful. More voluptuous. Certainly more compliant. But never one as unpredictable and headstrong and guarded as the woman sitting across from him.

And smart.

Which fascinated him most of all.

"Do stop staring at me," she murmured.

"I can't help it. You look very pretty, especially with the sunlight shining through the window, turning your hair to gold."

"Actual gold? It must be very heavy."

"Alas, more of an illusion than a reality."

She popped a pinch of bread into her mouth and watched him watch her chew and swallow it. "And my eyes? Does the sun make them especially sparkly?"

"Like green fire."

"And give my skin a glow of vitality?"

"It does."

"Are you totally smitten, then?"

"I fear I am."

Laughing, she lifted a palm. "Enough. Or I shall lose my lunch." But she said it with the first true smile since he'd asked about Smythe.

Amused, he filed away another clue: Lucinda Hathaway was uncomfortable with compliments. Odd in a woman so attractive. He resolved to give her several more, just to see her squirm.

The waiter arrived to replace their empty luncheon plates with dessert cups—a thick, rich custard topped with a caramelized sugar crust. They ate in a companionable silence, once more at ease with one another.

To keep from staring at the woman across from him, Tait watched diners come and go, saw none who resembled Smythe's description, and turned toward the window. Beyond it, the distant dome of Blue Knob rose like the back of a sleeping bear. Fields gave way to thick stands of hemlock, oak, and maple, and water trickling down rock faces or running in creeks beside the tracks reflected bright flashes of sunlight as they rolled past. All around them, the land showed signs of awaking after a long winter's rest.

It reminded Tait of spring back home, where the Smokies of the southern Appalachians bridged the border between Tennessee and North Carolina. Except here, no fog curled over the ridges or rose out of the wooded valleys like lingering drifts of smoke from ancient fires.

He took a deep breath and let it out, thinking how much easier it was for him to breathe the farther away they traveled from the bustle of Manhattan. Had he been in the city so long he'd forgotten the taste of cool mountain air, the feel of open sky above him, or the silent hush of a deep forest?

He'd heard there were even more dramatic mountains farther west. Thousands of feet taller than these, where the air was so thin and crisp it hurt to breathe, and where there were still a few valleys so remote they had yet to bear the track of man.

The Wild West. It was luring people by the thousands.

Looking across the table at Lucinda, he wondered if that was where she was headed, and if so, what she would do if he offered to ride along.

An unexpected notion. And once formed, impossible to ignore.

"What happened after your parents died?" he asked, risking another blunder rather than deal with that troubling thought.

A wistful smile curled her lips. Pressing the bowl of her spoon into her custard, she said, "A guardian angel saved me."

"And who was that?"

She shook her head. "I'll not reveal a name and put anyone at risk."

"At risk how?"

"Doyle is a vengeful man."

He reared back in his chair, insulted by the implication. "You think I'd tell him?"

She lifted one shoulder in a shrug. "Your first loyalty is to him. Why wouldn't you?"

Too angry for restraint, he slapped his napkin down beside his plate. "My first loyalty is to my conscience! And I don't carry tales, Miss Hathaway."

She studied him in silence. He could read the doubt in her eyes. Could see she wanted to believe and trust him. But something rose up between them and held her back. As it always did.

He was weary of it.

Leaning across the narrow table until his face was a foot from hers, he spoke with quiet emphasis. "I've said it before and I'll say it again. I am not your enemy, Lucinda. I never have been. And I never will be."

He watched a great sadness come over her face and something close to tears glitter in her eyes. "And yet you're here, Tait. What am I to make of that?"

Tait. It was the first time she'd called him by his given name. "I'm here to protect you."

"From whom? Smythe? You didn't even know about him until after you arrived. Doyle? If that's the case, you should have stayed to stop him, rather than coming after me. Instead, you've trailed me like a hound on a blood scent. Why would you do that?"

For you. The unspoken thought exploded in his mind.

I came for you.

Those words shocked him, cast his mind into turmoil. And suddenly, in that confused state, he saw himself through her eyes: a lonely man chasing after a woman who was married to another—a woman who neither trusted him nor seemed to welcome his attentions. What kind of fool would do such a thing?

The answer was so clear he couldn't deny it.

One who couldn't give up until he knew the truth—about her feelings for Doyle, about her past, about his own feelings for her.

You idiot.

Teeth clenched, he rubbed a hand over his brow where a tiny tick of pain was building between his eyes. "All I want is the truth, Lucinda." But even as he said it, he knew it was a lie. He wanted everything. In every carnal and emotional and intellectual way, he wanted to break through all her barriers and find the woman beneath.

"I told you the truth," she reminded him.

"Not all of it."

"Well, it's all the truth you're ever going to get." Folding her napkin, she took care to line it up next to her dessert plate. "Some things are best left unspoken, Mr. Rylander. This is one of them. Please do not ask me about it again. Now if you will excuse me."

She started to rise.

"Don't." He clapped a hand over hers, pinning it to the table. "Don't run from me." Realizing the inappropriateness of his action, he forced himself to take his hand away. "My apologies. I didn't mean to pry."

She stared at him, her eyes wide and unblinking, her body poised for flight.

"Okay, that's not strictly true," he conceded with a smile that felt more awkward than reassuring. "I did mean to pry, Lucinda. Just not so clumsily. But I assure you it won't happen again."

Her shoulders relaxed slightly. She pulled her hand back and rested it in her lap. "What won't happen again? The prying? Or the clumsiness?"

"Both. Either." He leaned back in his chair before he did something else foolish. Even touching her hand in such an impersonal way had sent his heart into a fast, hard rhythm. "Would you care to visit the Parlor Car, Miss Hathaway?"

"Perhaps another time, Mr. Rylander. I think I would prefer to rest a bit before we reach Altoona."

"Of course." Rising, he helped her out of her bench seat, then picked up her valise and walked her to their compartment. As he set the valise beside her couch, he saw that in their absence George had been in to raise the beds and tidy the room. He offered to lower her berth so she could nap, but she declined, saying the couch would suffice.

So formal. So distant. So coolly proper.

It infuriated him. They were sharing a room, for God's sake. He had spent half the night listening to her breathe and wondering what she wore—if anything—beneath that tent of a robe. Now after one foolish misstep, she couldn't even treat him civilly? *Hell.*

Okay, perhaps it was two foolish missteps, but he had apologized all he was going to. He wouldn't grovel, even for her. So after telling her he would return to escort her to dinner once they reached Altoona, he bid her a pleasant afternoon rest and left the room. *Damn woman.*

What did he have to do to break through that reserve and bring her to heel?

The absurdity of that ever happening made him laugh. He'd never met a more elusive, prickly, secretive, hardheaded woman in his life. He had as much chance of bringing her to heel as she had of keeping him under her thumb.

Still . . . it would be fun to try.

Good humor restored, he continued down the hallway, out the back of the sleeper car, and into the Parlor Car coupled behind it. A quick glance told him none of the men who were lounging on the plush couches matched Smythe's description.

Then where the hell was he?

Disgruntled, he settled onto one of the swivel chairs, stretched out his legs as best he could, and mentally composed the wire he would send to Doyle as soon as they reached Altoona.

He wouldn't mention that he had found Lucinda—Margaret. He would say only that he had tracked her to Philadelphia and was now on his way to Pittsburgh. He wasn't sure he should ask about Smythe until he knew for certain what the man was up to. He would close by saying the train would leave Altoona at ten o'clock tonight and if Doyle had a response, send it by then. Hopefully he would get one. Then maybe he could decide what to do about Lucinda Hathaway.

With a sigh, he tipped his head against the backrest and closed his eyes.

He had no legal right to force her to return to her husband.

But he had no moral right to keep her with him, either, especially feeling about her the way he did.

Nine

"You smell good," Rylander said later that afternoon when he helped her off the train at the Altoona, Pennsylvania, depot. "Like flowers."

Unwilling to let on how much his words pleased her, Lucinda busied herself retying the bow securing her horsehair bonnet. The wind had picked up with the approach of dusk and was playing havoc with her ribbons. Once she was satisfied that both the hat and her blush were under control, she scanned the platform one last time, saw no sign of Smythe, and happily put him from her mind. Smiling, she took the arm Tait offered and let him lead her out of the station and into the heart of Altoona.

It was the ultimate railroad town. Carved out of the wilderness only twenty-one years ago, it existed for a single purpose—to service the Pennsylvania Railroad with its machine shops and foundries and miles of tracks.

Carefully stepping over one imbedded in the middle of the street, she turned to Rylander and, just to needle him, asked, "Which flowers?"

"Something sweet and . . . flowery."

"Hyacinths, perhaps?"

"Perhaps."

His arm felt solid and warm beneath her gloved hand, and she allowed herself to brush against his shoulder ever so slightly. There was a calm steadiness about Tait Rylander that she appreciated—craved, almost. It seemed she had spent all of her life fighting for balance. With him, she had only to lean against his arm to find it.

She was sorry they had argued earlier. She disliked having to so blatantly dodge his questions. But she had no intention of baring that unspeakable part of her past to anyone's scrutiny. Especially his.

So to ease any lingering awkwardness, she badgered him with playful teasing, just to see him smile. "Lilacs?"

"Maybe."

"Lavender? Violets?"

"Something purple."

"Purple?" She glanced up to find him fighting a smile. "Why purple?"

Looking quite smug, he motioned to his mauve vest and her pale cerise walking dress. "It's your favorite color."

"You're guessing."

"A safe presumption."

"A presumptuous presumption. And you're wrong. The color of this dress is more pink than purple, and the scent I'm wearing is Attar of Roses."

A labored sigh. "Miss Hathaway, you wear me out. I had no idea offering compliments to a woman could be so exhausting. Can we not simply agree that you smell good and look pretty?"

"But it's important to be precise, even when—"

Deep laughter cut her off. The vibration of it passed all the way down his arm and into her chest.

"Rather than accept a compliment as your due," he scolded with a grin, "you would argue with the devil himself, wouldn't you, my dear?"

My dear. She liked that. "I'm not sure what the devil—"

"See? You're hopeless. If you'll just say, 'Thank you, Tait,' so we can put an end to it, I promise I'll never compliment you again."

"Thank you, Tait. But I never said I didn't want you to—"

Another burst of laughter, and she looked over to see his head was thrown back, his fine teeth showing in a wide-open grin. As her gaze drifted up his strong neck to the shadowed underside of his square jaw, she thought she had never seen a more attractive or compelling sight than Tait Rylander in an unguarded moment of delight.

She liked that he wore a bowler rather than a top hat, which would have made him impossibly tall. She liked that there was enough wave in his dark hair to make it curl over his ears and at the back of his neck. She liked that his smile was slightly one-sided and reached all the way up to his arresting eyes.

But most of all, she liked the way laughter burst out of him without restraint or artifice, like a bright bubble of un-abashed joy.

"We'll stop at the telegraph office first," he said in that dic-tatorial way of his that she liked somewhat less. "I need to send a wire to Doyle."

She stiffened.

He must have felt it because his head swung sharply toward her. "I'm not telling him I found you, Lucinda," he said in a reassuring voice. "Only that I tracked you to Philadelphia and I'm continuing on to Pittsburgh."

She nodded, still a bit confused by his motives. Granted, southern gallantry ran deep in him, and until her old nemesis was dealt with, he probably wouldn't want to leave her alone, even if it took him hundreds of miles out of his way. But why would he withhold the truth from Doyle? He had nothing to gain by doing so, and everything to lose.

He must have sensed those doubts, too. The man was becom-ing entirely too adept at reading her thoughts. "He expects to hear from me. If he doesn't, he might become suspicious."

"Of what? What have you done wrong?"

He didn't answer but scanned the street, his lips pressed in a tight line.

The wind gusted, and she pulled her new shawl closer around her shoulders, wishing she had worn her traveling cape instead. But if she had, her new gown would have been hidden from view, and she wanted to look her best in case Tait noticed.

Tait. When had she starting thinking of him as Tait?

The silence grew. They walked almost two blocks before he spoke again. When he did, it was to say something so shocking and unexpected it changed everything.

"I wish I had met you first."

Seven words. Expressing a sentiment so innocent yet so weighted with meaning it threw her thoughts into disarray.

I wish I had met you first.

She didn't know what that meant—or what she wanted it to mean—or how to respond. So, as was her habit when feeling unsure, she retreated into the safety of humor. "Actually, you did. Although 'met' might be too generous a word."

He turned his head and looked at her, and what she saw in his eyes made her heart change rhythm and her mind soar to places it had never been. "Mrs. Throckmorton and I were attending a gathering—I don't remember where—outside, I think."

"The Wallingfords'."

She nodded in surprise. "Yes. The annual Wallingford garden party." Did he remember, too? Facing forward again, she matched her pace to his and allowed herself to lean against his arm. "We were watching the croquet game, as I recall. Mrs. Throckmorton was complaining about the cloudiness, the bugs, the stale sandwiches, and the warm lemonade—although she wouldn't have missed it for the world—when you swept by with a striking brunette on your arm."

"Swept? Hardly sounds manly."

She laughed. "I assure you, one had only to look at your companion to put to rest any doubts about your manliness."

"I'm pleased to hear it. She was beautiful, then?"

"Very. Tall and regal. Quite the belle of the gathering. I remember thinking she must have been raised in a much colder climate, because despite the cool breeze, it seemed not to bother her in the least—or you, either, judging by the avidity of your stare—that her chest was almost completely exposed."

"Avidity? Surely not."

"I fear so. In truth, I was quite embarrassed for you."

His chuckle was a song in her ear. "I don't remember her. But I do remember you. You were coming down the steps with Doyle, your blond heads together, laughing over some quip he had made. You were wearing a purple dress that brought out the green in your eyes. I thought you were the most beautiful woman I'd seen all day."

"Only that day? What about the other three hundred and sixty-four?"

"Just say, 'Thank you, Tait.'"

Keeping her head tucked so he wouldn't see her foolish grin, she murmured, "Thank you, Tait."

"You're welcome, Lucinda."

"But just to be clear, it was lilac, not purple."

"Can't help yourself, can you?"

Laughing, she pointed at a Western Union Telegraph sign in the next block. "It appears it's still open."

"The conductor said they kept a telegrapher on duty at night because of the railroads. We'll stop there first, then find the restaurant he recommended."

As they stepped inside the small telegraph office, the clerk looked up from the chicken leg he was gnawing, then hastily set it aside and wiped the grease from his fingers. "Help you?" he asked, throat bobbing as he swallowed.

"I need to send a wire," Tait said.

"Sure. Just fill this out."

Taking the tattered notepad the clerk shoved across the counter, Tait began to write.

Lucinda considered sending a wire to Mrs. Throckmorton, too. She hadn't done so earlier when they'd stopped in Harrisburg, but now that she had the opportunity, she had reservations. What if Smythe—or whoever was tracking her—traced it back to Cyrus Quincy, her guardian's contact at the Merchant's Bank? And then through the banker to Mrs. Throckmorton? That might put her in jeopardy, too, and Lucinda couldn't risk that.

She wondered what Tait was writing but refrained from peeking. She wanted to believe he wouldn't tell Doyle he'd found her, but blind trust was hard for her, especially now, when her life might be at stake.

Tait finished writing, then offered the paper for her to read. "Let me know if there's anything I should add." *See? You can trust me,* his gaze said.

She could have shown that she did trust him by returning the wire to him unread. But unable to take that step, she took the paper from his hand.

No news. Heading to Pittsburgh. Send further instructions by ten P.M. Rylander.

Short and sweet. The most dangerous, nerve-wracking,

astonishing three days of her life boiled down to a few simple words.

"Do you want me to mention Smythe?" he asked.

"No." She returned the note. After the telegram was on its way, Tait told the clerk to bring any responses to him at the Oak Bar Restaurant, then picked up Lucinda's valise and motioned toward the door. "Shall we?"

The Oak Bar must have been one of the town's earliest gathering places. It had that comfortable, slightly worn look of an established eatery that catered more to local patrons than travelers passing through. The paneled walls were cluttered with memorabilia, from drawings of the horseshoe curves west of town to uniform patches worn in the war and photographs detailing the construction of the rail yards, shops, and iron works needed to keep the Pennsylvania Railroad expanding west.

By the time they took their seats, it was after eight o'clock and there were only a few diners left. Unlike Manhattan, where the streets stayed busy long into the night, railroad towns retired early, it seemed. Their table was near the back, beside a window and separated from the next table by a tall, leafy potted plant. An intimate candlelit setting, more suited to lovers than two near strangers who were still struggling to come to terms with one another.

As Lucinda removed her bonnet and set it on the corner of the table, Tait opened the menu.

"The conductor recommended the pork chops," he said scanning the offerings. "Although he said the buffalo steak was tasty, too."

In the end, Lucinda chose roast chicken and Tait ordered the pot roast. It was a quiet meal, neither of them saying much yet enjoying the relaxed atmosphere where they didn't have to talk over the constant clatter of wheels beneath their feet, or worry about their plates dumping into their laps whenever the train hit a bump. They were finishing dessert when the cashier brought to their table a message that had just been delivered by the telegrapher.

With some trepidation, Lucinda watched Tait open the envelope. He read the contents in a single glance, then, his face grim, handed the telegram to her.

Allan Pinkerton taking over. Return on next train. Kerrigan.

She stared at the clipped sentences, having to read them twice before they made sense. "You're leaving." The finality of those two words carried more weight than Lucinda could ever have imagined. When had she come to care so much for the man who had once been her greatest aggravation?

Looking up, she found him studying her with that intense concentration that only a week ago would have goaded her into saying something she might have later regretted. But now . . .

Now, she didn't know what to think. About him. About what she was feeling. About what she should do. She had heard of the Chicago-based Pinkerton National Detective Agency with its dramatic calling card: a wide-open eye with the caption, "We never sleep." She had read of Allan Pinkerton's relentless pursuit of the Reno Gang, and knew if Rylander had found her in a day it might be only a matter of hours before they tracked her down. Even now, agents could be halfway between here and Chicago, racing to apprehend her in Pittsburgh.

With a shaking hand, she passed the telegram back to Tait. "What do I do?"

"You could go back. Try to work something out with Doyle."

She didn't even have to think about it. "No."

"Or I could take the stock certificates back, try to convince him—"

"No. They're mine. He gave them to me and I need them."

He sighed, clearly as weary of this argument as she was. "They were intended for his wife. No court would ever—"

"I know what his intent was!" Realizing her sharp retort had drawn the attention of the few remaining diners, she leaned forward in the chair and lowered her voice. "His intent was to use me as a screen for his underhanded dealings. Well, I won't have it. If he forces me back, I will never sign the shares over to him or let him cast any votes in my name. When I can, I will repay him. That's the best I can do for now. You may tell him so when you see him."

"Lucinda."

Fearing he would see her disappointment, she turned her head and looked blindly out the window, but all she could see was the reflection of herself and Tait in the dark glass. She was such a fool. She had actually begun to trust this man. Had even allowed herself to think of him as a friend. Perhaps even more than a friend. But it was obvious that to him it was all about retrieving the stock certificates.

After a long, tense silence, Tait said, "I'll wire him back, tell him I found you, and to call off the Pinkertons."

"And then what? You drag me to New York against my will?"

"Then I let you escape."

She turned back, daring to hope when logic told her it was a reckless plan that might put them both in jeopardy. Doyle might forgive her defection since she had never meant that much to him. But he'd never forgive Tait's. "Would he believe such a ploy?"

"For a while."

"And when he realizes you lied?"

He shrugged as if this betrayal of his partner and friend and one of the most ruthless men in Manhattan were a small thing that wouldn't carry a huge price. "Hopefully, by then it will be too late. And you'll be safe."

She was stunned. "You would do that for me?" Perhaps he did care for her, after all.

Silence.

"But why?"

He sighed and rubbed his fingers over the furrow between his eyes. When he took his hand away, he looked weary and sad and almost . . . defeated. "Because I'm not your enemy, Lucinda. I pray someday you'll believe that." Taking his napkin from his lap and dropping it onto the table, he pushed back his chair. "Now if you'll excuse me, I need to send a message to the telegraph office."

She grabbed his arm before he could rise. "Don't, Tait. He'll never forgive you for deceiving him, and you'll never forgive me for forcing you into it."

"You're not forcing me, Lucinda."

"But your friendship with Doyle—"

"Is not your concern," he cut in. Then seeing the hurt she wasn't able to hide, he softened his voice. "But if it eases your conscience, our relationship has been under a strain for a long time. Perhaps this will provide the means I've been seeking to end it."

She took her hand away. "I fear he's a vengeful man."

"I can take care of myself, Lucinda." At his unyielding tone, Lucinda realized if the occasion warranted, Tait Rylander could be every bit as dangerous as Doyle Kerrigan. "I'll settle our bill and send that wire. Or if you're ready to leave, we can stop by the Western Union office on the way back to the train."

Unwilling to stay in the dining room alone, Lucinda rose with him. Tossing her shawl over her arm, she looped the drawstring of the reticule over her wrist, then picked up her bonnet. "I would like to freshen up," she said, and walked ahead of him out of the dining room and down the dim hallway leading to the rear of the restaurant and the ladies retiring room by the back exit. At the door, she paused, wondering if he intended to accompany her inside. "If you'd like to settle the bill, I'll only be a moment."

After attending her needs, she loosely knotted the shawl across her shoulders and checked the pins in her upsweep. She debated donning the bonnet but decided against it since Tait seemed to admire her hair. Satisfied, she pushed open the door and stepped into the hall, almost plowing into a figure blocking the hallway.

A stocky figure. Shorter than Tait. Holding a knife in a hand that was missing the last two fingers.

"You've been a naughty girl, Cathleen. Ready for your punishment?"

Smythe.

She whirled, a cry rising in her throat.

A hard slap knocked her into the wall.

She staggered, the reticule swinging at her wrist, the bonnet slipping from her grip. Then stinging pain exploded through her scalp as he grabbed a handful of her hair from behind and yanked. Something sharp jabbed into her back.

"Not a sound, you whore, or I'll send this knife into your liver." Kicking open the exit door, he pushed her ahead of him into the alley.

Cold air swept over her. The reek of rotting food almost made her gag when he thrust her between two trash bins behind the restaurant.

Fear sent her heart into a frantic rhythm.

Tait. Where was Tait?

Shoving her into the wall, Smythe pressed his body against hers from behind. "Ready for some fun, dolly?" Letting go of her hair, but keeping the knife against her side, he slid his deformed hand down and rubbed her bottom.

She froze, gasping in terror—trapped between the wall and his filthy body, between the past and the present—her mind spiraling back into that of a brutalized twelve-year-old, too frightened to fight and dreading what was to come.

"You'll pay for leaving me to burn, you rancid bitch. But first—" He bucked hard against her, driving her into the rough bricks. "A last bit of sport for old time's sake."

Spinning her roughly around, he clamped his hand on her head and shoved her down. "On your knees, whore."

Pain shot through her legs when she hit the cobblestones. Only his grip on her hair kept her from falling into him. "You know what I want, Cathleen." He shoved his crotch into her face. "Do it."

She cried out, tried to turn her head away, but he jerked her back. "Make it good and you'll die easy, whore."

"N-No—"

"Unbutton me!" He jabbed the tip of the knife against her neck. "Now!"

She lifted her left hand and forced her shaking fingers to work the buttons on his trousers. With her right hand, she dug frantically in the reticule. Her fingers closed over cold metal. Yanking the tiny pepperbox pistol free, she jammed the barrel into his groin.

He froze.

"Release my hair!" she choked out.

"You bitch—"

She ground the barrel against him. "Now!"

He let go of her hair.

With the gun still pressed against his crotch, she sat back on her heels and glared up at him. "Drop the knife."

He looked down at the gun. A wobbly sneer split his ugly face. "It ain't cocked."

"You won't be, either, if you don't drop the knife into the garbage bin."

He didn't move. She could almost see his foul brain trying to calculate if she would really fire before he could plunge the knife into her throat.

"Do it!" She gave a hard jab that almost doubled him over.

He dropped the knife into the bin.

"Now step back," she ordered, the pistol shaking almost as badly as her voice.

Cupping himself, he stumbled back. "This ain't over, Cathleen," he said in a strained voice. "I found you once and I'll find you again. And when I do—"

From inside the restaurant a voice called her name.

Tait.

She turned her head to call back when a vicious kick sent her flying.

"I'll be back, bitch," Smythe snarled as he fled into the darkness of the alley.

She was struggling to rise when the door opened, and suddenly Tait was there. "Jesus, Lucinda. What happened?"

Lifting her from the hard cobblestones, he stared into her face. "Are you hurt?"

"H-He was here. He had a knife."

She felt his body stiffen. "Smythe?"

He gathered himself to rise, but she tugged him back. "It's too late. He's gone."

"Did he hurt you?"

She could hear the panic in his voice, and it almost cracked the brittle shell that was all that held her together. "No. He didn't hurt me. Thanks to this." She lifted the hand holding the pepperbox pistol, her fingers shaking so badly she could barely keep a grip on it.

"You shot him?"

"I w-would have." She tried to laugh but it didn't sound right. "If I had remembered to load it."

Tait was almost numb with fury. It took all of his control to remain calm enough to get Lucinda back on her feet and help her straighten her clothing.

"Here," he said, handing her the bonnet he'd found in the hallway. He'd forgotten it was still in his hand and was unsettled to see that he'd gripped it so tightly the brim was a twisted ruin.

She tossed it into the garbage bin and pulled the shawl over her head, hiding the red mark he could see forming on her cheekbone.

They walked back through the restaurant and out onto the street, where he whistled up a cab waiting outside a hotel two doors down. After helping her into the seat, he told the cab to go to the telegraph office, then climbed in beside her.

"I'm sorry," he said, not knowing what else to say. This was his fault. He should have guarded her better. He knew Smythe was out there. He should never have let her out of his sight.

"For saving my life?"

He looked down, his mind still churning with rage. She was smiling up at him, which added to his guilt. "For not teaching you how to load the pistol. For taking you off the train when I knew Smythe was still a threat. For not waiting in the hall while you—"

"Would you have gone into the lavatory with me, as well?" She said it lightly, but he heard the quaver in her voice. "You were there when I needed you, Tait. And I'm grateful for it."

"But I—"

"Just say, 'Thank you, Lucinda.'"

Instead, he pulled her hard against his chest. "If anything had happened to you . . ." He couldn't finish the thought. Pressing his lips against her hair, he breathed in her flowery scent, his head so overrun with conflicting thoughts and emotions he couldn't make sense of anything.

How had he allowed this to happen? When had this woman taken control of his mind and his heart so completely that just the thought of harm coming to her sent him into panic?

"We're here."

He looked through the small door window and saw they had stopped outside the telegraph office. Reluctantly, he let her go. "You should come in with me."

"I'll be fine with the driver here. Hurry or we'll miss the train."

He hurried, and before the operator had finished tapping out the message, he was climbing back into the buggy.

"Are you cold?" he asked, using that as an excuse to put his arm around her and pull her against his side.

"Not now."

They arrived at the depot as the conductor called the "all aboard." Another train was waiting on a second track, pointing in the opposite direction. As they crossed the platform toward their Pullman car, Tait studied other returning passengers and the faces in the coach windows but saw no one matching Smythe's description. He walked Lucinda to the compartment, checked the room, and saw that George had readied both berths and lit the candle sconces. "Do you have an extra key?" he asked. "I don't want to wake you when I return."

Fear flashed over her face. "George only gave me one. Where are you going?"

"Just down the hall. To allow you some privacy. I won't be far."

He waited until he heard the lock click, then went looking for George.

"Have you an extra key to our compartment?"

George unlocked a door built into the wall and lifted a key marked with a three off the hook. As he handed it over, Tait asked if he'd seen the "brother" again.

The porter hadn't.

"He bullied Miss Hathaway in town tonight. If he asks about her or you see him hanging around, let me know."

"I will, sir. Is Miss Hathaway all right?"

"Yes." But barely, and that realization made it hard to draw a breath. No other woman had ever made him feel this way—desperate, driven, confused. Just the thought of how close he had come to losing her still drove him into a blind panic. It was irrational. Unexplainable. He wanted to shake her, lock her in his arms, bind her to him forever so he could keep her safe.

"Is there anything I can do, sir?"

He stared blankly at George, his thoughts leaping ahead to places they shouldn't. What if he was misreading her actions in the carriage? What if she had only reached out to him in fear?

But what if it was more than that?

"Don't suppose you have any preventatives locked away somewhere."

George opened a drawer, rummaged for a moment, and came out with a packet of Dr. Power's French Preventatives. "Will one packet be sufficient, sir?" he asked, his face carefully blank. "I believe it contains two. They're reusable."

Masking his distaste, Tait slipped the packet into his coat pocket. "How long to Pittsburgh?"

"It's not that far but it takes a while, since we have to go slow through the horseshoe curves and stop often to cool the brakes. Eight hours. Maybe ten."

"Best make it two packets, then."

Doing a poor job of hiding his skepticism, George handed over a second packet. "Have an enjoyable journey, sir."

Tait ignored that. After stopping by the lavatory to wash up, he went back to the compartment. Using his key, he opened the door.

The room was dark, and for a moment he thought she had already climbed into her bunk. Then he saw her standing at the window in her robe, staring at the eastbound train.

He crossed toward her. It wasn't until he reached her side that he realized she was watching a couple on the other train, framed by candlelight in their compartment window.

They were making love.

The woman was facing the window, her dress gaping open as the man reached from behind to cup her unbound breasts. Her head was tilted back against her lover's neck. Her eyes were closed. Tait watched the man's hands tease and stroke, watched the woman arch to his touch, her lips curved in a half smile. It was the most erotic thing he had ever experienced, standing there in the dark, watching them and knowing Lucinda was watching, too.

Heart pounding, he looked over at her, expecting to see shock, perhaps even disgust. Instead, she stood frozen, her gaze fixed on the couple across the way. He could tell by her breathing that she was aroused, too.

"Lucinda." He stepped closer, brushed his battered knuckles lightly across her cheek. "Sweetheart."

"He must love her very much," she said as the woman leaned back against her partner, the dress slipping low on her shoulders, opening her body to more of his touch. Her breasts were small and dark-tipped, the man's hands dark against her pale skin. "It's in the way he touches her. Like she's something rare and precious."

Puzzled by the wistful tone in her voice, Tait looked back at the couple on the other train.

The man's hands slid down below the gaping waistline of the dress to stroke low against the woman's belly. Her mouth open, she twisted against him, turning her head to meet his kiss. When he tried to push the dress off her hips, she broke away and, with a laugh, reached up to snap the drapes closed.

Lucinda stared at the dark window a moment longer, then said, "I almost died today. And I've never been touched like that. I've never known what that woman is feeling right now." She turned her head and looked at him. In the dim light cast by the gas lamps lining the tracks, her eyes looked wet and sad. "Is it so wrong to want that? Just once."

His mouth was so dry his tongue felt clumsy. "Doyle—"

"Never touched me like that."

"He's your husband. It's his right—"

"No," she cut in, her voice sharp. "He has no rights to me. This is something I decide."

He knew he'd blundered again. He could feel her drawing away, could almost see the walls coming up, and knew if he didn't act now, she would slip away from him forever.

He brushed a loose curl off her bruised cheek. "Are you asking me to make love to you, Miss Hathaway?"

He felt a shiver run through her. Nerves? Fear? Anticipation?

"You misunderstand, Mr. Rylander," she said with a shaky smile. "This has nothing to do with love. I'm not seeking a grand passion like in one of those lurid dime novels."

"Then what is it you want?"

She shrugged. "An experience. A memory. Since it's unlikely I will ever share a marriage bed with a husband, I thought I would—"

"Use me, instead?" He smiled, despite the sadness in his heart. He had hoped for so much more. Lifting a hand, he pulled loose the first bow in the row of ties down the front of her robe.

"'Use' is rather a harsh word, don't you think?" she mused.

He heard the tremble in her voice, felt it against his fingers as he pulled the next tie free. His heart kicked in his chest. "Is it?"

"I implore you not to read more into this than is there." She gave a laugh that sounded forced. "I'm not some timorous virgin, you know."

"A woman of vast experience, are you?" Another tie. Then

another. Then another. How many damn bows did one robe need?

She moved restlessly as his knuckles grazed the tip of her breast. "Not vast. Just once, in fact. The greengrocer's son. Over a dozen years ago. It was all rather sordid. And painful. Shouldn't you remove your coat at least?"

She was babbling. Which meant she was nervous. Which made him even more determined to do this right and take his time. "Was that your decision, too? Dallying with the greengrocer's son?"

"I thought if I weren't a virgin, men would no longer want me."

Tait didn't even try to make sense of that one. "Poor lad. He probably never knew what he had." Tipping his head down, he whispered into her ear, "Rest assured, I do," and pulled the last bow loose.

That shiver again. It made him smile. Having set his course, all doubt left him, and he began to see the humor in her attempts to keep this on an impersonal level. If she were thinking clearly, she would know that was impossible for either of them. This moment had been coming for a year. And it wouldn't be some brief dalliance.

He pushed the robe off her shoulders. It landed with a sigh on the thick rug. Heat rose off her body, filling his mind with the scent of flowers and woman. It robbed him of thought.

He watched his fingertip trace the soft rise of her right breast and felt the tip pucker beneath the thin cloth of her gown. "So now you choose me?" When she didn't answer, he lifted his head to find her looking back at him out of eyes that carried too much fear and doubt and pain. "Or will any man do?"

"Not . . . any man."

A tear rolled down her cheek. He leaned down to lick it away, then drew his tongue along the seam of her lips, letting her taste the salt of her own tears. It took monumental effort not to pull her body against his and wrap his hands in her hair and feel the pulse of her heart beneath his lips. "You'll have to ask me, sweetheart. So we'll both know this is your decision." He watched her face as he moved his hand to her other breast, felt her frantic heartbeat against his palm. "Say, 'Tait, I want you to make love to me.' That's all."

She leaned against his hand, her breath coming short and

fast. Her eyes fluttered closed. "Tait . . . I want you . . . to make love to me."

"You're sure?"

"Yes . . . I'm sure."

He took his hand away. "I'll have to think about it."

Her eyes flew open.

He laughed. And before she could start arguing, he cupped her face in his shaking hands and kissed her like he'd been wanting to do ever since the Wallingford garden party over a year ago.

Ten

"You still have on your coat," she reminded him when he finally let her come up for air.

Grinning and a bit winded himself, he spread his arms wide. "Have at it."

She stripped him bare to his waist, then seemed to suffer a maidenly attack of nerves.

Just as well. He didn't know how much more he could take without embarrassing himself.

"How is this going to work?" she asked, glancing around.

He sat on the couch and began unlacing his shoe. "Three ways, at least. Maybe four if you don't wear me out."

"No. I mean where will we do this? Trying to fit both of us onto one of those tiny berths would be like trying to fit a family of clowns into a steamer trunk. It would probably come crashing down and wake up the whole train."

Clowns? Surely not. "We're intelligent people. We'll figure a way." He already had several in mind. Kicking off one shoe, he started on the other.

"The couches are too small, too. I know sometimes people use chairs for this purpose, but those arms seem too high. I doubt it would be very comfortable."

Good God. What had that greengrocer's son put her through? And how did she even know about such things? "We'll come up with something." He almost popped the buttons on his fly as images burst into his mind. Lucinda nude, draped over the couch, one leg hooked over the back, the other—

"Standing seems impractical, too, don't you think?"

He was beyond thinking. Rising on bare feet, he motioned her aside.

"What?"

"Move over there." He pointed toward the windows.

When she stepped out of the way, he pulled both pads off the berths and tossed them side by side on the floor between the couches. "How's that?"

She frowned at the rumpled bedding. "I suppose it will do."

"Good." Picking up his coat from where she'd dropped it on the couch, he dug through the pockets. After retrieving matches and the packets of preventatives, he dropped the packets on the table within reach, lit the candle on the wall above it, then pulled the drapes closed. Turning, he found her studying him with an appraising look.

"No wonder you could carry Mrs. Throckmorton up three flights of stairs."

Taking that as a compliment, he smiled. "Take down your hair."

"It might get tangled."

"I'll brush it later." More images—her sitting naked in his lap, her long blond hair trailing over her breasts as he—

"But it knots easily."

"I'll brush out every snarl. I promise."

"But—"

"Now?" He threw up his hands, caught between laughter and aggravation. "You want to argue about your hair now?" Shaking his head, he slipped off his trousers, then started on the tabs on his drawers. The woman could wear down stone.

"I'm not arguing," she argued. "I'm simply saying that my hair—you're taking off everything?"

"It works best that way." He stepped out of his linens, tossed them aside, then straightened to find her gaping at him again. This time it was more in shock than admiration, he was disturbed to note. "What's wrong? I thought you said you'd done this before."

"I have. But . . ." She cleared her throat. "But you're . . . well . . ." With a backhanded wave at his groin, she looked away. "Different."

"From a green kid? I hope so."

"Actually, he was seventeen," she said to the wall. "And rather well built. What I saw of him, anyway. Although not as well built as you, of course."

The train lurched. Stumbling for balance, he caught her around the waist before she fell. He kissed her, almost lost his footing as the train moved forward, then kissed her again. "Take off your gown."

She pulled away. "Is that really necessary?"

He watched her chin set and her arms cross over her chest in that defiant pose. Sensing this was about more than just the gown, he kept his voice mild. "What's wrong?"

She shrugged. "I don't like being on display."

What display? "It's just me, Luce. Me and you. That's all."

A look of impatience crossed her face. "All right. If you insist." She started to pull off the gown.

He put a hand on her shoulder to stop her. "No, I don't insist. Anything we do here is because you want it, too. Whether you take off your gown or not is entirely your decision." He took his hand away and stepped back, hoping for once she would trust him.

I'm not your enemy.

She studied him in that assessing way of hers, then gave a hesitant smile. "All right," she said, and pulled off her gown.

Breath left him. She was even more beautiful than he had imagined. Perfect. All a man could ever— "What happened to your knees?"

She looked down at the puffy bruises. "I fell." Suddenly shy again, she dropped down onto the pallet and scrambled under a sheet. Then she dragged a blanket over the sheet. Then she grabbed the other blanket and thrust it toward him. "Here. You must be cold. Standing there . . . like that."

He was anything but cold. In fact if he didn't get the preventative on soon, it might be too late. Turning his back, he went to the table and opened the packet.

"What are you doing?" she called.

"Putting on a preventative." He hoped he wouldn't have to explain what that was. Getting the thing on was distracting enough without having to go into a detailed explanation of how it worked.

"You carry one around with you? That's a bit presumptuous, isn't it?"

"More hopeful than presumptuous. I got them from George."

"You planned this all along?"

"Planned it, fantasized about it, plotted it, and executed it in my head about a thousand times over the last year."

"The last year?"

"Ever since the Wallingford garden party." *Christ.* Goodyear must have been a sadist to dream up this thing. "You have any oil?"

A rustling behind him, then she appeared so suddenly at his side he almost fell into the table.

"That looks uncomfortable. Does it hurt?"

Dumbfounded, he blinked at her.

"Can I help?"

Heat rushed up his neck. "I appreciate the offer, but I assure you I've done this before."

"Oh, really?" She smirked at him. Actually smirked. "Well, your part there seems to be getting smaller. Perhaps that'll ease the fit."

Good God. Recognizing the absurdity of the situation—him standing there, with his shrinking, half-dressed cock in his hand, while she offered helpful solutions as if he were trying to choke a chicken rather than suffering through the most humiliating attempt at seduction in his entire life—he had to laugh.

And laugh.

"What's so funny?"

"You. Us. This. You astound me."

"Not equal to your fantasies, I take it?"

He looked down at her perfect body. "Hardly equal. Much better."

She gave a tentative smile, as if she wasn't sure she should believe him, then held out a small glass vial. "This is the only oil I have. Attar of Roses. Where do you want me to put it?"

With those words, images flooded his mind. His cock bounced back to life, and suddenly he was on track again. "Here," he said and pointed.

"It's perfume."

"I don't care. Just hurry." He inhaled sharply when her

fingers found him. "Or not," he added on a gasp. "In fact, sweetheart, take all the time you need."

"There," she said a moment later. "I believe it's on as far as it will go. Shall we?"

He blinked at her out of dazed eyes. "Shall we what?"

She pointed toward the pallet on the floor.

"Oh. Sure. Okay." Struggling to bring his body under control, he took several deep breaths to clear his mind, then followed her to the makeshift bed.

He had never felt this way. This . . . involved. Or pressured. It occurred to him that his feelings for this woman were stronger than he had thought—stronger than he had ever felt for any woman. And with that realization came the determination to do it right, take his time, and give her the sweet memory she sought. Perhaps then, he could break through her distrust and create even better memories.

So he kept his hands slow, and his voice soft, and his tongue anywhere she would let him. The rocking of the train added its own music and motion, and when she was breathing as hard as he was, and urging him on with gentle touches and whispered words, and her restless movements told him she was ready, he took them both to a place of pure sensation, where control shattered, and the world lost form and color, and rapture began.

Nestled against Tait's side, Lucinda yawned as she idly ran her fingers through the dark hairs on his chest. Beneath her ear, his heartbeat sounded like the distant thud of a hammer against a plank wall. Steady and sure. Like the man himself.

He smelled like roses. They both did. The room, too. They'd probably used up the whole bottle. Thankfully, during the night, Tait had risen to push aside the drapes and crack open a window just enough to pull out some of the overpowering scent. She remembered laying there, watching his long, strong form move against a spray of stars and thinking how much she had come to care for this contradictory and complicated man.

She knew him better now—in ways she had never imagined—both physically and emotionally. His quirky sense of humor. His playfulness. His fiercely intelligent and curious mind, and that unyielding sense of right and wrong. In the dark, after the candle had burned out, she had even been brave enough to learn his body as well as he'd learned hers—that ticklish spot behind his knees, the puckered bullet scar on his thigh, the slick band of skin on his neck where the rope had burned, his poor battered hands. He was hers now—if not in fact, then forever in her memory—as the man who had given her back the part of her soul that Smythe and Horne had stolen from her so many years ago.

Smiling, she stretched up to press a kiss against his damp neck, then settled back, replete and happy. Contented. She wondered if the woman on the other train was as deliciously worn out as she was. Probably not.

Beyond the window, the first hint of dawn revealed that the earth had flattened out. From their bed at floor level, she could see no hills rising above the sill, no silhouetted trees rolling past. Soon they would be in Pittsburgh and decisions would have to be made.

"Do you know Franklin Horne?" she asked, gently stroking his chest.

He yawned. "Somewhat."

"What do you know about him?"

He thought for a moment. "Not much. Drinker. A bit dodgy in his business dealings, as Doyle would say, even though he's considering investing in some branch line Horne is pushing. I know he has political ambitions, but I'd never vote for him. Why?"

Political ambitions. Was that the reason? "How high are these ambitions?"

"Albany. Maybe higher."

"High enough that a scandal would bring him down?"

"Depends on the scandal," he said drily. "Boss Tweed has proven corruption and greed are no deterrent to political office, so it would have to be something pretty bad. Why are you asking?"

Like depravity. Bestiality. The murder of innocent souls.

Suddenly, it all made horrifying sense. She knew what Horne was—a user of children, a beast, a man who was so depraved the screams of his victims had echoed through the filthy halls of the most notorious brothel in Five Points. No wonder he was after her. He couldn't allow her to tell what she knew, especially if he thought she would come back to Manhattan and assume her position in society as the wife of a powerful and ruthless man.

It was Horne who sent Smythe.

God help me.

She pressed her face against Tait's chest, tears burning in her eyes. Horne would never rest until he found her. There was no way out now. Her stomach churned and spots of color and light danced before her eyes.

As long as he knows I'm alive, I'll have to keep running or die.

Tait lifted his head and stared down at her. "You're shaking, Lucinda. What's wrong?"

She could never tell him . . . not about Horne . . . not about Smythe . . . not about Mrs. Beale's. She would rather live without him than see the disgust in his eyes. "It's nothing. Just a chill." Fighting tears, she snuggled closer and tried to keep her voice light. "This was rather a good idea, I think."

His head dropped back. "It was. You're an amazing woman."

She poked his side. "I was talking about putting the pads on the floor."

"Ah. That, too, then."

"George will be scandalized."

"I doubt it."

"What are we going to do?"

"About George?"

"About this." When he didn't answer, she tipped her head back to see him staring up at the ceiling. His face was set in those austere lines that had once irritated her. "Regrets, Tait?"

"About this? Never." He leaned up to press a kiss to her brow, then let his head drop back to the pad. Bristles shadowed his face and his hair was a tousled mess and he had never looked more beautiful to her. "I'm just trying to figure out the best way to handle Doyle."

Doyle again. It struck her that no matter what they did, or how far they ran, Doyle Kerrigan would always be there with them—like a sore that wouldn't heal. They were doomed—by both Franklin Horne and Doyle Kerrigan. "Doyle is my problem, Tait. Not yours."

"I just made love to his wife. That makes it my problem, too."

Only a man as honest and loyal as Tait would see it that way.

A blighted marriage, a betrayed friendship—the guilt of that would haunt him all his life.

At least she could ease his mind on one score. Sitting up, she pulled the blanket around her shoulders, then turned to face him. "Doyle and I aren't married."

"You may not want to be, but I was there, remember? I watched you give your vows." Smiling, he ran his hand under the blanket and up her inner thigh.

She blocked her mind to it. "Did you sign the marriage license as a witness? Did you see that it was registered?"

The hand stopped. "No. I thought the priest did that. Or Doyle. But then you went missing, and everything was confused and . . ." Frowning, he sat up. "It was never legally registered? How can you be so certain?"

She took a deep breath and let it out. "Because I have it."

He went still. She could almost see the thoughts racing through his analytical mind, retracing the events of that day— the ceremony, the signing, Doyle giving her the stock folder, Mrs. Throckmorton taking sick, carrying her up to the suite, Lucinda following, the folder in her hand.

And she knew the exact moment he came to the wrong conclusion.

The teasing light left his eyes. His face settled in those implacable lines. "What are you saying, Lucinda? That you planned it? All of it? From the very beginning?"

"No," she said, stung by the accusation. "I didn't even realize the license was in the folder until I went to the bank in Philadelphia. It all happened so—"

"Happened?" His eyes turned glacial. "Like your guardian *happened* to fall ill at the right time, and there *happened* to be a disguise on hand, and you *happened* to slip the license into the stock folder?"

"Tait, it wasn't like that—"

"And the stock certificates? How did you *happen* to know about them?"

"I didn't. Not until Doyle gave them to me." Suddenly terrified of where this was headed, she reached for his arm.

"It was all an elaborate deception, wasn't it?"

"No. It wasn't like that at all."

"I can't believe this." He abruptly rose, hands clenched at his

sides. "How could I have missed it? The stocks, Mrs. Throckmorton's fake illness, the widow's disguise to escape the hotel.
You planned it all, didn't you?" He spun toward her. "And this?"
He slashed a hand at the tangled bedding where they had made
love through the night. "Was this part of your plan, too?"

"No. If you'll just listen, Tait, I can explain."

"Not now, Lucinda—or Margaret—or whoever the hell you
are! Jesus." With savage efficiency, he began yanking on his
clothing.

Panic sent her off the pallet. "Tait, please." She tried to grab
his arm again.

"Don't!" He whirled, palms up. "I can't talk about this right
now."

She stepped back, so shocked she could only stare as he finished dressing and began gathering his belongings. Thank God
she hadn't told him about Mrs. Beale's. He would never have
understood. He was too quick to judge. Too convinced he alone
knew what was right and what was wrong.

By the time he had stuffed everything he wasn't wearing into
his valise, her despair had hardened into resignation. It was
over. He was leaving her. It was what she wanted. What needed
to happen.

So why did it hurt so much? The unfairness of it rocked her,
turned the bleakness into fury.

"So that's it? You're walking out? Without even giving me a
chance to explain?"

"I just need . . . time . . . to think about this." Picking up the
valise, he turned toward the door.

"Take all the time you need," she snapped. "But meanwhile,
give me the key." She held out her hand, surprised to see it was
steady.

Reaching into his pocket, he pulled out the extra key and
tossed it onto the rumpled bed. Then he held out his own hand.
"And you give me all the stocks you have left. At least I can
return that to Doyle."

"No."

Anger flared again. "No?"

"That's between me and Doyle. It doesn't concern you."

He opened his mouth to argue, then clamped it shut and
stalked to the door. He yanked it open, then hesitated, his big

form blocking the faint light from the candles mounted along the hall. Without facing her, he asked in a tight voice, "Is there even a Smythe? Or is that all a fabrication, too?"

She pressed a hand to her stomach. "Believe what you will, Tait," she said to his back. "But I have never lied to you. Ever."

He turned his head and looked at her. "I would have fought Doyle for you. Given you everything I had. I could have loved you." He gave a harsh laugh that belied the pain in his eyes. "Hell, I probably already do. And I don't even know who you are." A last look, then he stepped into the hall and closed the door.

Her hands shaking, Lucinda picked up the key he'd left on the pallet and locked the door. Then, strength deserting her, she tipped her head against the cool wood and let the tears fall.

Not up to sly looks from George, Tait turned away from the porter's alcove up front and headed toward the end of the car and the open vestibule between their Pullman and the Parlor Car at the end of the train.

Cool, coal-scented air washed over him. The noise and rocking was worse over the couplers, but he welcomed the distraction from his turbulent thoughts.

Jesus, he must be the world's biggest fool to have been so blind.

After a moment, his head cleared enough that he could think again. Crossing to the Parlor Car, he opened the door and stepped inside. Luckily, it was empty at this early hour. With a weary sigh, he set his valise on the floor, heard movement behind him, then flinched when something sharp jabbed into his back.

"You smell like a bloody flower garden, you buggering toff," an accented voice growled in his ear. "Put yer hands where I can see 'em."

Raising his hands to shoulder level, Tait slowly turned. A stocky man with thinning gray hair and the last two fingers on his knife hand missing grinned back at him. "Smythe," Tait said.

The man laughed, showing gaps in yellowed teeth, his breath rank and reeking of rum. "She told you about me, did she? Did she give you a good lickin', too?" He mimicked the motion, his tongue rolling over his bottom lip like a fat, pink slug. "That's what she's best at. Lickin'. Taught her myself."

Tait's hands clenched into fists as the realization slammed into him. She hadn't lied. Smythe was real. Maybe everything else was, too. *Oh, hell.* What had he done? "What do you want?" he said through stiff lips.

"Not here. Don't want to mess up the pretty rug. Out there." He tipped his head toward the rear door of the Parlor Car. "And get your bag. Don't want anyone wondering why you'd leave it behind."

Guessing that meant the bastard intended to throw him off the train, Tait picked up the bag with his left hand so he could keep his right free. His mind racing, he walked down the narrow aisle between the plush seats. If he could get Smythe to come at him with the knife, he could block it with the valise, swing under it with his right, and finish him with a left hook. Roundhouse left, undercut right, left hook. He'd done it a hundred times. His palms tingled at the thought.

"What do you want with her?" he asked over his shoulder. A talking man might be easier to distract.

"With Cathleen?"

The train lurched, making him stumble. *Cathleen?*

A sharp jab in his back sent him forward again. "I'm here to shut her up. Permanent like. But the bitch owes me a lickin' and I intend to get it before I gut her. Open the door. Slow and easy now."

Tait opened the door onto the narrow rear vestibule. Cool air blasted his face. Beyond the railing, the tracks stretched toward a faint purple smear across the eastern horizon. On the right, a rock wall rose out of sight; on the left, as best he could tell in the dawning light, the long rubble-strewn slope ended in a wide canyon with a river running down the middle.

He turned, putting his left side and the valise toward the open rear railing so he would have room to swing it. "What do you want?"

"Yer money fer starts." Smythe held out a dirty palm. "Ye'll be dyin' either way, so you might as well hand it over. Might put me in a merciful mood."

Tait eyed the knife, a short, fat-bladed skinning knife that could do a lot of slicing damage but wouldn't go deep enough to hit anything major. Or so he hoped. Bracing his legs, he reached toward his pocket with his right hand, then feinted with his shoulder as he swung the valise with his left.

Smythe jumped back, whipping the knife in a wide arc.

Tait heard a scraping sound as the blade slashed through leather. Teeth clenched, he drove his fist up into the Englishman's soft belly.

Smythe twisted, took the blow in his side. Grunting, he fell back against the railing.

Tait lunged forward, swinging the valise as hard as he could. It hit the brake wheel protruding above the rear railing instead. The handle snapped off. The valise flew past the Englishman to crash into the rocky wall behind him.

Before he could regain his balance, Smythe leaped forward, slashing.

Tait felt a searing pain across his chest. He staggered back, blood running.

But Smythe kept coming, the blade whipping back and forth.

Another slice on his right shoulder. His left arm. Stumbling out of reach, he looked frantically for an opening. Then suddenly he was up against the railing on the canyon side.

With a cry of triumph, Smythe rushed. Tait sidestepped too late. The Englishman plowed into him. The railing gave. Realizing he was falling, Tait locked his arms around Smythe and dragged him over the side with him.

Smythe hit first. Tait landed on top of him, then rolled. And kept rolling.

He clawed for a handhold, found only grass and loose rocks. Over the roar of cascading stones, he heard Smythe scream, but he couldn't stop the downward tumble. Faster and faster, rocks pelting his face, crashing into his flailing body. He couldn't see. Couldn't breathe. Just as his lungs felt about to explode, he slammed to a stop against a tree.

He lay gasping, choking on dirt and blood.

The roar of falling rocks ended. Over the frantic drumbeat of his heart, he heard the sound of the departing train fade into the rush of moving water. Shuddering with pain, he opened his eyes to see the first rays of sunlight crown the tops of the trees before darkness dragged him down.

* * *

Lucinda watched daylight creep over the fields beyond the window before she finally accepted that he wasn't coming back.

I could have loved you.

She pressed a hand over her eyes, tried to block the image of Tait's bewildered face. Maybe she should go after him and try again to explain. But if he still didn't believe her, what then? Go back to New York and try to clean up the mess she had left in her wake? Or put it all behind her and continue on?

Letting her hand drop, she swiped away tears of disgust. This was what came of trusting. Of hoping. She should have known better.

I don't even know who you are.

She gave a broken laugh. She didn't know, either. Nothing made sense anymore. She felt battered and beaten and so drained it was an effort to think.

Staring numbly at the bed on the floor, she fought a sudden urge to stomp it, stuff it out the window, tear it to shreds with her bare hands. But she hadn't the energy or the will.

Or the time.

She had to figure out what to do next. It was obvious Tait wasn't coming back. She was on her own, and it was up to her to deal with Smythe and the Pinkertons. She could feel them closing in, and knew if she was to avoid either, she would have to act now, before the train reached its next destination.

Resolved, she rose and began gathering her things. She would get off at the last water stop before Pittsburgh. She would pay George to carry her valises into the station, wait until the train started again, then slip off at the last moment. Hopefully, Smythe wouldn't see her. If he did, and left the train to come after her, she would scream that he was accosting her. In the confusion, she would escape into the street. If that didn't work, she always had the pistol, loaded now and ready in her purse.

From the water stop, she would take a public coach on into Pittsburgh. There, she would come up with another disguise—perhaps spectacles and a wig under a coal scuttle bonnet, a farm woman's boots, and a calico dress stuffed with extra clothing to make her look heavier.

From Pittsburgh, she would go on to Columbus, and from

there, either travel northwest to Chicago or southwest to St. Louis.

If she made it that far.

Wearily, she began to pack.

Later that afternoon, Byron Hildebrand leaned against a post, picking his teeth as he scanned travelers entering the Pittsburgh station. He'd been there all day, watching every train in and every train out. There weren't that many.

He glanced across the benches to where Mark Weyland watched women coming in and out of the ladies' lavatory. He looked bored as hell, too.

There had been some sort of ruckus earlier about a missing passenger on the run from Altoona. But that had been a man, and they were looking for a woman. Young, blond, pretty—or so her husband had described her to the Pinkerton office in New York. Within an hour, alerts had gone out to all the Pinkerton offices along the Pennsy line.

But she might have disguised herself as an elderly woman or even a boy, and for that reason, he and Weyland had been instructed to carefully watch every suspicious young man and every woman who came through the depot—old, young, pretty, veiled. It was tedious work, not at all like the glamorous adventures portrayed in the detective dime novels.

Out on the platform, the conductor made his final call for passengers bound for Columbus, which would be the last train out today. If they didn't see her board, or notice anyone even remotely suspicious, they were to await further orders. Hildebrand hoped it wouldn't involve travel. He was supposed to go to his daughter's first communion that night.

A quick, sharp whistle caught his attention, and he looked over to see Weyland motioning to a farm woman moving through the station doors and out onto the platform. She fit neither description, but he studied her hard anyway, wondering what had drawn Weyland's suspicion.

Heavyset and stoop-shouldered, the woman moved stoutly along, the brim of her bonnet obscuring most of her face, a traveling case hanging from one hand.

Pushing away from the post, Hildebrand angled toward her,

so if need be, he could intercept her just before she reached the train. As he approached, he saw a few wisps of white or blond hair showing beneath the bonnet at the back of her neck—an unlined neck, the skin firm and pale.

"Ma'am?" he called, reaching out a hand to stop her.

She turned to glare at him from behind wire-rimmed spectacles, her eyes so distorted by the glass he couldn't tell their color. She wasn't as old as he'd thought. Nor was she what one would call pretty, either, with that dirty face and jutting chin.

"What?" she barked, her lips drawn in a tight line.

"I'm with the Pinkerton National Detective Agency, ma'am. I'd like to ask you a few questions, if I could."

"Ask somebody else. I got a train to catch." Yanking her arm from his grip, she resumed walking.

"Please, ma'am. It'll only take a moment." He was reaching out again when someone elbowed him so hard it sent him staggering.

"You leave her alone!"

Hildebrand regained his balance to see a burly farmer looming over him, hands the size of hams gripping two valises. "Look here," Hildebrand began, then stopped when Weyland ran up, clutching a yellow telegram.

"It's all right, Byron. They found her. Sorry for the misunderstanding, sir," he said to the farmer, waving him on his way. Turning back to Hildebrand, Weyland handed over the telegram. "The client's partner found her in Altoona. He's taking her back to New York. We're done here."

Hildebrand scanned the wire, then frowned, watching the couple climb the steps onto the train. "I don't know. There's something about that woman . . ."

"Aw, let it go, Byron. It's over. We're off the case."

For now, maybe. But Hildebrand had a feeling the case was far from over.

"Thank you, Mr. Olafson," Lucinda said to the hulking farmer outside her sleeping compartment door.

"You sure you'll be alright, ma'am? That man in the station—"

"A case of mistaken identity," she cut in. "You heard him.

I'm sure everything is fine. You may set my other bag by the couch."

He did, then looked around. "You staying in here all by yourself?"

"No, my sister will be joining me at the next water stop. Thank you again."

After ushering him out the door, Lucinda turned the lock, then yanking off the spectacles, collapsed, shaking and nauseated, onto the couch.

She didn't know which had terrified her more—that Pinkerton man in the station or not being able to see through the distorting spectacles. Thank God for Mr. Olafson. He had seen her almost fall down the steps of the horsecar, and if he hadn't taken one of her valises and helped her into the station, she might be in the custody of the Pinkerton detectives right now.

A sudden knock on the door sent her scrambling for the spectacles again. Making certain her disguise was in place, she went to the door and opened it.

A new George smiled back at her—older, grayer, fewer teeth in his welcome smile. "Welcome aboard, ma'am. Just makin' sure eve'ything all right. Need anything 'fore we start rolling?"

Lucinda thought for a moment, then decided to risk it. "As a matter of fact, George, there is." She fabricated a story about a stocky gray-haired man with missing fingers who had been overly forward toward her in the station. "So rather than expose myself to more of his attentions," she went on, as she reached into the reticule still hanging from her wrist, "I was wondering if I might be able to take my meals here in my compartment?" As she spoke, she pulled out a twenty-dollar double eagle.

George's grin widened. "Sho' can. Want I should bring you a menu?"

"That's not necessary. Whatever the main offering is at each meal will be fine." She pressed the coin into his pink palm. "You'll tell me if you see him?"

"Yessum, I will. Don't want none of my peoples bothered, no, ma'am, I don't."

"Thank you, George. I appreciate the fine care you're taking of me."

After making arrangements for the porter to bring the evening meal at six thirty, Lucinda returned to the couch with a deep sigh. At least it seemed Tait's telegram had reached Doyle, and the Pinkertons were no longer on her trail. Now all she had to worry about was Smythe. Was he still after her? She hadn't seen him in the station.

And she hadn't seen Tait, either.

Had he taken the train back to New York?

Would he tell Doyle the truth?

Weary and heartsick, she curled up on the cushions and let exhaustion overcome her.

She arrived in Columbus without further incident. Still undecided whether she should go on up to Chicago or down to St. Louis, she stood in the ticket line and studied the board on the wall of the depot while keeping an eye out for the persistent Mr. Olafson.

He had stopped several times by her compartment. It wasn't until late this morning that she was finally able to convince him that she was fine and her husband would be meeting her in Columbus. But just to be certain, she had discarded the farm woman disguise in favor of a plain frock under her green cape, and had hidden her blond hair beneath the green bonnet. Seeing neither the kindly farmer, nor any men who looked like they could be Pinkerton agents, nor Smythe, she moved forward to the ticket agent. "Have you any private sleeping compartments available on tomorrow's train to Chicago?" she asked the ticket clerk.

"No, ma'am."

"How about to St. Louis?"

He thumbed through the dog-eared papers strewn over the ticket counter. "There's several stops between here and there, but, yes, ma'am. We have one Pullman compartment left that goes all the way. Leaves in ten minutes."

The decision made, Lucinda paid for the ticket, picked up her valises, and walked out to where the conductor was arguing with an auburn-haired woman beside the waiting train.

"How can there be no more berths available?" the woman railed in a cultured English accent. "I specifically reserved a private compartment all the way through to St. Louis. I have the voucher here in my hand."

The elderly conductor studied the ticket, then pointed out that it was issued by a different railroad company than the one traveling on to St. Louis.

"So I was duped? This is most vexing. Do you Colonials not communicate with each other at all? How am I to ride in coach with all this equipment?" She waved a hand at the mound of boxes and crates and valises piled at her feet. "I must have a compartment. Surely you can see that."

"I'm sorry, ma'am."

"Oh, bother!"

The woman looked to be near Lucinda's own age, clean, well dressed, and on the verge of tears. Or temper. Her color was so high, Lucinda wasn't certain which. Deciding to take a chance, and thinking having a traveling companion might ease the boredom as well as provide an element of disguise, Lucinda stepped up with a smile. "I couldn't help but overhear. There is no one but me in my compartment, ma'am, and if it would help, I would be pleased to share."

The woman blinked at her out of round brown eyes, then broke into a bright smile that turned her unremarkable face into one of rare beauty. "Oh, you dear thing. It would help immensely." She held out a gloved hand, saw Lucinda was gripping the two valises, and let it drop back to her side. "Madeline Wallace, but I prefer Maddie. From Scotland. Or rather, London. Or perhaps, both, really. Oh dear, if I don't stop babbling, you're sure to change your mind. Thank you so much. I am in your debt."

Lucinda nodded. "Lucinda Hathaway of New York." And seeing the woman was a bit out of her element, she aimed a dimpled smile at the conductor. "I know you're anxious to rectify your mistake, sir, so I'm sure Miss Wallace will appreciate your tending to this straightaway . . . at no charge, of course. Please have one of the station boys bring her belongings to compartment four on the second Pullman Car." Leaning closer, she added in a lower voice, "And be advised there has been a man following me." She gave a brief description of Smythe. "Please don't tell him our compartment number, and alert me if you see him. I would be ever so grateful." Another smile, then before the befuddled conductor could argue, she made a last check for Smythe then nodded toward the boarding steps. "Come along, Miss Wallace. I believe we're delaying the other passengers."

As they moved down the narrow hall toward the last compartment on the right, the woman called from behind her, "Actually, it's missus—Mrs. Angus Wallace. At least I think it is. He left some years ago, you see. He's a soldier. Scottish, although he's an officer in the British cavalry. Or was. I supposed if he had died, I would still be a missus, don't you think? It's all most vexing."

Lucinda smiled, her spirits rising. At least she wouldn't be bored.

And so far, no sign of Smythe.

If not for the empty ache in her heart, she might have thought it a grand day.

Tait floated in pain. Relentless, inescapable pain that was so encompassing he didn't know where it ended and he began.

Dimly, out of the darkness came voices. A woman's—not Lucinda's—and a child's. Occasionally a man's. He tried to call to them, tell them to help him and make the pain stop. But he couldn't seem to form the words, and the effort of trying brought even more pain.

Sometimes someone forced water into his mouth. Did things to his body that sent his mind spiraling into darkness.

Day? Night?

Was he alive or dead?

He didn't know. Didn't care. He just wanted the pain to stop.

Someone sang. A high, child's voice, singing a tune he remembered from long ago. In desperation, he turned toward it. A faint light, no bigger than a pinprick, showed in the distance. He struggled toward it through smothering blackness that was even more terrible than the pain.

The voice grew louder.

The light grew brighter, then suddenly burst into his mind like fire.

"Lucinda," he gasped and opened his eyes.

"Ma!" the child shouted. "He's awake!"

Eleven

Lucinda had never had close friends, either as a child or an adult. In Ireland, there had been a few neighbor children that she vaguely remembered. But the desperation of those times and the unrelenting hunger and despair had left little energy or inclination for childish play.

At Mrs. Throckmorton's home, the only children Lucinda ever saw were those of servants or tradespeople, and such associations were not encouraged. Naturally, her guardian knew nothing about the greengrocer's son. And because of fears that Lucinda's Irish heritage would cause her to be ostracized, Mrs. Throckmorton had kept her somewhat isolated from children of the upper classes, as well.

So instead of sharing confidences and giggles in the schoolroom, or trading advice on dresses and hairstyles and boys as an adolescent, Lucinda had remained quietly in the shadows, reading, watching, and taking daily lessons from her nanny and tutors on how to cast aside her base Irish nature and imitate proper behavior. She learned how to handle servants, stitch a sampler, and choose the correct fork at a formal dinner. And over the last year, through observation during those long dinners with Doyle and Tait, she had gained knowledge in business—how to read accounting books, assess weakness in an investment opportunity, evaluate risk and potential profit, and how to negotiate—although with Doyle, negotiation was more like threat and manipulation.

But never had she been taught how to be a friend.

It was a novel experience—the instantaneous familiarity and rapport that sprang up between her and Maddie Wallace. In truth, the overtures of friendship were mostly on Maddie's part—not that Lucinda wasn't pleased or flattered, but her natural reserve and lack of experience made it a bit awkward. Yet it was difficult not to be swept along by the Englishwoman's natural vivacity.

Perhaps it was that bright outlook that gave Maddie the daring to journey halfway around the world on her own while dragging in her wake enough luggage to fill most of her side of the tiny compartment. Lucinda had traveled only a few hundred miles, and she was already exhausted and apprehensive of what might lay ahead.

But then, Maddie didn't have a vicious degenerate, an irate groom, and several Pinkerton detectives hounding her footsteps, either.

"Do you plan on staying in America long?" Lucinda asked, eyeing the stack of crates and boxes in the corner of their compartment as she shook out the next day's dress and hung it on a hook beside her couch.

"I had only intended to be here two years," Maddie admitted. "And that time will be up in a few months. Although I have to say, there is such a wealth of material here in your vast country I could easily stay for another two."

"Material?"

Maddie gave a bright smile that was almost childlike in its enthusiasm. "I've already done the Colonies and some of the Civil War sites, and now I'm off to the Wild West. I can scarcely wait." She must have seen Lucinda's confusion. "Did I not mention that I'm an expeditionary photographer? Although I prefer portraiture, don't you? But one must do as one's publisher insists, I suppose."

"A photographer?" Lucinda was astounded. She had never heard of a female photographer. Perhaps Maddie Wallace wasn't such a bubblehead after all. "Is that what's contained in all these crates? Your photography equipment?"

"Yes, but not to worry." Maddie patted Lucinda's shoulder,

which startled her into a flinch. Lucinda tried to cover it with an awkward smile but could see Maddie had noticed. Having suffered enough pawing at Mrs. Beale's, Lucinda had a well-earned aversion to being touched by strangers. Oddly, though, it hadn't seemed to have bothered her with Tait.

"I keep all the dangerous chemicals and emulsions in closed containers," Maddie went on in reassurance as Lucinda took a seat on the couch on her side of the room. "We're in little danger of an explosion. Unless the train derails," she added with a gay laugh.

Lucinda glanced at the crates again, wondering if in her impulsive generosity she had signed her own death warrant.

"I daresay that won't happen. It hasn't yet, anyway." Maddie checked a watch pinned in her skirt pocket, then almost lost her balance when the train jerked into motion. "We're on our way, it seems. And luckily, only three hours late." Almost falling onto the couch across from Lucinda's when the train gave another lurch, she straightened her skirts and heaved a great sigh. "Well," she said, folding her hands in her lap and smiling at Lucinda. "We still have several hours yet before dinner, so why don't we become better acquainted? I assume you're not married, which I must say, astounds me, considering how beautiful you are. So if not an angry husband, then who is it you're running from?"

Lucinda's jaw dropped. "I beg your pardon?"

Maddie made a face. "Too forward? With you Colonials, one never knows. Perhaps I should go first, then. I'm running from an indifferent marriage, myself. A lovely man, but from a rather tiresome family—except for Glynnis, of course. But really, after only one visit and three letters in six years, what else was I to do? Molder in that drafty old castle forever? As if. So naturally, when the opportunity presented itself, thanks to Mr. Chesterfield, my publisher at *The Illustrated London News*, I jumped at the chance to rekindle my interest in photography and come here. Now it's your turn."

"A castle?" Good heavens, was she sharing quarters with royalty?

Maddie made an airy motion with one graceful hand. "I know. It's utterly absurd. The thing should have been modernized years ago, but the old earl insists everything remain the same as it has been for . . . well . . . forever. The Scots do cling to their traditions. Now you."

"Now me what?"

"Where are you headed? Is Columbus your destination, or will you be traveling farther? I'm going to the Rocky Mountains in Colorado Territory. Have you ever been there? I've seen photographs and it looks like magnificent country. Wouldn't it be lovely if we were to travel that far together? It gets rather lonely traveling alone, I've found. But you can no doubt surmise that by the way I keep running on."

Lucinda had to laugh. What an engaging, cheerful, and artless person Maddie Wallace was. She was just what Lucinda needed to lift her spirits and take her mind off Tait. It would be nice sharing the long hours in such pleasant company. "As a matter of fact, I was heading west, myself," she said, acting uncharacteristically on impulse. And why not? Where else had she to go?

"Oh, how marvelous," Maddie cried, clapping her hands in delight. "I think we shall get along famously, even if you snore. Angus sometimes snored, and I often find I miss it, which is strange, insomuch as we spent only a few nights in each other's company." A sad look crossed her lively features, then was quickly masked behind another bright smile. "But that's neither here nor there. We're off to make new starts and put the past behind us, you and I. And what an adventure we shall have!"

Lucinda smiled. *A new start.* Hopefully this one would be her last.

Tait floated in and out of awareness, sometimes shivering with cold, at other times feeling so hot he thought he was on fire. And always thirsty.

Gradually the pain dwindled to a constant deep ache, mostly on his right side and down his left leg—and a sharp burning across his chest, and shoulder, and face. His head never stopped pounding. He felt cocooned in wrappings, and wondered how badly he was broken.

He didn't know where he was or who the woman was he often found hovering over him when he awoke. He didn't know how long he had been there or where Smythe was or if Lucinda was safe. He didn't know how he could hurt this bad and still live.

"You must drink," the woman said.

He opened his eyes—his left one, anyway. The right was trapped beneath a thick bandage that covered the side of his face from jaw to temple. "Who . . ."

"Martha Yoder. My son, Levi, found you by the river. My husband brought you back here to our home."

"How . . . long?"

"Three days ago. Drink this." She pushed a tin cup against his lips.

He drank as much as he could. When she took the cup away, he studied her. She looked near his age and might once have been pretty. But a hard life had left permanent lines around her brown eyes and bracketing her full mouth. Her hair was pulled into a severe knot at the back of her head and was partially covered by a white cap. He noticed silver threads in the dark brown.

My son, she had said. Not our. Yoder was a common name in this area. He remembered it from his Army days. "Are you Amish?" he asked.

"My husband is."

"Not you?"

"Can you drink more? You lost a lot of blood." She offered the cup again.

He drank. By the time the cup was empty, he was trembling with weariness. "Did you find the other man?" he asked as blackness loomed at the edges of his vision.

"What other man?"

"By the river . . . gray hair . . . missing two fingers."

"We only found you."

"He's there," he insisted weakly as he began to sink. "He has to be."

Tait slept most of the rest of the day, awakening to bright afternoon sunshine, a grumbling belly, and a head full of questions. His watchdog, a brown-haired boy no more than ten—Levi?—alerted his mother, and while Tait was still trying to clear his muddled head, Mrs. Yoder came in with a pitcher of water and a bowl of watery oatmeal. The boy followed behind her with Tait's clothing, which appeared to have been cleaned and all the knife cuts mended. Levi set the garments on a chest at the foot of the bed, then leaned against the foot post, watching.

After finishing both the water and the oatmeal, Tait started with his questions, the foremost being, how bad was the damage. He couldn't lie here forever. He had to find out what happened to Smythe, and if Doyle had called off the Pinkertons, or if Lucinda was even now being dragged back to New York. He had no idea what Doyle would do when he found her, but Tait did know what he was capable of doing, and for that reason he was desperate to get there before things got out of hand.

"You'll live," Mrs. Yoder answered, her quiet voice interrupting his racing thoughts. "When infection sent your fever so high, we thought you might not. But it broke yesterday, and your wounds show no more infection."

He lifted a hand to the bandage on his face.

"A deep cut," she said before he could ask. "I stitched it. Luckily your eye wasn't damaged, but you'll have a scar." She went on with a long list of his other injuries—dozens of cuts and abrasions, bruised ribs on his right side, stitches where Smythe had cut him across his chest and shoulder and arm. "All that will heal fairly quickly. I don't know about your leg."

His leg? Lifting the covers, Tait saw his left leg was splinted and swathed in wrappings from thigh to shin. "Is it broken?"

"I don't think so. But your knee is very swollen and there are surface scrapes and deep bruising. I thought it best to keep it splinted until the swelling goes down. Maybe then I can see how bad the damage is."

Tait let the covers fall back over him. He had never been tended by a woman before and was glad he still had on his drawers at least. "You sound like you have experience with this sort of thing."

She shrugged one shoulder, as if she was too weary to lift both. "I helped during the war. One learns fast on a battlefield."

A man appeared in the doorway. Big, bearded, except for the forbidden mustache, his broad shoulders and worn hands proclaiming him a farmer. "Mrs. Yoder," he said in a thick Dutch accent, "the roast is burning. Levi, tend your chores."

The man stepped aside as they filed silently out, his eyes never leaving Tait. Once they were alone, he walked closer to loom over the bed. He had a hard face—not cruel, but set in stern lines. Tait guessed there wasn't much laughter in this household.

"My wife tells me you are healing," the man said.

Tait nodded, wondering if he was about to be sent on his way and how he would manage as weak as he felt. "Thank you for taking me into your home. I doubt I would have survived otherwise."

"I am Abram Yoder." Instead of offering his hand, he held out Tait's leather money case. "This was in your coat. Nothing has been taken."

Tait took the case and set it aside without opening it. "Tait Rylander."

Yoder shifted from one foot to the other and looked over to the open window beside the bed. Tait followed his gaze and saw several milk cows grazing in a pasture behind a big, stout barn. As he watched, Levi walked out of the barn with a feed bag over his shoulder. Chickens rushed him in a clucking frenzy as he began tossing grain. Beyond the barn was a large garden with newly planted rows laid out in straight, precise mounds. There were even two budding fruit trees. Tait wasn't sure what kind. Like this plain, unadorned room, everything he could see, inside or out, was neat and clean and carefully tended. A prosperous self-sufficient place, the Yoder farm. Yet a feeling of defeat hung in the air.

"I will do my duty by you," Yoder said, drawing Tait's attention away from the window.

Tait nodded and tried to smile as best he could with a bandage covering half his face. "I'm grateful for what you and your family have done."

"I do not know how you came to be by the river," he went on in a measured, toneless voice, as if he'd carefully rehearsed the words. "But your injuries show you are a man of violence. Such is not welcome here." His brown eyes bored into Tait. "This is a house of God, Mr. Rylander. We want only peace. Once you are healed, you will leave. Until then, now that you are awake, Levi will tend you, as is proper."

"I understand."

"Good." He pronounced it *goot*. "You will tell me when you are strong enough to travel, and I will take you to town."

"How far are we from Pittsburgh?"

"At least twenty miles. I can take you to the nearest settlement. It is half that distance. From there you can take the coach into the city."

"Thank you."

The farmer studied him for a moment, his face betraying nothing, then he turned and left the room.

Over the next few days, determined to regain his strength as quickly as possible, Tait ate as much as his stomach could tolerate and drank prodigious amounts of water. The day after talking to Yoder, he pulled the bandage off his face, hoping that having use of both eyes might ease the dizziness. The cut by his temple ran down past his cheekbone, and the stitches were beginning to itch. The knife wounds on his chest and shoulder and arm were itching, too, which meant he was starting to heal. It was still difficult to sit up or move with the restrictive bandages around his ribs, but that soreness was easing, too.

His leg was another matter.

With the boy's help, he removed the splint. The leg looked straight, although his knee was still swollen and tender to the touch. Holding on to the bedpost, he slowly rose and put weight on it. It hurt like hell but didn't fold beneath him, and when he tried to bend it, it moved as much as the swelling would allow.

Not broken, but definitely damaged. It felt strange, like it was stuffed with something that didn't belong there, and he hoped that would go away when the swelling subsided. He had the boy help him replace the splint and wrappings, then tried to stand again. Better, but still too painful to walk on yet.

The boy must have told Yoder, because the next day, the farmer appeared with a wooden crutch he'd made from a sturdy branch with a cross branch fitted across the top. Mrs. Yoder had padded it with thick scraps of quilting, and although it was short by an inch or so, it enabled Tait to walk without putting his weight on the injured knee.

That night, dressed in his clean and mended clothes, he took dinner with the family in the kitchen.

It was a quiet meal. Tait didn't know if that was because of his presence or if such was the usual case in this somber household. It wasn't until they were halfway through the meal that Yoder finally spoke.

"We will take the buggy into town on the morning after tomorrow. I already went once this week, but I will go again so you can be on your way."

Tait nodded, hoping he would be up to a ten-mile ride in a buggy, then another ten miles by coach.

"When I was there earlier," Yoder continued, "I heard talk about a man missing from the train. Is that you?"

"I'm one of them."

"They said there was blood and signs of a scuffle."

Tait set down his fork. Resting his hands beside his plate, he leveled his gaze at Yoder, hoping the farmer would see the truth in his eyes. "A man attacked me and tried to throw me off the train."

"Or maybe you attacked him and threw him off first."

"No. There was a woman I was trying to protect. The only way I could do that was to take him with me when he pushed me off."

"And yet, only you were found."

"Lucinda?" Mrs. Yoder asked.

Tait looked at her in surprise.

"You know this woman?" Yoder asked his wife.

"He mentioned her when he was fevered."

Frowning, Yoder turned back to Tait. "Why did we find no other man where we found you?"

"Maybe you didn't look hard enough."

Yoder didn't respond to that, and nothing more was said.

But dire thoughts kept circling in Tait's mind. He had heard Smythe scream. How had he escaped and where was he now? Had he found his way back onto the train somehow?

That unleashed a torrent of other questions—ones that haunted Tait's nights and chased him through the day. Where was Lucinda now? Was she safe? Or had Smythe found her again?

He had no answers, and his sense of desperation built by the hour.

The morning they were to leave, Tait was in the kitchen, finishing breakfast, while Yoder hitched the buggy. It was the first time he had had an opportunity to speak to Mrs. Yoder alone, but he wasn't sure what to say. He sensed undercurrents in this family, especially between Yoder and his wife. Although it was none of his business, he didn't feel right leaving her and the boy in what might very well be a bad situation without at least trying to help her.

"Mrs. Yoder, I owe you my life. Is there anything I can do to repay that debt?"

"There is no debt. You owe me nothing."

She moved briskly about the kitchen, pulling a bowl from the cupboard and filling it with steaming oatmeal. He'd already eaten eggs, a thick slice of ham, and two pieces of buttered bread. But she made the best oatmeal he had ever tasted, so he wasn't about to pass it up.

She set it on the table in front of him, then went quickly back to the stove, as if fearful of being too close to him.

Tait frowned, not liking the implication. Picking up his spoon, he stirred the oatmeal to cool it, then said, "Maybe you and Levi should go into town with us."

She turned from the stove with a sharp look, her back stiff, her hands gripping her apron. "Why would we do that?"

"You seem . . . troubled. If there's anything I can do to help . . ."

She opened her mouth, closed it, then turned back to the stove. Tait ate in silence while she busily stirred this pot and that.

In the pasture beyond the window, a calf ducked against its mother as Levi held a handful of grain through the rail fence.

"Abram is my second husband," she said without facing him. "He may seem harsh, but in his heart he's a kind and generous man."

Tait didn't respond.

"He's been good to me and Levi. I have no complaints."

Tait had never met a wife who had no complaints. Nor a husband who hadn't earned some. It was in the nature of marriage, he supposed.

"After my first husband died and we lost the farm," she went on, still facing away, "Levi and I moved into town. The only work I could find was at Kahler's store. He's a hard man, and didn't pay me much, but with a son to feed, I was grateful for the job."

She looked out the window at Levi, who was still trying to entice the calf with the grain. A small, gentle smile softened her face. "Abram often came into the store. He saw the way Mr. Kahler looked at me and the harsh way he treated Levi. It bothered him. So he married me and brought us out here. At great cost to himself, I think."

"Does he beat you or Levi? Mistreat you?"

She whipped toward him, her face more animated than he had ever seen it. "Of course not! He's a good man. A decent, honorable man. He would never raise a hand against us."

"I'm glad to hear it." Tait spooned up another bite of oatmeal and watched her as he chewed.

"He married me against his faith, and has been shunned because of it," she blurted out, her hands twisting in the apron. "People he lived among all his life, now no longer speak to him. He's an outcast. Forever. Because of us."

"His choice."

"On impulse. And out of pity. I think he's come to regret it."

Tait scraped up the last of the oatmeal and thought of Lucinda and the stricken look on her face when he had wrongly accused her of the vilest deception. He knew all about impulses and regrets. It had probably cost him the best thing that had ever come into his life. Somehow, he had to find her and make that right.

"We all do things without thinking them through," he said as he pushed back his empty bowl. "But no man—no matter how good and decent and honorable he is—takes on the burden of a wife and another man's son out of pity. Especially if it goes against a lifetime of religious teachings."

A sound caught his attention and he looked over at the door into the hall. It was partially open, and in the narrow gap, he saw Yoder standing in the shadows, watching them. The expression on his bearded face as he looked at Mrs. Yoder confirmed what Tait was beginning to suspect. It wasn't pity that made Yoder marry her—and it wasn't regret he was feeling now when he looked at his wife.

Leaning down, Tait picked up the crutch Yoder had made for him. He pushed back his chair, then with one hand braced on the table, and the other gripping the crutch, pulled himself up on his good leg. Once he found his balance, he looked at Mrs. Yoder. "So I'll ask you again, ma'am," he said in a voice that would carry into the hall. "Do you want to go with us into town or not?"

"No, Mr. Rylander," she said with calm certainty. "We're happy here with Abram. He may have regrets, but I don't. And I'll stay as long as he wants me."

Tait nodded, then shifting the crutch under his arm, limped toward the door.

"I hope you find your Lucinda," she called after him. "Because I think you're a good man, too, Mr. Rylander."

When Tait hobbled outside, Yoder was backing a sturdy mule into the traces of a black four-wheeled buggy with a canvas top and sides. After securing the harness, Yoder helped Tait climb in, then stowed the crutch behind the bench.

"If you get cold, there's a blanket behind the seat."

"Thank you." Sliding the money case from his inside coat pocket, Tait peeled off several bank notes and held them out toward Yoder.

The farmer gave him an offended look. "Put that away. I do not want payment for doing my Christian duty."

"Then think of it as a gift. Or set it aside for the next needy person you stumble upon." Seeing the obstinate set of the Dutchman's jaw, Tait tried a different approach. "You saved my life, Mr. Yoder, and used up precious supplies doing so. If I were well enough, I would stay a while to split rails or dig post holes or cut firewood or do whatever else I could to show my gratitude. But I can't. So please allow me to thank you the only way I am able right now."

After a long hesitation and with great reluctance, the farmer took the notes and shoved them into his pocket.

"This, too." Tait extracted a calling card from the case and handed it over. "If you find the other man, or hear anything about him, would you please send word to me here? I'm very concerned about the woman he was threatening."

"Lucinda."

"Yes. Lucinda."

Nodding, Yoder slipped the card into his pocket. "I will ask around." Then turning, the big farmer walked back to the porch where Mrs. Yoder stood.

As Tait watched, Yoder reached out and rested a hand on his wife's cheek. He said something, then bent and pressed his lips to hers. Tait could see Mrs. Yoder was startled by the action.

But she was smiling when her husband turned and walked back to the buggy. And Yoder was, too.

Before they even reached Indianapolis, the next big stopover after Columbus, Lucinda and Maddie had become fast friends, which was odd, insomuch as they were the exact opposite of one another.

Maddie, the optimist. Lucinda, the cynic. The English-woman's unbridled cheerfulness might have grated on Lucinda had she not caught glimpses of a sharp intelligence beneath the bubbly personality. Plus, Maddie seemed innately kind. But what set her apart even more was her ability to see through the armor most people wore—Lucinda included—to the goodness, rather than the ugliness, of the person within. It was apparent in every photograph she showed Lucinda, whether the subject was an old woman sharing her lunch with pigeons in a park or a tattered soldier begging on a street corner or a mist-shrouded cemetery next to a charred plantation home. She saw beauty everywhere. That was her gift, and through her tintypes, she was able to share it with anyone who took the time to look.

But the dear woman needed a keeper. She was forever forgetting her reticule or her gloves, or charming strangers with her ready smile. She had no idea of the dangers awaiting the unaware, so it was left to Lucinda to take on the task of being her watchdog and protector. Besides, she was the one with the gun.

With some reluctance, she had told her traveling companion about Smythe. Nothing missed Maddie's observant gaze, and she had asked several times who Lucinda was expecting. The dear woman had a right to know that a dangerous deviant might be lurking about.

"You mean you actually poked his . . . lower person . . . with a gun?" Maddie had asked that first night as they sat in the dining car, enjoying a lovely dinner of roast capon, rice, and string beans—when the rocking of the train wasn't sliding their plates all over the table. "You brave thing!"

"More furious than brave." Lucinda hadn't shared all the details—such as why Smythe had attacked her or that Tait had come to her aid. She couldn't talk about Tait yet. Maybe she never would. And she would never talk about those horrible days in Five Points.

"Nonetheless," Maddie insisted, "I find you a most remarkable woman. I admire you tremendously."

Lucinda hid her smile behind a forkful of rice. No one had ever said that to her before. It was nice. Having a friend was nice. She resolved to work hard to be deserving of Maddie's admiration.

By the time they arrived in St. Louis, over four hundred miles and several days after leaving Columbus, Lucinda was convinced she had made her escape. With grim determination, she put Smythe . . . and Tait . . . behind her, and looked ahead to her grand new life.

They would be changing trains in St. Louis, and she and Maddie had decided to take a break from travel and enjoy at least one night on solid ground. Maddie was anxious to take photographs of the plush gambling riverboats plying their trade on the Mississippi River, and Lucinda had things she needed to attend to, as well. So, after hiring a cart and a trustworthy boy to help Maddie with her equipment and keep an eye on her, Lucinda picked up her valise of railroad shares and headed to the nearest bank.

Bankers in St. Louis, she found, were not as particular as those in Philadelphia, and were even more susceptible to female manipulation. Probably because there were fewer women available the farther west they traveled. Using the same ruse she had employed at the Girard Bank—but with less bosom flaunting— she was able to exchange five more of the twenty-share certificates for another line of credit. It was absurdly easy and made Lucinda wonder how banks ever stayed in business. In less than an hour, she was back on the street, fortified with four more stacks of crisp bank notes and several rolls of double eagles, and headed for the nearest Western Union office.

After sending a wire to Mrs. Throckmorton, assuring her that she was well, in the company of a dear lady, and headed toward the mountains, she went to round up Maddie for supper.

She found her surrounded by gawkers, mostly men, and taking a portrait of four scantily clad women hanging their plump assets over the railing of a riverboat gambling den moored at the busy wharf.

"Oh, Lucinda," she cried, when she saw her marching toward her. "I have met the most astounding people."

"I can see that. Are you ready to go? It's getting late."

"We might as well. I'm almost out of albumenized paper. Isn't this marvelous? I so adore the West."

"How can you be sure?" Lucinda asked drily, as she helped her pack her camera and folding table onto the cart she had hired. "We're not even there, yet."

"Truly? Well, I adore it anyway."

Twenty-four hours later, they were seated in the dining car of the westbound train, steaming toward Kansas City and the setting sun.

Lucinda's spirits continued to rise. Her escape had been successful; she had seen no sign of Smythe or lurkers who might have been Pinkerton men. Their George said no one had been asking about them. In fact, she thought, glancing around the crowded dining car, no one even remotely suspicious seemed to be taking the slightest interest in them.

"Do you see him?" Maddie whispered, leaning across the table.

"See who?"

"Whoever it is you keep looking for." Maddie grinned and popped a slice of stewed carrot into her mouth. "I know it's not Smythe. I've been watching for him, too, and have seen no one even remotely matching his description. Besides, he never brought that melancholy look to your face. So it must be someone else. Your lover? A smitten swain you're trying to forget?"

"I have no idea what you're talking about."

The Englishwoman laughed. "You're a terrible liar, Luce. And far too beautiful not to have a dozen brokenhearted men in your wake. So who are you trying to avoid?"

There was only one man in Lucinda's past that mattered, and it was she who had been left with the broken heart. But realizing her companion wouldn't rest until she heard at least part of the story, Lucinda admitted to being nearly a bride.

"How near?"

"I realized at the last minute he was not for me," she hedged, not wanting to go into a lengthy explanation about the unregistered marriage license. "So I left him at the altar, so to speak."

"Never!" Maddie blinked at her through eyes as round and bright as new brown buttons. "What did he do?"

"He sent Pinkerton detectives after me."

"No. I mean what did he do to make you change your mind?"

Lucinda thought for a moment. "He was harsh with his employees. He saw me as little more than his entree into society and a screen for underhanded business dealings. And he had an unsavory past, which I only learned of as we were about to begin the ceremony. In short, he wasn't the man I thought he was."

"Well." Maddie sat back against the cushions, her expression one of utter amazement. "You are quite the bravest person I know. I wouldn't have dared."

Lucinda refrained from rolling her eyes. "This from a woman who crossed an ocean and half a continent by herself, rather than 'molder in a drafty castle.' That's brave." Or foolish. Lucinda still wasn't certain which.

Maddie waved the notion away. "I've found that putting one's person in peril is not nearly as frightening as putting one's heart at risk. In the former, one might only endure a momentary injury. While with the latter, there is the possibility of suffering a lifetime of loneliness and regret. Unless one died, of course. Then that would make loneliness rather a moot point, don't you think?"

Lucinda sipped from her glass, then returned it to the table. She might not be as observant or perceptive as her new friend, but she knew regret when she saw it. "You still love your soldier husband, don't you?"

Maddie stabbed her pork chop when a sudden lurch almost sent it sliding off her plate. "Perhaps. But that's all in the past."

"And if he realizes his mistake and comes after you?"

The Englishwoman took a tiny bite and chewed thoughtfully. After swallowing, she dabbed her mouth with her napkin and sighed. "I very much doubt he would—realize his mistake, that is. Being a military officer, he would probably perceive my leaving as a treasonous act of desertion, rather than a natural consequence of his neglect. But should he attempt reconciliation"—a crafty smile came over her face as she speared a green bean—"he will have to woo me all over again before I would even consider taking him back." The smile faded. "Although I hope he doesn't. He's a very good wooer, and I'm dreadfully weak where he is concerned. I should hate to go through all that heartache again."

Lucinda understood that kind of weakness all too well. She wondered what she would do if Tait realized his mistake and came after her. Would she ever be able to trust him again? Would he trust her? Probably not, unless she told him everything about her shameful, sordid past, which she would never do. Seeing the disgust in his eyes would be a crushing blow, one from which she would never recover.

No. Better to be alone. She didn't need a man to give her life meaning. In fact, now that she was rich, she didn't need a man at all.

Tait arrived in Pittsburgh so sore he could barely hobble into the Grand Park Hotel. Since there was no screw railway available, he rented the largest accommodations available on the ground floor, then asked the concierge to send a physician, tailor, barber, and a full meal to his suite as soon as possible.

The physician came first. Deciding Tait should leave in the neat stitches Mrs. Yoder had put in his chest, shoulder, and arm for a few more days, he checked Tait's head wound, which he said was healing well, although there might be a few headaches now and then. His bruised ribs no longer needed support, but his knee was still too swollen to properly assess, so he advised keeping it splinted for a few more days. Pronouncing him well enough to travel, the doctor gave Tait a bottle of laudanum for the pain, then left, much richer than when he arrived.

The tradesmen came next. Once Tait was shaved, trimmed, and measured for new clothing—for which he had to pay double to ensure that they would be ready by the following afternoon—he ate a full meal, washed it down with a goodly dose of laudanum, then collapsed on the bed for his first painless, dreamless night in almost a week.

By seven the next evening, he was on the train back to New York, determined to find out who had hired Smythe and why, and wondering how he could convince Doyle to give up on his runaway bride and the five hundred shares of Hudson and Erie Railroad stock she just *happened* to take with her when she left.

Twelve

The first thing Tait did after stepping off the ferry onto Manhattan Island was to hire a hansom cab to take him to Mrs. Throckmorton's Sixty-ninth Street brownstone.

He was convinced Lucinda would stay in touch with her guardian. She had seemed deeply concerned when Mrs. Throckmorton had taken ill after the ceremony. So concerned, in fact, Tait was beginning to think her worry might have been genuine and that it had been the old lady who had instigated the escape and not her ward.

Or maybe that was just what he wanted to believe.

Either way, he was certain if anyone knew whether Lucinda was all right or where she might be headed now, it would be Mrs. Throckmorton.

When the cab stopped at the curb in front of the brownstone, Tait wrestled out the makeshift crutch, then used it to pull himself up, almost pitching forward on his face when it slipped into a crack in the walk. He straightened, cursing under his breath, and vowed that as soon as he finished here, he would see a doctor about his knee. The swelling had gone down somewhat after several days of sitting idle on the train, but it was apparent he had suffered substantial damage to the joint. He figured his last waltz was behind him. He just hoped he'd still be able to sit a horse.

Finally making it up the steps, he knocked on the front door. It was several minutes before Pringle, Mrs. Throckmorton's stuffy butler, swung it open. Masterfully veiling his surprise at Tait's battered appearance, he raised bushy white brows in his usual expression of pinch-lipped disdain. "Yes?"

"Is Mrs. Throckmorton at home?"

"She is."

When it was obvious the pretentious bastard had said all he intended to, Tait lost his patience. "I need to see her. Now."

Pringle's expressive nostrils twitched. "May I say who's calling, sir?"

"Goddamnit, Pringle, you know who I am." Thrusting the end of the crutch past the butler, he shoved open the door and hobbled inside. "Just get her. I'll be in the front room."

With a sniff, Pringle closed the door, and moving at a snail's pace to show his affront at such harsh treatment, he turned toward the stairs. "I'll see if she's available."

"Tell her it's about her ward."

Pringle's speed increased to a turtle's pace.

Tait limped into the front receiving room, where coals were glowing in the grate even though the early April afternoon was sunny and mild. Not wanting to go through the painful process of sitting, then rising again when the old lady arrived, Tait crossed to the window. Leaning on the crutch, he stared blankly out at the street, troubled thoughts running through his mind.

It had been a difficult decision to come back to New York rather than go after Lucinda. In the railroads' rush to cross the continent, rail service became less dependable and the schedules more erratic the farther west they pushed the tracks. With fewer trains running each week, even assuming he correctly guessed her route, he might have had to travel for weeks before he caught up to her.

But after giving it much thought, he decided he would be more help to her if he came back here and convinced Doyle to give up on recovering the stocks and let her go. Plus, here in New York, he would have a better chance of finding out who had sent Smythe.

He didn't see how the bastard could still be alive. But if he had survived the fall from the train and the tumble down the slope, where was he now?

"Pringle says you have news of Margaret?" a voice snapped behind him.

Moving awkwardly, Tait turned to find Mrs. Throckmorton glaring at him from the doorway. When she saw the crutch and the stitched cut on his face, her scowl deepened. "Were you accosted?"

"I fell off a train."

The thin, blue-veined hand not gripping her cane flew to her throat. "Margaret? Is she—"

"She's fine," Tait cut in. "At least she was when I left her."

"Left her where? Where is she now?"

"I was hoping you could tell me."

"Oh, dear. I think—oh, my—I need to sit down."

Alarmed by the sudden paleness in the elderly woman's face, Tait hobbled over to assist.

She curtly waved him aside. "Stay back before you fall on me and end us both." With a groaning sigh, she collapsed into one of the two chairs flanking the fireplace. When Tait continued to linger nearby, she impatiently motioned to the other chair. "Oh, do sit down. I detest hovering."

As soon as Tait was settled, she leaned forward in her chair, hands clasped on the head of the cane positioned by her knees. "You went after her, didn't you? I thought you might. Did that Irish parvenu send you, or did you go on your own?"

"I—"

"On your own, I suspect. I saw the way you looked at her, you sly thing. Tell me everything that happened."

Tait leaned forward in his own chair. "Have you heard from her, Mrs. Throckmorton? Is she all right?"

The pale blue eyes widened. "Why wouldn't she be all right? You're here—that nasty Irishman is here—why wouldn't she be all right?"

"Have you heard from her?" Tait pressed. He could see his tone alarmed her, and tried to soften it. "It's important, Mrs. Throckmorton. I need to know she's all right."

"Oh, dear." Slumping back in the chair, she let the cane lean against the cushions by her hip and pressed a hand to her neck. "Something's happened, hasn't it?"

"I hope not. When did you last hear from her?"

"Several days ago. She sent a wire to my banker to pass along to me. She was leaving St. Louis in the company of an

Englishwoman she had met on the train. They were heading west toward the mountains."

"Thank God." If she had made it all the way to St. Louis, then Smythe was probably no longer a threat. Closing his eyes, Tait let out a deep breath, only then realizing that he'd been holding it. It was shocking, the depth of his reaction. And revealed to him in the starkest, most elemental way how important Lucinda's safety was to him—how important she was to him.

"You care about her, don't you?"

He opened his eyes to find that sharp gaze fixed on him in a manner that reminded him of Lucinda. Despite her age, this woman was almost as astute as her ward. "I do."

"Then tell me why you left her. And why you think Margaret might be in danger."

"Lucinda." He smiled wryly. "Lucinda Hathaway is the name she's using now. Clever lady, your ward. Full of surprises." His smile faded. "But I wasn't the only one following her."

"What do you mean?"

He told her about tracking Lucinda to Philadelphia, and how the conductor on the train to Harrisburg had said another man had been asking about her, too. "English, gray-haired, missing two fingers. Said he was looking for his sister."

"Margaret has no brother. Or any blood relatives, as far as I know. And I have certainly never met anyone by that description."

"Lucinda has. Said his name was Smythe."

"Smythe!" She seemed to shrink in the chair, her skeletal fingers plucking at the lacy collar of her dress as if it cut too tightly into her throat. "Oh, dear heavens . . ."

"Ma'am, are you all right?" Tait struggled to rise, afraid this time the crafty old woman truly was sick. "Shall I send for Pringle?"

With a trembling hand, she waved him back into the chair. "No, no. He's useless anyway." Raising her voice, she called toward the door. "Do you hear that, Pringle? I know you're out there, eavesdropping. Do make yourself useful and bring me a cup of tea." She glanced at Tait, then added, "And that bottle of Scotch whiskey the judge kept in the drawer of his desk."

A low muttering as footsteps shuffled down the hall.

Mrs. Throckmorton turned back to Tait. "Are you certain it was Smythe?"

"Lucinda seemed convinced it was." Seeing her color had returned, Tait settled cautiously back, keeping his injured leg stretched straight before him, which seemed to ease the pain a bit. "You know him?"

"I know *of* him. Oh, poor Margaret. She must have been terrified."

"She was. Why? What did he do to her?"

The blue eyes shifted away. "What did she tell you?"

"Only that there was a fire fifteen years ago, and she thought he'd died in it. Who is he?"

"Someone from her past. A horrible man." Mrs. Throckmorton sighed and shook her head. "If she wants you to know more, she'll tell you. Who sent him after her?"

"That's one of the things I'm here to find out." Tait felt like he was stumbling around a snake pit in the dark. First Lucinda, and now Mrs. Throckmorton. Why wouldn't they answer his questions? "How can I keep her safe if you won't tell me who's a threat to her and why?"

"Dear boy, I would if I could." Tears shimmered in the pale blue eyes. "But I cannot. I promised her I would never speak of it."

Seeing that Mrs. Throckmorton was becoming more agitated, Tait struggled to curb his frustration. What in the hell could have happened in that fire? Lucinda had been little more than a child fifteen years ago, yet it haunted her still.

An abrupt knock announced Pringle's return. Conversation ceased as the old man entered, bearing a silver tray upon which sat a cup and saucer, a steaming teapot, a cut glass tumbler, and a half-filled bottle of amber liquid. In silence they watched his shuffling progress across to the table beside the fireplace, where he set down the tray and with great ceremony poured out the tea and whiskey, then presented them with a flourish to Mrs. Throckmorton and Tait.

Tait doubted the tea was even warm anymore.

"If that will be all, madam?"

"For now." She waved him toward the door. "And no more eavesdropping, Pringle. I would hate to have to put you on the street at your age."

"Thank you, madam." With a sniff, the old man sidled out, closing the door with a resounding thump to show what he thought of her threats.

"Cantankerous old fool," Mrs. Throckmorton muttered.

Tait took a swallow and almost choked on cheap rye whiskey instead of the expected Scotch. Old fool, indeed.

"How could you have left her with that horrid man skulking about?" Mrs. Throckmorton accused, picking up the conversation where it had left off. "You said you cared about her."

"I didn't leave her," Tait said wearily as he set aside his glass. "Smythe pushed me off the train."

He told her about Smythe's attack on Lucinda in the alley, and his later assault on Tait in the Parlor Car. "He said he'd been sent to silence her. Because I was in the way, he intended to kill me, too. When he tried to push me over the railing at the back of the train, I took him with me. That's the only way I could think of to protect her."

"Mercy. It's a wonder you survived."

"I almost didn't." He described the fall down the slope, hearing Smythe scream, then waking up at the Yoder farm three days later. "They said they saw no one else on the slope. But I don't see how Smythe could have survived."

"Margaret's wire mentioned none of this."

"She didn't know." Which troubled Tait almost as much as Smythe's disappearance. What was Lucinda thinking? That he had deserted her? Just walked off the train without looking back? But what else would she think after the things he'd said.

"So what do you intend to do?"

At least that part was clear to him. "Stop Doyle from pursuing her further. Then find out who sent Smythe." And do what he must to stop him.

"You're that certain your Irish friend didn't send him?"

"Doyle? I don't think so. At least I hope not."

She made a derisive sound. "I don't know how you can associate with such an underhanded man. He was never going to be worthy of my Margaret. He would have made her life miserable."

"Is that why you convinced her to go along with your plan?"

That evasive look again. "I don't know what you're talking about."

"Don't you?" He'd known it all along. It had just been easier to believe it was clever Lucinda's doing rather than this duplicitous old lady. "It was all your idea, wasn't it? Faking the illness, the widow's disguise, taking the certificates and marriage license."

"Marriage license? I know nothing about that."

Tait noticed she didn't deny the rest of it. He wondered again how he could have been so blind. "She still has it. It was never witnessed or registered, which means they're not legally married."

A tremulous smile lit the wrinkled face. "So Kerrigan has no hold over her?"

"Not legally. At least as far as the marriage goes. But the stock certificates are a different matter. Look, Mrs. Throckmorton." Tait leaned forward again, determined to get answers from her before it was too late. "I know Lucinda is Irish. I know what happened to her parents, and that when she learned Doyle was a runner like the one who destroyed her family, she felt she had to leave."

"She told you that?"

He nodded.

"Then you also know what kind of vile person your friend must be to do that to his own kind. So how can you be so sure he didn't send Smythe after her?"

"Because he cares less about Lucinda than he does his stock certificates. And he won't get them back if he kills her." Just saying the words aloud made him half sick.

Fresh tears clouded Mrs. Throckmorton's eyes. "I am the one who put them in her traveling case. If I hadn't—"

"It wouldn't have mattered," he cut in. "Smythe wasn't sent to retrieve the stock certificates. He was sent to silence Lucinda."

"By whom? And what could she possibly know?"

He shrugged. "Maybe it's something she saw or heard fifteen years ago when she last saw Smythe. Or maybe she knows who set the fire. But if you won't tell me about her past, I don't know how I can help her."

"Oh, dear." Fresh tears fell. She plucked at a handkerchief in her lap.

Tait could see she was caught in a dilemma she couldn't resolve, but he didn't care. He would do whatever was necessary to protect Lucinda. He owed her that after what he'd accused her of. Reaching over, he placed a hand on the restless fingers. "Please talk to me, Mrs. Throckmorton. Help me before it's too late."

She took a hitching breath and hiked her chin. "I would if I could, Mr. Rylander. I gave her my word I wouldn't. But go ask the Papist. Father O'Rourke was there. He saw it all."

By the time Tait left the brownstone, it was too late to hunt up either Father O'Rourke or a doctor, so he went directly to Doyle's townhome.

It was lit up as if a party were in progress, although the rooms behind the open drapes looked empty of revelers and only one carriage sat parked in the street. Tait knew Doyle didn't like darkened rooms—a legacy of the horrific crossing from Ireland, when rats would come out at night to feast on the fevered flesh of the starving immigrants stuffed like cordwood in the dark, dank hold of the overcrowded ship. Even now, Doyle's fear of vermin was so strong he wouldn't even venture near the docks after dark.

Tait told the coachman to wait, then hobbled up the steps to the front door.

Buster Quinn—a retired Pinkerton detective hired by Doyle just before Margaret left, and who served more as a security advisor than a butler—opened it to Tait's knock.

"Good evening, Mr. Rylander. Welcome back." Then he saw Tait's face and the crutch, and his smile faltered. "Come in, sir."

Tait hobbled over the threshold. "I saw the carriage outside. Company?"

"Only Mr. Horne, sir. I'll get Mr. Kerrigan."

"Thanks, Quinn."

Before Tait had hung his bowler on the hall tree, he heard brisk footsteps coming down the hall.

"*Dia duit*, my friend," Doyle called out as he crossed the marble foyer. But like Quinn's, his smile faded when he saw Tait's battered condition. "I'd like to see the other fellow, so I would. Jasus, boyo. What happened?"

"Long story."

Doyle looked around. "Where's Margaret? Your wire said you were bringing her back."

"I intended to." Unwilling to show his hand before he found out who had hired Smythe, Tait gave a shorter version of what he'd told Mrs. Throckmorton, saying only that a man had attempted to rob him and in the ensuing struggle, they had both fallen off the train. He didn't mention names . . . either Smythe's or the new one Lucinda was using.

"Will you be all right?"

"Eventually."

"And Margaret? Was she involved in this?"

"No. She was on another car at the time."

"So where is she?"

Tait shrugged. "She could be anywhere by now. I was laid up for a week on an Amish farm before I was well enough to travel."

"Faith!" Doyle cut loose several Irish curses as he paced the foyer. "If I ever get my hands on that—"

"Forget it, Doyle," Tait cut in before the Irishman's temper got away from him. "You don't need her. Just get an annulment and let her go."

Doyle threw his hands up in disgust. "It's not her I want, Tait. It's the damned certificates. The vote is fast approaching."

"What vote?" a voice interrupted.

Doyle muttered something in Gaelic.

Tait turned to see Franklin Horne coming toward them. He tried to hide his distaste. There was something unsavory about the man. Almost reptilian, with that darting tongue and those small, close-set eyes that never seemed to blink. "Evening, Horne."

In a show of camaraderie, Doyle clapped an arm around Tait's shoulder. The smell of alcohol was strong on his breath. Drinking and sharing confidences with Franklin Horne—a bad combination, in Tait's view.

"Tait fell off a train, Frank. Can you imagine anyone being that clumsy?"

Horne studied Tait, those eyes bright with speculation. "Train where?"

"Near Pittsburgh." Tait watched to see if the other man showed any reaction, but Horne's expression didn't change.

"Horne, here," Doyle went on in a jovial voice, "has plans to be our next governor. Be nice having a friend in Albany to cover our backs, don't you think, Tait?"

The last person Tait wanted covering his back was Franklin Horne.

Taking his arm from Tait's shoulder, Doyle motioned toward the rear of the house. "Let's go back to my office for a drink and we'll discuss how best we can help each other."

Tait shook his head. "Perhaps another day. I haven't even been home yet. Just wanted to tell you I'm back." With a nod to Horne, he told Doyle he'd be by in a day or two, and returned to his waiting cab.

Tait's own townhome was in an older but still fashionable area of the city, and was smaller and less showy than Doyle's sprawling mansion. Situated in a row of similar homes on a quiet street lined with trees, it had a solid, almost staid feel to it, due in part, because Tait had furnished it more for comfort than show, and also because most of his neighbors were older.

Insomuch as his various investments and board positions took up most of his evenings—and when he was home, Tait preferred privacy and quiet—he didn't often entertain large groups, but restricted his gatherings to a few close friends in for dinner from time to time. Thus, he didn't require a large staff, and his simple needs were easily met by Elder and Ceily Rice, an older Negro couple he'd found sitting on the steps of a nearby church three years ago.

Both had been house slaves. But like thousands of other freed men and women who had fled the South hoping for a better life up north, they had found even less opportunity awaiting them above the Mason-Dixon Line. They had eagerly taken up Tait's offer to manage the house he had recently bought. It was an amiable arrangement that had worked out well for all of them. And through the years, as sometimes happens between people torn from places they've known all their lives and thrust into unfamiliar surroundings, a bond had formed between Tait and the Rices that transcended skin color or background or education. Perhaps it was the sound of the south in their speech or the love of common regional foods or the shared memories of things found only in the place they'd left behind. Whatever the cause, Tait and the Rices had become family. And that evening, as Tait wearily entered his home and saw their familiar, welcoming faces, it was like a weight had been lifted from his heart.

"Oh, Mr. Tait," Ceily cried when she saw him hanging his hat on the rack by the door. "Elder, come quick! What in heaven's name happened to you, child?"

"I fell off a train."

"Mercy sakes! Elder, grab his arm there, and let's get him to the kitchen. Fell off a train. Lawd, if that don't beat anything I ever heard."

As was her habit when faced with a crisis, Ceily offered food. Leftover cornbread and molasses, baked beans simmered with molasses, sweet tater pie made with molasses. Ceily had a bit of a sweet tooth, and molasses was her favorite cure for everything from homesickness to boils.

Knowing he would have to eat something whether he was hungry or not, Tait chose pie. As he settled in a chair at the kitchen table, his leg stretched out before him, she plunked down a thick slice of pie and a glass of milk . . . milk being her second favorite cure. But just to be triply sure, she rushed off to get the medicine basket she kept in her and Elder's quarters at the back of the house.

As soon as she left, Elder took another seat, folded his arms atop the table, and studied Tait hard. Being as quiet as his wife was talkative, he kept his questions brief. "Drunk?"

"Robbed."

"You let him?"

Tait shrugged. "Not much I could do against a knife. At least when he pushed me off, I took him with me."

Elder ruminated on that while Tait finished up the pie and downed the last of the milk. "When she come back," he advised in a whisper, "tell her you tripped. Otherwise, we never hear the end of it."

"She'll know when I ask her to take out the stitches."

"Leave them in."

"They itch like hell."

"We in trouble, then."

Thirty minutes later, stitches removed, every bruise and half-healed cut slathered with salve, his knee wrapped, and his actions thoroughly chastised, he was finally allowed to go to his room.

It was on the third floor.

Even with Elder's help and Ceily's fussing, he was in such pain by the time he reached it he knew it would be a while before he could sleep. Sending them on to their own beds, he stood at the window and looked out at the city he had called home for almost five years. Yet tonight felt more like a prison.

The next morning, he took a hansom cab to Father O'Rourke's church near the tenement district of Five Points. It was a dismal place. Here, a world away from the wealthy streets toward the other end of the island, struggling immigrants lived in crowded, tight-knit conclaves where English was rarely spoken and grinding poverty opened the door to drunkenness, prostitution, and hopeless despair.

This was the landscape from which Doyle Kerrigan had sprung, and Tait could only imagine the cruel forces that had helped shape the Irishman into the man he was today. For that reason, more even than the debt he owed Doyle for saving his life, Tait had overlooked some of his partner's more unprincipled traits.

But now, with Lucinda caught between them, he could no longer look away or make excuses or distance himself. He had to protect her—even from his friend and partner. Even from himself, if necessary, by staying as far away from her as he could, rather than leave a trail back to whoever it was who wanted her dead.

But first, he had to find out who that enemy was, and what her pursuer thought she knew or saw that had made her his target. Hopefully, Father O'Rourke could help him with that.

St. Columban's Catholic Church was a small, unimposing structure on a block crowded with other unimposing structures, yet there seemed to be a fair amount of foot traffic going in and out of the arched oak doors. The coachman was reluctant to wait in such a questionable section of the city, until Tait showed him the extra half eagle he would earn if he stayed.

Luckily there was a handrail on the front steps, and using that along with the crutch, Tait was able to make it up to the door without too much difficulty. But once inside, his luck ended.

Father O'Rourke was in Ireland, Father Michaels told him. "He goes back every two years," the red-cheeked young man explained in a lilting Irish accent, "to help orphaned immigrant children reestablish contact with their relatives in Ireland. Unlike Reverend Brace of the Children's Aid Society, Father O'Rourke thinks these poor lost angels would be happier among their own in their homeland rather than being shipped off to strangers all over the country."

Biting back his frustration, Tait looked out the window to see two of the lost angels trying to relieve his coachman of his money purse. "When will he be back?"

"Two, perhaps three months."

Lucinda might not have three months.

Returning to the cab just as two more little angels ran up to bedevil the coachman, Tait climbed in and directed the driver to take him to Sixty-ninth Street. Mrs. Throckmorton would have to answer his questions now.

But Mrs. Throckmorton wasn't at home, either, Pringle was delighted to inform him when he finally answered Tait's insistent knock. "She is not expected back until early afternoon," he intoned, somehow managing to look down his blade-shaped nose at Tait even though he was half a foot shorter. "Shall I tell her you called, Mr. . . . ." He let the sentence hang, his brows raised in question.

"Oh, for the love of God," Tait snapped, and whirling as best he could on a crutch, stumped back down the stairs.

With nothing left to do but wait, he directed the coachman to the East Eighty-second Street office of Dr. Alvin Greenwall, an ex-army surgeon who had treated him during his recovery at Harrisburg, and who he had later run into here, in Manhattan. Greenwall's early years as a physician, coupled with his grisly experiences as a battlefield surgeon had made him one of the most knowledgeable and sought-after doctors in the city, despite his gruff manner and odd sense of humor.

Tait caught him just as he was finishing lunch, and was able to see him without the usual long wait.

"Haven't seen you in . . . what? Two years, sergeant?" the doctor asked as Tait stepped out of his trousers and sat down on the end of the examination table. Greenwall was better with faces and rank than he was with names.

"At least."

Pulling a wheeled chair from the corner, Greenwall hooked the earpieces of a pair of thick magnifying spectacles over his ears, then sat down. "What the hell did you do this time?" he asked, idly chewing on a fancy toothpick as he poked a finger at the old bullet wound in Tait's thigh. "Did a good job here, it seems."

"You did. But I'm more concerned about my knee."

"Hmm." The doctor shifted his attention to Tait's other leg. "What the hell happened?"

"I fell down a slope." Tait winced as Greenwall twisted his lower leg to the right, then the left. "Actually, I fell off a train first, then fell down the slope."

"Hmm." The doctor rolled the toothpick to the other side of his mouth. Back in the war days, he had combated the stench of the surgeon's tent by holding in his teeth a slim piece of wood to which a wad of cotton soaked in oil of eucalyptus had been tied. It had become a habit, although now Tait saw he favored the more fashionable imported toothpicks with carved grippers and spiral shafts that were made of Portuguese orangewood.

Pushing the spectacles up on top of his head, Greenwall looked hard at Tait. "You a drinker now, sergeant? Or just goddamn clumsy?"

"I was pushed."

"By the lady's husband?" Pleased with his quip, he gave a short bark of laughter that almost shot the toothpick out of his mouth before he clamped down on it with his teeth. "Well, however the hell it happened, you definitely did something to yourself." He gave the swollen knee one last thump that almost sent Tait off the table, then sat back. "The knee is a complicated, complex joint with a lot of connective tissue. Seems you've either torn some loose, or stretched them good. Can't tell which unless I cut it open."

"Cut it open?"

"I know, I know," Greenwall broke in before Tait could add further protests. "You'd rather walk with a limp the rest of your life than risk losing your leg on the cutting table. Understandable. But how the hell else are we surgeons to learn what works unless we get to operate on the living? Goddamn cadavers don't heal all that well." Another bark of laughter.

"So you can't help me?" Tait asked once the doctor's merriment faded.

"I look like your goddamn fairy godmother, soldier? Hell, no." Suddenly all business again, Greenwall checked the watch in his coat pocket, then rose. "As long as there's pain, keep it supported with wrappings, stay off it, and elevate it as much as you can until the swelling goes down. If it's not better in three months, come see me again. And quit falling off trains. That's just goddamn stupid. Pay on your way out. Dismissed, sergeant."

Three months. *Hell.*

Thirty minutes later, Tait was hobbling back through his front door, wondering why he'd ever left in the first place. O'Rourke gone, Mrs. Throckmorton gone, and no help for his knee. It had been a wasted day.

He was just finishing a lunch of cold cuts, sliced tomatoes, and cucumbers, followed by a piece of pecan pie with molasses, when Elder came in with the day's post. In it was a letter from Abram Yoder. Tait quickly tore it open.

Smythe had been found buried under a pile of rubble halfway down the slope. *If the authorities come,* Yoder wrote, *I will show them where. If not, we will leave him to rest where God put him. Abram Yoder.*

Smythe was dead. Lucinda was safe.

Tait pressed his palms against the table as a sudden rush of emotion left him almost lightheaded.

Thank God.

Elder hovered at his shoulder. "You all right, Mr. Tait?"

"They found him." Tait held up the letter. "The man who tried to rob me. He's dead."

"Thank the Lawd for that."

Tait pushed back the chair and reached for his crutch. "Whistle up a cab for me, will you, Elder? I have one more errand to run."

This time, he didn't wait for Pringle to go through his routine, but shoved past him as soon as the old man opened the door on Sixty-ninth Street. "I have news for Mrs. Throckmorton," he said, heading directly to the front room. "If she's not here, I'll wait."

A few minutes later, Mrs. Throckmorton came in, worry clouding her pale blue eyes. "Pringle said you had news? Is it about Margaret? What's happened?"

"Smythe's body was found."

She lifted a hand to her throat. "Dead?"

Tait nodded.

"Oh, my." She seemed to waver, her hand tightly gripping the head of her cane. "So Margaret is safe?"

"For now."

"Thank heavens." Crossing to her chair beside the unlit hearth, she sank down with a sigh. "I wish there was some way to tell her that. I know she's probably worried, although she never mentioned him in her wire."

Tait took the seat across from her and laid his crutch on the rug beside his chair. Resting his elbows on the armrests, he studied the elderly woman. "You have no way to contact her?"

"How could I? She's always traveling. Until she reaches the mountains and settles in one place for a time, I won't know where to send a letter or even a wire."

Tait thought for a moment, plotting her route in his mind. If she went west out of St. Louis toward Kansas City, she could take the Kansas Pacific all the way to Colorado Territory. Once there, she might have to take small branch lines farther west, or even a stagecoach here or there. But if she hadn't tarried along the way, it was possible she could be nearing the Rocky Mountains any day now.

"Do you think she'll stop when she reaches the mountains?" he asked.

"Possibly. We spoke of it, but she never said for certain."

They sat for a time without speaking. Tait contemplated the strange alliance he had formed with this stubborn old woman. It was obvious a strong bond existed between her and Lucinda, and Tait admired her sense of loyalty. But until the person who sent Smythe was in the ground, too, Lucinda would never be completely safe.

"Did Margaret ever mention a man named Franklin Horne?" Tait remembered Lucinda asking about him that last night on the train, but she hadn't told him why. In fact, she'd shied away from the subject when he'd pressed.

"The gentleman rumored to be seeking the governorship?"

"That's the one."

Mrs. Throckmorton gave it some thought, then shook her head. "She may have mentioned the name once. But I don't remember what she said, or even if it's the same man. This old memory fails me sometimes, you know."

Tait smiled to reassure her. "It's not important. By the way," he added, watching her carefully, "I went by Father O'Rourke's church today. A priest told me he was in Ireland and may not be back for several months."

"Is he?" Mrs. Throckmorton stared down at her clenched hands. "I wasn't aware."

An evasion if he ever saw one. Leaning forward in the chair, Tait gave her a hard look. "So unless there's someone else I might ask, ma'am, you're the only one who can answer my questions about Margaret."

The frail hands clenched tighter. "I told you I cannot."

Defeated, he sat back.

"But if she sends me a way to contact her," she offered after a moment, "I will ask her if you can correspond directly with her. Then you can ask your questions, yourself."

Tait sighed. "Then let's hope she writes soon. I have a feeling once this unknown enemy realizes Smythe is dead, he'll send somebody else after her."

Thirteen

"Two weeks. Here. Surely they're jesting." Ignoring the men gawking from the windows of the Red Eye Saloon, Lucinda set her two valises down on the boardwalk in front of the Heartbreak Creek Hotel and looked around.

It was scarcely even a town. A string of unpainted buildings—many of which were boarded up—along a single street sandwiched between a rocky canyon wall on one side and a tumbling creek on the other. A second set of structures—mostly patched tents and tilting lean-tos—sat deeper in the canyon where the creek spilled down a rocky slope. High above it, the spindly scaffolds of a mining operation clung precariously to a thousand-foot-tall rock face.

"I wonder what they mine," Maddie said, squinting up at the figures moving about on the high platforms.

"Nothing lucrative. This place is one breath away from being a ghost town."

"A ghost town! How marvelous."

As the other passengers stepped off the wagon that had transported them from the stranded train five miles beyond the mouth of the canyon, Lucinda asked Maddie to watch her cases, and marched over to the conductor, who stood in the open double doorway into the hotel, shuffling through his passenger list.

"Does this happen often?" she asked.

He looked up, his gray brows drawn in a line above a bulbous red-veined nose that proclaimed him a drinker. "What?"

Raising her voice over the tinkling piano music coming from the Red Eye Saloon next door, she said, "The trestle washing out. Does it happen often?"

"Every spring. Name?"

"Then why don't you reroute? Why not come through the canyon here?"

He scowled at her, clearly out of patience. "Have you tasted the water in Heartbreak Creek?"

"Not yet, but—"

"Trains run on coal and water. You fill the tenders with water as hard as what flows through this town, the pipes and valves and gauges would be fouled in a week. Name?"

Realizing she would get no more from him, Lucinda gave her name.

He read carefully down the list, stuck the tip of his tongue past the gray mustache that looped around to join equally bushy sideburns, primed his pencil with spit, then marked off her name. "Go on inside, ma'am. Yancey there at the front desk will give you a key."

Lucinda glanced through the open doors, grimacing with distaste at the peeling wallpaper, frayed carpets, and stained upholstery on the worn chairs scattered around the lobby. "Is there indoor plumbing?"

"Of course," he said, with some indignation. "A full water closet and bathtub on the ground floor."

"Only the one?"

Clearly offended, he didn't bother to answer. "If you'll move on so others can—"

"Have they any suites with two bedrooms?"

"One, I think. Number twenty. But it costs double, and the railroad won't pay it. You'll get a regular shared room like all the other—"

"Number Twenty will do nicely," Lucinda cut in with her best smile. "I will happily share it with three other women, which should not add to the cost for the railroad. Thank you so much, you've been most helpful." Then before the harried man could argue, she turned and walked back to where Maddie stood guard over their valises and her photography equipment.

"I hope it's acceptable with you to share quarters with two other women," she said as she picked up her valises. "The place is questionable, and I thought we might at least have safety in numbers."

"Not at all," Maddie said cheerfully. "Perhaps we could ask the two ladies we met earlier—the mail-order bride and her Negro traveling companion?"

"Precisely what I was thinking."

An odd pair, Edwina and Prudence. Both were southerners, which might account for it. Apparently in her desperation to escape the excesses of the reconstruction in Louisiana, Edwina had answered an advertisement in the *Matrimonial News* placed by a Colorado widower with four children. Having married the man in a proxy ceremony, she was now suffering grave doubts about her decision.

Lucinda didn't blame her. Her own recent experience with Tait had only strengthened her belief that men were intractable, unforgiving creatures incapable of viewing the world through any perspective other than their own. She couldn't imagine the disappointments awaiting poor Edwina at the hands of a complete stranger. At least she would have Prudence, her traveling companion, beside her for moral support.

But by the time she and Maddie made it into the hotel lobby, Edwina and Prudence had already received their assigned room and were stepping up to the front desk to be issued their key.

"Room number?" the grizzled clerk asked.

"Twenty," Lucinda answered, cutting in front of them with an apologetic smile. "I hope you don't mind sharing a suite with Maddie and me," she added in a whisper. "It'll be safer with four of us." Without waiting for a response, she turned to the slack-faced clerk. "Where do I sign?"

The man gaped and sputtered and stuttered. It was intriguing to watch, considering the gaps in his rust-stained teeth. "But that—that's the Presidential Suite," he finally managed. "And you're not the president."

"Alas, no." Another broad smile, a deep breath that brought his gaze to her bosom, followed by one small lie, and they were heading up the stairs behind Billy, the freckle-faced bellboy, who was laden with fresh linens and a pitcher of the murky water they had been warned not to drink.

"Are you really Ulysses Grant's niece?" Edwina asked as they neared the "big suite" at the end of the hall.

Lucinda laughed. "That old drunk?" Ignoring Edwina's look of puzzlement, Lucinda stepped into their suite, relieved to find it in surprisingly better condition than the rest of the hotel— probably because of the rarity of presidential visits to Heart-break Creek.

"Is this the water we're not supposed to drink?" Edwina asked, peering down into the pitcher the bellboy had left on the bureau.

"I'll stick with brandy," Lucinda muttered, moving toward the bedroom she and Maddie would be sharing. She would have preferred champagne but doubted there was such a thing in Heartbreak Creek.

On her way past, Maddie stopped beside the pitcher, took a look, and shuddered. "It looks used. How vexing."

"I wonder what's wrong with it?" Edwina asked with that puzzled look again. "With a creek running right through the middle of town, how can the water be so bad?"

"Probably the mine." Prudence hung her coat on a hook beside the door and straightened the cuffs on her dress. She was always fussing with something, Lucinda had noticed. "They often use harsh chemicals," she went on in her low, melodious voice, "to leach gold or silver from the raw ore. If it seeps back into the ground, it can taint the entire water table."

Edwina stared at her companion. "How do you know these things?"

"I read."

Watching through the open doorway of the bedroom she was to share with Maddie, Lucinda had to smile. Never having had a close friend until meeting Maddie, she found their gentle bick-ering amusing. The two acted more like sisters than compan-ions, although they seemed opposites in every way. Edwina Brodie, thin almost to the point of brittleness, her lively blue eyes so filled with life her energy seemed to charge the room. Prudence Lincoln, calmer, despite her fussy attention to details that betrayed her need for order. More prone to thought than reckless action, Pru seemed highly intelligent and well edu-cated, in addition to being one of the most beautiful women Lucinda had ever seen. She might once have been part of Edwi-na's southern household, but Lucinda doubted the woman had ever been a slave. There was something about her and the way she carried herself. Pride, perhaps. Or a lack of illusion. Prudence struck Lucinda as a woman who knew her place in a white-dominated male world, but rightly placed her self-worth much higher.

Impulsive, high-spirited Edwina and thoughtful, fastidious Prudence. Lucinda liked them both.

"Why would you read about mining practices?" Edwina asked, clearly astounded that anyone would find the subject in the least interesting.

"Why wouldn't I?" As she spoke, Prudence set herself to rights, straightening her sleeves, brushing her skirts, running a hand over her tightly pinned hair. "I'm only guessing, of course. But since the mine is upriver of the town, and I did see some sluices and a thick canvas pipe running down from one of those waterfalls to what I assume is a concentrator, I can only deduce the water is being used to leach out unwanted chemicals." She paused in thought, one long, graceful finger gently tapping her full lower lip. "Or maybe it's for a water cannon. I'll have to check."

"Oh, please do." Shaking her head, Edwina walked into the bedroom she was to share with her Negro companion.

An hour later, their clothing unpacked, their beds made, and as refreshed as four women could be sharing one pitcher of cold water between them, Lucinda marched back into the sitting room with her valise in hand and Maddie on her heels. "We're famished," she announced. "Shall we brave the cooking in this place and go down to the dining room?"

"Dare we?" Edwina asked.

Prudence straightened her collar and checked her buttons. "I'm willing."

"Excellent."

It was far from excellent. But at least the company was enjoyable.

When they returned after choking down the barely edible meal of something mostly brown, they found a folded note had been shoved beneath the door. It bore the name Edwina Brodie, written in bold script.

"Who is it from?" Prudence asked, as Edwina bent to pick it up.

"Not bad news, I hope." With a deep sigh, Maddie sank into one of the worn wingbacks by the flyspecked window. "I deplore bad news."

"Do you, Miss Ever Cheerful? How odd." Grinning, Lucinda took the other chair. But seeing the stricken expression on Edwina's face, her smile faded. "What's wrong?"

"He's here," she burst out, shaking the note in a tight fist as if she had whoever "he" was by the scruff of his neck. "And he expects me to meet him outside the hotel tomorrow morning. Tomorrow!"

Maddie turned to Lucinda. "I'm assuming she means her husband-by-proxy."

Edwina had told them about her mail-order husband, Declan Brodie, and his four children, and her growing reservations about marrying a stranger. Maddie had tried to reassure her by explaining that arranged marriages were not uncommon in Britain. "Although mine wasn't, of course. Ours was a love match."

"And see how well that turned out," Lucinda had remarked, adding, "Married or not, men are as steadfast as a loose woman's virtue."

"What should I do?" Edwina asked now in a quavering voice.

"Run," Lucinda advised.

"Meet him," Maddie countered. "He deserves at least that."

"Pack," Prudence said flatly. Moving to the wardrobe in their bedroom, she pulled out her carpetbag from beneath the bed and began folding garments inside.

Watching her, Lucinda realized that after their departure tomorrow, she might never see either woman again. The notion saddened her more than she would have thought. Sharing their company for this short while had been a novel and delightful experience. The prospect of losing Maddie's companionship at some point in the future was even more depressing.

Edwina smoothed out the note and studied it again. "Perhaps he just wants to talk. Pay his respects. Perhaps he doesn't intend to actually leave tomorrow." She looked hopefully at Lucinda and Maddie. "That sounds reasonable, doesn't it?"

Lucinda shrugged.

"What does he say exactly?" Maddie asked.

"'Eight o'clock in the morning outside the hotel. Brodie.'"

"Chatty fellow, isn't he?" Lucinda said drily.

"Twelve hours. That's all I have left."

"It could be a grand adventure," Maddie consoled. "This marriage might be all you've ever dreamed."

To sweet Maddie, every cloud was woven with golden threads and sprinkled with diamonds. Lucinda wondered how much of it was a front to mask her disappointment in her own lonely situation. "Surely you don't believe that, Maddie," she challenged, unable to let it pass. "Have you ever seen a truly happy couple?"

"Angus and I might have been, had he ever stayed around long enough for us to get to know one another."

"Or you might have been utterly miserable. Three letters and one visit in six years. The man should be shot."

"Maybe he was. Maybe that's why he hasn't written." Maddie sent Lucinda a worried look. "Surely I would have been notified if he had been, don't you think? I wouldn't want him to be dead."

Edwina wandered into the bedroom and plopped down on the bed beside the valise Prudence was packing. "Why is he in such a hurry?" she complained. "He could have waited a few more days."

With a deep sigh, she flopped back across the ratty counterpane. "Such haste is unseemly. I'm not a cow to be herded around. I'm a gently bred lady."

"You're a nitwit," Prudence muttered. "That's why we're here."

"Nonetheless, I deserve better. I had better."

"You've been married before?" Maddie called.

"And she's doing it a second time?" Lucinda muttered.

"We married just as the war broke out," Edwina said, staring up at the stained ceiling. "Shelley was such a sweet boy. And so handsome in his sword and sash."

"One does get pulled in by the uniform," Maddie mused. "Angus is with the Tenth Hussars. Assuming he's still alive. What happened to your Shelley?"

"He marched off the day after our wedding, only to return four months later, minus a leg and dying of a hideous infection. It near broke my heart." Her voice cracked. "Oh, why did everything have to change? I wish that wretched war had never happened."

Prudence paused in her packing to look at her.

"Except for the slavery thing," Edwina amended with a half-hearted wave of one hand. "Naturally I wanted that to stop."

"We English ended that nasty practice years ago, thank heavens," Maddie said.

"After," Lucinda pointed out, "you introduced that nasty practice here."

"No matter how it ended," Prudence cut in, "on behalf of freed slaves everywhere, I just thank the Lord it's over."

"On behalf of Yankees everywhere," Lucinda quipped, "you're welcome."

"Ha!" Sitting up, Edwina glared at her traveling companion. "You were never a slave, Pru, and don't pretend you were."

"My mother was."

"And our father was a slave to her."

Our? Lucinda saw the warning look pass between the two women and finally understood. They were half sisters, sharing the same father. That explained the strong bond between them.

"Please, Pru," Edwina said, wearily. "Let's not get into that again. The war's been over for five years. There's even a man of color in Congress. Can't we finally put slavery to rest?"

"Half color. And Mr. Revels was never a slave." Pausing in her folding, Pru looked at the far wall, her expression troubled. "I try. But then I see all those bewildered Africans wandering through the towns we pass, and I get angry all over again. They can't read or write, Edwina, and some barely speak English. They have no training to start new lives. Someone should help them—do something to right that terrible wrong."

Edwina flopped back again. Lucinda hoped the lacy cobwebs on the stained ceiling that swung to and fro over her face weren't inhabited. "I just want to put it all behind me," the southerner said in a wobbly voice. "All that pain and death. I don't want to think about all those new graves. Is that so wrong? To want to leave the past behind and start over?"

Wasn't that what they were all trying to do? Lucinda wondered. Maddie, deserting her neglectful Scottish soldier to start a new life; Edwina and Pru, fleeing the destruction of their entire way of life; herself, trying to escape her aborted marriage and memories of her dalliance with Tait?

Escape? Who was she trying to fool? Tait still hovered in the back of her mind. He haunted her nights and plagued her days. She would never be able to leave the memories of him behind.

"No, love, it isn't." Sinking onto the edge of the bed, Prudence patted Edwina's hand. "I'm just not sure marrying a man you never met is the way to go about it."

"Well, what choice did I have?" Edwina complained, sitting up again. "A Klansman or a carpetbagger. It seems all the men I knew were either married, so defeated they couldn't go on, or so angry they couldn't let the killing end. I can't live like that any longer. I won't."

Prudence rose and resumed packing. "Eldridge Blankenship was unmarried and was neither Klansman nor carpetbagger. He would have made a fine husband."

"Or a beaver," Edwina argued. "Did you see those teeth? Besides, he wanted children."

Maddie tipped her head to study Edwina through the open door. "You don't want children?"

Edwina shrugged.

Lucinda had a sudden image of Tait struggling with the preventative. All those muscles, all that athleticism and intelligence, defeated by a little piece of rubber. She had to smile, even as something shifted deep inside her at the memory. How could he just walk away without even giving her a chance to explain?

"How do you plan to stop them from coming?" Maddie asked.

Angry with where her thoughts had taken her, Lucinda gave a bitter laugh. "Oh, there are ways. A man named Charles Goodyear has invented a rubber sheath that fits over—"

"Lucinda Hathaway!" Prudence gave her a look that would have done her name proud. "I cannot believe you would discuss such a thing!"

"Fits over what?" Maddie asked. Then her eyes went round. "My word! You're talking about French letters, aren't you? They're made of rubber? I thought they were made of linen or silk or animal intestines."

"Intestines? Good Lord. You Scots truly are backward."

"I'm English, Lucinda, as well you know."

"Be that as it may, rubber sheaths have been around for at least a decade." In fact, she still had an unopened packet that

Tait had left on the train. She wasn't sure why she'd kept it. "Apparently neither you nor your Scottish husband ever used one."

"There was no need."

"No need? You mean you didn't—"

"Of course we did," Maddie cut in. "Many times. In the same day, in fact. But prevention wasn't an issue. I wanted children very much."

"You two astound me."

Lucinda looked over to see Edwina peering wistfully through the bedroom doorway. "Why?"

"You say whatever you want. Travel where and when the mood strikes you. Follow your dreams wherever they take you. Instead of just being someone's wife."

"Oh, being a wife isn't so bad," Maddie allowed. "I rather liked it. Until he abandoned me to his family and left, of course. Ghastly man, that earl."

"Earl?" Edwina sounded shocked. "You're married to an earl?"

"His father is the earl. Angus is only third in line, which is why he is in the military, of course."

"Edwina, you wouldn't last two minutes on your own," Prudence said, responding to her earlier remark. "You can't even cook."

"Who cooks?" Maddie said airily. "I'm sure your new husband will be delighted with you, Edwina, whether you can cook or not."

Lucinda smiled sadly, her mind slipping back into rose-scented memories even as a bittersweet pain wrapped around her heart. Would Tait have cared that she couldn't cook? Would he have expected her to fit into the perfect wifely mold, as Doyle had? Or would he have welcomed her insights and ideas?

Sadly, she would never know.

"I shall miss them," Maddie said later that night as she and Lucinda prepared for bed.

They had already said their good-byes to Edwina and Prudence, and even Lucinda was battling a feeling of loss. How odd that after going most of her life without close friends, she would become so quickly attached to these women she barely knew. "We're supposed to be stranded here for at least two weeks. Perhaps they'll come back to town during that time."

"Why would they bother? As you said, this place is a ghost town."

Lucinda moved to stand at the window that overlooked the dirt road behind the hotel. A full moon highlighted a sheen of seeping water on the canyon wall behind the creek and gave a pale, angular shape to the canvas awning outside the Chinese laundry. Except for light spilling through the rear window of the Red Eye Saloon next door and lamplight in the office of the livery several buildings down, the town looked deserted. Yet the plinking of an untuned piano drifted in pine-scented air that was blessedly free of coal smoke and rotting garbage, and every now and then she could hear the call of a night bird. Not since Ireland had she seen a night so quiet. There was a peaceful feeling to it.

"It's too bad," she mused. "This could be a pretty little town if somehow it could be made prosperous again."

"It certainly has character," Maddie agreed, coming to stand beside her at the window. "Everywhere I look, something of interest catches my eye. I hope we stay long enough to order more supplies. I would hate to miss such a wonderful photographic opportunity."

"I suppose we don't have to leave when the trestle is rebuilt," Lucinda said, surprising herself almost as much as she seemed to have surprised Maddie. But why not stay awhile? She needed a place to stay—hide, really—until she found out if Smythe was still trailing her, and no one—certainly not Doyle and his Pinkertons—would ever think to look in a place this far away from civilization. And for some unfathomable reason, she actually liked this dismal little town. If she were given to whimsy, she might even think it needed her.

Or, perhaps she needed it. An interesting thought.

"You're serious, aren't you?"

Lucinda shrugged. "It's not as if we have anywhere else to go just now, so why not stay as long as we want? You can have your supplies sent here, and meanwhile, when Edwina and Prudence come to town for supplies as surely they must, we can find out how Edwina's arranged marriage is going, and if Prudence has been able to teach her to cook, and what the children are like. I certainly don't have any pressing reason to keep heading west at the moment. In fact, I'd enjoy a rest from that bouncing train. How about you?"

Maddie didn't even give it a thought. "I adore the idea. Let's do it!"

"Excellent. We'll tell Edwina and Pru in the morning."

But they overslept, and when Lucinda saw the other bedroom was empty, she thought they were too late. Then she noted the traveling cases stacked inside the sitting room door waiting for Billy, the bellboy, to carry them down, and realized her friends hadn't yet left. "Wake up," she said to Maddie as she quickly changed out of her night clothes. "They're still here. If we hurry, we'll be able to see them before they go."

They were just about to rush out the door when Prudence came in, trailed by Billy. "He's here," she said with a breathless grin. "And oh my goodness. Edwina is in for it now."

"What does that mean?" Maddie asked, tossing a shawl around her shoulders.

"You'll see."

A moment later, they trooped down the stairs to find Edwina leaning across the front desk, whispering to the clerk, Yancey. Other than a big man skulking in the open double doorway, the lobby was empty.

Lucinda studied him, thinking he looked a little like the man in the tintype Edwina had shown them last night, insomuch as both men had dark hair and eyes, and neither seemed capable of smiling. But instead of wearing a banded drover shirt and a dark coat like in the tiny photograph, this man wore a battered sheepskin jacket over an unbleached work shirt and worn denims, and a three-day growth of dark beard on his scowling, square-jawed face.

"Is that her husband?" Maddie whispered.

"God help her if it is."

He stalked forward, spared them barely a glance, and said to Edwina, "You ready? The washout and a busted wheel have already cost me an extra day. I need to get back. Now." Picking up the valises, he turned toward the door.

Edwina's lips pinched tight.

"We're right behind you, sir," Prudence answered, shoving Edwina forward.

"You poor thing," Lucinda muttered, falling into step behind them.

"Oh, it's not so bad," Maddie whispered. "I think your husband is rather handsome, Edwina. And big, like Angus."

"He's not my husband."

Pru stopped pushing. "He's not?"

Edwina giggled. "That's Big Bob." She drew out the name, adding a flourish, like a barker at a county fair announcing the prize hog. "At least, that's what Yancey called him. I assume he's been sent to fetch us." Seeing Pru's frown, she quickly added, "But don't fret. The clerk said he was once a sheriff, so we'll be fine. I think." Turning, she gave hugs to Maddie and Lucinda. "I shall miss you," she said, blinking hard.

"Me, too," Lucinda murmured, quickly pulling back, always uncomfortable with emotional displays.

"But not for long," Maddie announced. "Since we're staying. We decided last night."

"Staying? Here? In Heartbreak Creek?"

"Only for a while," Lucinda warned, even though she couldn't help but smile at the befuddled expressions on their friends' faces.

"But why?" Edwina asked.

"Why not?" Maddie grinned and looked around, her eyes alight with excitement. "This is the perfect place to start my photographic expedition. The real West. And besides, I have to order more supplies and it might be a month before they reach me. And this way, if Luce and I stay together, rather than traveling on alone, we'll both be safer."

"And also," Lucinda added, with a nod toward the tall figure heading down the boardwalk, "if this foolish proxy marriage of yours doesn't work out, we'll be close by to spirit you away."

Fourteen

As had become his habit soon after returning to Manhattan, Tait called on Mrs. Throckmorton several times a week. He told himself it was because he enjoyed her lively company and acerbic remarks. Plus, he often dined there, and Mrs. Throckmorton set a fine table. But in truth, his main reason for stopping by so often was because the old lady was his only link to Lucinda and it was his hope that when Lucinda finally gave her guardian a way to communicate with her, he might be able to establish a correspondence with the woman he had so wrongly accused.

His foul behavior preyed heavily on him. He had overreacted badly. Probably because his feelings that night had been a confusing mix of guilt and lust and something he still couldn't define. He remembered awakening to the rose-perfumed dawn, wondering what he should do now and how he should settle this with Doyle, and how he could have lost so much of himself to a woman about whom he knew so little. Such indecisiveness was abhorrent to him, and in that moment of confusion, he had lashed out at her rather than at himself. He had to tell her that and try to mend the damage he had done.

But first he had to find out where she was.

"You took your time getting here," Mrs. Throckmorton complained when she entered the front receiving room on a bright afternoon during the second week in May. Then seeing Tait's look of confusion, she gave a huff of exasperation. "You didn't receive my message, did you? I vow I'll cast that Pringle out on the street. You hear that, Pringle?"

"Thank you, madam," came the muffled reply as footfalls shuffled slowly toward the back of the house.

Waving away Tait's offer of assistance, she propped her cane against the armrest of her chair and sank into the cushioned upholstery.

Tait did the same with his cane and settled across from her. He had given up the crutch a week ago. Although his knee was still weak, as long as he kept it wrapped and took care on stairs, he got by. But he doubted he'd ever run again.

"You have news?" He tried to keep from sounding too anxious. It had been almost a month since Lucinda's telegram to Mrs. Throckmorton. Tait was starting to worry that something might have happened.

"I do. And you may not like it." Reaching into her pocket, she pulled out an envelope. But instead of giving it to him, she spread it flat on her lap. "Three weeks ago, not long after your first visit, I received another wire from Margaret, telling me she was fine and that she was anxious to hear from me. She included an address where I could reach her."

Tait sat upright. "Three weeks ago? Why didn't you—"

"Calm yourself." She waved him back into his chair. "I know I said I would give you her direction as soon as I heard from her. But how could I do that without her permission? Margaret is a very private person."

He knew that well enough. Biting back his frustration, Tait motioned to the letter in her lap. "Is that her response? What does she say?"

"She's in a safe place. A small mining town in the mountains. Her English friend is with her, so she's not entirely alone."

"Where?" he demanded. He needed to write to her straight away. Words were already forming in his head. Questions, regrets, apologies. The need to talk to her, even by letter, was burning a hole in his mind. "Where can I write to her?"

"She asked me not to tell you."

Tait blinked. "What?"

"I will read what she wrote in regard to you. If you wish to respond, you may include your pages with mine when I write back to her. I'm sorry, but that's the best I can do."

"She actually said I couldn't correspond directly with her?" She gave him a pitying look.

Damnit! He would have lurched from the chair if he'd thought his knee would hold him. How could she shut him out this way? Why wouldn't she at least listen to what he had to say?

But wasn't that precisely what he had done to her?

Christ. With a sigh, he slumped back, his hands gripping the armrests. He'd hear what she wrote, then send a response back. It rankled to have to go through her guardian, but he would do it, and gladly, if that was his only choice. "Read it, then. Please."

Mrs. Throckmorton unfolded the letter, scanned down several lines, then began. "'I was sorry to hear that Mr. Rylander was injured.'" Pausing, the old lady looked up to explain, "I told her that you and Smythe had fought, and that when you fell off the train, you were injured."

Tait nodded, and waved for her to continue.

"'Please tell him I appreciate his efforts on my behalf.'" Another pause. "Of course, I didn't tell her that Smythe was dead, since at the time I wrote, you hadn't yet heard from Mr. Yoder. Nor did I mention that Smythe had been sent by someone else to silence her. Until we have further information, I think it's best not to add to her worries, don't you agree?"

Just read the damned letter, Tait wanted to shout. "Yes. Continue, please."

She looked back through the script to find her place. "Here comes the part about you. 'But I must warn you to be wary of him,' she writes. 'Mr. Rylander has a charming and amiable way about him that invites trust. But there is also an unyielding, unforgiving side of his nature that prevents him from seeing any view of the world other than his own.'"

Mrs. Throckmorton sighed and shook her head. "I think that's rather harsh of her, don't you?"

Tait forced a smile, even though impatience was churning in his gut.

"Yes, well." Clearing her throat, she continued. "'I had counted him a trusted friend but was deeply disappointed to learn he held no trust in me, which caused us to part on less than cordial terms. For that reason, please do not give him my direction. I am starting a wonderful new life here and have no wish to drag into it any unpleasantness from the past.'" Mrs. Throckmorton set down the letter and gave Tait a look of regret. "I'm sorry, Mr. Rylander."

Unpleasantness? Their parting was probably the worst day in his life—other than when he was shot and hanged, of course. He had insulted the woman who had haunted his thoughts for a year, fought a knife-wielding brute on the back of a moving train to protect her, then had taken a fall that would probably leave him permanently crippled. And now she wouldn't even speak to him?

He had never met a more hardheaded woman.

It was probably a good thing she wasn't standing in front of him. He might have shaken her hard enough to loosen her teeth. "That's it?" he managed through tight lips, a rebuttal to those absurd statements already forming in his mind. "That's all she wrote?"

"Oh, she goes on about her friend—did I tell you she was a photographer? I've never heard of such a thing, but Margaret seems to like her very much. Apparently she's estranged from her husband, a Scottish soldier or some such. They've also befriended two other women, half sisters, one of whom is Negro—can you imagine that scandal?—and the other who is a mail-order bride to a rancher with four children. Southerners, both, so I guess we shouldn't be surprised. Oh, do forgive me—I forgot you're southern, too. At any rate, Margaret is apparently doing well, and we should be happy about that."

Something in Tait's expression caused the elderly woman to reach over and pat his hand. "Don't be too disappointed, Mr. Rylander. After all, she did say you were charming and amiable, didn't she?"

Tait showed his teeth in what he hoped would pass for a smile. "Yes, she did. Bless her heart."

The next day he returned to the Sixty-ninth Street brownstone with several pages of script sealed in a small envelope. "When will you be posting this?" he asked as he handed it to Mrs. Throckmorton. He hoped she didn't intend to delegate the task to her irascible butler. Pringle was beyond incompetent.

The crafty old lady gave him a sly look. "And I suppose

you're hoping I'll give it to you to post so you can take a peek at the address."

"Not at all," Tait lied. It was disturbing that he was so transparent even a doddering old lady could see through him. But he'd been greatly distracted of late, fretting over this thing with Lucinda, positioning himself to end his partnership with Doyle while still staying close enough to learn what the Irishman intended to do about his runaway bride, and trying to figure out who had sent Smythe. His life had fallen into such disarray he wasn't sure what he was doing, or where he was headed half the time. But he sensed that everything in his future hinged on Lucinda. And that disturbed him most of all.

"By the way," Mrs. Throckmorton said, regaining his attention. "I've been thinking about that man you asked about. That politician, Franklin Horne. And I do think Margaret mentioned him. Right after the wedding, in fact."

"What did she say?"

"I don't remember her exact words, but as I recall, it was something about overhearing two men talking about Kerrigan being a runner in his youth. One of them was Franklin Horne, and she said he and Smythe were cut from the same cloth. She seemed quite upset about it. Does that help?"

"It might." Or it would if he knew what Smythe's connection to Lucinda had been. But so far, neither Lucinda nor her guardian nor the absent Father O'Rourke had told him anything.

"I shall post this today," Mrs. Throckmorton said, slipping his letter into her pocket. "But don't expect an immediate reply. Even with mail going by rail now, it takes time. And she may not answer you. For such a gentle-appearing creature, Margaret can be quite strong-minded at times."

Tait nodded, well aware of that trait but finding it strangely appealing—when it wasn't directed at him.

Almost three weeks after her arrival in Heartbreak Creek, Lucinda awoke with an idea blossoming in her mind. The seed had been planted that first day when she and Maddie had decided to stay on in Heartbreak Creek. It had quietly germinated since then, and now that the railroad trestle had been repaired and the other passengers had moved on, it burst into full bloom.

Rising from the bed, she went to the window of the bedroom in the Presidential Suite that she had taken over after Edwina and Pru had left. It was another lovely day. The clarity of the skies in Colorado Territory never ceased to amaze her. She had never seen such a vibrant blue, and there was so little haze in the air she could see for miles once she left the narrow confines of the high canyon walls. Despite the ramshackle appearance of the town, the surrounding landscape was shockingly beautiful— high peaks, stark bluffs, and tall, stately firs and spruces crowded against the frothy creek. And east of town, where the canyon widened into a long rolling valley that stretched all the way to distant slopes, the view seemed to go on forever. For a woman who had spent so many years locked in a city, the openness of it struck a chord within her.

Smiling, she thought of Mrs. Throckmorton and how drawn her guardian seemed to be toward this country. It wasn't surprising. The Rocky Mountains were magnificent—raw and savage and untamed—a stark contrast to the gentler peaks of the Appalachians. At times the sheer size and scope of these mountains seemed a bit intimidating, yet, despite that, she felt a kinship here, a sense of belonging. Perhaps because everything was new and untainted by the past, or because the vastness of it hinted at limitless possibilities, or because the challenge of it called to her spirit. Whatever the reason, it breathed life into her.

And hope.

Here, she could start over for the last time, and maybe, in doing so, she could find the home she'd been seeking. But first, even if it took every dollar she'd gained from the railroad shares, she would have to create a home worth having.

Resolved, she hurriedly dressed, then tiptoeing past Maddie's closed door, went downstairs.

"Yancey," she said, rousing the elderly man from a doze behind the front desk. "Who owns this hotel?"

The old man yawned and squinted an eye and scratched at his bald pate. Thinking was always a chore for Yancey. "Used to be owned by a fellow from Denver. But last I heard the bank took it over. Might ought to check with Emmet Gebbers."

"The mayor?"

Lucinda had met most of the people in town when she and

Maddie had attended services at the Come All You Sinners
Church of Heartbreak Creek. Pastor Rickman and his wife,
Biddy, had proudly introduced them to the choir ladies; the
mayor and his wife; a handful of merchants and ranch families;
Doc Boyce and his wife, Janet; and the few miners from the
Krigbaum Mine who didn't spend all their free time in Red Eye
Saloon. It wasn't a robust community.

"Emmet's also the banker," Yancey told her. "Heard he and
the missus used to be missionaries, but after they lost their only
son in the war, they sort of lost the calling. Yep. I think the bank
owns the hotel now. Why you asking? Know someone who
might be interested in taking it over?"

"I might." Smiling, she turned toward the wide hallway leading toward the dining room. "If Mrs. Wallace comes down, tell
her to join me for coffee."

"Think whoever buys it might still let me work here?" he
called after her.

"You never know."

A while later, when Miriam—the maid, cook's helper, waitress, and general workhorse of the hotel—came to clear the
dishes, she handed Lucinda a thick envelope Yancey said had
just been delivered by the mail courier from Denver.

Lucinda recognized the spidery handwriting as that of Mrs.
Throckmorton. Delighted, she tore open the seal. A second
envelope fell out, along with several sheets of script in her
guardian's hand. She stared in consternation at the name
Lucinda written in bold letters across the second envelope. Only
one person acquainted with her guardian knew her as Lucinda.
Heart pounding, she set it aside and opened Mrs. Throckmorton's missive first.

May 1870

My dearest daughter,
    *I hope this finds you in good health and spirits. I am
glad you are making new friends—but a mail-order bride
and her mixed-blood sister? Even for Southerners, that
seems a bit eccentric, don't you think? The Englishwoman
sounds nice, although regrettably near to being a blue-
stocking.*

Maddie? Hardly. Prudence, perhaps. She was certainly the smartest.

> *As you instructed, I did not give Mr. Rylander your direction, but have allowed him to enclose his pages with mine. I do not know what caused the rift between you, but he seems anxious to mend it. I advise you to consider what he has to say, especially in regards to the dangers that surround you.*

Lucinda frowned. What dangers? Was Smythe still after her?

> *Since his return to Manhattan, Mr. Rylander has become a frequent visitor in my home. I find him most pleasant—much more so than that Irish hooligan—and I am convinced he has only your best interests at heart.*

Ha! Don't believe it. He's simply trying to wheedle information from you.

> *The weather has been quite unsettled of late, with heavy rains and high winds that have caused my old bones to ache. Cook has been ill with a bad cold this past week, and Pringle remains his usual irascible self. Were he not so enamored of me, I would be forced to let him go. I am simply too soft of heart, I suppose.*

Lucinda chuckled. Since when?

> *Do please tell me more about your beautiful mountains in your next letter, my dear, so I can picture you standing before them in my mind.*

> *As always your devoted guardian,*
> *Ida Throckmorton*

Lucinda carefully folded the letter and tried to breathe past the clog of homesickness that gripped her throat. She vowed that someday, when all this was behind her, she would bring the dear woman to Colorado to see these magnificent mountains for herself.

But homesickness quickly changed to anxious anticipation when she broke the seal on the second letter. With trembling fingers, she unfolded the pages and began to read.

Lucinda—

No salutation, no date, only her name. Arrogant toad.

> *You call me unforgiving? If so, then it is a trait we seem to share. But in my defense, please allow me to express my deepest regrets for my reprehensible behavior when last we were together. I offer no excuses for there are none that would justify the cruelty of my parting words.*

He was certainly right about that, at least.

> *I can only say that, as usual, you caught me off-balance. You're very good at that.*

So now he's saying it was her fault? Ridiculous.

> *And although my final statement was true—I still don't know who you are—over the weeks since I made that ill-advised comment, I have come to realize that who you are— or were—is not as important as it once was. Not because I no longer care—you know that's impossible, don't you?— but because it no longer relates to your safety.*
> *Smythe is dead.*

Air rushed from her lungs. Dead? Smythe? Lucinda let the letter fall to her lap and pressed a hand over her racing heart. When? How? Had Tait killed him when they fought on the train? With trembling hands, she lifted the letter again.

> *I only recently learned he did not survive our fall from the train. And even though he is no longer a danger to you, the man who sent him to silence you still is.*

What man? Doyle? Horne? Staring blankly out the dining room window, Lucinda probed her mind for a reason why Doyle

Kerrigan, or Franklin Horne, or anyone else would want to "silence" her. Had she seen or heard something at the engagement party or at the wedding that she didn't even remember? Or did it go all the way back to those terrifying days at Mrs. Beale's? But what? And who? Smythe and Franklin Horne were the only two people still alive that she remembered from that horrible time, and until that shocking moment at the engagement party, she hadn't seen or spoken to Horne in fifteen years. What could she possibly know that would suddenly make her a threat to him? Or anybody?

Unless it wasn't Doyle or Horne who had sent Smythe, but someone else.

Like Mrs. Beale. Perhaps she wasn't dead. If Smythe had survived the fire, maybe that evil woman had, too.

Filled with dread at that thought, Lucinda continued reading.

> *If you are unwilling, or unable, to answer my questions, I will not press you. But be warned I am committed to learning the identity of your pursuer, if only to assure myself of your safety.*

Thank you for that, at least, she told him silently.

> *As for this method of communication through Mrs. Throckmorton—I will, of course, do as you wish in that regard. And although I will also do my best to avoid mention of the extreme closeness we enjoyed during that final unforgettable evening on the train, I cannot be certain a chance word won't alert your guardian should she "accidentally" look through my letters before forwarding them on to you.*

Why, that blackmailer!

> *But be advised, Lucinda. We are not finished, you and I. Unlike your greengrocer's son or Doyle Kerrigan, I will not let you go that easily, nor will I walk away without at least trying to convince you to give me another chance to win your affections.*

Win my affections? After all the pain he caused me? Never!

> *Until then, I will be thinking of you—and the way your skin glowed in the candlelight, and the little sounds you made when my hands moved over your beautiful body.*

> Tait

> *PS: Below is my address should you wish to correspond directly with me, rather than through your guardian. I await your reply.*

That scoundrel! That unrepentant cad! How crass of him to mention—what sounds? The man was incorrigible.

Yet, as she stuffed the letters back into the envelope, she couldn't help but smile. How like him to try to manipulate her, first with flowery apologies, then coercion, and finally, with blatant sexual references.

As if that would work on her.

"What has put you in such a happy mood?" a voice asked.

Startled into another blush, Lucinda looked up to see Maddie coming toward her. She was dressed for photography, with a heavy canvas apron tied over her dress, auburn curls sliding out from beneath her bonnet, and her stained work gloves hanging halfway out of her pocket. "Off to make tintypes?" she asked.

"*Cartes de visite* of the miners. At least until I run out of albumenized paper. Hopefully the supplies I ordered will arrive today. What are you up to?"

"I'm heading over to the bank. I have an investment idea I'd like to discuss with Emmet Gebbers."

Maddie raised her brows in surprise. "Here in Heartbreak Creek?"

"Why not?"

"Does that mean you intend to stay?"

"Perhaps."

Maddie chuckled. "I knew it. You're thinking of buying the hotel, aren't you? I heard you questioning Miriam and Cook the other day. Come." Taking Lucinda's arm, she guided her out of the dining room and across the lobby. "While we walk to the bank, you can tell me why buying a rundown hotel in a near ghost town would appeal to you, of all people."

Lucinda smiled weakly. Maddie's astuteness always caught her off guard. The Englishwoman showed such a carefree, cheerful nature it was easy to assume she harbored few serious thoughts. But Lucinda knew that was patently false. Maddie was quite observant and, with her sharp artist's eye, was often able to see straight to the heart of a matter, while a slower mind might never make the connections. What might appear shallow or even ninny-headed at first glance was actually unguarded honesty. Maddie never hid what she felt and let every emotion show on her expressive face. She was as different from Lucinda as anyone could ever be—and Lucinda loved her for it.

"You think I'm foolish for considering it, don't you?" Lucinda asked as they stepped off the boardwalk and into the dirt street.

"Not at all. You have to be from somewhere, don't you? Why not here? Plus, it's an excellent place to hide."

Lucinda was so distracted by that comment she almost stepped into a fresh pile of horse droppings. "Hide? Who's hiding? I'm not hiding."

That soft chuckle again. "You're on holiday, are you? Shall we expect other New York socialites with valises of money to come knocking on the door?"

Lucinda's distress must have shown, because Maddie's smile faded. Reaching over with her free hand, she gently squeezed the arm linked through hers. "I'm sorry, Luce. I know you detest prying. And whatever your reasons might be for buying the hotel, I fully support you. In fact, I've toyed with the idea of staying in Heartbreak Creek for a while longer, myself."

"You have?"

Maddie nodded. "My publisher has hinted that he is so pleased with my first shipment of portraits and tintypes and panoramic photographs that he might consider lengthening my stay from two years to three. If so, I would need a permanent place—one from which I could venture out on photographic expeditions, and also a place where I could have supplies delivered. The hotel would be perfect."

When they stepped up onto the boardwalk in front of the bank, Lucinda stopped and faced the kind-hearted woman who had become the first and dearest friend she had ever had.

"Heartbreak Creek isn't a terrible place," she said impulsively. "It just needs a helping hand. And I . . ." Her words faltered. It was difficult to admit, even to herself, how much this broken little town had come to mean to her in just a few short weeks. In some odd way she didn't fully understand, she felt a kinship to this poor, dying community of misfits. It was as if in helping to heal Heartbreak Creek, she might also be able to heal herself.

A fanciful notion, to be sure. But still . . .

"We can do good here, Maddie," she burst out. "I have the resources and the business acumen to bring prosperity to this town. You have the artistic vision to make it beautiful again. Together we can make it a place we would both be proud to call home. And I . . ." Again, she faltered.

But Maddie seemed to understand. "And you need a home," she finished with a gentle smile. "As do I. So." Her smile grew until it involved her entire face. Lucinda would have sworn the sun shone out of her lovely brown eyes. "Let's have a go at it, shall we? You and Mr. Gebbers do whatever that business thing is, and I'll document the transformation for the world to see. A town reborn. It has a nice ring to it, does it not?"

"It does."

"Although," Maddie added thoughtfully, "if the mine fails, we'll have to come up with another way to bring prosperity back to Heartbreak Creek."

"I know. And I already have an idea."

"Of course you do. You're brilliant, Luce. I have no doubt you can make this happen. But . . ." She sighed. "There's still the problem of the water."

"There is," Lucinda agreed. "But I have a plan for that, too."

Two hours later, Lucinda left the bank with papers that proclaimed her the proud owner of a rundown hotel and a silent partner in the newly formed Heartbreak Creek Development Company—led by Emmet Gebbers, president and minority stock holder—which already held two deeded right-of-ways through the canyon.

Fifteen

Mr. Rylander—

Despite your insistence that we continue our acquain-tanceship, I advise you to prepare for disappointment. Although our brief encounter was pleasant, in no way should you view it as a commitment toward—or even an interest in—a further relationship. I will never return to Manhattan, and I cannot see a man such as yourself ever making a home away from the city. In addition, a sound friendship must be based upon mutual trust and respect, which I fear is sadly lacking between us.

I regret that you came to harm on my account, and am sorry for any distress Smythe caused you. But now that he is no longer a threat, there should be no need for further contact between us.

I wish you well,
Lucinda Hathaway

PS: And just to be clear—it was you making those sounds, not I. In fact, at the time I thought perhaps you were suffer-ing a mild case of dyspepsia. I'm relieved to learn it was just an overabundance of ardor.

Dyspepsia? Overabundance of ardor?

Tait was so astounded he could only stare at the words until they finally made sense.

Then he began to laugh.

Lucinda—

Dyspepsia aside, it is physically impossible for me to utter notes that high. So unless some mechanism on the undercarriage of our sleeping car was squeaking rhythmically and loudly, I feel certain the noises in questions came from your own person. Not that I am complaining, of course. To bring a woman as guarded as yourself to a full-throated squeal is something in which any man could take pride, and I am certainly no exception.

As to your comment that I would never make a home away from the city, I fear you are wrong about that, as well. I grew up in the shadow of the Smoky Mountains, and can assure you that I have spent many happy times in the wilds. In fact, after hearing Mrs. Throckmorton read aloud your glowing testimonials about the Rocky Mountains, I am seriously considering taking a trip out there myself. Should I do so, I will certainly do my utmost to spend time with you.

Until then, I shall have to content myself with memories of you and how perfectly your breasts fit into my hands. As I recall, you enjoyed that very much. As did I.

Tait

As summer approached, Tait's knee continued to improve, especially after Greenwall prescribed a series of exercises designed to strengthen the muscles supporting the joint. Tait wasn't able to completely discard the cane yet, but as his leg grew stronger, he began to rely on it more for balance than as a crutch. To compensate for his limited activity, he added his own exercise regimen of rowing a small skiff thrice weekly along the shore of the East River, which helped wear out his body but did little to quiet his restless mind.

He scarcely slept through the nights anymore, either awakening with a choking sensation, as if the noose were tightening around his neck, or with rose-scented images of Lucinda so strong in his mind he could almost taste the salty tang of her skin, feel her legs wrapped around him, and see her rising above him, her round, full breasts swaying with the motion of the train.

Overabundance of ardor, indeed.

His relationship with Doyle was faring no better. Lucinda now stood between them, and often, when Tait looked at his partner, he felt as if he were seeing him through Lucinda's eyes, and all the flaws and dodgy behavior he'd overlooked in the past now stood out in stark relief.

Doyle must have sensed the growing distance between them, but he said nothing about it until a meeting in Doyle's office in early June when Tait advised against investing in yet another railroad—this one almost two thousand miles away and much too close to Lucinda.

"Jasus, Tait!" Doyle exploded, slamming a fist down on his desk. "What's going on with you? Did you lose your balls in that fall, too?"

Horne snickered.

Tait turned his head and looked at him until the other man's gaze slid away. He wasn't as bothered by Horne's sly attempts to undermine Tait's influence with Doyle as he was by that vague, but undeniable, feeling of disgust that flared up whenever he was around the man. He had no name or cause for it, but it was so persistent he could hardly look at Horne without wanting to hit him.

Turning back to Doyle, he kept his tone mild. "The railroads are expanding too fast. Rumblings of corruption are starting to shake up the money markets. I wouldn't be surprised if, in a year, maybe two, it all comes tumbling down. We don't want to be caught under it when it falls."

Doyle made a dismissive gesture with his cigar—an affectation he'd taken up to fit the railroad mogul image he was trying to portray—then poured another splash of whiskey into his glass, even though it was barely past noon. "Gould is still investing. You're saying you know more than the nation's leading financier?"

Another snicker from Horne.

"But why so far away, Doyle? Why Denver?"

"It's booming, Tait. Faith and now that they've settled the Indian problem and men are finding gold in the hills, people are moving there by the droves. Just last week the Denver Pacific completed the run from Cheyenne, and the Denver and Rio Grande is already laying tracks south. It's ripe for investment, boyo. Horne, here, thinks if we can find a way across the lower Rockies, we'll own the southern route to the coast. It would be worth millions."

"You're starting another line? In Colorado Territory?"

"So I am. And we're calling it the Wichita Pacific."

We. So Horne was in on it. Tait sighed, wondering when Doyle would ever have enough—enough money, enough respect, enough distance from his impoverished beginnings. "How can you manage an operation that far away and still keep up with what you have going here?"

Doyle emptied his glass, then leaned forward, cigar clamped in his teeth, arms folded on his desk. "That's the beauty of it, Tait. There is no operation. We don't have to actually lay the tracks—just control the right-of-ways."

"And how do you intend to do that?"

Doyle poured another drink. "Horne, tell him."

"I've already got a fellow scouting the area," Horne said, his small eyes darting back and forth between Tait and Doyle. "The Kansas Pacific crossed the Missouri into Colorado Territory several weeks ago. By the time it reaches the city of Pueblo, the Denver and Rio Grande should just about be there from Denver. If we can find a negotiable canyon or pass through the mountains directly west of that point, we'll be able to open up the entire southwest all the way to the Pacific coast."

All these railroads and spur lines and crisscrossing routes were giving Tait a headache. "But I thought the Atlantic and Pacific was laying the southern route."

"They are," Doyle cut in, his eyes whiskey bright. "But if we can give them a route through the mountains, rather than around them, it could save them time and money. A lot of money."

"Which we would get a percentage of," Horne added, "by selling them the right-of-ways."

"Do you even have a route picked out yet?" Tait asked. This scheme was starting to look more farfetched with every word.

Horne shifted in his chair, his pointed pink tongue flicking nervously along his bottom lip. "There's several that look promising."

"So you haven't even started buying up the right-of-ways that you're hoping to resell?"

"This fall there'll be another statehood convention in Denver," Horne defended. "I'm hoping to have everything bought and a proposal ready by then."

That was over three months away. A lot could happen during that time. By then, Tait might know exactly where in Colorado Territory Lucinda was, and who had sent Smythe to silence her.

But what if it was Doyle? Or even Horne? Or someone he'd never met?

"So, Tait," Doyle pressed, an unspoken challenge in the slurred words. "You in or not?"

Rather than arouse suspicion by refusing, Tait decided to play along to see what they were up to. "Let me think about it." Of late, he had been trying to divest himself of speculative holdings, not add to them. It seemed he had neither the interest nor the inclination to play the money game anymore. Maybe he needed a new challenge, a deeper purpose than just amassing wealth.

Or his fall had shaken him up more than he'd thought.

Or he was just tired.

Retrieving the cane from the floor beside his chair, he rose. "I'll get back to you on it."

"Don't take too long," Doyle advised. "Horne will be busy soon with his campaign for governor, so he will. And we'll want the right-of-ways in hand when the Colorado statehood convention meets this fall."

Promising to have a decision soon, Tait left Doyle and Horne discussing campaign strategy. As he crossed the foyer, Quinn, Doyle's bodyguard-butler, held open the front door. "Afternoon, Mr. Rylander. Shall I whistle up a cab for you?"

"I'll walk. Doctor's orders." But as he stepped out onto the entry porch, he paused and turned back. "Does Mr. Kerrigan seem to be drinking more than usual of late, Quinn?"

The older man's gaze slid away. "I don't know about that, sir."

"Do you know if something is troubling him?"

Tait thought Quinn would evade that question, too, but after a hesitation, the ex-Pinkerton lowered his voice and said, "His wife, I think. Something about her past. Whatever it is, he's determined to find her. Even called in the Agency again."

Tait stared at him in surprise. "The Pinkerton Agency? Why?"

"Wants a full report going all the way back to the twinkle in her daddy's eye. But you didn't hear that from me."

"Thank you, Quinn." Tait continued down the steps to the street, his thoughts racing. Because Doyle hadn't mentioned Lucinda in weeks, Tait had assumed—hoped—he'd decided to let the issue rest. Apparently not.

What had he heard? And from whom? Horne?

He quickened his pace as much as his knee would allow. The Pinkertons and now this sudden interest in Colorado. He didn't like the sound of that. After giving it some thought, he decided he wouldn't tell Lucinda about the Denver project until he knew more about it, but he had to warn her about the Pinkertons. Hopefully then she would finally tell him what he needed to know to keep her safe. If not, he might have to go to Colorado, himself.

June 1870

My dearest daughter,

You bought a hotel! How exciting. It sounds as if you will have much to do to return it to its former glory, but I am certain you will accomplish that in short order. Hopefully, Denver will have all that you need to bring it up to snuff. If there is anything I can send you from here, let me know.

Mr. Rylander continues to come by regularly and is excellent company. He shows great interest in your letters, and is ever hopeful that you will someday allow him to correspond directly with you. I think he is quite smitten with you.

The days have turned unseasonably warm, even for June. We are in desperate need of rain, although with the drier weather, the ache in my joints is much improved.

I see from the society pages that Mr. Kerrigan is stepping out again, although he maintains the fabrication that his wife is visiting relatives in the Midwest. Your leaving was a terrible embarrassment to him, and I fear it will be many a year before he lives it down. I cannot in all honesty

> *say I am sorry for that. Mr. Rylander continues to urge*
> *him to forget about the stock certificates and you. But*
> *I doubt the Irishman's pride will ever allow him to do*
> *that.*
>
> *You are never far from my thoughts,*
> *Ida Throckmorton*

Tait put it off as long as he could, but in mid-June he finally told Doyle and Horne he would be passing on the Denver project due to other commitments.

Doyle accepted his decision without argument. But Tait sensed it further widened the distance between them that seemed to grow a little more every day. That bothered him. Not because the friendship was crumbling, but because for Lucinda's sake, he needed to know what Doyle was up to.

He could almost feel the danger closing in around her—Doyle, the Pinkertons, whoever sent Smythe. Her friends couldn't watch over her twenty-four hours a day. He needed to either stop the Denver project from moving forward and find whoever had sent Smythe, or go to Colorado and protect her himself.

Toward that end, he went to Doyle's townhouse in the last week of June. "Afternoon, Quinn," he said, removing his hat. "Mr. Kerrigan in?"

Quinn glanced at the hallway behind him, then made a tipping motion with his hand as if he were drinking from a glass. "He's in, sir," he said in a low voice. "But I'm not sure he'll be making much sense."

Tait set his hat on the carved entry table. "Drunk?"

"Getting there. And laughing. Kind of odd, you ask me."

Tait frowned in the direction of the long hallway that led to Doyle's office. "What set him off?"

"Something in the latest Pinkerton report, I think. Should I have Cook send in food? That might help settle him down."

Tait nodded. "And tell Mrs. Bradshaw a big pot of coffee, too."

"Mrs. Bradshaw left over two months ago." At Tait's expression of surprise, Quinn leaned forward to whisper. "Mr. Kerrigan blamed the housekeeper for his wife leaving. Had quite a row, I heard. Don't know all the details since I came after, but it was bad enough that half the staff left." He straightened. "I'll see you get coffee, sir."

Doyle had always been a drinker. In the past, Tait had rarely noticed alcohol altering his behavior. But the humiliation of his wife's desertion had left him with a moroseness that often erupted in anger he seemed barely able to control. Tait sensed it was only a matter of time before the Irishman hurt himself or someone else in one of his drunken rages.

But today, Tait noticed as he walked into the office, Doyle seemed a happy drunk, so whatever news was in the Pinkerton report, it couldn't be all bad.

"Tait!" Doyle called jovially when he saw him come through the door. *"Conas tu?"* He held up the bottle of amber liquid. *"Ar mhaith leat uisce beatha?"*

Assuming he'd been offered a drink, Tait shook his head. Taking a seat in one of the chairs across from Doyle's desk, he set his cane on the floor, stretched out his game leg, then sat back, hands resting idly on the arm rests. "You're certainly in a fine mood today."

"And so I am, laddie." Grinning, Doyle slapped his free hand on the folder sitting on top of his desk. "I found her."

Tait felt a coil of tension tighten in his chest. "Margaret?"

"Lucinda Hathaway. That's the name she's using now." Doyle studied him over the rim of his glass as he took a sip. He set the tumbler back onto his desk and smiled—less in friendliness than in challenge. "But you knew that, didn't you, boyo?"

"That she was calling herself Lucinda Hathaway?" Tait nodded. "I did."

"Why didn't you tell me? It would have saved the Pinkertons a lot of time."

"I didn't know it signified. Or that the Pinkertons were still on the case. Last I heard, you had called them off."

Doyle studied him a moment longer, then making one of those abrupt changes in mood, laughed. "No matter. I've got her now. It's like God Himself has put her in my hands, so it is."

"So where is she?" Tait asked, hoping Doyle didn't hear the urgency in his tone.

"Town in Colorado Territory called Heartbreak Creek."

Another laugh, this time laced with menace. "An apt name, I think, considering how she'll feel when I'm through with her."

The coil tightened. "You're going to Colorado?"

"Not yet. I'll keep her watched to make sure she doesn't try to run again. Then once this Denver deal gets going, maybe I'll go over there—pay her a little visit. What's that saying about killing two birds with one stone?" He emptied his glass and set it down with a thump. "I've heard the Rocky Mountains are so big a person can disappear into them and never be seen again."

"What are you going to do?"

The Irishman shrugged.

"Hell, Doyle, why don't you just let it go?"

"Let it go? She stole from me, man! How can I let that go?"

Realizing his fingers were digging into the upholstered arms of the chair, Tait forced his hands to relax. "But you don't even need her shares anymore," he said, hoping to mask his desperation under a tone of reason. "The vote last week went your way anyway."

"After I had to buy almost half of them back, damn her to hell!" Doyle lifted the glass, saw it was empty, then drew back his arm as if he intended to throw the tumbler across the room. Instead, he set it carefully back onto the desk. "Did you know she took out loans against the certificates in Philadelphia and again in St. Louis? Even discounted, it cost me a fortune to get them back."

"If you have the stocks, why pursue her? Why not put this behind you and move on?"

"Never!" Doyle slammed his fist so hard onto the desktop papers bounced. "She had a grand time, so she did, making a fool of me and spending my money. Well, now the piper must be paid. We Irish have a saying. *'Fillean meal ar an meal-laire'*—evil returns to the evildoer. But it's not just going to return, boyo, it's going to rain down on her head. I swear on my mother's name, Tait, by the time this is over, Margaret Hamilton, or Lucinda Hathaway, or whoever the hell she is, will regret the day she ever crossed Doyle Kerrigan."

"Doyle—"

A knock interrupted him. Quinn stepped in with a tray of sandwiches and a pot of coffee.

"Take that away," Doyle ordered when he saw it. "And get me another bottle, Quinn. I'm in a drinking mood, so I am."

Seeing he could talk no sense into the drunken Irishman, Tait left and went directly to the brownstone on Sixty-ninth Street.

As soon as the door opened, he shoved past Pringle. "Get her. Now." Without waiting to see if the butler obeyed, Tait went straight into the front room. Too agitated to sit, he stood at the window, one hand resting on the head of his cane, the other in his pocket, idly turning a coin in his fingers.

At a sound behind him, he turned to see Mrs. Throckmorton coming through the doorway. "'Get her'?' What am I—a sack of potatoes in the pantry?" But her pique faded when she saw his face. "Oh, my dear boy. What's wrong?"

"He found her. Doyle knows she's in Colorado Territory. In a town called Heartbreak Creek. He's sending Pinkerton agents to watch her."

Her color faded so abruptly the two lightly rouged spots on her cheeks stood out like round, rosy bruises. "Oh, no . . ."

Seeing her falter, Tait limped forward. It was a measure of her agitation that this time the old lady allowed him to assist her into her chair.

"What are we going to do?" she asked, once Tait settled across from her.

Before he could answer, the door opened and Pringle shuffled in with the usual tea and whiskey tray. This time, the liquid in the bottle was the color of horse piss. Tait figured by the end of the week, he'd be drinking straight water.

"Shall I set another plate for dinner?" Pringle asked in a bored tone.

"Is Cook still ill?"

"So she says, madam. Although she seemed well enough earlier in the day when she departed with a carpet bag in her hand. Shall I count the flatware?"

"She left?"

"I do not know. There is, however, a consensus below stairs that she has eloped. But rest assured, madam, the upstairs maid has whipped up something for your dinner. I cannot say for certain what it is. She's Scottish, you see. Something boiled, I think. With an odor of fish."

"Oh, dear."

"That's all right," Tait cut in. "I won't be staying long."

After Pringle made his excruciatingly slow exit, Tait said, "If you're short of personnel, Mrs. Throckmorton, I know of an excellent housekeeper who might be seeking employment. In fact, you probably met her at the wedding. Mrs. Bradshaw."

"I do remember her. The hooligan's housekeeper, wasn't she? I wondered why any decent woman would stay in his employ."

"He pays well."

"He would have to, I daresay. All right, you may send her around."

Tait said he would see if the woman was available, then turned back to the more pressing matter. "We must warn Lucinda that Doyle knows where she is and that he's sending Pinkerton agents to report her movements. I'll write to her directly."

"First you should probably read these." She pulled three envelopes from her skirt pocket. "They all came on the heels of one another. I started to send for you, then remembered you said you'd be working on some issue up north for a couple of days."

Tait had gone up to Newburgh to assess an accident in a machine shop he and Doyle owned. Luckily, no one had been hurt and the damages were minimal. He'd returned home the next day.

She handed an envelope to Tait. "This came late last week. The next arrived two days ago. The third, this morning. Read that one first."

With some apprehension, Tait pulled out the letter and began to read.

Dearest Mrs. Throckmorton,

It was lovely hearing from you again. Your letters always give me a lift.

My Heartbreak Creek family continues to grow. Not long after I bought the hotel, Edwina and Pru came into town, bringing with them the entire Brodie brood, along with a striking Indian gentleman named Thomas Redstone. He looks very fierce in his Cheyenne Dog Soldier regalia, and appears to be quite taken with Pru.

Robert Declan Brodie, Edwina's husband—who also carries the nickname of Big Bob because of his imposing stature—seems an honorable, dependable sort. From all appearances, his marriage to Edwina is working out well, although the children are somewhat resistant to the idea of a new mother. (Did I tell you their natural mother was killed by Indians several years ago?)

Maddie continues to take the most astounding photographs. Her editor is hinting that he may publish a bound copy of her work. Naturally, she is thrilled with the prospect. She recently commissioned the construction of a little wagon that she plans to use for her photographic expeditions. I fear for her safety, but she insists she has always been greeted with great courtesy wherever she goes, so I try not to worry too much.

The hotel restoration goes slowly, but a thorough cleaning, a fresh coat of paint, some furniture wax, and a few potted plants have already done wonders. I long for you to see it.

As always, I miss you terribly.
Margaret

Tait folded the letter and slipped it back into the envelope, wondering what the urgency was. Granted, Lucinda's letters to her guardian were more newsy than those she wrote to him, but still, he saw nothing in the missive to account for the anxiety he saw in Mrs. Throckmorton's eyes.

"Now read this." The frail hand held out the second letter. Tait took it and read:

Dear Mrs. Throckmorton,

I am writing this two days after my earlier letter. An awful thing has happened!

While the Brodies were in town, their ranch was attacked by a renegade war party of Arapaho Indians led by a terrible man named Lone Tree. And now, Pru has been abducted by the same vile creature!

Edwina is in a terrible state, as are we all. Although wounded in the abduction, Thomas Redstone, the Cheyenne warrior I mentioned earlier, has gone to find her. And this morning, Declan Brodie left with a dozen army troopers to search also.

*I can scarcely believe this dreadful thing has happened—
especially now that Edwina has just informed me that this
Lone Tree person is the same man that Declan thinks killed
his first wife. It sounds like a plot in one of those lurid western dime novels, does it not? But sadly, it is all true. I will
write more when we have news.*

*Please keep us in your prayers,
Your devoted Margaret*

Tait looked at Mrs. Throckmorton in astonishment. "A
woman's been abducted? I thought the Indian trouble had been
settled over a year ago. My God, is Lucinda in danger?" He
didn't realize he was halfway out of his chair until Mrs. Thorn-
ton motioned him back.

"Relax, dear boy. The woman's been found. Read on." She
held out the last envelope.

Dearest Mrs. Throckmorton,
  So much has happened here I hardly know where to begin.
  *First of all—wonderful news! Pru has been saved! She
will not talk about her ordeal, which we can see weighs
heavily on her, but we respect her wishes and rejoice that
she is still alive.*
  That is the good news.
  *The bad news is that Declan Brodie returned with
another woman who had been taken captive by the same
Indian. His first wife, Sally!*
  *You can imagine our shock. With the return of his previ-
ous wife, Declan's marriage to Edwina becomes invalid. To
complicate matters further, it was immediately apparent
that the poor woman was dying of consumption. How can
Declan cast her aside now?*
  *Then two days ago, Lone Tree attacked again! This time,
he broke into the hotel, gave Sally a mortal beating, and
took Edwina and Declan's seven-year-old daughter, Brin,
hostage.*
  *Luckily he didn't get far before Declan put an end to
him. So now Sally is resting in the church graveyard, and*

*we have a wedding to plan. And soon! Since we only recently
learned Edwina is in a family way.*

*So all's well that ends well. A harrowing experience, and
one that serves to remind us how fragile life is, especially in
the Wild West. I am so grateful my Heartbreak Creek family
is safe—and am now even more determined than ever to
make this town a happy place once again.*

*Toward that end, I am pleased to report my efforts are
progressing nicely. And just in time, since the mine is closing. We have already garnered interest from two railroads.
I will give you more details as they come to fruition.*

Thank you for your prayers.

*Devotedly yours,
Margaret*

*PS: Alas, if it's not one thing, it's another. Apparently some
man has been tracking Maddie. I suspect it is her long-lost
husband. But if he expects to find the same docile little wife
he deserted back in Scotland, he'll be mightily surprised.
I'll keep you apprised. M.*

Tait looked up, his mind spinning from all he'd read. Indian
attacks, abductions, wives coming back from the dead, hus-
bands stalking wives . . . good God. What kind of place was this
Heartbreak Creek? "What is this plan she has to save the town?"
he asked, passing the letter back to Mrs. Throckmorton.

"I don't know. But it sounds as if it involves a railway, does
it not?"

That's what Tait was afraid of. Surely her little canyon wasn't
the same one Doyle and Horne were considering. That would be
too coincidental. Yet he knew there weren't that many passes—
or canyons—through the southern Rockies that would be suitable for a railroad. God help her if they were working toward
the same route; the best way to send Doyle into a murderous
rage was to get between him and his money.

"I've got to go to her," he burst out, reaching for his cane.
"Warning her about Doyle won't be enough. I should be there."

"Why?"

"Why?" Tait looked at her in astonishment. "To stop her

before this railway venture puts her in the path of her enemies. To protect her from Doyle."

"And who will protect her from you, Mr. Rylander?"

"Me?" Yet even as he said it, Tait felt the heat of guilt rush up his neck.

"I'm not a fool, dear boy. I know you're in love with her. I also know you are obsessed with her past. If you expect to win her, you must put that aside. For her sake, as well as your own. If you are unable to do that, don't go after her."

"I assure you, Mrs. Throckmorton, your ward has nothing to fear from me."

"No?" The old lady smiled in a way that reminded him again how astute she was. "Then perhaps I should be worrying about protecting *you* from *her*."

As soon as he reached home, Tait went directly to his office, sat down behind his desk, and pulled out several sheets of stationery.

His frustration was at a boiling point. After much argument, Mrs. Throckmorton had convinced him not to go haring off to Colorado but to stay in Manhattan where he could watch Doyle and search for whoever had sent Smythe. Yet the drive to do something almost overwhelmed him. He needed to see her. Talk to her. Make certain she was safe. But instead of being able to touch her to reassure himself, all he had in his grasp was a piece of paper.

Dipping his pen into the inkwell, he began to write down everything he wanted to say to her. Using words he might never have been able to speak aloud, he told her about the lonely days and restless nights, the ache in his heart that never seemed to go away, the need that consumed him and made a mockery of his empty life. He wrote how much he admired her intellect, her courage, and that smirky smile that made him laugh. He told her he loved her and was convinced she loved him, too, and that they were destined to be together. He told her everything that was in his heart, and for an hour, he bled inky letters across the white pages.

When at last he put down the pen, he felt drained and emotionally exhausted, but also relieved to have finally sorted through the chaos in his mind.

He loved her. Had loved her for over a year. Would continue to love her.

Despite everything.

And that was that.

Balance restored, he read through the letter one more time, wadded it into a ball, and tossed it into the unlit grate.

Then he picked up the pen and began again . . . and this time, he wrote from his head rather than his heart.

He still had some pride, thank God.

Sixteen

"How is Edwina today?" Maddie asked as she peered through the back of the camera while twisting the lens mounted on the front.

"Vomiting. Why are you taking a photograph of a mule's eye?"

"It's beautiful, is why. I swear if you look into it you can see to infinity."

Lucinda mentally rolled her eyes. "Of course you can. The sky is reflected in it. Are you coming to work on the schoolhouse this afternoon?" Cal Bagley from the mercantile had sent word that the paint had arrived, and Lucinda wanted to get the project completed. She had a lot to do before going to the statehood convention in Denver.

"Of course. I think it's having a salubrious effect on Pru, don't you?"

"One never knows." It had been several weeks since the Great Turmoil—as Lucinda had begun to think of the time stretching from Pru's abduction to that final horrid confrontation between Declan and Lone Tree and Edwina up on the mine scaffold. Now Sally lay in the fenced graveyard at the Come All You Sinners Church, and Declan was out at the ranch, working to repair the damage from the Indian attack, and Pru was back where she belonged.

But things hadn't settled back to normal, and Lucinda

wondered if they ever would. Pru was still not speaking of her ordeal—although she seemed quite excited about Edwina's idea of turning one of the abandoned cabins into a school where she could teach reading and writing to anyone who wanted to learn. Thomas was moping about like a lovesick Indian, which he surely was. And Declan had hardly spoken to Edwina since Sally's funeral. Granted, he'd been busy with the house and settling any lingering animosities with Lone Tree's tribe, but really. Was the man ever going to come back to town and remarry Edwina so their union would be legal, or did he plan to leave her at the hotel forever?

Lucinda was wearing herself out worrying over all these people. She didn't have time for it. In addition to preparing the proposal to present to the various railroads when they were in Denver at the statehood convention, she was trying to refurbish a dilapidated hotel and start a business project that she hoped would save the entire town now that the mine was closed down. It was exhausting.

"There," Maddie said, her voice muffled by the black drape that protected the plates from premature exposure. "Now hold Buttercup's halter, will you, Luce? And keep her head as still as you can."

Lucinda did as instructed.

Buttercup didn't. And with a snort of disgust, she pulled the halter free and walked haughtily away, her swishing tail almost catching Lucinda across the face.

"You rude thing," she scolded the retreating mule.

"Damn and blast!" Maddie muttered, flinging back the drape. "I will never get that stubborn creature to stand still."

"Well, she is a mule," Lucinda observed, checking her palm for mule dirt, although she secretly thought Maddie was the more stubborn of the two. One would have to be, she supposed, to be a photographer. Either that or infinitely patient—which in some ways, was the same thing. "So I guess you're done for the day?"

"I might as well be." Maddie began loading her various supplies into the pushcart she used to transport her photography equipment around town. "Do you think Edwina will feel up to going with us to the schoolhouse?"

"She's not sick, Maddie. She's pregnant. And it's her own fault. I gave her a preventative."

The Englishwoman straightened to blink at her. "A French letter? Why would she want one of those?"

"In case she was serious about not wanting children."

Edwina was convinced that madness ran in her family—an opinion Lucinda didn't question, having seen the scars both she and Pru bore—and the poor woman was naturally fearful of passing along tainted blood to her own children. A sound decision, Lucinda thought, since Edwina was Southern, and who knew what sort of inbreeding might have occurred in the past.

"Besides," she went on to Maddie, "every woman should have one. Even you."

"Me? But I'm not—that is to say, I haven't—what I mean is, my husband isn't even in the country."

"Exactly. So if you meet some handsome—and understandably lonely—miner or mountain man or mule skinner or whatever, you will have no worries about conception."

"But that . . . that means I would have to be . . . intimate with them."

"Well, that's the point, dear."

A sudden commotion arose as a rider charged into town at breakneck speed, hauled his lathered horse to a stop outside the hotel, tossed a pouch to Yancey, then tore off again.

"Looks like the mail courier has brought something." Perhaps there was a letter from Tait. She hadn't heard from him in several weeks. "When you're finished here, come to my room, Maddie. If Edwina has her head out of her bowl by then, we'll go on to the school and start painting." And feeling suddenly perky, she walked briskly back to the hotel.

There was, indeed, a letter from Tait. But this time it came directly to her, and not through Mrs. Throckmorton. Had her guardian told him of her location? Filled with a sense of foreboding, Lucinda carried it into the empty dining room. Taking her usual seat by the window overlooking the dirt track that ran between the back of the hotel and the woods along the creek, she opened the envelope, pulled out several sheets of fine stationery, and began to read.

Lucinda—

Doyle knows where you are. As you can see by this letter, I do, as well. So I trust we can dispense with the tiresome game of writing through your guardian.

Doyle also knows the name you call yourself now, and about the loans you took against the shares. He learned all this through Pinkerton detectives. I was not aware they were still in his employ. Since Doyle and I are not as close as we once were, he does not confide in me as he did in the past. But I know he is very angry and intent on getting his money back. Even now, he has sent Pinkerton Agents to report your every move back to him.

I worry about you. I care about you. I am working hard to convince him to let you and the stock certificates go. But if I fail in that, I will come to Heartbreak Creek to protect you. It is my duty. And my right. You hold my heart in your hand, and therefore, your safety is my own.

Fondest regards,
Tait

She sat staring at the bold handwriting, her mind struggling to accept what she had read. Pinkertons were still after her? Watching her? A sudden prickle between her shoulder blades brought her whipping around to check the room behind her.

But it was only Miriam, laying fresh tablecloths over the tables. She saw no one but Yancey in the lobby, and no shadowy figures lurked in the trees bordering the creek.

She wondered if she should alert Declan Brodie. Surely he would know if any strangers were in town. But he was no longer sheriff, and was miles away at the moment, doing repairs on his ranch. Thomas Redstone was here, but he probably knew fewer faces than she did, despite being Declan's temporary deputy for a while. The new sheriff would likely laugh at her. No, she would have to take care of herself.

Reaching down, she felt the hard shape of her little pistol in her skirt pocket. Since the Indian trouble, she never went anywhere without it.

And anyway, from what Tait had written, the Pinkerton men

were only there to watch and report back to Doyle. They weren't an actual threat to her.

She glanced back over the letter again. *I worry about you. I care about you. You hold my heart in your hand.*

A fanciful notion. But one that brought an empty ache in her chest.

I could have loved you, he had said that day on the train. *Hell, I probably already do. But . . .*

There would always be that "but," she knew. The past would ever stand between them, poisoning any chance they might have had, and she needed to accept that. So she would. Slipping the letter into her pocket, she rose.

And anyway, being a spinster might not be so bad. She would be accountable to no one but herself—an excellent inducement— and she would be surrounded by these dear friends who were becoming her new family. She could enjoy their children without the bother of having her own. She could become the town matriarch, Lady Bountiful, the fairy godmother who made all the kiddies' dreams come true. It could be a good life. Certainly better than the one she might have had with Doyle.

And if her friends drifted away into their own lives without her?

She wouldn't think about that.

Resolved to be happy, she went back to her office to make her pantry lists and linen lists, set up work schedules for Miriam and Yancey and Billy, and plan menus for Cook. And later, after the ladies came back from the schoolhouse and dinner was over and the hotel had settled down for the night, perhaps she would write a short note to Tait, telling him she didn't need his protection, and in view of the lack of future between them, thought it best if she held neither his heart—nor any other of his body parts—in her hand.

Then she would climb into her lonely bed and cry herself to sleep.

August 1870

Dear Mrs. Throckmorton,

Wonderful news! We are finally going to have a wedding! It promises to be quite the spectacle, with a fully costumed Cheyenne Dog Soldier standing as best man, four restless children crowded around the little altar of the Come All You Sinners Church, and of course, the pregnant bride. I just hope Biddy Rickman, the pastor's wife and choir director, doesn't become so enthusiastic in her accompaniment that she falls off her piano bench. (It's happened before.) After the ceremony, we will all retire here to the hotel for a grand wedding feast.

I regret that this letter will be so short, but I have much to prepare and only a short time to complete the decorations, menu, etc. (In deference to Edwina's delicate condition, we thought it wise to hold the nuptials as soon as possible.)

I so wish you could be here to celebrate with us and meet my wonderful friends. Perhaps soon.

Much love,
Margaret

PS: I forgot to relay my other good news. We have purchased five more right-of-ways! Let's hope with the mine shut down and the water cannon no longer in operation, Heartbreak Creek's water problem will resolve itself. If not, I fear we shall have to have Edwina find us a new water source (I did tell you she's a water douser, didn't I? A remarkable woman). M.

"Do stand still, dearest," Maddie mumbled around the pins clamped between her lips. "Or I'll never get the fit right."

"What fit?" Edwina looked dejectedly down at her body. "I look like I've got a bustle strapped to my stomach."

She had a point, Lucinda thought, looking up from the wedding veil she was hemming that would eventually be attached to the beaded coronet Pru had almost completed. Before she had begun increasing, Edwina had been so slim she had scarcely cast a shadow. Declan was constantly reminding her to eat so the eagles wouldn't carry her off. But now, she truly did look like she was wearing a bustle on the wrong side. Ignoring Pru's please-don't-get-her-started look, Lucinda grinned and said, "I'd advise you not to fit it too tightly, Maddie. At the rate she's expanding—"

"Well, thank you so much for noticing!" Edwina's moods—while always a bit mercurial—had, of late, become downright volatile.

"Well, really, dear," Lucinda said in a soothing tone. "How could I not? You're either carrying a rather substantial baby—which, considering its size, I fervently hope is a boy and not a girl—or you're mistaken about when conception took place."

"Lucinda!" Maddie said, aghast.

"Oh, dear." Pru, shaking her head.

Undeterred, Lucinda pushed on. "I only say that because if it happened sooner than we've calculated, then the baby isn't so oversized, after all."

"Oversized?" Maddie glared at her over her shoulder. "Truly, Lucinda? You want to use that word around a bride—*enceinte* or not?"

"I know exactly when conception took place," Edwina announced. "And when and where it happened is none of your business, Lucinda Hathaway!"

"Where? Hmm . . ." Lucinda cocked her head. "I didn't think to question where it happened. But that raises some interesting possibilities, does it not?"

"Enough of your troublemaking, Luce," Maddie scolded. "You'll have her in tears, and you know how that upsets Declan."

"Then let's talk about the next wedding, shall we?"

"Next wedding?" Maddie stopped pinning. Edwina looked confused. Pru bent over her beading.

Lucinda laughed. "I mean Pru's and Thomas's, of course."

Edwina's mouth fell open. "You and Thomas are getting married, Pru? Why didn't you tell me?"

Pru raised pink palms in a slow-down gesture. "Because there is nothing to tell. I swear it. Thomas is a good friend, and that's the extent of it."

"And yet . . ." Lucinda put on a puzzled look. "You did spend all that time with him in the mountains in that—what did he call it?—oh, yes, sweat lodge."

"He was just trying to help me," Pru defended. "I was upset about . . . what happened. He believes sweat lodges have great healing powers."

When she saw that haunted look had returned to Pru's dark eyes, Lucinda could have kicked herself. She had only meant to lighten the mood, not remind Pru of her ordeal at the hands of that madman, Lone Tree. Leaning over, she rested her hand on Pru's shoulder. "I'm sorry, Pru. That was thoughtless of me to make light of your pain. Please do forgive me."

"There's nothing to forgive." Pru reached up to pat the hand on her shoulder. "You ladies are my dearest friends. I wouldn't have survived any of this without you. And my friend Thomas, of course."

"Well, anyway," Edwina cut in with forced joviality. "I'm not sure Indians believe in marriage. Or kissing. Or any such goings on."

Lucinda laughed. "Oh, I'll bet they do. How else would you account for all the little Indians running around? What do you think, Pru?"

"I heard from my publisher again," Maddie broke in with another glare at Lucinda.

"About extending your stay?" Lucinda didn't know how she would bear it if Maddie went back to England.

"No, about that man inquiring about me."

"What man?" Edwina asked.

"I think it's her husband," Lucinda told her. "The wretch probably just now noticed she has decamped. What did he want, Maddie?"

"It appears he went to the newspaper and questioned my publisher directly. Mr. Chesterfield described him as 'tall, over-bearing, and unpleasant.' He also called him 'persistent and determined.' That does sound a bit like Angus. He could be quite imposing. Especially in his uniform."

Pru tied off the last knot, inspected her handiwork, then nodded in satisfaction. Closing the tin of beads, she set the coronet aside for Lucinda to attach to the veil, and folded her hands in her lap. "I wonder how he found you. Since you sign your work A. M. Wallace, rather than using your full name, how would he know to go to your publisher?"

"Precisely my thought."

"Did your publisher tell him where you were?"

Maddie shook her head.

"Sounds like someone you'd do well to avoid," Edwina remarked. "If he tracked you to the newspaper, I wouldn't be surprised if he showed up here."

Maddie's eyes grew round in her lightly freckled face. "Surely not."

Lucinda finished the slip stitch around the top of the veil and pulled it into loose gathers she could attach to the coronet. "We shall have to keep an eye out for him." And she definitely had some questions for the bounder—assuming he was Maddie's husband and he showed up here in Heartbreak Creek—such as why he had treated her dear friend so shabbily.

"I'll be sure to tell Declan," Edwina said. "Now that he's sheriff again, he should know of any strangers lurking about."

Lucinda wondered if that extended to Pinkertons. She would ask but was afraid of arousing suspicion. Declan was too smart not to question why detectives would be watching her, and the poor man had enough on his mind right now. The wedding, his wife's delicate condition—which was why he'd temporarily moved the family back to town and taken the sheriff's position again—the upcoming statehood convention to which he was a reluctant delegate, and dealing with out-of-work miners who spent far too much time in the saloon.

Lucinda was delighted to have the Brodies back in town, of course. Now that she counted Declan and his brood as part of her family, she wanted them all close by. Besides, the children needed schooling, and once the schoolhouse was finished, Pru would be able to teach them every day. From what Lucinda had seen, she was an excellent—and thankfully, patient—teacher.

But now, if the man inquiring about Maddie was indeed her soldier husband and he showed up here expecting to take her back to Scotland, Lucinda wasn't sure what she would do. Without even meeting the man, she already disliked him intensely.

"Then I shall simply have to see that my little gypsy wagon is finished as soon as possible." As she spoke, Maddie pinned up the last section of hem on Edwina's ivory underskirt. "That way, if he does come to Heartbreak Creek, I shall be long gone on a photographic expedition. Do stop fidgeting, Edwina."

"I can't help it. I have to use the water closet."

"Again? At this rate I'll never get this dress finished."

"It's not as if I enjoy traipsing back and forth, you know. Declan said last night I must have woken him up five times. But then once he was awake," she added with a sly grin, "he rolled over and commenced—"

"Please. Spare us the details." Lucinda made a shooing motion. "Go. And if you see Miriam, ask her to bring another pitcher of lemonade."

"Oh, grand. That's just what I need. More lemonade."

As the door closed behind her, Maddie plopped into a chair with a deep sigh. "Trying to get that woman to stand still is like . . ." She paused, searching for the right words.

"Lassoing a cyclone?" Pru supplied with a chuckle. "That's what my momma used to say. Edwina has always been like that. Declan's settled her down some, but he's lucky to have four children around to help drain off some of that energy."

"Nonetheless, they do seem quite happy with one another," Maddie observed. "Who would have guessed, after that first awkward meeting."

"Awkward? Lord, you don't know the half of it. I felt like I was caught in the middle of a dog fight. And those children certainly didn't help. They came at her like chickens after a June bug."

Lucinda laughed. "Yet she prevailed. I admire her for that. For having the courage to jump in with the sharks, as it were."

"More like landing in a nest of Louisiana alligators."

"All this to-do reminds me of my own wedding," Maddie said, a dreamy look in her eyes that meant she was thinking about that rogue Scotsman.

"Oh?" Lucinda teased. "Were you pregnant, too? Was your Angus a widower? Did he have four rowdy children?"

"You are a cold woman, Lucinda Hathaway. I daresay you haven't an ounce of romance in your heart."

"I should hope not. Romance is for fanciful novels and gullible young misses." Yet, even as she spoke, Lucinda felt that spark of melancholy flare up again. Ignoring it, she sewed another stitch in the veil she was attaching to the coronet.

The door opened and Edwina came back in, trailed by Miriam, bearing a fresh pitcher of lemonade and a plate of tiny sandwiches and pastries. Seeing that Edwina was tiring, Lucinda suggested a break while they ate, and had Miriam set up a table and bring in another chair from the office.

"Our first Heartbreak Creek wedding," Maddie mused.

"But hopefully not our last." Edwina raised her brows at Pru, then Lucinda.

Lucinda shook her head. "Don't look at me. I'll never marry."

"Why not?" Edwina was so in love with her husband she thought everybody should have one. "You're beautiful, rich, pointy—any man would be lucky to have you."

"Pointy?"

"Don't ask," Pru muttered under her breath.

"One lucky man almost did," Maddie said.

Lucinda sent her a warning look.

Which she ignored. "Our Lucinda is the original runaway bride. Left him standing at the altar, so to speak."

Seeing the curious looks headed her way, Lucinda knew she would have to respond or Edwina would nag unmercifully. "Actually, I left him after the ceremony but before the signing of the marriage certificate. Since it was never duly filed, we are not legally married. I think that disqualifies me as a bride."

"But, Lucinda! You gave your vows. Before God."

Poor Edwina. She actually thinks God cares. But unwilling to be dragged into some theological discussion about God and sin and everlasting damnation or whatever it was Southerners believed, Lucinda put on a regretful smile and said, "He was not the man for me. Luckily I came to my senses in time and was able to save us both from a lifetime of unhappiness and heartache."

That was a bit of a whitewash, but Edwina and Pru seemed to accept it, and although Maddie's skeptical expression told Lucinda she didn't, she said nothing more, for which Lucinda was deeply grateful.

Happy to change the subject, she asked Maddie how her little gypsy wagon was coming along. In truth, she thought the idea of a woman traveling around the wilderness taking photographs was patently absurd and potentially dangerous. But she and Maddie had had this discussion several times in the past, and each time Maddie had stood firm. It was, after all, her life and photography was her passion. So how could Lucinda interfere?

"I am assured it will be ready in time for a short expeditionary trip before we all leave for the statehood convention."

Most of them would be going to Denver. The only ones not attending were Pru, who would be watching over the children, and Thomas, who would be taking over deputy duties in

Declan's absence—and watching over Pru. As a delegate to the convention, Declan was going there to cast the town vote on the statehood issue, and because he couldn't bear to be parted from his wife in her delicate condition, he had insisted Edwina come along, as well. He was such a dear.

Lucinda was attending to meet with railroad investors about a route through Heartbreak Creek Canyon, and Maddie was going along to photograph the proceedings.

It sounded like a grand adventure.

"Maddie, you're actually going into the mountains alone?" Pru looked more admiring than shocked, which disappointed Lucinda. She had hoped for an ally.

"How else will I find trappers and mountain men and miners and buffalo hunters? Besides, I won't be alone. Wilfred Satterwhite is coming with me for protection."

Edwina blinked at her in astonishment. "Wall-eyed Willy?"

"You might as well take a corpse," Lucinda muttered. "The man must be ninety."

"He's a lively seventy-three," Maddie countered, then added with a grin, "But not too lively, if you take my meaning. I would hate to have to fend off unwanted advances."

"From Wall-eyed Willy?" Edwina gave a dramatic shudder. "Just the thought of that gives me the shivers."

"Despite his unfortunate appearance," Maddie defended, "Wilfred Satterwhite is a very nice man. Now stand up, Edwina. It's getting late and we need to get this dress finished before you outgrow it."

"And we still must decide on the menu," Lucinda reminded them.

"And what decorations you want," Pru added.

With a labored sigh, Edwina pushed herself out of the chair and went back to stand on the crate so Maddie could finish the hem. "What a bother all this is becoming," she said wearily. "It's a wonder anyone ever gets married."

"My sentiments exactly," Lucinda muttered. Yet, somewhere deep inside, the thorn of envy pricked her, and she wondered if she would still feel so disheartened about marriage if instead of walking down the aisle with Tait Rylander, she had been walking toward him.

Lucinda—

I am in receipt of your return letter, and I must say I was delighted to read that you have been thinking of my body parts. Was there one in particular that stood out for you?

I freely admit I think of yours almost constantly—that dimple in your left cheek, that freckle on the underside of your left breast, and that tiny strawberry-colored birthmark high on the inside of your thigh. What? You didn't know about that? Then it is my fondest hope that you will allow me to point it out when next we meet. (Incidentally, it tastes nothing like strawberries. More like . . . well, never mind. Just another thing we'll have to explore together, won't we?)

Until then, and with the lovely image of you stretched beneath me, your head thrown back in abandon, your rose-bud mouth open on a sigh of bliss, I shall retire to my lonely bed and dream of you. As always.

Tait

Seventeen

September 1870

My dearest guardian,

How this summer has flown. Even though the days are still warm and sunny, the nights are growing so cool the fur on Maddie's mules is starting to thicken.

I am happy to report that the wedding was a huge success. I vow I have never seen a lovelier bride, despite the fact that she sobbed throughout the entire ceremony. (Apparently it's not unusual for some women to become extremely emotional during the prenatal state, especially at their own weddings.) Declan took it all in stride, although the children got into a bit of a flap when a bee took an interest in Brin's bouquet. Thomas Redstone looked magnificent in his warrior costume and Pru—along with every woman in the church except for Biddy Rickman and the choir ladies—couldn't seem to take her eyes off of him.

As for me, the day was a bittersweet reminder of my own wedding—which started with such high hopes, and ended so badly. And yet, without that sad sequence of events, I wouldn't be here today among dear friends, building a wonderful new life. My greatest regret is that you are not here to share it with me.

I am sad to report that yesterday Maddie left in her new wagon on her first photographic expedition, heading north to the Alamosa River where gold was recently found. She takes with her a little dog she recently acquired, and an elderly man who will drive the wagon and watch over her. I daresay the dog, which is quite the yapper, will be better protection, although Maddie, who is the most courageous woman I've ever met, still insists she will be safe.

Seeing her wagon drive away was difficult for me. She has become the sister I never had and I shall miss her terribly. At least I will have Edwina and Pru to keep me company, and the upcoming convention in Denver to occupy my mind.

Missing you, too,
Margaret

Tait knew something was wrong as soon as Quinn opened the door to Doyle's townhome late in the afternoon during the last week of September.

The man looked as if he hadn't slept in days. There were shadows beneath his eyes, his suit was rumpled, and several day's beard stubbled his chin.

"Good God, man, what's happened? Is it Doyle?"

Tait hadn't seen the Irishman for almost three weeks. He had come by on several occasions, but each time Quinn had reluctantly refused him entrance, obviously at Doyle's instruction. But now with time running out, and the Colorado statehood convention looming in the near future, Tait was determined to find out what was going on.

"Another Pinkerton report?" he asked, handing over his hat and cane.

Quinn nodded. In a low voice, he said, "I've never seen it this bad, Mr. Rylander. I'm supposed to turn you away, but—" A crash from the rear of the house brought his head around. Turning back, he gave a deep sigh. "I don't know what to do, sir. He's run off most of the staff, and now with Mr. Horne gone—"

Tait stilled. "Gone where?"

"Colorado." Quinn made a weary gesture. "Some railroad thing. Maybe you can talk some sense into him, Mr. Rylander. He's liable to hurt himself, or someone else, he keeps this up."

Tait gave the other man's shoulder a pat. "I'll see what I can do, Quinn. Send in a pot of coffee, will you?"

"Doubt he'll drink it. He threw the last one through the window."

"Bring it anyway. And stay close, in case I need you."

"I will, sir. And you take care. He may be drunk but he's still quick. Harry's got the eye to prove it."

The reek of whiskey hit Tait as soon as he opened the door into the darkened office. Pausing on the threshold, he looked around. The room was a shambles. Chairs overturned, broken glass littering the marble hearth, more shards clinging to the mullions in the leaded-glass window that overlooked the back garden. Flies darted in and out of the shattered panes, while others buzzed lazy circles above whiskey spills and food drying on plates stacked on the side table.

"Doyle?"

Tait caught movement in a chair beside the hearth and turned to see Doyle push himself to his feet. He stood swaying, a half-filled whiskey glass dangling from one hand, a bottle from the other.

"If it's not my good friend, Tait Rylander, loyal as the day is long, so he is."

"Jesus, Doyle." Tait gestured at the filthy room. "What are you doing?"

"*Ag ol uisce beatha*—drinking whiskey. It's what we Irish do, don't you know?" Laughing, Doyle wove toward his desk and plopped into his chair with a groan. After clumsily refilling his glass, he held the bottle high. "Would you care to join me, boyo?"

"No." Picking his way through scattered books, papers, and empty bottles, Tait crossed to Doyle's desk. As he lit the lamp, he saw a folder beside it with the distinctive Pinkerton open-eye logo printed on the front.

A sense of inevitability came over him. A certainty that what lay inside the folder would put an end to this poisonous friendship built on greed and guilt and obligation. It was an ending he both welcomed and dreaded—the final irrevocable confrontation with this damaged, driven man.

It had been a long time coming. Since before Margaret. Perhaps even beginning the day Doyle had cut Tait down from the hanging tree and said the words he would repeat many times throughout the years—always with a laugh and a clap on the back, as if it were a joke, when they both knew it wasn't.

You owe me, boyo.

Well, no more.

Bending, Tait picked up one of the toppled chairs and set it back on its feet before Doyle's desk, then sat down, relaxed yet ready, every sense so focused on what was to come he could almost feel the nerves jumping beneath his skin.

It reminded him of his fighting days.

He studied the Irishman. It was apparent the man hadn't shaved or bathed or changed clothes in days. From the look of it, he hadn't slept, either. Tait had seen this dark side of Doyle only one other time—after he'd lost a business deal to another man and had realized it had all been a setup and they had been laughing at him the whole time. It had taken all of Tait's skill as a lawyer and negotiator—as well as a hefty chunk of his cash— to keep Doyle out of prison.

But this time, it looked even worse. "What's wrong?"

The Irishman didn't answer.

"A problem with the Denver venture?" It had to be, if Horne was already headed there. Just the thought of that bastard being anywhere near Lucinda made Tait's jaw lock. He had to go to her. As soon as he finished here, he would make the necessary arrangements. He just hoped he hadn't waited too long.

"The Denver venture. Hmm . . ." Tipping his head back, Doyle squinted up at the ceiling. "Aye, there's a problem, so it seems."

Tait wondered what demons frolicked in the Irishman's head tonight. Like a child with a cruel streak and a trapped butterfly, Doyle did like his games. "What kind of problem?" he asked.

"Competition. It seems someone is buying up the right-of-ways we need." Turning his head, he looked at Tait, and what Tait saw in the Irishman's eyes heightened his senses even more. "That wouldn't be you, would it, laddie?"

Not the question Tait had expected. "I passed on Denver, remember? I don't even know what route you've chosen."

Doyle studied him a moment longer, then looked away. "No matter. Horne will take care of it."

"Take care of what?"

Before he got an answer, a knock sounded. Quinn came in with a pot of coffee, two cups, and a plate of sandwiches on a tray. Tait told him to put it on the desk, which he did, then left, closing the door behind him.

"You should eat something." Tait offered the sandwich plate.

Doyle surprised him by taking one. But after one bite, he set it aside. Tipping his head against the backrest, he closed his eyes.

Silence. Tait poured a cup of coffee and shoved it across to Doyle. "Here's coffee."

Doyle ignored it.

Two minutes stretched to five. Tait wondered why he was staying.

Then finally, in a voice so flat and weary Tait scarcely recognized it, Doyle said, "Why, Tait? Did you think I wouldn't find out?"

"Find out what?"

"That you were fucking my wife."

Tait rubbed a finger across his battered knuckles and imagined driving them into Doyle's face. But knowing calmness, not violence, was the only way to reach Doyle when he was drunk, he kept his fury under control. "She's not your wife."

Doyle opened his eyes and looked over at him.

"The marriage certificate wasn't witnessed," Tait explained. "Or registered. Margaret is not, and has never been, your lawful wife. And if you ever speak about her that way again, I'll put you on the ground."

Doyle continued to look at him. A sneer slowly curled his chapped lips. "You stupid bastard. You're in love with her, aren't you?"

Tait didn't answer.

Which made Doyle laugh. "Well, here, boyo." Slapping a hand on the folder, he shoved it so savagely across the desk it would have fallen to the floor if Tait hadn't caught it. "Read all about your little love."

Tait looked at the folder in his hands. He could guess what was inside. Dates, names, every private thing she had worked so hard to conceal. The Pinkertons would leave no corner unprobed, no relationship undissected, no action unexamined. It was an invasion of the foulest kind.

God help him, but he wanted to open it. To finally have all

his answers laid before him. All he had to do was open it and
the puzzle that was Lucinda would be revealed to him, and he
would know all her secrets at last.

He took a deep breath, let it out, and put the folder back on
the desk. "I already know all I need to."

"Do you, now?" Leaning forward, Doyle folded his arms on
the desk. "And did you know she's Irish? Or that she's no kin to
the Throckmorton bitch? Or that her true name is Cathleen
Donovan? Did you know that, boyo?"

Tait could see the Irishman was enjoying himself, and that,
more than anything Doyle could have said or done, killed any
lingering respect Tait might have harbored for this cruel and
soulless man.

Doyle laughed. "So you know about Mrs. Beale's, do you?
And the auction for little Cathleen's virginity? And the fine
training she received at Smythe's hands? Ah . . . I can see on
your face you didn't know that part. Horne said she had a talent
for satisfying a man. A gift, really. He said—"

Tait's fist drove the words back down the Irishman's throat
with enough force to send his chair crashing into the bookcase
behind the desk. Lucky for Doyle, Tait had had to lean over the
desk to deliver the blow, or Doyle's jaw would have been
shattered.

The door opened and Quinn rushed in. He gaped first at Tait,
who was trying to staunch the blood from his torn knuckles,
then at Doyle, who was struggling to disentangle himself from
the chair amid an unending string of Irish curses.

"Send in a bowl of warm water and some clean rags, would
you please, Quinn?" Tait asked.

"Ah . . . yes, sir." He hurried away.

"Ciarch ort," Doyle mumbled, wiping a hand over his
bloody mouth.

"I warned you." Picking up the Pinkerton file, Tait walked to
the fireplace. Bending down, he struck a match and held it to the
corner until the paper caught.

"Feis ort."

As the flames engulfed the file, Tait dropped the folder into
the grate, dusted his hands, and rose. He hadn't wanted this to
deteriorate to physical violence. The Irishman was no match for
him in size or experience or strength, and Tait found it

repugnant to use his fists on a man who was so drunk he could hardly stand. But the images Doyle's words had planted in his mind had had such an explosive effect Tait had reacted purely on instinct. And rage.

"Sit down, Doyle," he ordered as he walked back to the desk.

Still muttering under his breath, Doyle righted his chair, then sank down just as Quinn returned with a bowl of steaming water, a tin of ointment, and a stack of clean rags.

As he set it on the desk, Quinn's gaze swept over the bleeding Irishman before settling on Tait. "Do I need to stay, Mr. Rylander?"

Less of a question than a subtle warning. Which surprised Tait, even though it made him respect the ex-Pinkerton even more for his loyalty to his employer, however misplaced. "No, Quinn. It'll be all right."

"I'll be outside, should I be needed." With a last glance at Doyle, he left, this time leaving the door slightly ajar.

A good man, Quinn. Tait wished he'd known him under other circumstances.

After tending his knuckles, Tait wrapped them tightly with a strip of cloth, then shoved the bowl and ointment toward Doyle. "Clean yourself up."

"Pog mo thoin."

"Just do it."

Tait waited until Doyle had mopped up most of the blood streaming from his nose and split lip before he spoke. "We both know you don't give a damn about Margaret. So we'll put that aside and get to what's bothering you the most."

Doyle glared at him in silence.

"How many stock certificates are left unaccounted for?"

"Why?"

"So we can end this, here and now. How many?"

Thirty minutes later, the negotiations were complete, the debt paid, and Lucinda was safe. At least from Doyle. Tait rose, a feeling of disgust churning in his stomach. But already this sordid scene was slipping behind him and his thoughts were racing ahead to what he needed to do.

Two weeks—maybe less, if he didn't make any stops—and he would be there beside her. That thought sent such a rush of emotion through Tait it swept away all the pain and despair that hung in this room. He felt new again. Hopeful. Like the moment he'd been awaiting all his life had finally arrived.

"Good-bye, Doyle," he said, and turned toward the door.

"Faith, and you're an ungrateful bastard. I saved your life, so I did."

Tait stopped. Curbing his impatience, he turned back. "Yes, you did. And I thank you for it."

"You *thank* me?" With a bitter laugh, the Irishman spread his hands in a gesture of disbelief. "You owe me more than that, so you do!"

"And I've repaid you. Many times. But you're a bottomless pit of need and greed, Doyle, and nothing I can say or do will ever fill you up. So I quit trying."

"I made you rich!"

"No! I made you rich," Tait shouted back. "Do you know how many times I had to give my personal surety on your dodgy deals? No one wanted to do business with Doyle Kerrigan unless they knew Tait Rylander was standing behind him."

"They hate the Irish—"

"They hate a liar! A man whose word is worth less than the breath used to give it." Seeing the sullen look in the Irishman's face, Tait let some of his anger go. This was getting him nowhere. He didn't know all the forces that had shaped this man he had once called friend, and he no longer cared. He had other things to do and places to go. A woman to win.

But in deference to their long years together, he tried one last time to reach through the bitterness and selfishness to the man he hoped still dwelled behind the empty eyes and seducer's smile.

"You left your soul in Ireland, Doyle. I suggest you go back and try to find it before it's too late."

"Go back?" Doyle laughed and reached down for the bottle beside his chair. "Just walk away from all I've built here? *Pog mo thoin.*"

Tait opened the door. He looked back at the man slumped in the chair, head tipped back, the glass raised to his lips. "Then I pity you."

Doyle's words kept circling in Tait's head as he hurried down the street. . . . *Her training at Smythe's hands* . . .

. . . Horne said she had a talent . . .
. . . He held an auction for her virginity . . .

He shook with rage.

If the Pinkerton report was right that both Horne and Smythe had been at Mrs. Beale's when Lucinda was there, then he now knew who her enemy was. The same man headed her way now.

Franklin Horne.

A sense of urgency quickened his limping stride.

He had no firsthand knowledge of the Beale whorehouse since it had burned down long before he'd come to Manhattan. He had still been in North Carolina back in fifty-five, a young man of nineteen, newly orphaned by a freak flood and struggling to hold on to his parents' store while studying the law. But Mrs. Beale's reputation as the purveyor of the most debased and vile entertainments in Five Points was legendary. He could only imagine the depravity Lucinda might have witnessed or been forced to participate in, or the cruelties she had endured at the hands of Smythe and Horne. Not the kind of appetites a man running for a governorship would want made public.

Now, along with who, he knew why.

But he couldn't let his mind go further than that. It was too much. He couldn't bear to think of Lucinda suffering what she must have with no one there to protect her.

But when he caught up with Horne . . . *God* . . . he would pay.

On his way to Mrs. Throckmorton's, he stopped at a Western Union office and sent a wire to Lucinda in care of the Heartbreak Creek Hotel. He kept it simple and to the point: *Do not go to Denver. I'll be there soon. Tait.*

If he had time, he might write her a more detailed letter later. But for now, he hoped this warning would be enough.

It was full dark when he arrived at the Sixty-ninth Street brownstone. But even in the dim light of the street lamps, it was apparent Pringle was in a snit. He didn't bait Tait at all but did as he was told without a single sniff or snort or haughty glare. Tait understood why as soon as Mrs. Throckmorton came into the receiving room, looking every bit as cheerful as her butler was dour.

"You are such a dear, Mr. Rylander," she gushed, fluttering a lace-edged hanky in greeting as she swept into the room. "I cannot thank you enough."

"For what?"

"For Mrs. Bradshaw, of course. The woman is a gem. A miracle worker. An absolute joy. Even Pringle is afraid of her." Abruptly she stopped fluttering when her gaze fell on the stained rag around Tait's hand. "Oh, dear! What have you done to yourself now?"

"I just came from Doyle's. He knows everything. That she's Irish, and her name was Cathleen, and about . . . everything."

She seemed to deflate. "Mrs. Beale's, too?"

He nodded. He hadn't been sure of how much Mrs. Throckmorton had been aware, but if she knew about Mrs. Beale's whorehouse, then she probably knew all of it. He didn't know what to say. What to think. What he was supposed to do with all this rage churning inside him.

The old woman sank into her chair. "How?"

"The Pinkertons are very thorough."

Damn them. The idea of strangers—men—pouring over the salacious details of the abuse Lucinda had suffered made Tait want to hit something.

Slumping into the chair across from Mrs. Throckmorton, he propped his elbows on his knees and dropped his forehead into his hands. How could this have happened? To Lucinda? To any woman, much less a child?

It shamed him. As it should shame any man.

"It was Horne who sent Smythe after her," he said once he'd gotten himself in hand. "I'm sure of it. He was there . . . back then. She probably saw or heard . . ."

He couldn't complete the thought. Letting his hands drop away, he looked up and saw his own pain reflected in Mrs. Throckmorton's watery blue eyes. "She was just a child. How could she bear it?"

Mrs. Throckmorton blotted her tears with her hanky, then gave him a tremulous smile. "Because she's strong. Because she's a survivor. And she never let it defeat her. Nor should you." Reaching out, she took Tait's undamaged hand in both of hers.

Her fingers felt brittle against his, her skin cool and papery. But their grip was surprisingly strong.

"Don't fail her now, Mr. Rylander." She stared hard into his eyes even as tears slid down her rouged cheeks. "If you do,

I shall allow Pringle to push you down the steps as he's been pining to do all these weeks."

Tait smiled grimly, despite the sudden sting in his own eyes. "I have no intention of failing her, madam. I intend to marry her."

"Humph." Releasing his hand, she sat back. She took a moment to smooth a wrinkle from her skirt, then hiked her chin. "You shall have to ask my permission first, of course."

"I'm asking for it now, ma'am. But only as a courtesy. I will have your ward as my wife, with or without your blessing."

"Cheeky."

"Determined."

"She won't be easy to win."

Tait smiled. "I have my ways." Picking up his cane, he rose. "I'll be leaving on the first ferry to Paulus Hook in the morning. But I could delay that should you want to go to Colorado Territory with me."

The old lady's eyes clouded again. "I should like to, but you will travel faster alone, and it's imperative that you reach Margaret as soon as possible."

Tait couldn't argue with that. "If you decide to come later, I urge you not to travel alone. Bring Mrs. Bradshaw. She would be excellent company."

"But scant protection. And that would leave Pringle with no one to keep an eye on him."

"Then let him go," Tait suggested. "He's hardly indispensable." *Not with that attitude.*

"Oh, I couldn't. The man dotes on me, you know. I suppose I could have Cyrus Quincy from the bank check on him."

Tait thought for a moment, then stepping to the escritoire against the window wall, pulled out a piece of stationery and a pen. After scribbling down a short note, he handed the paper to Mrs. Throckmorton. "I would feel better if you had more protection. Contact this man. I can vouch for his trustworthiness and experience. Buster Quinn would look after you well. Meanwhile, if you need to reach me, send a wire to either Pittsburgh or Columbus or St. Louis, and ask them to hold it for my arrival. I'll check with the Western Union offices in each town as I travel through."

She studied the paper. "Buster. An absurd name. But perhaps I will."

Leaning down, Tait braced his hands on the armrests of Mrs. Throckmorton's chair. He gave her a solemn look. "You will come, dear lady. And soon. Because there is no other but you that I and Lucinda Hathaway or Margaret Hamilton or Cathleen Donovan would have at our sides when we wed."

She batted at his chin with her hanky. "Don't hover."

Laughing, he bent lower, pressed his lips to her soft cheek, then straightened. "Thank you for your kindness, madam. I value it highly."

"You should. Now go. My daughter awaits."

Tait made one more stop on his way home. Even though the bank was closed at this late hour, he and his banker shared a long friendship, and Tait was comfortable dropping by his house uninvited.

Luckily Geoffrey Brisbane was home. And it was even more fortunate that he had a safe in his study. Accepting Tait's note in exchange for two thick envelopes of bank notes, he quickly wrote down all of Tait's instructions relating to his Manhattan home and various accounts.

"I don't know when I'll be back, Geoff," Tait said, once all the transactions were completed and they were walking into the foyer. "But I thank you for disposing of the house and clearing any outstanding debts. As for the Rices, you have my instructions. If there is any problem or if you have questions, you can contact me in Heartbreak Creek."

When they reached the front door, the older man paused. "I have to say, Tait, all this seems rather impulsive. Especially for such a deliberate man as yourself. What has made you decide to take such a leap now?"

Tait had to laugh. "You want me to say it, don't you?" Geoff had long been after him to sever ties with Doyle and find another purpose in his life other than chasing the next business venture. "Okay, you were right. About Doyle. About settling down. About everything. You're brilliant."

Geoff laughed. "Perhaps so. But I didn't intend that you

should go all the way to Colorado to prove it." His smile faded
into an expression of affection. He gave Tait's shoulder a final
squeeze, then opened the front door. "I shall miss you . . . both
as an investing partner and a friend. I wish you luck, Tait."

"I'll need it."

Before Tait made it up the steps of his home a half hour later,
Elder had the door open. "Ceily was wondering if you was coming home for supper tonight. Want I should have her set a plate
in the dining room?"

"Have you eaten?"

"Just fixing to."

"Then I'll eat in the kitchen with you. I need to talk to you
both."

"That don't sound good."

A few minutes later, after Ceily had served up plates overflowing with collards, pork chops, mashed sweet potatoes—
with molasses, of course—fluffy biscuits, and huge slices of
pecan pie—also made with molasses—they were all seated
around the worn table in the kitchen of Tait's house.

He looked around, a feeling of homesickness already moving through him. This had been his first real home since enlist-
ing in the Union Army and leaving North Carolina forever. It
had been a comfortable, happy place—mainly due to the efforts
of these two people sitting here with him. They had anchored
him, worried over him, and provided a safe refuge when the
pressures of his business life seemed to weigh him down. He
would miss them.

"I'm leaving Manhattan," he said.

Ceily froze, a forkful of sweet potatoes arrested in midair.
"Forever?"

"Probably." Tait braced himself for the tears, admonish-
ments, and appeals that were sure to come.

Instead, Ceily let her fork clatter back to her plate and
clapped her hands. "Praise the Lawd! See, Elder, didn't I say
everything work out? When, Mr. Tait?"

It was a moment before Tait could form a response. "Actually, I'm leaving tomorrow, but—"

"Wonderful! What about the house?"

Leaning back in his chair, he studied the faces beaming back at him, a bit put off by such giddy delight at their impending separation. "Mr. Brisbane at the bank will be arranging for its sale. But you can stay on—"

"Sho' 'nuff, we'll stay on and keep an eye on it. Ain't that so, Elder? How long you think that'll take, Mr. Tait?"

"I'm not sure. Perhaps a month or two."

Ceily looked questioningly at her husband.

He nodded back.

They both grinned like possums eating persimmons.

Resting a bony hand on Tait's arm, Ceily gave him a broad smile. "That be fine, Mr. Tait. 'Cause we leaving, too. Been trying to get up the nerve to tell you." Laughing at Tait's look of surprise, she launched into some garbled account of her sister down in Alabama who had inherited a big house and wanted their help to turn it into a boarding house catering to rich folks who came to the Gulf on holiday.

"Got it from a white woman—can you credit that, Mr. Tait? Just up and left it to her. Lawd, these times are a'changing, just like Mister Revels say. We been saving up a long time, and this the perfect place to spend it. Be a good life, Mr. Tait. Having our own house, maybe a little patch where I can grow me some vegetables, put up a chicken roost, maybe get a milk cow or two. We been thinking on it for a long time."

It struck Tait how far removed his life was from theirs, despite living in the same house. This was the first he'd ever heard of their aspirations, and it shamed him that he had never bothered to ask. But at least now, he might be able to help.

Reaching into his coat pocket, he pulled out the envelope marked with their names. "Then I'm pleased to help you realize that dream," he said, setting the envelope on the table by Ceily's plate. "For all that the two of you have done to ease my life over these last years, I thank you."

Ceily glanced at her husband, then back at Tait, then down at the envelope. "This for us?"

"It is."

Picking up the envelope as if it might come alive and bite her, she lifted the flap and peeked inside, then screamed so loud Tait thought his windows would crack.

"Oh, Lawd—Lawd—sweet Jesus!" Clutching the envelope

of bank notes to her chest, she slumped in the chair and would have toppled to the floor if her husband hadn't caught her.

Tait spent most of the night preparing for his departure early the next day. Mr. Brisbane would see that the furnishings and books went to local charities and churches, so all he had to pack were items of a personal nature, which Elder would send on to Heartbreak Creek. It amounted to only a single trunk. Not much to show for five years of his life.

By dawn, after an emotional parting from the Rices, he was steaming across the Hudson toward New Jersey, the crisp fall air cold against his face as he stood at the rail. Now that he was finally on his way, a sense of impatience gripped him and thoughts of Lucinda filled his mind.

Would she welcome him? Or would he have to woo her again? He smiled, strategies already forming in his mind. As long as he was with her, nothing else mattered.

Several days later, when he checked the Western Union office in St. Louis, he found a telegram from Mrs. Throckmorton awaiting him.

"Kerrigan gone. Quinn, Bradshaw, and I leave next week. Don't tell Margaret. T."

Eighteen

"There he is," Lucinda whispered, nodding toward the tall man talking with Declan in the hallway outside the dining room. "I think it's him. I wish Maddie was here to tell us for sure."

She had sent for Edwina and Pru as soon as the stranger had disappeared into the washroom with his nasty dog. Now the three ladies were seated at Lucinda's usual table in the dining room, which presented a fine view of the hallway and adjacent lobby.

"He's too old," Edwina decided.

Lucinda shook her head. "Don't let the gray in his hair fool you. Up close, he looks about your husband's age. And he has a very strong Scottish accent. I'm sure it's her Angus, even though he introduced himself as Lord Ashby to me." A false name if Lucinda ever heard one. And she should know.

As if he had read her mind, the man turned and looked directly at Lucinda.

She scowled back, trying to remember what color Maddie said her husband's eyes were. This man's were as green as Ireland—a lighter, mossier shade than her own.

Declan continued to speak over the huge rough-coated dog sprawled at their feet, his long legs spanning the hallway. The man's gaze swept over Pru, paused on Edwina, then swung back to Declan.

He was almost as tall as Edwina's husband, but leaner. His clothing was well made, his bearing stiffly erect. An ex-soldier. Lucinda was certain it was Angus Wallace.

"What exactly did he say?" Pru asked.

"That he had news of Maddie's family, but he wouldn't tell me what. I don't trust him."

"Why?" Pru asked, surprised. "What has he done?"

"He let his muddy dog into my lobby. And he was impertinent. Far too bossy for my liking. No wonder Maddie left him."

"I think he's handsome. With that gray hair and those dark brows, he's quite striking. Not as striking as Declan, of course, but then who would be?"

Tait Rylander, for one. But Lucinda kept that information to herself.

"Thomas has a lovely smile," Pru offered.

"Does he?" Edwina smirked at her half sister. "I wouldn't know, since you're the only one he ever smiles at."

"That's not true. He smiles at the children all the time."

"Look," Lucinda cut in. "He's leaving. Wave Declan over so we can find out what they were talking about."

Edwina put on a face. "Good luck getting information from that man. He's only marginally more talkative than Thomas."

"Thomas talks all the time."

"Not to anyone but you, Pru."

"Have a seat, sheriff," Lucinda called as Declan strode up. She hoped the chair he reached for was one of the newly repaired. The man was as big as a house. "So what did he say?" she asked once he was safely settled.

"About what?"

"See?"

"Hush, Edwina, let the man talk."

Lucinda waved the sisters to silence. "Who is he, why is he here, and what does he want with Maddie?"

"Didn't ask his name. Said he had news of her family. And I don't know what he wants with her. Any coffee left?"

"Like talking to a rock," Edwina muttered.

Lucinda motioned to Miriam to bring another cup. "What kind of news?"

"Didn't say."

"He must have said something. You were talking to him for a good five minutes."

Declan scratched his bristled chin. "We talked about his dog some. An Irish wolfhound. Impressive animal."

Almost choking on frustration, Lucinda refrained from banging her forehead on the table. "How can you bear it?" she asked Edwina.

"He has other compensating qualities." Edwina grinned at her husband.

He grinned back. When he did that, he was almost as handsome as Tait, Lucinda thought, then turned back to her questions. "What did you tell him? And don't deny you said anything, Declan Brodie. I saw your lips move."

"I asked if his dog was dangerous and told him I didn't want him to upset you ladies and that Maddie was headed up to the Alamosa River. Thanks, Miriam," he said as the waitress set a steaming cup before him.

Lucinda was aghast. "You told him where she was?"

"Don't worry." The sheriff gave that lopsided smile that made Edwina sigh. "He doesn't hurt women. Said so, himself."

"Good heavens."

"Is he going after her?" Pru asked.

"Didn't say."

Lucinda swiveled toward him, fists planted on her hips. "If he does anything to Maddie—harms a single hair on her head, Declan—I swear I'll—"

"Are you threatening my husband?"

Pru rolled her eyes. "Oh, dear."

"That's sweet, Ed. But I can handle her, I think."

Dear Mrs. Throckmorton,

Why is everybody trying to ruin my happy little town? First Tait wires that he is on his way to Heartbreak Creek and orders me not to go to Denver! (Does he truly think I will alter all my plans on his account when he wasn't even invited to come here in the first place? Honestly.)

Then I find out someone else is buying up right-of-ways in the canyon, which will ruin my plans. And now some rude, arrogant man with a huge dog, who thinks he's a lord or

*some such (the man, not the dog) is chasing after Maddie—
and our sheriff actually told him where she was! Men can
be so obtuse. Except for the late judge, of course.*

*Luckily I have time to straighten all this out before we
leave for Denver. Worst case, I might have to go into partnership with whoever is buying the right-of-ways, which I
would rather not do. It is most upsetting.*

*Well, enough of my complaints. How are things with
you? Is the new housekeeper working out? I have great
respect for Mrs. Bradshaw and am delighted she has found
a more agreeable situation with you.*

*A guest left an old newspaper behind, and I read where
Doyle has apparently absconded to Ireland after several
business ventures failed. Good riddance, I say. It is quite a
relief to know I no longer need worry about that man and
his Pinkertons.*

*Well, I must run. I have much to do before we leave, and
with all this fretting I find I'm not sleeping as well as I'd
like.*

*I hope all is well with you,
Your devoted Margaret*

Maddie returned late one afternoon almost a week after Lord
High Pockets left for Alamosa to find her . . . and she didn't
return alone. Lucinda met her at the back door into the hotel and
barely mastered her dismay when she saw that same Scottish
person and his oversized dog standing behind Maddie.

"I have the most dreadful news, Luce," Maddie cried, stepping over the threshold. "Mr. Satterwhite died. His heart, I
think. It was so unexpected."

"I don't see how." Lucinda glared at the dog and his owner
as they crowded into the narrow space. "The man must have
been at least a hundred."

"Seventy-three. He was only seventy-three, and quite vigorous for his age." Maddie set down her little lap dog, which
immediately charged toward the lobby and the two women
coming through the front doors. "What are Pru and Edwina
doing here?"

"I sent for them when I saw your wagon go by." Lucinda closed the back door. "I thought we could dine together and hear all about your trip. And poor Mr. Satterwhite, of course."

"I should like that." Calling to her friends, Maddie went to greet them, leaving Lucinda standing in the hall with the frowning Scotsman.

"Of course, you're welcome too, Mr. . . . Ashby, was it?"

"Lord Ashby."

That cool smile changed his austere face for the better, Lucinda noted. And those green eyes were definitely his finest feature, although he wasn't nearly as handsome as Tait. But then, who could be?

"Perhaps another time," he said, rolling the *r*s in his thick brogue.

"I've asked Sheriff Brodie and Thomas Redstone to join us," she added so he wouldn't think her forward. "So you needn't fear being overrun by ladies."

"As fearful—and intriguing—as such a fate might be, I must decline." Shifting the heavy saddlebags slung over his shoulder, he glanced at the closed door into the washroom. "However, if I might trouble you for a bottle of your finest and use of your washroom . . ." He let the sentence hang on a hopeful note.

Her gaze flicked over his rumpled, mud-spattered clothing. "Of course. You'll find hot water on the stove and drying cloths in the cabinet. Please don't use them on your dog. If you need your clothing laundered, put them in the burlap bag on the hook behind the door and Billy will take it down to the Chinese laundry later. I'll send Yancey with the bottle." She started away, then turned back. "Will you be needing a room, as well?"

"Best check with my—with Madeline."

Clearly an evasive answer. But before Lucinda could question him further, he reached past her to open the washroom door. "Come, Tricks."

Dinner was a somber affair, partly out of deference to Mr. Satterwhite's passing but also because everyone was waiting for Maddie to explain who the Scotsman was and what his news was concerning her family. Edwina, ever impatient, finally broached the subject. "So? Who is he?"

For a moment Lucinda thought Maddie might try to dodge the question. Then she sighed and said, "He's my husband."

"I knew it!" Lucinda threw her napkin onto the table. "That wretch lied to me! He said his name was Ashby. Lord Ashby."

"It is."

"But . . . I thought Angus Wallace was your husband."

"He is. But he recently came into the title of Viscount Ashby."

"Oh, my goodness gracious." Pru's smile lit up her strikingly beautiful face. "I suppose that makes you a viscountess, does it not?"

"A viscountess?" Edwina clapped her hands and laughed. "Well, if that isn't the most exciting thing. Our Maddie a real English Lady. Should we curtsy, do you think?"

Lucinda masked her growing unease behind a teasing smile. "Are we now to call you Lady Ashby?" She didn't want Maddie to go. But with a grand estate and title awaiting her in Scotland, how could she stay?

Declan studied Maddie over his coffee cup. "Why is he here?"

"He wants to take me back to Scotland."

Lucinda felt as if her stomach had dropped to the floor. Voices rose in protest, drawing glances from the other diners. But Declan continued in his calm, reasonable way. "Do you want to go back?"

Maddie gave a helpless shrug. "It's complicated."

"But I don't want you to leave," Edwina protested.

"She will not go." Pushing his empty plate aside, Thomas Redstone folded his forearms on the table.

Usually when he was in town and acting as Declan's temporary deputy, he dressed in his "whitewashed" attire—meaning trousers rather than leggings, a collarless work shirt and blue army jacket in place of breechcloth and war shirt, and instead of a topknot with an eagle feather, his long black hair and narrow temple braids pulled back and tied with a strip of leather. But Edwina had mentioned earlier that Thomas had just returned from another of his mysterious forays into the mountains and had not taken time to stop by his room in the Brodies' carriage house to change out of his Indian garb. He looked quite fearsome, Lucinda thought. Perhaps fearsome enough to run off a Scotsman.

Studying Maddie through eyes as black as chips of basalt,

Thomas said in his flat, solemn voice, "Unless it is what Madeline Wallace wants, he will not take her away. I will not allow it."

Maddie regarded the Cheyenne with alarm. No one was quite sure when he was joking, and when he was not. "It's all right. He is my husband, after all."

"Then you must do as he says. Always. It is your duty."

Pru shot him a look.

"Ho." Thomas gave that startling smile that curled women's toes. "Have I ruffled my little brown dove's feathers?" Which earned him another look.

A strange man, Thomas Redstone. One quarter white, three quarters Cheyenne, he straddled two cultures but seemed to belong to neither. He had gained the respect of his people by suffering the ordeal of the Cheyenne sun dance ceremony, then had gone on to earn a place with the Dog Soldiers because of his courage as a warrior. But through adversity and tragedy, he had forged a stronger bond with Declan, and when the tribes had been driven from the territory, Thomas had stayed behind. Now he watched over his new tribe in Heartbreak Creek.

He was a welcome addition to Lucinda's growing little family, and if he wanted to chase off the Scotsman, she wasn't about to try to stop him.

"Ash would never force me to go back," Maddie defended. "But it's either go to Scotland or petition for a divorce. And because Ash is now a peer, a divorce would require an act of Parliament, which could take years."

"Then why doesn't he stay here?" Edwina asked.

"He can't. As next in line, he has duties to the earldom and the lands that go with it." She gave a sad smile. "And Ash has ever been a creature bound by duty."

"Well, I don't give a fig," Edwina announced. "He treated you shabbily by not writing or coming to see you, and for that, he doesn't deserve another chance."

"He had reason."

"Such as?" Lucinda challenged.

Maddie shrugged. "He was injured, for one thing. And still suffers because of it. He's not a bad man, Luce. I wouldn't want any of you to think that."

After the way he had behaved toward his wife, how could they not? But Lucinda kept that thought to herself.

The gathering broke up soon after. Before dispersing, Edwina invited everyone to Sunday dinner at the Brodie house the next day, and suggested they hold a short memorial for Mr. Satterwhite after services. "I thought we would eat at two. And be sure to bring along Lord Ashby or Angus Wallace or whatever he's called," she told Maddie. "I have some questions for the fellow."

"Oh, dear," Prudence murmured.

"Now, Ed," Declan seconded as he helped his pregnant wife from her chair. "Don't you start anything."

"Oh, hush. As if I would." Edwina narrowed her blue eyes at her overgrown husband. "But aren't you just the littlest, teensiest, weensiest bit curious why he did what he did? It near broke her heart."

"I can hear you," Maddie chided. "I'm standing right here. And my heart isn't that broken." As the other four filed out, she turned to Lucinda. "She's gotten so big. Will she be up to the trip to Denver, do you think?"

"Edwina will do what Edwina will do." Lucinda motioned for Miriam to clear the table. "I doubt I'll be able to attend dinner tomorrow. And don't give me that look, Maddie. It's not because I think your husband is a cad for treating you the way he did—injured or not. But I have to ready my presentation for Denver. Now that the Denver Pacific has completed the main line from Cheyenne, they might be seeking a southern route across the Rockies, rather than relying solely on the Transcontinental. This will be my best chance to convince them to come through our little canyon."

"Ash intends to accompany us to Denver," Maddie said as they walked toward the lobby. "He thinks I need protection."

"Perhaps he's right." She paused by the front desk. "I'm assuming you and your husband will want the big suite. That way you would have your own bedroom, in case you don't . . . well . . ."

"The big suite will be fine," Maddie said, avoiding Lucinda's gaze.

After finding the key, she told Yancey to move Maddie's things to the big suite, then turned her attention back to the upcoming convention. "Hopefully with Grant in office there will be no more vetoes. But if this attempt to gain statehood fails, there could be violence. We might need every protector we can get."

"I hope not." Retrieving her coat and little dog from the room behind the front desk, Maddie said her good nights and went down the hall to the back door.

Lucinda felt that stab of dread as she watched her go. She resolved to try to be nicer to Maddie's Scottish lord. Maybe if she made him feel welcome, he might not be in such a hurry to drag her friend away.

They left for Denver several days later. It was an uneventful trip, other than an incident with a man and his young simpleminded brother who shared their camp one night. Apparently a third brother was missing, and since Maddie had photographed him, they thought she might remember where she had last seen him. But Maddie couldn't recall, and the next morning they were gone. It turned out they were imposters and claim jumpers, which they learned the next day when Thomas rode up with the missing man's real brother—a reverend—in tow.

It was all very confusing. Lucinda happily left it to the others to sort through while she concentrated on polishing her proposal. She was committed to selling the idea of a railroad coming through their canyon, sensing it was the town's best chance of survival.

Denver was a bustling town ready to blossom, due to all the mines sprouting up in the hills. Miners, gamblers, and all manner of ruffians crowded the streets, as well as those who catered to them. Declan and Lord Ashby thought they would all be safer out of the commercial district, so they found a boarding house not too far from the government buildings.

Lucinda's first appointment was with the gentlemen of the Denver Pacific, and as she climbed up onto the driver's bench of Maddie's little gypsy wagon the next morning, she was almost vibrating with excitement.

"Are you ready for your meeting today?" Maddie asked, taking her seat between Lucinda and Chub, the boy Lord Ashby had hired to drive them into town. Declan had ridden ahead to his earlier convention meeting, while the Scotsman had stayed behind to keep an eye on Edwina and their belongings. Thomas and the reverend would be leaving for the area where Thomas thought the missing brother's mine might be located.

Lucinda patted the thick, ribbon-tied folder in her lap. "All that's missing is the paperwork on the water test."

"I thought you already took care of that."

"I did. But the results weren't as good as I'd hoped so I'm having it tested again." The water in Heartbreak Creek was its major drawback, as was proven by the stained teeth of most of the longtime residents. The high mineral content was equally damaging to pipes, gauges, and valves on steam-driven locomotives, and for that reason, the railroads had avoided Heartbreak Canyon when they had laid tracks through this part of the territory several years earlier. But their alternate route presented its own problems, including a steep grade up Henson's Loop and the trestle over Damnation Creek, which washed out each spring.

But now, with the mine shut down and the water cannon no longer in operation, Lucinda was convinced the mineral levels in Heartbreak Creek's water would be substantially reduced, which might induce the railroad to reroute through their canyon rather than go through the costly and time-consuming task of rebuilding the trestle every year.

"And if the new results are still not favorable?" Maddie asked.

"I'll have Edwina use her willow sticks to find a water flow, then dig a new well." Edwina had already found a new water source at the ranch—hopefully she could find one for the town, too.

"Won't that be a terrible expense?"

Lucinda wished she could make her friend understand why this was so important to her. "I'm committed to this, Maddie. I want to see Heartbreak Creek flourish again so we can be proud to call it home."

And the longer she stayed in Heartbreak Creek, the more resolute she became. Edwina and Pru had lost their plantation home in Louisiana, but they still had each other, and now both women had men who adored them. Maddie still had her Scottish rogue, although they had yet to establish a home, either in Scotland or here. But Lucinda had nothing except her new friends, a stack of railroad shares that was rapidly dwindling, and her hopes for Heartbreak Creek. And she was determined to succeed.

Her morning meeting with the Denver Pacific went beautifully, although it wasn't until she finished her proposal that she learned the two men she had presented it to were not the final decision makers. However, their enthusiasm was gratifying, and before she left, they had set up another appointment with the gentleman in charge of routing and construction. She wasn't able to put her proposal before the board of the Kansas Pacific yet, but managed to garner a luncheon meeting with Edgar Kitchner at the Grand Hotel the following day. In her estimation, the day had been a huge success.

That evening, another odd thing happened when Lord Ashby or Mr. Wallace—the man had entirely too many names—found one of the claim jumpers who had had intruded on their camp earlier, Silas, the simpleminded younger brother, hiding in the little barn behind the boarding house. It seems he had been ordered to watch Maddie while his older brother and a cohort followed the reverend and Thomas to the missing brother's claim.

"Thomas could be riding into an ambush," Mr. Wallace said. Determined to warn him, he rode out, trailed by his giant dog, leaving Declan in charge of the ladies and young Silas.

Silas seemed a sweet young man, and had been clearly abused by his brother, so the ladies were happy to fix up a place for him in the barn and bring him food.

Mrs. Kemble, the boarding house owner, was less happy.

The next morning, Declan sent Maddie and Lucinda into town without him, while he stayed behind to watch over Edwina. When the Scotsman returned with Thomas and the reverend that afternoon, he would ride into town and cast his statehood vote.

This trip into town was even more nerve-racking for Lucinda than the one on the previous day. She saw it as her last chance to tout her proposal, since the convention ended that afternoon with the final vote, and the Brodies would want to leave soon after to return to the children. She had scarcely slept, and as they headed into the commercial district, she was so nervous she thought she might toss up her breakfast.

"How do I look?" she asked Maddie when Chub stopped the wagon before the Grand Hotel where she would be meeting with the gentleman from the Denver Pacific, then later lunching with Kitchner of the Kansas Pacific.

Maddie brushed a piece of lint off Lucinda's green traveling cape and straightened her matching bonnet. "Beautiful. You'll win the day for certain."

"I pray you're right." Her heart pounding wildly, Lucinda climbed down, checked her cape and skirts, then with a wave to Maddie, walked into the lobby, her head high and her folder under her arm.

Three hours later she came back out on the verge of tears, the folder a mangled mess from fidgeting with it while she waited for appointments that never happened. Stopping outside the hotel doors, she read the note gripped in her trembling fingers.

It is with regret that we must pass on your proposal. DP

That was it. Less than a dozen words on Denver Pacific stationery. No salutation. No signature. And how could they pass on her proposal when the man she was to meet with hadn't even seen it? It made no sense.

She considered marching back in and demanding an explanation. But the thought of facing that officious secretary again made her stomach roll. He actually seemed to enjoy destroying her hopes and dreams.

What had she done to chase them off? Yesterday the advance men had seemed so enthusiastic. Then this morning, this abrupt note? What had happened between then and this morning?

Her mind numbed with disappointment, she wandered several blocks before she was able to bring her thoughts into focus. It was just one railroad, she reminded herself. She still had her meeting with Kitchner. Surely that one would go better.

It didn't.

In fact, Kitchner didn't even do her the courtesy of canceling their luncheon himself. He sent an underling—this time an overweight, buck-toothed man with hair sprouting from his ears—to tell her he wouldn't be meeting with her. Ever.

Battling tears of utter despair, she walked listlessly down to the government offices where Maddie said she would be working through the morning.

"What are you doing here?" Maddie asked, holding a box of photographs she was about to pass up to Chub, who stood at the top of the back steps, stowing her equipment and supplies into the wagon.

"I thought I'd ride back with you."

"What about your luncheon?"

"Canceled." Fearing she might burst into tears if she said more, Lucinda picked up a small crate of negative plates and handed them up to Chub. "Anything else to load?"

Maddie looked around. "I think that's it."

They rode in silence for a while, then Maddie put her hand over Lucinda's and gave it a comforting squeeze. "I can see you're upset, dearest. Tell me what happened. Perhaps I can help."

Weakened by that simple act of support, Lucinda looked away, blinking hard to hold back tears. Once she had regained control, she gave the hand holding hers a pat, then released it. "I don't know what happened. It's as if overnight I've become a pariah."

"Perhaps they had conflicts."

"That's what I thought. But when I tried to schedule another meeting with the Kansas Pacific, the assistant informed me that Mr. Kitchner would be unavailable . . . permanently. What do you make of that?"

"Obviously he's a fool. Just as well you won't be doing business with him. He'll come to regret missing this wonderful opportunity, mark my words."

Lucinda absently plucked at the tattered edge of the folder in her lap. "I might have agreed, had he been the only one to cancel."

"The men from the Denver Pacific dropped out, as well?"

Lucinda nodded. "Yesterday the two men I met with seemed so enthusiastic about my plans. Then today no one spared me a glance."

"They gave no reason for their change of heart?"

"Their minions gave a few mumbled excuses. Overextending. Labor shortages. Right-of-way issues. The usual. All polite ways of saying they're no longer interested. I just can't figure why." Feeling the prick of tears again, she blinked hard. "Something's not right. It's as if someone has warned them off."

"Are there no other railroads you could talk to?"

"One. A newly formed group out of New York called the Wichita Pacific. But I know nothing about them."

"Perhaps you should find out," Maddie suggested. "You've come too far to give up now."

Lucinda gave a halfhearted shrug. She wasn't feeling hopeful.

Declan came out to meet them when they rolled up to the stable. "What are you doing back so soon?" he asked Lucinda as he helped her down from the driver's box.

"I had no reason to stay." She explained about the canceled meetings, adding, "I think this whole trip has been a waste of time."

"The vote for statehood doesn't look promising, either."

"Any word from Ash or Thomas?" Maddie asked.

"Nothing yet," Declan said, helping Chub unharness the mules.

The back door slammed. Mrs. Kemble marched purposefully toward them.

Lucinda thought the woman was kindly enough but rather autocratic. However, she set a good table, which greatly appealed to the men. She looked even angrier now than when she'd found out about the simpleminded boy, Silas.

"Trouble," Declan muttered.

"I need to talk to you people." The heavyset woman stopped before them, feet braced, hands planted on her aproned hips. "First you bring a Red Indian to my house, then that giant dog roaming everywhere, and now I have a simpleminded boy living in my barn. I don't know what kind of establishment you think I'm running here, but I've about had it with your shenanigans."

"What shenanigans, ma'am?" Declan asked in his calm way.

"Comings and goings at all hours of the night, that's what. People disappearing, then others showing up, and now strangers hounding me with their questions. I don't need this aggravation. I run a respectable place."

"What strangers?" Lucinda asked, wondering if the Pinkertons were back on her trail, even though Doyle had fled to Ireland.

"I'm sure I don't know. Some fellow asking about Miss Hathaway. He didn't leave his name. I told him you would be in town all day, and sent him on his way. But now here you are.

And your wife, sheriff, says the other three—the reverend and that Scotsman and the Indian—will be back this evening. Do you people have any idea how difficult it is to plan meals when I never even know who all's going to be here? Now I'll have to go back to the market for two more chickens. I've a mind to send every one of you packing."

"What was he asking?" Lucinda cut in, her mind still caught on the stranger inquiring about her. Could it be Tait? He'd written that he was on his way. The thought of seeing him again made it suddenly hard to draw in a full breath.

"I'm sure it's none of my business," Mrs. Kemble snapped. "Something about a railroad. He had beady eyes is all I remember."

Lucinda frowned, wondering who he could be and with what railroad.

"Is that simpleminded boy expecting to eat, too?"

"I'd appreciate it, ma'am. I can put him to chores to pay for it, if you'd like." Declan gave her the smile he used to charm Edwina. It seemed to have little effect on the landlady.

"You people," she muttered, stomping back to the house. "No telling who or what you'll bring around next."

As soon as she was out of earshot, Maddie turned to Lucinda. "Do you suppose it could be someone from that new railroad, the Wichita Pacific?"

"I don't know." But the thought was intriguing enough to push Tait out of her mind. Temporarily, anyway. It seemed he never strayed far.

"If he's interested enough to come asking about you," Maddie persisted, "perhaps you should make inquiries of your own."

"You're right." Sudden energy shot through her. She grinned at Declan. "I've decided to go back into town with you this afternoon, Sheriff. I've come too far to give up so easily."

"Good," Maddie said with an approving smile. "I'll stay with Edwina until Ash returns with Thomas and the reverend."

The afternoon was as discouraging as the morning had been. When Lucinda finally found out where the representative from the Wichita Pacific was staying during the convention, the concierge told her that he had already left but added that he believed the man had plans to visit Heartbreak Creek later in the month. In addition to that disappointment, the statehood vote failed yet again.

In morose silence, she and Declan rode back to the boarding house.

And into utter chaos.

Edwina and Silas stood weeping on the back stoop beside an irate Mrs. Kemble, while in the yard a U.S. marshal stood over what appeared to be the dead body of a man sprawled halfway between the barn and the house.

"Oh, my word," Lucinda cried. "What happened?"

"Go to Ed," Declan ordered her, hauling the team to a stop. Jumping down, he rushed over to the man in the yard.

Lucinda ran to Edwina. "Are you all right? Who is that man? What's going on? Where's Maddie?"

"You people are insane, that's what's going on," Mrs. Kemble burst out, her color high and frizzy curls framing her face. "I want you out of here before you ruin me completely. I run a proper boarding house. Now I got dead bodies in the yard, strangers and Indians in my barn, that vicious dog running around, and who knows what else." Whirling, she stomped into the house. "Wait 'til I tell Ruby!"

Lucinda put her arm around Edwina, who had her arm around Silas. Both were still crying. "Who is that?" she asked, staring in horror at the bloody body Declan and the marshal were examining.

"Silas's brother," Edwina blubbered. "It's all about that mine in Maddie's photograph. He was convinced Maddie knew where the claim papers were, but she didn't, so he hit her and blood went everywhere. Then Ash rode up and shot his ear off just before Maddie shot him in the stomach with that little pistol you made her carry—shot the brother, not Ash—then his giant dog ran up and attacked the man and Ash stuck him in the throat with a big knife—the man, not the dog. Then Ash fell down, and Maddie was crying and—it was horrible, Lucinda. Just horrible. And Ash said Thomas has been shot."

Lucinda looked around but saw neither the Cheyenne nor Maddie nor Mr. Wallace. Terror clutched at her. "Where is Maddie? Is she all right?"

"She and Ash are at the trough out back trying to wash off

the blood and clean his dog. You should see her poor nose, Lucinda—that's where he hit her—and something's wrong with Ash, his head or something, although he doesn't seem injured. He said Thomas is with the reverend and they're on their way back, but I don't know how bad Thomas is hurt. I need Declan." And shoving the crying Silas toward Lucinda, she waddled off, wailing for her husband.

Just when things were starting to settle down, the reverend arrived in a buckboard with Thomas lying, unconscious, in back, and things got crazy again.

Because Mrs. Kemble didn't want Indians in her house, they had to put Thomas in Maddie's little wagon. The doctor came and said Thomas would recover if fever didn't get him, and Maddie would look worse than she felt for a while.

Meanwhile, Mr. Wallace was suffering a debilitating headache from his old injury and had collapsed upstairs, and Maddie looked as if she had a pound of sticking plaster stuck to her face. Silas was still crying, Declan had his hands full settling down Edwina, and Mrs. Kemble continued to rant.

The only ones not in near hysterics were the dog, who was sleeping happily despite tearing up a man's throat; the reverend, who had generously offered to take Silas under his wing and was even now packing up to go back to his brother's cabin; and Lucinda, who was a master at putting on a calm front even when she was screaming inside.

She felt like she'd fallen into the middle of a night terror.

Finally, after questioning everybody who could sit long enough to talk to him, the marshal decided he didn't know who to arrest for killing Silas's brother—Maddie for shooting him, the dog for tearing up his throat, or Wallace for finishing him off with a bayonet. So he left, taking the body with him.

It didn't feel real. Any of it.

It was a subdued group that headed back to Heartbreak Creek the next day. Lucinda felt like her entire world had spun out of control. At that moment, she didn't care about railroads and broken dreams or Pinkertons or Doyle and Horne or even her poor battered family . . . she just wanted Tait.

Nineteen

Tait arrived in Heartbreak Creek late in the afternoon during the last week of October. He'd had to ride the last twenty miles by horseback, and when he swung out of the saddle, his knee was so sore it almost buckled beneath him.

But he was here. Finally.

He limped into the Heartbreak Creek Hotel, not sure what to expect after Lucinda's descriptions to Mrs. Throckmorton. But it was as nice as any of the western hotels where he'd stayed, and a damn sight cleaner.

He could see Lucinda's touch in the potted plants and the chair cushions and the fringe hanging off the shade of a floor lamp beside the front desk. It was purple, and seeing it made him smile.

The desk clerk looked up as he approached. "Help you?" he asked, showing gapped, brown-tinted teeth in a friendly grin. The child sitting on top of the counter beside him swiveled to regard Tait out of curious gray eyes a shade lighter than his own. With the slouch hat and tattered overalls, Tait wasn't sure if it was a boy or girl.

"Is Miss Hathaway available?" he asked.

"Nope."

"When will she be?"

"Hard to say."

Tait wondered if a cuff upside the man's bald head might jar loose a more helpful answer.

"Who are you?" the child asked before he could act on the impulse. A girl, he guessed. And destined to be a beauty if she ever cleaned herself up.

"A visitor."

"Visiting who?"

"Miss Hathaway."

"What's wrong with your leg?"

Tait hadn't much experience with children and found it disconcerting to be grilled by one. Which seemed to amuse the desk clerk no end.

"Chick has a peg leg," the girl went on. "Made of pine. What's your leg made of?"

"Skin and bone."

"Like Ma, when she's not growing babies." She sent a sage nod to the clerk. "Talks funny like Ed, too." Turning back to Tait, she said, "Can I see it?"

"No."

"Why not?"

"Enough, Brin. If you've come for the doings," the clerk said to Tait, "the wake is over. Even all those funny-talking Scots are gone, wanting to be clear of the mountains before the big snows come. Miss Hathaway is in back with the other ladies cleaning up. They should be done soon. Need a room?"

Tait hoped not. He had plans to share one with Lucinda. "Is the dining room open?"

"Nope."

"They got pickled eggs and pig feet in there," the child chimed in, pointing toward a door in the staircase wall, through which Tait could hear the plinky notes of an out-of-tune piano. "Tastes like do-do, R. D. says. Yancey likes them, though, even if they make him gassy as old Cooter Brown. Right, Yancey?"

"Brin, mind your words. Your ma would come at you with a bar of lye soap she heard such talk coming out your mouth. And Cooter Brown was a drinker, not a farter."

"Probably trying to get rid of the taste of pig feet. They live in do-do, you know."

Wondering if he'd walked into a lunatic asylum by mistake, Tait turned toward the door in the staircase wall.

"Can't go through there," the old man called. "Miss Hathaway locked it permanent. You'll have to go around front."

Glad to escape, Tait went back out the double doors and turned toward the splintered sign swinging above the boardwalk that read RED EYE SALOON and showed at least a half-dozen bullet holes.

The saloon was smoky and noisy and surprisingly crowded for such a deserted-looking town. Most of the tables were filled with dirty men wearing the high boots and slouch hats and frayed homespun that Tait had seen in other mining towns. But sitting at a corner table in back, two well-groomed men met his gaze with curious glances of their own.

Definitely not miners. Pinkertons? But why would Pinkertons still be on the job if Doyle had fled the country?

Tait angled toward the bar, which sported a big jar where chunks of tattered flesh-colored meat and boiled eggs hung suspended in a pale yellowish liquid.

His appetite fled.

The barkeep, a burly man with a bald head and the widest mustache Tait had ever seen, sauntered up. "What'll you have?"

"Brandy?" he asked hopefully.

The man stared at him for a moment, then burst into laughter. "You're joking, right?"

"Rye, then."

"Coming up."

He hated rye whiskey but had found it the common fare in the poorer establishments. He figured it couldn't be much worse than Pringle's watered-down swill.

He took a sip, shuddered, then looked into the cracked mirror behind the bar to find the two men at the corner table staring back at him. They were hard to miss. Both were big. And both were clean. A rarity, it seemed. One had dark hair and eyes and an air of authority about him; the other had gray in his hair despite his youthful face, and dark brows and stubble. He was also wearing a kilt. They both rose and started his way.

Not sure what to expect, Tait braced himself, making sure his right arm was free and his bad knee was slightly flexed. But he doubted even in his prime fighting days he could have handled both men, as big as they were. He wished he hadn't given up his cane. It might have evened the odds a bit.

But instead of coming up on each side, as they would have if they meant mischief, they came to his left side, and stood waiting for him to acknowledge their arrival.

Tait gave a friendly nod.

"You a Pinkerton?" the man with gray in his hair blurted out, rolling the *r* in a thick brogue.

Tait shook his head.

"Did you hire the Pinkertons?" the larger man asked. "We heard there might be some in the area."

"No." Then Tait saw the badge on the man's vest and it all fell into place. "You're the sheriff, aren't you? The one married to the pregnant lady." Turning to the other man, he added, "And you're the photographer's Scotsman. Lord something or other."

"Bluidy hell."

"And who are you?" the sheriff asked.

Tait grinned. "Tait Rylander."

They stared at him without recognition, which was a bit deflating. "From New York."

"Oh, aye," the Scotsman slurred, nodding to the sheriff. "The one Miss Hathaway left at the altar. Maddie told me all about it, so she did."

"That was my business partner," Tait corrected. "She changed her mind after she heard he was a runner and ran off, so he sent Pinkertons to find her. But now that he's gone back to Ireland, there shouldn't be any agents still hanging around."

Judging by their expressions, he hadn't explained that as well as he might have. "So what are you doing here?" the sheriff asked.

"I've come to marry her."

"Miss Hathaway? Blond? Owns the hotel?"

Tait nodded.

"Bluidy hell."

The two men looked at each other, then back to Tait. "Does she know that?"

"Not yet."

"I think I need another drink." Lifting a hand, the sheriff motioned toward the table he and the Scotsman had left. "Join us, Mr. Rylander?"

Tait couldn't tell if it was an order or an invitation, but he nodded anyway.

After they had taken their seats and the barkeep had delivered a bottle of Scotch whiskey—from the Scotsman's private reserve, it seemed—the sheriff introduced himself as Declan Brodie, owner of the Highline Ranch and temporary sheriff of Heartbreak Creek, and the Scotsman as Angus Wallace, Lord Ashby, or Ash, as some folks called him, an ex-cavalry officer and now the new Earl of Kirkwell. "That's why he's wearing a skirt."

"'Tis no' a skirt. 'Tis a kilt, ye daft numptie." Scowling, the Scotsman took a deep swallow.

Tait gave his name again, and added that he was late of Manhattan Island but expected he would be residing in Heartbreak Creek from now on.

After carefully setting down his glass, the earl folded his arms on the table and gave Tait a hard look through alcohol-reddened green eyes. "So . . . you're no' a Pinkerton, then?"

"No," Tait said patiently, wondering if the man was a heavy drinker. He was certainly doing a fine job of it tonight. "I'm a lawyer and railroad investor. Or was. Not sure what I'll be doing now." Other than reacquainting himself with Lucinda, and hopefully soon.

"I always wanted to be a Pinkerton, so I did."

"You haven't always wanted to be a Pinkerton," the sheriff argued. "You only recently found out about them. And I doubt you could be one anyway, since you're a lord."

"Bugger that." The Scotsman slapped a big hand on the table. "I'm a soldier and bluidy peer of the realm. I can be any fookin' thing I want, so I can."

Sheriff Brodie sighed and turned to Tait. "Forgive the language. He's had a hard day. We just laid his brother to rest."

"I'm sorry to hear that," Tait told the Scotsman.

"Aye . . . well." A deep sigh. "'Twas time, I suppose. The puir bastard's been dead these six months, so he has."

"And you're just now burying him?"

The earl reared back, his dark brows drawn into a scowl. "Dinna be foul, ye bluidy foreigner. He's buried in Scotland as he should be."

Between the thick accent and the slurring from drink, Tait could scarcely understand the man. But he thought maybe he'd just been insulted.

Brodie rested a staying hand on the ex-soldier's broad shoulder. "Today was more of a memorial," he told Tait. "Ash piped him to his rest this morning. And this afternoon, before his Scottish family headed back home, the ladies cooked up a nice feast in honor of the new earl and countess."

"Aye." The earl slumped back in his chair. "Donnan was a guid brother, so he was. I'll miss the bastard. Verra much."

Tait looked over as three boys shuffled hesitantly into the saloon, their eyes round as marbles as they looked around the smoky room. They were obviously too young to be regulars, although the oldest was tall and gangly and sported a bit of dark fuzz on his top lip. He seemed vaguely familiar to Tait. The other two—a blond, who had stopped to gape at a poor painting of a nude woman, and a smaller boy, whose face was partially hidden by a fall of brown hair—bore little resemblance to the older boy.

"Hell," the sheriff muttered, catching sight of the newcomers as they angled toward the table where the three men were seated. "What are you boys doing in here?"

The blond gave Tait a hard study. "Who are you?"

"Mind your manners, Joe Bill." Brodie waved the youngsters forward. "This is Mr. Rylander, boys. Tait, these are my sons. Robert Declan Junior is the oldest, although he prefers R. D. Best shot in the family."

Tait saw why the boy looked familiar. With his dark hair and eyes, the boy was a younger, ganglier version of the sheriff.

"This one's Joe Bill." Brodie gave him a sharp look. "Best watch him. Never seen a kid run faster, especially when he's in trouble."

Apparently taking that as a compliment, the boy grinned, showing a hodgepodge of baby teeth, permanent teeth, and missing teeth. "Ed know they got nekkid ladies in here?" he asked his father.

The Scotsman perked up. "Naked ladies. Where?" He swiveled in his chair to study the room. "I dinna see any."

"Over there." Joe Bill pointed to the painting.

"No, she doesn't," the sheriff said sternly, gripping the boy's shoulder in warning. "And she'd best not find out, or I'll know how. Lucas, step closer."

The youngster with the brown cowlick moved forward and

regarded Tait out of solemn eyes that seemed to take in everything.

The sheriff pushed the hair off the boy's wide, intelligent forehead. "You need something figured out, come to Lucas, here. Helluva thinker. And tinkerer."

A pleased flush stained the boy's cheeks. He mumbled something Tait didn't catch.

"Now what are you boys doing in here?" the sheriff asked. "You know you're not allowed."

"Ed's looking for you," the oldest, R. D., said.

"She's getting cranky," Joe Bill warned. "You better come."

Before Brodie could respond, a woman's voice rose on the other side of the closed door leading into the hotel. "Declan Brodie, if you're in there, you better come out right now. The boys have run off, and I'm tired, and Brin is ready to go home. And Ash, you better watch out. Maddie's looking for you. Tricks chewed one of Lucinda's potted plants."

"Bollocks."

"His dog," the sheriff explained to Tait as he rose. "R. D., bring the buckboard around and you boys load up."

As the youngsters trooped out, the earl rose with a weary sigh. "A bad day just keeps getting worse. And I had such grand plans for tonight, so I did."

"In your condition?" The sheriff chuckled. "I doubt it."

The Scotsman drew himself up to parade stance. "I'm a fookin' Hussar, ye daft cow herder. We can do anything, anytime, anyplace. Just ask us. Or my sweet lass." Then he threw back his head and laughed so hard he almost toppled over.

"You go on." Tait waved them toward the door. "I'll pay up. And if you see Lucinda, don't tell her I'm here. I want to surprise her."

The Scotsman grinned, and bending over, lowered his voice to a stage whisper. "Then try the hallway behind the front desk, third door on the right." Frowning, he straightened. "Or maybe the left. I canna remember."

"He mixes up his rights and lefts sometimes," the sheriff said, shoving the Scotsman toward the door. "It's on the left. But I'm not sure you should go barging—"

"It'll be fine," Tait cut in, and hoped that was true. "I told her I was coming. Just not when."

The lobby was deserted when Tait entered with his saddle-bags after taking his horse down to the livery. Grateful not to have to contend with the desk clerk and curious Brin, he went down to the third door on the left and opened it.

It was an office. Her office. He would know that Attar of Roses scent anywhere. Moving inside, he closed the door, set down his bags, and looked around.

It was well furnished with a desk and chair, several book-cases, a table by a tall window, and a couch. Efficient, feminine, tasteful. Just like Lucinda. On the wall beside the desk, a door stood ajar. He crossed over and peered inside.

Her bedroom. Deserted. The thick red robe he remembered well lay thrown across the brass foot rail. Heart pounding, he stepped into the room.

It was lit by a single lamp. He saw slippers by the bed, a hair-brush on the night table, a familiar vial of perfume on the bureau. His body instantly reacted to memories of it. A sound caught his attention. Every sense alert, he turned toward a closed door with a light showing along the bottom. From behind it came the sounds of splashing water and a woman humming softly.

He closed his eyes as images burst into his mind—Lucinda, slick with water, her blond hair piled up on her head, loose tendrils sticking to her damp neck. A soapy cloth moving over her shoulders, down to her breasts, circling . . .

With a curse, he opened his eyes. The urge to see her, to assure himself that he had finally found her again, almost sent him across to that closed door. But he would wait. Let her come to him. This was too important to rush.

Reluctantly, he left the bedroom and returned to the office. Standing at the window, he stared blankly out at the darkening sky and wondered what he would do if she sent him away. He had banked everything on this moment, this woman. There was nothing more important to him right now than Lucinda.

It seemed forever before he heard soft footfalls approaching from the bedroom. Then a gasp. Bracing himself, he turned. "Hello, Lucinda."

"Tait!" She stared at him, her hands pressed against the robe over her stomach, her expression showing both shock and . . . panic. Why?

She was even more beautiful than the woman who had drifted through his dreams for over a year.

"You're here," she blurted out.

"I am."

"Why?"

That threw him off balance. There were countless reasons, but he decided to give the most urgent. "To protect you."

"From what? I read that Doyle has fled to Ireland."

"From Horne."

That panic again.

"He was in Denver," Tait explained. "That's why I didn't want you to go there. But being you," he added with a wry smile, "of course, you went anyway."

She didn't smile back. "What was he doing in Denver?"

"Promoting some railroad venture he and Doyle were putting together. And to find you." Why were they talking about Denver? Why wasn't she rushing over to throw her arms around him? And why did she look so afraid?

"Find me?"

Hoping the direct approach would end this wary dance, he said, "I know it was Horne who sent Smythe to silence you, Lucinda. And why."

She seemed to shrink into herself. Color left her face except for the green of her eyes. Terrified eyes. The hand at her waist tightened into a fist.

Regretting his bluntness and wanting to reassure her, he took a step toward her, but when she flinched, he stopped, confused. "I won't let him hurt you any more, sweetheart. I'll protect you."

"Wh-what else do you know?"

That was the question he dreaded. But he wanted no more secrets between them. "Everything."

"How?"

"Doyle had a Pinkerton file."

"Oh, God." She whirled away and almost stumbled into the table by the window.

"Luce." He started forward again.

"Don't! Stay away!" She stood slightly hunched over, her back to him, her arms crossed at her waist.

He stopped, uncertain what to do, wondering what was going through her mind. Was she that upset that he'd come?

Worried about what he might have read in that cursed file? "I didn't read it, Lucinda. I burned it."

"Then you don't know everything, do you?" She straightened. Let her hands fall to her side. Slowly turned. The expression on her face was such a mix of emotions he could scarcely sort them out. Grief. Fury. Even sadness. "And I can see all those questions are still eating away at you."

"No, they're not. I have no—"

"Questions? I doubt that. Not after the way you've hounded me with them all this time." Her smile was a grimace of bitterness and despair. "Shall I satisfy your curiosity, then?"

"Lucinda, don't—"

Rage erupted. "No! You listen! You wanted to know all about my past, so now you listen!"

Tait felt a sick coldness move through his chest. He didn't want to hear this. He didn't want to watch her lips form the words because he sensed once she said them, they would stand between them forever like an unbreachable wall.

"Shall we start with the question I can see you're dying to ask? Was I a whore? That's what you want to know, isn't it? Did I service the fine gentlemen who came to Five Points to feed their depravity? Like your friend, Franklin Horne."

"Luce—"

A bitter laugh cut him off. She was shaking, her eyes glittering in her pallid face. "Yes, I was a whore. I serviced them. I was their little plaything. But since Mrs. Beale intended to auction my virginity, they weren't allowed to make use of my body. Only my hands and my . . . mouth."

"Lucinda, stop. Please." He couldn't bear this. The words. Her pain. The images that seared his mind. "You don't have to—"

"But I did have to," she cut in savagely. "Or I was beaten, starved, made even more wretched by Smythe's visits." She began to pace, her trembling hands reaching out to touch this or that, as if to assure herself that if she could feel something with her fingers, then it was real and she was real.

"And your next question," she went on, plucking from a shelf a beautiful china figurine of a shepherdess with a lamb at her side, "would be why didn't I run away? You're thinking any sane person would, right?"

She turned the figurine this way and that to study it. Tait had a sense she was offended by its innocence and beauty. That she wanted to throw it against the wall. Smash it into tiny pieces. Instead, with great care, she set it back on the shelf, then flattened her palm against her skirt.

"I tried. I did. But how far can a twelve-year-old run? And to where? Who would help a starving, filthy little runaway from Mrs. Beale's?" She made a sound—part laugh, part sob. "No one, that's who. Not a single person."

She began to pace again, her legs stiff, her heels coming down hard, as if to crush whatever was underfoot. "Perhaps they were afraid. Perhaps they didn't care. Perhaps no one thought I was worth saving."

Tait watched her, silently battling his rage, knowing there was nothing he could do but listen. He could see it was important to her that she say the words. And important for him to hear them. This was what he had wanted to know—the secrets he had been desperate to fit into the puzzle. Well, now he had them, and his punishment was to stand there in helpless silence and watch the pain pour out of her like bile.

"The last time Smythe caught me"—she stopped at the window, keeping her back toward him, as if she couldn't bear to see the effect her words were having—"he beat me and put me in a closet. For a week, maybe more, I'm not sure, I lived in the dark, with only a sliver of lamplight shining beneath the locked door, or a short burst of blinding light whenever he opened it to bring me food or take away my waste pail.

"But I was fed. I had blankets. I had a roof over my head. I was safe."

Turning abruptly from the window, she wandered aimlessly to the desk, then on to the bookcase. "For two years Smythe tutored me—that's what he called it—and paraded me through the downstairs rooms and let them touch me—but not enough to damage the merchandise, of course."

Tait watched a shudder ripple through her, and felt his own stomach roll. He wondered what he was supposed to do with this knowledge. This rage.

"Then on the day of the auction—you knew about the auction? I can see by your disgust that you did. After all, that's the most important piece of the puzzle, isn't it?" She continued to pace. "Smythe came for me. He made me take off my clothes—

rags, really—and put on a sheer nightdress. He brushed the tangles from my hair and put paint on my face and told me what was going to happen to me. When I began to cry, he laughed and said before it was over, I would wish I was back at Mrs. Beale's with him."

She stopped pacing and finally faced him. There was fire in her eyes, fed by a hatred so intense it seemed to heat the room. "I wanted to kill him. Claw out his eyes. I wanted to die and be with Mam and Da and my baby brother."

She began to cry, her hands opening and closing at her sides, an awful soundless despair twisting her mouth and distorting her beautiful face.

"Lucinda . . . sweetheart . . ."

"When he finished and I looked into the mirror and saw what he had done—what he had made me into—I felt . . . gone. Like Cathleen Donovan had ceased to exist, and this pitiful, painted thing had taken her place. I wasn't even aware that I had picked up the lamp and thrown it at him until I heard him scream and saw the flames. Then I ran." Shoulders heaving on silent sobs, she dropped her face into her hands.

"And you're still running." On wooden legs, Tait walked over and stopped in front of her. He was shaking with the need to touch her, hold her, cry with her. But he knew she would have to come to him. Her decision. Her terms. When she was ready. "Aren't you weary, Luce?" he asked gently. "Don't you want to stop running and rest . . . just for a while . . . with me?"

"I-If only I had—"

"The fault is with them," he cut in, incensed that she could think any of it was her doing. "What happened to you was unthinkable. An affront to God. And to me. You're not to blame for any of it."

She let her hands drop away and looked up at him with an expression of such anguish it felt like a punch to his chest.

"Give me all that pain and fear," he said. "Let me carry it for you, sweetheart, and I promise I won't ever let anything like that happen to you again."

She stood shaking, tears streaming.

"Please. Let me protect you. Let me love you like you deserve."

"Love me?" Her voice was filled with self-loathing. "How could you love me after what I did . . . what I was?"

"I do. And have. And will. Always."

An expression he couldn't define crossed her face. She reached up, and with a trembling hand, brushed her fingertips across his cheek. "You're crying."

Tait wasn't aware of it. But he wasn't surprised. He had never hurt this bad.

"No one has ever wept for me."

"They should have. What happened to you was wrong. What they did was wrong." His voice faltered and for a moment he couldn't speak. Desperate to touch her, he cradled her face in his hands and looked hard into her beautiful eyes. "But look at you," he said with a wobbly smile when he could speak again. "You're an amazing woman, Lucinda Hathaway. You know why? Because you survived. No matter what happened to you, you survived. And I'm so grateful you did."

She wrapped her fingers around his wrists. He wasn't sure if she meant to push him away or keep him close. Her hands were cold. He could feel them shaking. "I might be a murderess. I might have killed Mrs. Beale in the fire."

"I hope so."

"Others may have died, as well."

"They shouldn't have been there."

New tears glittering on her cheeks, dripping from her chin. "I j-just wanted to make it stop. I wanted to die."

"I know." Unable to bear the pain in her face, or to let her see the despair in his, he pulled her against his chest. "But thank God you didn't. Thank God you lived so I could find you."

Surrender came slowly, and at great cost. But when she finally gave in to him and let her body relax against his, Tait knew he had won the greatest prize he would ever hold in his hands. Lucinda's trust.

Picking her up, he carried her to the couch and sat down with her in his lap and held her while she cried. It went on for a long time, as if she had stored up a lifetime of tears and pain, and she was finally able to let it go. With him.

He pressed his damp cheek against her hair, grateful to be there, determined to always be there, until finally, she fell into an exhausted sleep.

Hoping his knee would hold him, he rose. He carried her into the bedroom, gently laid her on the bed, and pulled a quilt over her. He watched over her until she settled back into deep sleep, then he went into the lavatory, sat on the water stool, and wept.

Lucinda awoke with a start, confused and disoriented. Then it all came rushing back. *Tait. He's here. He knows.*

She bolted upright, terrified that now that he finally had his answers he had left her, and this time, for good. Then she heard muffled sounds coming from the water closet. Rising, she stumbled to the door and threw it open.

He was bent over, wearing nothing but a towel, attaching something to his leg—a brace around his knee. He looked up, startled, then gave a crooked smile. "Did I wake you?"

She sagged against the door frame, so relieved she felt dizzy. "I didn't know where you were. I thought you might have left." Why did he need a brace? Were those new scars on his shoulder and arm?

He finished tying on the brace and straightened, and she saw another puckered scar across his chest. And one she hadn't noticed earlier on the side of his face.

"I've been in the saddle all day and smelled like horse. I hope you don't mind that I used your tub. Your ridiculously small tub."

"Did Smythe do that to you?" she asked, staring bleakly at a fresh red scar by his temple.

"My fists aren't much good in a knife fight. Don't worry. They don't hurt."

"And your knee?"

He looked down. "I hit a rock when I fell off the train. It's getting better. But I hope you're not partial to dancing." He said it lightly, but all she saw was the battering his beautiful body had taken on her account.

"I'm so sorry. If not for me—"

"If not for you," he cut in, "I'd be a soulless bastard, drowning in whiskey and greed like Doyle. You've given me a purpose, Luce. And hope."

"Hope of what?"

"A life with you." That crooked grin again. "I had planned to do this with a little more finesse. Or at least with more clothes on. But . . ."

With one hand braced on the edge of the cabinet, he stretched out his bad leg and lowered himself down on his good knee. Then he took her hand in both of his and looked up into her face. "Will you do me the honor of marrying me, Lucinda Hathaway and Margaret Hamilton and Cathleen Donovan?"

"Get up," she said, trying not to burst into tears again. "You look ridiculous. And your towel is gapping open."

He looked down at himself, then chuckled. "Impressive, huh?" But his grin faded when he looked back up. "Why are you crying? I thought you'd be happy to have finally brought me to my knee."

"I am happy. And impressed." She dipped down and pressed her lips to his, then straightened. "But are you sure, Tait? Horne might be the only one who—"

"I'm sure."

"Or Doyle might tell—"

"He won't."

"I wouldn't want to shame you—"

"For crissakes, Lucinda. Just say yes. My knee is killing me."

"Then, yes. I'll marry you, Tait Rylander," she said in a wobbly voice. "I am honored to do so. But we must wait until I can send for Mrs. Throckmorton."

His face fell. "Wait?"

"For the ceremony. The honeymoon can start now. Shall I help you up?"

His laugh swept away all the sadness in her heart. "Sweetheart, I'm already up. But you can give me a boost off the floor, if you want."

Loving Lucinda was better than Tait remembered, and more than he'd hoped. And not just because she insisted he not wear a preventative—*thank you, Lord*—but because she put away her distrust and fear and came to him with an ardor that matched his own.

Here. Yes, there. Harder. Slower. Faster. Again. Oh, God . . .

There was definitely something to be said for a woman who made her own decisions and who had no qualms about telling a man what she liked and disliked, and where, and when, and how often. He got the gist of it pretty quickly, then did what felt right.

In the end, she rode him like a bronc rider, her hair flying, her perfect breasts bouncing above him, those little sounds he loved spilling from her open mouth. If he hadn't been so distracted, he would have laughed with the joy of it.

Who would have thought such enthusiasm rested beneath that serene smile and logical mind and coolly regal exterior? An incredible woman, his Lucinda, and his love for her was a fire he couldn't quench.

It was a night spent in a blaze of delight.

He slept like the dead and awoke after dawn to an empty bed. Beyond the room, he could hear the hotel awakening to the day, and he smiled, thinking of his bossy little wife-to-be bustling about issuing orders to the staff.

But after he dressed and left her suite, he learned from her bald, brown-toothed desk clerk, Yancey, that she had left an hour earlier for the church.

Thinking she was already planning their wedding and glad to stay out of those preparations, he started toward the dining room for coffee when the clerk added, "Seemed sad. Like she was fixing to cry. I ain't never seen her cry, 'cept the time Billy mashed his finger in a door."

Tait turned back to meet narrowed eyes that carried more steel than he would have thought the old man had in him.

"Got any idea why she would be fixing to cry, Mr. Fancy Pants New Yorker? Oh, yeah, I heard all about you from Miriam, who heard Mrs. Maddie grilling that hungover, dress-wearing husband of hers this morning over coffee. So don't think you can get away with mistreating Miss Lucinda without having to answer to me and Billy and a whole lot of other folks."

Tait was so astounded he could only stare.

"So what exactly are your intentions, mister?"

"My intentions are to marry her . . . if that's any concern of yours."

"So why was she fixing to cry?"

"Joy?"

"I don't think so."

"Then I'd best go find out, hadn't I?"

"Yeah, you'd best."

Not sure how far the church was, Tait went to the livery for his horse, then following the directions that Driscoll, the livery owner, had given him, rode toward the mouth of the canyon.

He shivered, vowing to get a thicker coat. Maybe one made of buffalo hide. Lucinda would love that. City man to mountain man, he thought with a grin as he pulled the collar of his frock coat tighter around his neck.

Clouds were moving in from the west, skimming the tops of the peaks, and a gusty, chill breeze whispered through the spruce boughs and loosened what few leaves remained on the aspens along the creek. The air had a heavy, wet feel to it, and he wondered if it would snow. He wouldn't mind being snowed in with Lucinda for a couple of months.

As he neared the Come All You Sinners Church, he spotted a figure bundled up in a familiar green cape, sitting on a log bench in the little fenced graveyard. Dismounting, he tied his horse to a hitching post beside the fence, then went through the gate.

"Lucinda, what are you doing out here?" he asked as he approached.

She glanced up, and Tait saw the desk clerk was right. She did look sad.

"I couldn't sleep."

How could she not sleep after the night they'd just spent? Taking a seat beside her, he put an arm around her shoulders and pulled her against his side. He could feel her shivering. "Tell me what's wrong. Bad dreams? Worries about Horne? Regrets?"

"About you?'" She stroked a gloved hand over his cheek. "Never." Then with a sigh, she let her hand fall back to her lap. "It's Cathleen. She haunts me. Night after night. I thought once I talked about what happened at Mrs. Beale's, she might leave me alone."

"What does she do?"

"Nothing. She just stands there, crying, wearing that nasty gown Smythe put on her, and her poor little face painted like a wanton—"

"Wash it."

She turned her head and looked at him. "What?"

"Wash her face. Put real clothes on her. If you don't, Smythe will have her forever."

"But she's just a figment of my imagination."

"Then imagine washing her face. Try it. What can it hurt?"

He could almost see the idea taking hold in her mind. Her eyes lost focus. Her gaze turned inward. She grew still as her lids came down. For several seconds she sat without moving, then slowly, her frown gave way to a smile that curled the corners of lips still swollen from his kisses.

"What do you see under that paint?" he asked her.

"A beautiful little girl."

"What's her name?"

The smile spread, reaching all the way to the dimple in her left cheek. "Cathleen."

"Who is she?"

Her eyes opened and what he saw in their green depths wrapped like a gentle hand around his heart. "Me."

Lucinda was in a state of euphoria when they left the graveyard. Ever since yesterday, when she'd learned Maddie and Ash would be staying in Heartbreak Creek more or less permanently, she had been flying high. But now with Tait beside her, she felt lighthearted, loved, and so in love she was dizzy with it. He knew everything yet saw her no differently. She wanted to laugh. Dance. Hug the man beside her until her arms gave out.

She felt free.

"I fear I'm rather taken with you, Mr. Rylander," she said, smiling up at him as they walked arm in arm back to the hotel, the horse following behind on his rein.

"You should be. I broke Doyle's nose for you."

"Did you? You brave thing."

"I also defended you against a knife-wielding lunatic."

"And I love you for it."

He stopped, making her stop. When he looked down at her, his gray eyes were so intense she felt stripped bare. Not an unpleasant sensation, she recalled. Especially when he took his time at it, trailing kisses over whatever he exposed. And when he put his tongue—

"Do you?" he asked, shattering her pleasant musings.

"Do I what?"

"Love me? You never said."

She started to laugh, then realized he was serious. "Of

course I do. How could you doubt it after the way I . . . after last night?"

"Then say it."

Emotion clogged her voice. "I love you, Tait Rylander. More than I thought possible. More than I probably should."

"Why do you say that?"

She shrugged and started them walking again, needing to get herself in hand before she started crying again. She was amazed she had tears left. "Other than Mrs. Throckmorton, no one that I've cared about has stayed around long."

"I will."

"Will you?" She looked up at him. "Here, in Heartbreak Creek?" She had been afraid to broach the subject, terrified of having to leave this place she had grown to love. But if that's what Tait wanted . . .

Before he could answer, the drum of hooves drew their attention. She looked up, one hand shading her eyes from the morning sun. "It's Declan and Ash. I bet they're riding out to the site where the Wallaces are planning to build a house. I'll introduce them to you, then you can go with them."

"I met them last night. And I prefer being with you."

"Do you? How sweet. But you should go anyway, just to be nice."

"I don't want to be nice. I want to take off your clothes and lay you across the bed and—"

"Hush. They'll hear."

"You're trying to get rid of me, aren't you?"

"Of course not," she lied. Nor, she realized, did she want to mar this beautiful morning with a difficult discussion about where they would live after they married. "It's simply that I'll be busy with the ladies all morning and thought you might enjoy an outing with the men, although Thomas has gone up into the mountains, so I doubt you'll be meeting him today. Or possibly ever," she added with a look of disgust. "Since the foolish man shouldn't be up and about so soon after being shot."

"You haven't told your lady friends about me, have you?"

"Well, I . . . meant to. I am. I will. Right now, in fact. Hello, gentlemen," she called to the approaching riders. "What a lovely day for a ride."

"I agree," Tait muttered, with a look that sent heat into her face. Turning, he nodded to the men reining in beside them. "Looks like you're stuck with me for the morning, gentlemen, so Lucinda can explain to your wives who I am and why I spent the night in her bed and why she hasn't mentioned me before today."

"Tait Rylander!"

"Och, lass." The Scotsman pressed a hand to his brow. "Dinna shout. My head is bursting as it is."

Declan grinned. "Ed did mention she wanted to talk to you, Lucinda. In fact, I believe she and Maddie and Pru are all waiting for you right now in the dining room."

"Oh, dear."

"If you're coming, lad," the earl said to Tait, "best mount up before Tricks gets here. He can be fair exuberant, God love him."

Following his nod, Tait saw a huge gray dog streaking toward them, mouth open, tongue flopping. "Jesus," he muttered, stepping in front of Lucinda.

"Not to worry," the earl assured him. "He's verra fearful of the ladies. Especially this one. Would have made a fine sergeant, so she would."

Reining his horse away, the sheriff called over his shoulder, "Come along, then, Rylander. Feels like snow. You can help me watch Ash dig a foundation before it gets here."

Twenty

Lucinda had read once about a river in South America that was inhabited by small fish with large teeth, and any creature that happened into their midst would be completely devoured in a matter of minutes.

That was exactly how she felt when she walked into the hotel.

"You're in trouble," Brin shouted gleefully from an upholstered chair where it appeared she was trying to fit one of her dead doll's dresses on Maddie's little dog. The doll itself had been burned at the stake the previous year by Brin and her brother, Joe Bill, Edwina had informed Lucinda with a look of horror.

"Best turn around and leave while you can," Yancey advised from his stool behind the front desk. "They been honing their tongues in there for an hour."

"Ed made Pru come so she could fuss at you, too," Brin added. "I ain't seen her so worked up since she cracked an egg over Joe Bill's head for looking under her skirts for a devil tail. What'd you do?" Born into a family of three older brothers, then allowed to run wild for four years after her mother disappeared, Brin was a bit of a handful. Edwina was making a valiant effort, but Lucinda doubted she'd ever gain control over that indomitable spirit. Nor should she.

But Lucinda wasn't sure the seven-year-old should be on

hand for what was sure to ensue. In her present state, Edwina was too volatile, and the child was too curious—no telling what she might overhear, or repeat. "Where are your brothers?"

"Fishing."

"Don't you want to join them?"

"Ed said I had to stay here with Yancey. Besides, they're not really fishing. They're looking at postcards of nekkid women Joe Bill found."

Good Lord. "Well, stay in the lobby, then."

"What if the doggie has to pee?"

"Yancey."

"Yes, ma'am, I'll tend it."

Unable to delay further, Lucinda pasted on an innocent smile and marched bravely to her inquisition.

Edwina pounced the moment she saw her. "Lucinda Hathaway! You have some explaining to do!"

"Ed, calm yourself," Pru warned. "It's not good for the baby."

"Who is this Rylander person?" Maddie's expressive face showed more than a little hurt. "Ash said he came all the way from New York to see you, but you've never even mentioned him before."

"I wanted to." Lucinda sank into her chair beside the window that overlooked the woods bordering the creek. "But I thought it was over, that I'd never see him again."

"Why?"

"We had a falling out. A misunderstanding. But all is well, now."

"Apparently so," Maddie murmured with a knowing look.

Ignoring it, Lucinda poured a cup of tea from the pot on the table, then spooned in sugar. She took a sip and set it aside. "So how are you ladies this morning?"

The ploy didn't work.

"Is he handsome?" Ever the romantic, Edwina was.

"Extremely so. In fact, with his gray eyes and dark hair, he reminds me of your Brin. But only in appearance," she hastily added. "And he's southern, which I know will please you, although he's lived in New York since the war." She didn't mention that he'd fought on the Union side, which would please Edwina less and generate more questions.

Edwina leaned forward to peer intently into Lucinda's face. "Is that bristle rash?"

"Edwina!"

"Well, look at her, Pru. Her lips are puffy, she looks as if she hasn't slept a wink, and she's got red splotches all over her chin and neck and Lord knows where-all else. That's bristle rash. Trust me, I should know." Ignoring her sputtering sister, Edwina leaned forward again and lowered her voice. "You consummated, didn't you?"

Pru gasped. "Good heavens, Edwina!"

Lucinda felt heat rush up her splotchy neck.

"You did! I knew it! Didn't I say dear Luce has the look of a woman missing her man, Pru? Didn't I say that?"

"Actually, you said she seemed lonely and you thought we should find her a beau. To which," Pru hastened to add to Lucinda, "I heartily objected."

"Hush, you two," Maddie admonished. "So she can tell us who he is and why he's here."

Lucinda looked at the three pairs of eyes staring back at her with disturbing intensity, and was reminded again of those fish in South America. "His name is Tait Rylander. He's a lawyer and railroad investor, and he was my fiancé's business partner. I've known him for over a year, and he's the finest man I've ever known. He's asked me to marry him, and I've said yes."

Edwina squealed, which brought Brin and the dog running from the lobby.

Pru blinked at her in shocked delight. "Oh, my."

Maddie gave a troubled smile.

"How romantic," Edwina gushed, her eyes suspiciously bright. "He followed you all the way from New York just to profess his love. It's like a fairy tale. Although I must say it took him long enough. Brin, go back to Yancey, please."

"But I'm hungry."

Thinking it best to get the child out of the room before her stepmother made any more untoward comments, Lucinda nodded toward the kitchen. "If it's all right with your mother, I think Cook has some biscuits left from breakfast."

Brin waited hopefully for Edwina's nod, then dashed down the back hallway, the dog bounding behind her in her jaunty bonnet.

"Well, your swain is here now," Pru said, continuing where they had left off before Brin's interruption. "And that's what's important."

"Do you love him?" Maddie asked.

Sudden emotion flooded Lucinda. With a shaky smile, she reached over and gave her friend's hand a reassuring squeeze. "I do. Very much."

"Then I'm happy for you."

Lucinda felt wretched. There was so much more she wanted to tell them, especially Maddie. But to do so would only open herself to questions she wasn't ready to answer. Confessing all to Tait had been one thing—a good and necessary thing, she realized now, no matter how painful it was. But to reveal the sordid details of her past to her friends would change how they looked at her. They would be sad for her, and horrified by what she had suffered, and glad that she had put it behind her . . . but that knowledge would ever after be in their eyes whenever they looked at her. It might alter forever the connection they shared, and she couldn't bear that.

She would always be Lucinda Hathaway to them, and so she would remain. And if a twinge of guilt marred her happiness as she accepted their well wishes and congratulations, she hid it behind a smile. She loved and needed them too much to let the truth create a barrier between them.

"So when will the wedding be?" Edwina asked. "If you wait until the baby comes, I'll be able to dance again. I so love to waltz with Declan, even though he vows he hates it."

"Perhaps a month. Maybe two. I have to send for my guardian, Mrs. Throckmorton. It's very important to me that she be here for the ceremony."

Edwina eyed Lucinda's rashy neck with a smirk. "She had better hurry then, or you might be wearing my wedding dress when you go up the aisle."

Lucinda laughed, unnerved yet intrigued by the idea of a laughing, gray-eyed baby, even if he or she came a few months early. She wondered how Tait would feel about that, or if she would be as emotional as Edwina—although judging by the copious amount of tears she had shed the previous night, she might even become more so.

Movement caught her eye, and she looked out the window

beside her to see a man riding past the hotel toward the livery. There was something familiar about him. The set of his shoulders, the way his jowls spilled over his high, stiff collar, the hands gripping—

Then he turned his head and she saw his face.

Air rushed out of her. *Horne.*

For an instant she sat frozen, then a more terrifying thought sent her bolting from her chair. *Brin!*

Unmindful of the surprised voices calling to her, she ran into the lobby but saw only Yancey, dozing on his stool. "Where's Brin?" she cried. "Has she come back from the kitchen?"

The old man jerked awake, eyes slow to focus. "Brin?" Blinking groggily, he looked around. "She was right here, then her Ma shrieked and she—"

"What's wrong?" Maddie cried, rushing up behind her, Edwin and Pru on her heels.

"Brin's gone. We have to find her! Yancey, check the kitchen!"

"She's probably just outside," Edwina said as Yancey rushed toward the back hallway. "She wanders sometimes, but . . ." Her words trailed off when she saw Lucinda's face. "What's wrong? Oh, God. Something has happened to her?"

"Take a breath, Ed," Pru ordered. "Lucinda, what's going on?"

"There's a man," Lucinda cried, rushing out the front doors. "A terrible man. He just rode by. I have to find Brin." She spun, searching the boardwalk, but saw no one. "Brin!" she yelled. No answer.

She rushed back inside just as Yancey returned. "Cook said she went out back."

"Maddie, call your dog," Lucinda ordered. "Brin was playing with her earlier. Billy," she said when she saw the bellboy coming down the stairs. "Have you seen Brin?"

"No. ma'am. I been upstairs folding—"

"Can you ride?"

The boy nodded.

Lucinda grabbed him off the bottom step and shoved him toward the door. "Find a horse, any horse—steal it if you have to—and ride out to the Wallace's new place and get the men. Now! Tell Tait it's Franklin Horne."

"Who's Tait?"

"Just go!" She was shaking, spiraling into panic. Visions of Horne's cruel hands and fat, pointed tongue exploded in her mind. She ran into her office, grabbed the little pistol from her desk, and raced toward the rear door. "Keep looking," she called back to the others still milling in the lobby. "I'm going to the livery." Then bursting out of the hotel, she raced down the rutted track, whimpers of terror bubbling in her throat.

"I'd like to be a Pinkerton," the Scotsman mused, tossing another shovel full of dirt over his shoulder. "I'd be good at it, so I would."

"I told you they wouldn't hire you," Declan Brodie reminded him as he positioned another length of log for sawing. "You being a fookin' earl and all."

"Bugger off."

Tait looked up from the hole he was digging. "You're not going back to Scotland?"

"No' to live. This is my Maddie's home now, so this is where I'll stay. Yet a man must do something besides follow his wee wife about while she takes her tintypes. But if the Pinkertons willna hire me . . ." The sentence trailed off on a long sigh.

Tait paused in his digging. "Then start your own agency."

The Scotsman looked up, a fall of gray-brown hair shading his forehead. Tait could see the speculation in his green eyes. "My own detective agency?"

"Why not? With all the railroad activity around here, there must be a steady need for security."

"Aye. Security. Maybe."

They dug for a while in silence, then Wallace said, "I'm no' so good with paperwork. I couldna do it all on my own." He looked over, his rugged face showing a vulnerability Tait would never have expected in such a capable, confident man. "You said you're planning to stay in Heartbreak Creek?"

"If that's what Lucinda wants." Was he asking Tait to join in the venture? As Tait mulled that over, Brodie stalked up, a scowl on his face. "I said dig a hole, you two. Not a grave."

"A grave is a hole," Ash argued. "And if ye dinna stop ordering me aboot, ye'll learn that firsthand, so ye will."

Tait noticed that drink and aggravation made the Scotsman's

accent stronger. If he got much more irritated, he'd be speaking gibberish. Sticking his shovel point first into the pile of dirt beside the hole he was digging, he rested an arm across the handle. "Perhaps if you explained the ultimate purpose of the holes, we might be better able to excavate them to your specifications."

The earl stopped digging to stare at him. "You are the funniest-talking man I ever heard, so you are."

"Me? Hell, I can't understand half of what comes out of your mouth."

Tait realized he was becoming a bit aggravated, himself. He could be back at the hotel teaching his fiancée how to play strip poker instead of being stuck here, sweating like a field hand alongside these two cantankerous bastards. If they would spend as much energy working as trading insults, they could get this done and he might still have time for a couple of deals before dinner.

Or maybe just have dinner sent to the room. An interesting thought.

Brodie's voice broke into his delightful musings of round, dark-tipped breasts and naked thighs. "You see that log over there?" The sheriff pointed to what had once been a thirty-five-foot-long, two-foot-in-diameter cedar trunk that he had spent most of the morning sawing into eight chunks of equal length. "Those go two feet into the holes you're digging. The part sticking out will be the piers that will hold up your house. So unless you want to roll downhill every time you get out of bed in the morning, the holes have to be the same depth. How hard is that to understand?"

"Assuming, of course," Tait put in, "that the land is flat, which it doesn't appear to be."

"I already checked that with the water level. Now dig. Or you'll be waking up to the squeal of a stuck pig every morning."

Tait frowned at him.

"Bagpipes." Seeing Tait was still confused, he added, "Where else you think he and Maddie have been staying, but at the hotel? Hell, if the ladies had their way, we'd all be living there together like some lunatic inbred carnival family. Now dig."

"White people," a voice said. "Such a fuss over a tipi."

Tait turned to see an Indian sitting on one of the logs they would later use as a foundation beam, scratching the wolf-hound's ear. The missing Cheyenne Dog Soldier, he assumed. How had they not seen or heard him arrive? And why hadn't the dog warned them?

"Greetings, heathen," Ash called with a grin.

"Ho, Scotsman. Where is your dress?"

"'Tis a kilt, ye diaper-wearing savage."

Tait guessed the earl was referring to the loin cloth and leggings the Indian wore beneath his long leather tunic. At least, he hoped so.

"When did you get back, Thomas?" Brodie walked over to clap the Cheyenne on the back. "Pru's been worried. How's your side?"

The Indian lifted up the bottom of his beaded war shirt to expose a barely healed wound just below his ribs that corresponded to a round hole in his shirt. "I cannot see where the bullet went into my back, but it itches, so I know it is healing." He let the shirt drop. "*Epeva'e.* It is well." He glanced over at Tait. "*Nevaaso?*"

"Tait Rylander. He's come all the way from New York to marry Lucinda Hathaway. Tait, this is Thomas Redstone, my temporary deputy when he feels like it."

"And a hell of a scrapper, so he is. But sneaky." Ash nodded at Tait's hand. "I can tell you're a bare-knuckle fighter, as well, Rylander."

"Was," Tait amended. "Now I only fight when I have to." He gave the Scotsman a warning look.

The earl grinned back.

The Indian didn't, and solemnly assessed Tait out of coal black eyes set in a swarthy, expressionless face framed by beaded braids. Tait had a feeling that gaze missed nothing. After an almost imperceptible nod of acknowledgment, the Cheyenne looked back at Brodie. "How goes it with your skinny wife?"

The sheriff chuckled. "She's not so skinny anymore." His smile faded. He motioned to the unlaced V at the neck of the Indian's leather tunic. "Your pouch is gone."

"My dead wife and son rest in peace now."

"So it's over?"

"It is over."

A distant drumming drew their attention, and they all turned to see a horseman racing toward them. As he drew closer, Brodie said, "Looks like Billy."

Tait set aside his shovel. "Who's Billy?"

"Bellboy at the hotel."

The boy hauled the winded horse into a sliding stop. "Brin's missing!" He glanced at Tait. "You named Tait?"

As the other men raced for their horses, Tait stepped forward, dread building. "I am. What's wrong?"

"Miss Hathaway said to tell you it's Franklin Horne."

Lucinda raced up just as Driscoll was coming out of the barn. "Have you seen Brin?" she cried, struggling for breath.

"She was here a minute ago. Her and that little dog." He pointed.

Lucinda looked around, saw Maddie's dog digging in the manure pile, a tattered bonnet around her neck. But no sign of Brin.

"Did a man ride by? Middle years. Wearing a suit. Dark eyes, small and narrow set."

Driscoll nodded. "Said he lost his dog. Brin went to help him find it."

Terror almost doubled her over. "Which way did they go?"

"Up the mine trail. What's wrong?"

"He'll hurt her!" Lucinda whirled and ran toward the footpath that wound through the brush and trees beside the road, over the creek, and up toward the abandoned mine. "Get everyone you can to look for her. Hurry!"

Voices rose behind her but grew fainter as she stepped into the shadows bordering the road. Brambles caught at her skirts, scratched her face and arms. The rush of the creek ahead grew louder as she clambered over downed branches, sharp rocks, and around stumps and trees. She crossed the footbridge, then stopped and tried to listen, but all she heard above the rushing water was the pounding of her own heart and the rasp of air tearing through her throat.

If he hurt Brin she would kill him. She gripped the pistol tightly in her shaking hand. She would fire until she ran out of bullets, then tear out his eyes. Stomp his face to mush. Feel his blood run through her hands.

Never again, she chanted soundlessly, as she started running again. *Never again. Never again.*

She slipped on dew-slick aspen leaves, stumbled on. Fifty yards farther, she stopped, gasping, her chest pumping. Breath fogged the air, her throat ached. She was shivering so hard her teeth chattered—either from cold or fear—she didn't know. She should have found them by now. Had she taken a wrong turn?

God, don't let me miss her. Don't let me be too late.

Then she heard movement ahead and the crackle of brush. Brin's voice.

Frantic, she raced toward it, tearing blindly through the bushes, throwing branches aside.

Then suddenly she was on them.

Horne whirled, his pink tongue flicking.

"Hi, Miss Hathaway," Brin called. "What are you doing out here?"

Seeing the child was unharmed and had no idea of the danger she was in, Lucinda hid the gun in the folds of her skirt. She struggled to keep her voice calm. "Looking for you, honey. Your mother and father are worried. Everybody is looking for you." She shot a warning glance at Horne. "You'd better run back now before you get into trouble."

"But I'm helping him find his doggie."

"No, Brin. You must go back." She was shaking so badly, she was glad she hadn't cocked the pistol to pop the trigger out, or she might have accidentally squeezed off a round. "Now, Brin."

"I think not." Horne grabbed the child's arm. "You'll stay with me, won't you, little Brin?"

"Ow. That hurts." Brin tried to jerk her arm away, but Horne gave it a vicious yank that almost lifted her off her feet.

"Stop that!" Lucinda cried, rushing forward.

"Let me go!" Brin jerked again, her flailing arm catching him in the groin.

With a grunt, Horne stumbled back.

Lucinda yanked the girl from his grip and pulled her beyond his reach.

"Ow. You're squeezing my arm."

"Go to the hotel, Brin! Now!" Lucinda shoved her toward the trail.

"Why are you being so mean? I'm going to tell Ma." Rubbing her arm, she glared up at Lucinda as she stomped toward the trail. "And I don't care if you never find your stinky ole dog!" she shouted back to Horne as she disappeared into the brush.

Lucinda cocked the pistol. When the trigger popped into place, she curled her finger over it and aimed at the man hunched over, his hands cupping his crotch. Her heart drummed so hard she was lightheaded. Her legs felt numb, yet her arms wouldn't stop shaking. Hate rose in her throat like vomit.

Horne slowly straightened, then stilled when he saw the cocked pistol pointed at his chest. "What are you doing, Cathleen?"

"I'm going to kill you, you leprous maggot." She took a step, narrowing the distance between them to ten feet. In some dim, still functioning part of her brain, she remembered Tait had said she needed to be within five feet of her target for the gun to do any real damage.

She wanted to be nearer. She wanted to be so close she could smell his blood. Watch his last breath. See the light die in his eyes.

"I only have four bullets," she said, taking another step. "Where do you want them?"

"Cathleen, you can't—"

"I'd aim for the heart, but you haven't one." She was vaguely surprised by the steadiness in her voice despite the shaking of her limbs. "The groin would be too small a target, as I recall. So I guess it'll have to be the face."

"Put that away, you stupid woman."

"Mouth first? You were always partial to mouths."

He took a step back.

She took a step forward. An obscene dance to the music of their harsh breathing and the frantic drumbeat of her heart. "Eyes? Yours always reminded me of black holes that reached all the way down to hell."

"You can't do this!"

The panic in his voice told her he thought she might. She could almost smell his fear. It strengthened her.

"But I can. And I am." Another step.

Horne's control snapped. "You filthy whore! I should have killed you back then. I was going to, did you know that?"

She took another step.

He retreated, stumbled back into a tree. "I was going to buy you. Smythe and I had already stacked the bid. We were going to use you over and over, in every way we could, until you bled like a stuck pig and there was nothing left but raw—"

Lucinda squeezed the trigger. But she was shaking so badly the bullet missed and slapped into the tree behind him.

Horne gaped at her, his eyes wild with fear.

She took another step. "Don't worry, Horne," she ground out, desperately trying to bring her rage under control so she could aim. "I still have three more."

"D-Don't do this! I'm a rich man! I can give you—"

As she fired again, he lurched to the side. The second bullet missed his chest and plowed into his arm. The third went into his shoulder.

Crying out, he sagged against the tree, blood welling through the fingers gripping his shoulder. "You bitch!"

She stepped closer. Four feet separated them. One bullet left.

Breath caught behind clenched teeth, she took careful aim.

But Horne saw her finger tighten and lunged forward before she could fire. He would have plowed into her had a leg not shot out of the brush and tripped him.

As he fell, a hand reached around Lucinda from behind and yanked the gun from her grip.

"Enough, Lucinda," Tait said in her ear. "I'm here." His arms came around her, pulled her back against his chest.

Her legs buckled, but he held her fast, the hard, rapid thud of his heart vibrating against her spine, his labored breath warm against her temple. She felt the tremble in his body. Smelled horses and sweat and her mind started to spiral. "Oh, God . . ."

"You're safe. I've got you."

Ash stepped out of the brush, followed by Declan. "Is she all right?" the sheriff asked.

"Are you?" Tait asked, his voice hoarse in her ear.

"Y-Yes. No. Yes. Why did you stop me?"

"You're not a killer."

"But he shouldn't—"

"He won't."

Ash kept a booted foot on Horne's chest while Declan felt his pockets for weapons. When he found none, he rose and motioned for Horne to rise. Ash helped him . . . rather vigorously, Lucinda was happy to note.

Declan scowled at Tait and Lucinda. "All right, you two. What's this all about? You know this man?"

"She was trying to kill me," Horne blubbered, struggling to evade Ash's grip. "She has a gun! She—"

"*Haud yer wheesht,*" Ash ordered, driving his elbow into Horne's face.

Horne reeled, hands cupped over his bleeding mouth.

Tait took his arms from around Lucinda. "I'll take care of it, sheriff," he said in a hard, flat voice Lucinda scarcely recognized. Pulling out a handkerchief, he ripped it in two and began wrapping his knuckles. "My thanks to you and the earl for your help. Please take Lucinda back to the hotel. I'll be along directly."

Declan sighed. "That's not how it works, Rylander. I've got to follow the law. That's why I wear this badge. You're a lawyer; you should understand that."

"Bollocks," Ash burst out. "Take off the badge, then. Be a father, not a sheriff. He had your daughter, for God's sake."

Some of the color left Declan's face. "But he didn't hurt her, did he, Lucinda?"

"N-No. Not really. I don't think she even knew he was a threat to her."

Oddly, now that the danger was past, the shaking was even worse than when she was confronting Horne. She had been focused then, but now her thoughts felt scrambled and she was so dizzy she feared she might fall.

But she wanted to stay. She wanted to see Horne die. She wanted to know for certain it was over forever.

"Did he hurt you, Lucinda?" Declan asked.

She started to laugh. But it sounded broken and strange in her ear and her teeth were chattering again, so she made herself stop. "No, he didn't hurt me. Not today."

"Then we're done here, Rylander."

"No, Sheriff. We're not." Tait calmly tested the wrappings by clenching and straightening his hands. Apparently satisfied, he looked at the sheriff.

Lucinda had never seen his face so set. His gray eyes appeared lit from within with a fury he seemed barely able to contain.

"Horne will not leave these woods alive, Sheriff," he said in that terrible voice. "I owe that to Lucinda. And to your daughter. And to all the children he's hurt. It's a debt every man owes. Even you."

"But I can't—"

"Yes. You can. Just walk away."

"Aye, Brodie. Ye ken he's right. Think of what a trial would do to wee Brin."

Declan hesitated, his gaze moving from Tait to Ash.

"Don't do it, Sheriff!" Horne shouted, seeing the lawman waver. "If you leave, they'll kill me!"

When Ash rounded on him, he cowered, tears and sweat rolling down his face. "Please, Sheriff. Don't let them hurt me. I'm a rich man. An important man. You want a railroad through here? I can bring one. I can—"

"Dinna I tell ye to shut yer geggie?" Another blow sent Horne staggering back into the tree. He slumped against it, coughing blood.

Declan seemed to have reached his decision. He started to speak. But before he could get out a word, a whistling whisper cut through the air. Then a choking sound. Then they saw Horne slump to the ground, blood welling around the horn handle of a knife planted in his neck.

"Jesus," Tait said.

Declan blinked at the dying man, then spun around, anger crackling. "Thomas, is that you?" he yelled.

No answer except for the sigh of the wind through the boughs.

"Damnit, Thomas! I know it was you!" Declan stomped off into the trees. "You're a sworn deputy. What the hell are you thinking?"

"Bluidy fine throw," Ash said, studying the corpse.

For several moments Lucinda stared numbly down at Horne's body, nauseated by the reek of blood and spent gunpowder, her mind grappling with what had just happened. Horne was dead. It was over. She was safe. He could never hurt her again. As the reality of that sank in, she was gripped with a deeper emotion than fear. "I wanted to be the one to kill him. It was my right!"

"I know, sweetheart. But it's over now. Let it go." Tait's arm came around her shoulders and pulled her tight to his side. He bent to press a kiss to her temple, then whispered in her ear. "And if you ever do anything like this again, or scare me so bad, I swear to God, Lucinda, I'll—"

She whirled and threw her arms around his neck. "Oh, Tait. Th-thank you."

He tried to pull back, but she wouldn't let him. "For what?"

"You came for me. You would have fought him. For me." She drew back to give him a hard, fast kiss, then smiled up at him through a blur of tears. "No one has ever done that . . . and I thank you."

"You foolish woman. I love you. I would do anything—everything—for you." This time he kissed her. And it was the kind of kiss that rolled through her like a healing wind, sweeping away all the fear and pain, making her feel cherished and loved and safe, at last.

"Oh, for the love of Saint Andrew," a deep voice grumbled. "Should I be paying to see this, or is it a free show, I'm wondering?"

Lucinda jumped back, her cheeks hot for all sorts of reasons.

"Em, sorry," Tait said, adjusting his coat. "Forgot you were there."

"Did you now? And did you forget aboot him, as well?" Ash motioned at the man in the brush who was already drawing flies. "So now what?"

Tait shrugged. "So now I guess we dig another hole."

Twenty-one

Seeing that Lucinda was shivering, Tait sent her back to take a warm bath while he stayed with the earl to dispose of Horne's body. They were trying to figure what to do with it when the sheriff returned, bringing with him a horse, a piece of canvas, and two shovels he'd borrowed from the livery.

"No undertaker?" Tait asked, helping the other two men wrap Horne's body in the canvas and tie it with lengths of cord.

"Visiting his mother in Santa Fe. Any family we need to notify?"

Tait shrugged. "I'll send a wire to his banker. He'll probably know." And he might also know who Tait had to contact about the right-of-ways Horne and Doyle had bought. He wanted everything free and clear and in Lucinda's name as soon as possible. He wanted this behind them forever.

After loading Horne on the horse, they took a back trail down to the graveyard by the church where Tait had sat with Lucinda that morning. He didn't feel the bastard deserved to rest in holy ground, but Brodie said it wasn't all that holy since worse folks were buried there, including Lone Tree, the Arapaho who had tried to kill his family.

There were no prayers offered, and after they filled in the hole, they walked back toward town, Brodie leading the horse and carrying the borrowed shovels. The sky was so heavy it seemed to bend the tips of the firs and spruce trees lining the road, and made the clopping of the horse's hooves sound unnaturally loud in the hush. It didn't feel as cold as it had earlier that afternoon, but Tait was shivering by the time he saw the light shining through the lobby windows of the hotel up ahead. He wondered if Lucinda was through with her bath yet, and reminded himself to have a bigger tub made. A tub for two.

He had almost lost her today.

"You going to tell us what Horne was doing here, Rylander?" the sheriff asked, breaking into Tait's thoughts. "It was apparent you knew each other."

Tait took his time forming a response. Lucinda deserved her privacy, and although he sensed these two men would think no less of her if they knew the truth about her past, it wasn't his tale to tell. So he skirted all that and simply told them Horne had been a business associate of her former fiancé. "My guess is Horne saw the same railroad potential for Heartbreak Creek that Lucinda did. In fact, he's probably the one who's been buying up the other right-of-ways through the canyon."

"What does that have to do with Brin?"

Tait looked over at the sheriff and saw a man of such honor he was slow to recognize the lack of it in others. It was a refreshing change from Doyle. Both these men were. And Tait hoped after the grisly business that evening, he could count them both as friends. "Horne had a sick weakness for children. Lucinda knew that, and when your daughter went missing, she feared he might have taken her."

The sheriff looked away. Tait wondered if he was regretting his hesitation to kill the bastard.

"I wish the buggering whoreson was still alive so I could kill him myself," the earl complained.

"Do you have the knife Thomas threw?" Brodie asked him.

The Scotsman responded with such a look of innocence Tait almost laughed. "What knife? And how do you know Thomas threw it?"

Tait had seen the ex-soldier wipe off the blade and pocket the dagger, and he silently applauded the man for covering for the Cheyenne while at the same time saving the sheriff from having to arrest his friend and deputy.

"Then where is it?" Brodie pressed.

"I'm guessing it slipped out while we were moving him," the earl mused. "Do you want us to go back and find it?"

"It would be easy enough to recognize," Tait added, picturing the horn grip. "Especially with that fancy carved wooden handle."

"Aye," the Scotsman quickly agreed. "It couldna be the heathen's. Dinna his have a stock made of antler?"

"I believe you're right," Tait allowed. "Now that I think on it, it couldn't have been Redstone's knife that killed Horne. I'd swear to it, in fact."

"Bunkum." Brodie let out a deep breath that fogged the air for a moment before dissipating on a chilling gust. "Do you two actually think you're fooling me with that crap? Or that Thomas needs your protection?"

The earl turned to Tait. "Do you suppose it'll snow tonight, lad? There's a feel of it in the air, I'm thinking."

"I believe you're right about that, too."

It was dark when they walked into the lobby of the hotel. Brodie's wife and her half sister had already taken Brin to the sheriff's house on Mulberry Creek, so Brodie headed home, as well.

When Yancey told the earl his wife had retired, too, the big Scotsman gave Tait a quick good night and bounded up the stairs, obviously intent on making up for his drunken incapacitation of the previous night.

"Miss Hathaway's turned in, too," Yancey added. "Looked beat to hell. I didn't have the heart to wake her when the new guests arrived. Shoulda booted them out. Old lady demanded the best room. I told her it was taken, and she almost whacked me with her cane. But when I explained it was rented to an earl and his missus, she settled down somewhat. Cranky old broad, that one."

Tait grinned. "I know. Treat her well or you'll be answering to Miss Hathaway."

"Uh-oh. Family?"

"Guardian."

"Hell."

A single lamp burned in Lucinda's deserted office. Stepping in, Tait closed the door behind him, then crossed to the bedroom and looked inside.

Another lamp burned by the bed where Lucinda lay curled

under a mound of quilts, her damp hair spread over the pillow. He moved closer, needing to see her face to assure himself that she was safe and unharmed.

He had almost lost her today.

After all his promises and pledges of protection, he had still almost lost her to the enemy he knew was coming. The thought sickened him. Brought a rush of that same throat-choking panic he'd felt in the woods earlier when he'd seen Horne lunge toward her.

But now it was finally over. As far as he knew, there was no one left who was a threat to her. She was safe. That realization brought such a welcome relief his legs felt suddenly wobbly. Stumbling to the chair beside the window, he slumped down, his heart pounding.

He had almost lost her today.

Jesus.

Sitting in the dim lamplight, the fingers of one hand spread over his trembling mouth, Tait watched her sleep.

Lucinda awoke to a soft snore. Sitting up, she tracked it to the wingback chair beside the window, where a big form sat slouched, elbows sagging over the sides of the armrests, long legs outstretched and crossed at the ankles.

"Tait," she called softly.

He jerked awake, saw her sitting upright, and rubbed a hand over his face. "Did I wake you?"

"Come to bed."

He looked at her for a moment, then leaning forward, rested his arms on his thighs and stared down at his clenched hands. "I'm sorry. I should have gone after Horne instead of coming to you in Heartbreak Creek."

"Tait—"

"I knew he was in Denver. I should have gone there first."

"No. It happened as it should have. I needed to face him. And I couldn't have done that if he hadn't come here, or without you beside me."

"I was almost too late."

"Almost doesn't count. Now come to bed."

He rose and walked toward her. Leaning down he gave her a

slow, sweet kiss, then straightened. "I need to bathe. Wash the taint of death off my hands."

"Hurry, then."

When he came back into the bedroom several minutes later, his hair glistened damply in the lamplight, and he wore only a towel that did little to hide what his intentions were.

Laughing, she pulled it away so she could admire his lean form. He was all sinew and muscles and long, strong limbs. All hers.

She lifted her arms to him and drew him down to her side. "Lie back," she ordered. When he did, she began a slow exploration with her hands and lips and tongue.

He smelled of the pine soap she had left out for him, and tasted slightly salty, and felt like sleek, warm marble coming alive beneath her questing hand.

"You better stop that before it's too late," he whispered hoarsely.

Chuckling, she bent and circled his navel with her tongue. Muscles rippled. His breath caught, then came faster when her hand slid lower to close around him.

"Jesus." His eyes fluttered closed.

She knew what a man liked. She had been tutored in the most explicit and brutal way. And she had hoped that once she'd left Mrs. Beale's, she would never have to suffer this degrading act again.

But this wasn't any man—this was Tait. And because he demanded nothing of her, she gave more than she thought she could.

"Sweetheart," he said in a strained voice, his hips flexing. "You don't have to do this."

"Hush."

His hands fisted in the sheets. With a groan, he rose up to meet her. And as the taste and smell and feel of him moved through her mind, the past slipped back into the shadows and all that was left was the joy she could give him, and the love he gave back.

And it felt right. And good.

The next time Lucinda awoke it was to bright sunlight, a familiar voice in her office, and Tait's hands on her breasts.

"Oh, my God."

"I know," murmured a sleep-hoarse voice beside her. "It's a grand way to meet the day. Roll over."

"No. Listen!" She bolted upright, head cocked. She couldn't discern the words, but that cranky voice she would know anywhere. "She's here!" she hissed, thrusting his hands away. "Get up!"

"I am up. All you have to do is climb on."

"Not now! It's her! Mrs. Throckmorton. She's in my office. What if she finds you in here?"

He yawned and scratched his chest. "Then she'll force me to marry you."

"Tait!"

"Margaret?" a voice called from outside the bedroom door. "Are you awake? That nasty little creature in the lobby said I mustn't disturb you. As if. Are you decent?"

"Yes. No!" Lucinda called back. "Let me throw on my robe." In a lower voice to Tait, "Go hide in the water closet." Throwing back the covers, she jerked her robe from the foot rail, then picked up the towel Tait had worn last night and threw it at his chest. "Hurry."

"You're serious?" He blinked at her. "You want me to hide from your guardian? She already knows I'm marrying you."

"We're not married yet, so go." She shoved him hard.

"Margaret, dear, who are you talking to in there?"

"Myself. I'm just talking to myself. I can't find my robe. Oh, there it is."

Muttering, Tait stumbled toward the water closet door.

Lucinda yanked on the robe just as the door into the water closet closed and the door into the office opened.

To cover her discomfiture, Lucinda rushed over to give her guardian a hug. "You're here! You're actually here! I was going to send for you, but—"

The elderly lady drew back to study her. "What is that rash on your neck? You're not coming down with measles, are you?"

Lucinda's hand flew to her neck. "What?"

"Humph. Of course you're not. I know bristle rash when I see it. Did you think I was born yesterday?" Waving Lucinda away, Mrs. Throckmorton looked around. "And where is that scalawag?"

"In here, ma'am," Tait called through the door. "Just draining the pipes . . . ah . . . in case we have a freeze later."

Lucinda stared up at the ceiling and prayed for patience.

"Draining the pipes, my Aunt Fanny's bustle," the old woman muttered. "Come out, you rascal, and face the music."

The door opened and Tait came out, fully dressed and looking quite rakish with his morning stubble and crooked smile. "Mrs. Throckmorton, what a lovely surprise."

"Nonsense. You knew I was coming."

Lucinda spun toward him. "You did?"

He answered with a grin and a kiss on her cheek.

"It's apparent that you have anticipated your vows, you grinning rogue." Mrs. Throckmorton batted Tait away from Lucinda with her hanky. "I will not countenance such immoral behavior. You will marry today." To drive home her demand, she thumped Tait's foot with her cane. "Are we clear?"

"Yes, ma'am," Tait said.

"Excellent. Mrs. Bradshaw and that nice Mr. Quinn will handle all the details. Come, Rylander. You may beg my forgiveness for your reprehensible behavior over breakfast. I'm famished. You have ten minutes, Margaret."

Thus began Lucinda's second wedding day.

Again, dear Mrs. Bradshaw worked wonders. And with the help of Maddie and Edwina and Pru, as well as Biddy Rickman and the choir ladies, by late afternoon, all was in readiness, and the pews of the little Come All You Sinners Church were filled to capacity.

"Is this one more to your liking?" Mrs. Throckmorton asked Lucinda as they stood before the church doors, awaiting the signal to enter.

"Infinitely so. He's kind and thoughtful and endearing and smart and—"

"But do you love him?"

"To distraction."

"Excellent."

"And you, too, ma'am."

"Of course you do. You're my daughter. Chin up, and do stop crying. I get enough of that from your friend, Edwina."

The door opened a crack. Billy peered out at them. "Ready, ma'ams?"

"And near frozen," Mrs. Throckmorton barked. "Let's get on with it."

Billy opened the church doors wider, and Lucinda stepped forward on Mrs. Throckmorton's arm. A bit unorthodox, perhaps, being given away by her female guardian, but Lucinda would have it no other way.

As soon as she appeared on the threshold, the choir ladies burst into song and Biddy Rickman began beating on the piano.

The guests stood. Mrs. Throckmorton patted her arm in reassurance. And dressed in her lilac gown and Edwina's veil, with Maddie's blue lace handkerchief tucked in her cuff and clutching a tiny book of verse Pru had brought from home, Lucinda walked toward Tait and Pastor Rickman, and all of the beloved faces beaming from the front pews—the Brodies, Maddie and Ash, and Pru and Thomas.

Her family.

Never in all of her life had she been so happy.

She scarcely remembered the ceremony or the vows. Partly because Edwina was blubbering so loudly Lucinda couldn't hear them, and partly because Brin and Joe Bill got into a whispering match over who got to hold the hymnal. But mostly because as soon as she reached Tait's side, he bent down and murmured, "You're a vision of loveliness in that pretty purple dress."

"It's lilac," she whispered back.

"No matter, it's coming off in about two hours."

Instantly, scripture and vows and even Biddy's enthusiastic piano pounding faded under a hot rush of anticipation. Two hours. She wondered how she could bear waiting that long.

Then the church ceremony was over and they were walking back to the hotel under a darkening sky, laughing and talking amid salacious comments tossed at the bride and groom. Lucinda barely refrained from skipping.

When they reached the hotel, she told Tait she needed to freshen up and ducked into her office. Mrs. Bradshaw and several of the town ladies had cooked up a grand feast to mark this second Heartbreak Creek wedding, and they would be seating the wedding guests soon. But Lucinda desperately needed a few moments to herself.

Shutting out the babble of voices in the lobby, she leaned

back against the closed door, battling a sudden urge to cry and laugh and twirl across the floor.

She was a married woman now.

An astonishing, thrilling, almost frightening thing.

And sobering.

What kind of wife would she be?

Crossing to stand at the window in her office, she watched the day fade behind the peaks and tried to imagine what her life would be like now.

Luckily Tait—unlike Doyle—had shown no attempt to mold her to his demands. But Lucinda knew what was expected of her as a wife. No longer a hotel owner and business woman in her own right, she would be her husband's hostess, his lover, the mother of his children and keeper of his home. She would live where he lived, put her dreams aside for his, follow in his shadow. That was the way it was.

She accepted that, and gladly, because she loved Tait with all her heart and couldn't bear the thought of a life without him.

And yet . . .

The memory of those brief days on the run flooded her mind. Days of total autonomy and independence. A frightening, exhilarating, liberating time. The rush of it still swirled in her memory.

She would miss that thrill of accomplishment.

But she was a married woman now.

"So here's where you are," Tait said, coming through the door. "They're ready in the dining room." Moving up behind her, he pressed a kiss to her neck. When she was slow to respond, he stepped around to look into her face.

"What's wrong, Luce?"

The man could read her every thought, it seemed. She tried to cover her momentary melancholy with a bright smile. "Nothing. This has all happened so fast I'm just trying to sort it out and figure where we go from here."

His dark brows drew together. "Go?"

"We should probably travel back with Mrs. Throckmorton. That way I can be certain she doesn't overtire herself."

"Travel where? New York?"

Now she was the one confused. "Of course. That's where your business is. You have a house there. I assumed that's where you would want to live."

"Hell." He raked a hand over his face, then dropped it to his hip. "You're right. This has happened too fast. We should have had this conversation earlier."

"What conversation?" He was starting to alarm her. What had he not told her?

He spread his battered hands in a helpless gesture. "I sold my house. I closed my accounts. I have no business dealings in New York."

"You what?"

"It never occurred to me that you would want to return to Manhattan."

She blinked at him in astonishment, not certain she had heard him correctly. "Don't you want to go back?"

"Not particularly. Definitely not permanently."

"But . . ." Confusion gave way to hope. She pressed a palm over her racing heart. "You want to stay here? In Heartbreak Creek?"

"Why not?" He motioned toward the window, where stars were slowly disappearing behind a thick layer of clouds. "It's beautiful country. And now that I've seen it, I don't know that I'd want to live anywhere else." He let his hand fall back to his side. "And, of course, I also need to stay here to protect my investment." He grinned down at her. "You owe me quite a bit of money, Mrs. Rylander."

"For what?"

"The stock certificates."

She frowned in confusion. "How can they be yours?"

"I bought back the ones you took loans against. I even paid Doyle for the ones you still have. I wanted no clouds hanging over you. Over us. It was the right thing to do, Luce, and you know it."

She wasn't sure she agreed, but was too astounded to argue about it. "So they're yours? All five hundred shares?"

"Ours. And only the ones you still hold. I resold the others, and suggest you do the same with the certificates you have left. I don't trust this market."

She blinked up at him, her mind reeling. "I don't know what to say."

"A simple 'thank you, Tait,' would be nice."

"Thank you, Tait."

He laughed softly in that way that sent quivers along her nerves. "Your thanks is appreciated, sweetheart, but woefully insufficient. I expect you to pay me back. With interest, of course. Compounded daily. You can start tonight."

She batted at his arm to cover her tangled emotions. "You."

"Too sore? Then we could play strip poker until you're up to more vigorous games. Or go into partnership."

She reared back. "Partnership?"

"Equal shares. I want you working beside me, not for me. Although, of course, I'll have the final say. Do you agree?"

She didn't answer. Couldn't. Tears burned in her eyes and clogged her throat.

"And I'll expect you to show your gratitude every day," he went on. "At least once. You can start now, if you'd like."

Equal partners. She loved the sound of that. She loved that he thought her capable of keeping up with him in business matters. With his connections and railroad experience, and her vision and determination, along with their combined funds, they could turn Heartbreak Creek into a remarkable place. A real home. For both of them . . . and their children. She smiled, loving the idea of that, as well.

"I adore you, Mr. Rylander." Rising on tiptoe, she gave him a hard, quick kiss to seal the bargain. "And I accept your terms."

"What terms?" he said, his hungry gaze fixed on her mouth.

"You bring in the railroads, and I'll do the rest." She looped her arm through his and steered him toward the door. "We'll discuss benefits later."

"I'd rather discuss them now."

"Me, too. But they're waiting."

"Let them wait."

"Mrs. Throckmorton, too?"

He sighed.

As Lucinda took her place beside her husband at the head table, she glanced at Pru, speculating on whether she and Thomas would be the next Heartbreak Creek wedding.

But as usual, Thomas had disappeared, having little fondness for crowds and white gatherings, and Pru, even though she was smiling and appeared to be enjoying the festivities, seemed to have a melancholy air about her. Lucinda prayed the two mismatched lovers would find a common ground despite their vast differences. Then she pushed the thought aside for now. This was her wedding day. She would allow no unhappiness to mar its perfection.

After they had eaten and the dishes had been cleared, the tables and chairs were stacked in the lobby to make room for dancing. Lucinda allowed Yancey to unlock the door into the Red Eye just this once so the piano could be rolled in. Other instruments were brought out, and soon music filled the dining room and the dancing began.

It lasted less than two hours, until Billy brought news that snow was coming down fast and anyone having far to go had best leave now before the drifts piled up. Soon, the only ones left were Lucinda's Heartbreak Creek family—which tonight included Mrs. Throckmorton, Mrs. Bradshaw, and Buster Quinn—all of whom were staying the night at the hotel.

They gathered on the couches and chairs in the deserted lobby, exhausted but enjoying the quiet companionship. As there were no other guests in the hotel at the moment, Lucinda sent Yancey to bed and told Billy and Miriam to go home for the night.

Declan rousted his children from Lucinda's office, where they had been playing a ring-and-toss game, and ushered them upstairs to the suite assigned to the Brodies. When he returned, Ash proposed a toast to the bride and groom.

After filling their glasses with the champagne Mrs. Throckmorton had brought all the way from New York, he raised his high. "*Slainte mhòr agus a h-uile beannachd duibh.* Great health and every good blessing to you, my friends."

"Here, here," the others chimed in.

"I have a toast, too." Tait stood. The smile he sent Lucinda sent tingles all the way to her toes. "To my beautiful bride," he said softly, his glass held high. "The woman I loved before I even knew who she was. And to her guardian, Mrs. Throckmorton, who kept her safe until I found her."

Lucinda smiled and strove not to cry.

Mrs. Throckmorton sniffed into her hanky and leaned over to whisper loudly enough for all to hear, "You chose wisely this time, my dear. I approve."

Other toasts were offered, then as the last glass was emptied, Lucinda rose.

"I have something to say." Wiping her suddenly damp palms on her skirts, she smiled uncertainly at the people gathered around her.

She had thought about this all through the day, surrounded by these people she loved in this place she now thought of as home. They had opened their hearts to her. They had accepted her without question or doubt. They loved and trusted her.

She owed them no less in return.

She looked at her beloved Tait and the cranky Mrs. Throckmorton, and at all the dear faces waiting expectantly, and had to blink away a rush of tears.

"I love all of you so much."

At those words, Edwina began to cry and smile at the same time.

Pru and Maddie beamed.

The men looked uncomfortable.

"You're my family now." It came out weak and wobbly, and she was forced to pause and wait for the tightness in her throat to ease so she could continue.

Outside, the snow fell, slow and steady, building crescents in the corners of the windowpanes and reshaping the landscape with a soft blanket of white. The first true snow. Beneath it, the earth would sleep, undisturbed, awaiting a new spring and a new beginning. A time of rest and healing.

For her, as well. Perhaps this time the words would come easier.

She took a deep breath and let it out. A last glance at Tait, then buoyed by his strength, she smiled into the faces of the people she loved most in the world.

"A long time ago, I was Cathleen Donovan," she began. "And I was born two years before the Great Hunger came to Ireland . . ."

Epilogue

Pru knew he was there long before she saw him, or heard him, or felt his arms slide around her from behind. There was that unmistakable change in the air, like a breath caught and held . . . a subtle shift in tension that she felt all along her nerves.

"Eho'nehevehohtse," Thomas whispered in her ear. *"Neme-hotatse."* I love you.

Turning from her contemplation of the snow drifting past the window of her room at the hotel, she put her arms around his neck and kissed him. His lips were cold, his face damp with melting snowflakes. He smelled like horses and old smoke and life.

"I wasn't sure you would come." They had joined together only once. And that bonding was still new—a tender, fragile thing that she hadn't yet learned to trust.

"I will always be close by, *heme'oono.* You have only to call." His hand moved up to cup her breast, then hesitated when he felt the pendant beneath her gown. "What is this?" He pulled it out and smiled when he saw it was the piece of rose quartz he had carved into the shape of a heart.

"I missed you at the wedding feast tonight," she said.

"And I missed you, Prudence Lincoln. To prove it, I brought you a gift."

She looked where he pointed and saw tall, fur-lined moccasins and a buffalo robe lined with rabbit fur that was draped over the foot rail of the bed. "What's that?"

"Put it on."

"Are we going somewhere?" She looked down at the flannel gown draping her from neck to toe. "I'm not dressed to go out."

"Put this on and you will be." He held out the fur robe.

"I don't understand."

"You will."

She pulled on the robe. The slide of the silky rabbit fur lining against the thin flannel of her gown made her feel deliciously wanton. She glanced over at Thomas, wondering if he knew that even without touching her he had made her want him.

Once she had donned the boots, he led her silently down the stairs, past the hotel lobby, and out the back door where his spotted pony waited. He lifted her onto his blanket saddle, then swung up behind her. Pulling her back against his chest, he reined the pony toward the far end of town and nudged him into a fast, smooth walk. Soon, they left the few lights behind and moved deeper into the canyon.

Having been raised in the south, Pru had seen little snow except for the two short snowfalls in Heartbreak Creek last month that had melted within hours. As she rode before Thomas, his warmth at her back and the cold, soft snowflakes swirling in her face, she marveled that even with all the movement around her, the night could be so silent. The hush was broken only by the gentle thud of the pony's unshod hooves against the soft snow and the sound of Thomas's breathing by her ear.

Lifting her face to the sky, she caught a snowflake on her tongue and laughed. "It's so beautiful, Thomas. Thank you for bringing me out to see it."

"There is more, *Eho'nehevehohtse*. When the clouds part, you will see more stars than you ever dreamed there could be. And if we are lucky, as we rest in our warm, misty bed, we will see spirits dance across the sky."

"The snow's stopping?" she asked, unable to keep her disappointment from showing.

"For now."

They rode higher and higher, the rush of the creek fading on their left, the steep wooded slopes rising on their right. And still the snow drifted down, silent and thick and heavy. Because of the whiteness all around them and the pale clouds hanging just above the treetops, they were able to see where they were going. Although Pru saw there was little need for concern—the pony seemed to be following a familiar trail hidden beneath the snow.

When they finally stopped, she was chilled despite the warm robe. The horse's breath fogged the air and frost clung to the whiskers by his nostrils. As Thomas helped her down, she looked around, expecting to see a sweat lodge or tipi or some other reason why he had brought her out here on a snowy night. But all she noticed were tall trees and an eerie silence and tendrils of mist curling through the drooping frosted branches. A faint odor, like eggs, hung in the still air.

"Where are we?"

He didn't answer but took her hand and led her through the trees. The mist thickened. The odor grew stronger and reminded her of the rank-tasting water in Heartbreak Creek.

"What's that smell?" she asked him, ducking under a low branch.

"The warm breath of Mother Earth. You will get used to it."

"It's probably what gives the creek its distinctive odor and taste." Pru wrinkled her nose. "Is it this bad everywhere in the canyon?"

"Only from here down to your town. Farther up, it tastes better."

"Really? I'll have to tell Lucinda. If we can pipe the good water into Heartbreak Creek, the railroads will be more likely to come through the canyon."

He stopped so abruptly she stumbled into his broad back.

"I did not bring you here to talk about water and railroads and Lucinda Hathaway," he scolded gently. "You will think only of me."

"Will I?"

He grinned. "You will. I will see to it."

Turning, he continued through the trees.

She followed, stepping into his tracks to keep from slipping on rocks hidden beneath the deepening snow. It was slow going. She soon regretted not wearing more clothing when cold air crept up beneath the fur coat and her gown. She was about to complain to Thomas when they rounded a huge spruce.

She stopped, amazed.

A small clearing, ringed by tall firs, opened before them. In the center, a foggy cloud hung above a bubbling pool nestled in a rocky basin. A warm spring. Pru had heard and read of them but had never seen one. "How beautiful." Crossing toward it, she stared down into crystal-clear water that rippled and rolled with the stirring of an unseen current just below the steaming surface.

"It is a place of healing," Thomas said.

"It's amazing." Pru bent to study the tender plants clustered at the edge of the water despite the frigid air. Even the snow-flakes melted before they breached the rising mist. "It must be caused by a fissure that goes very deep."

"To the heart of Mother Earth. This is a sacred pool. Now it will be our pool." Dropping his coat to the ground, Thomas pulled his war tunic over his head.

"What are you doing?" she asked.

He sat on a rock and began unlacing the ties on his tall, fur-lined moccasins. "Take off your robe, Prudence."

"I'll freeze."

"I will not let you." Barefoot, he rose and loosened the tie around his lean waist so that his breechcloth and leggings slid down his sturdy legs. He stepped out of them and turned toward her, a scarred, proud warrior, his beautiful body dark against the falling snow. His smile reached across the mist and into her heart. "Take off your robe, *Eho'nehevehohtse*," he said again.

She took off her robe.

"Now your gown."

She hesitated, then did as he asked, gasping when cold air struck her heated body, yet enjoying the way his dark gaze moved over her and his breath caught.

Sweeping her up in his arms, he stepped into the pool.

Clouds of steam rose around them, filling her lungs, leaving tiny beads of moisture on his long lashes. She tightened her arms around his neck, shocked by the heat of the water against her chilled flesh.

The bubbling current caressed her, eddied around her limbs as he went deeper. Soon her body adjusted, and the water felt like a warm blanket sliding around her, and the smell no longer mattered, and the world was reduced to swirling mist and fall-ing snow and Thomas's strong arms holding her safe.

"I can't swim," she warned when he finally stopped, the

water so deep only her uplifted arms and her neck and head rose above the surface.

"You know I will let no harm come to you, Prudence."

She felt the vibration of his voice against her breasts, the warm, slick hardness of his body against hers. Her heartbeat quickened.

Awash in sensation, she dropped her head to his shoulder and breathed in his warm, male scent.

"*Nemehotatse, Eho'nehevehohtse,*" he whispered into her hair.

She lifted her head and smiled at him. "I love you, too, Thomas."

He kissed her. "You are *nahe'e*, my woman, Prudence Lincoln. My heart mate for all time. As I am yours."

Heart mate. Such a fanciful turn of phrase. But coming from Thomas it sounded right. Pressing her face against the pulse beat in his neck, she felt a cold emptiness spread where joy had been. Tears of regret filled her eyes. She had dreaded this moment, hated the words she must say, but knew their time had come.

"I will always be your heart mate, Thomas. No matter where our lives lead us." She lifted her head and looked into his dark eyes. "But I can't stay here with you."

He grew still. It seemed for a moment even his heartbeat stopped drumming against her breast. "Where will you go?"

How like him not to question her decision or try to talk her out of it. She would have preferred anger rather than this quiet acceptance. His expression showed her nothing, yet the pain was there in his beautiful eyes. "I'm not sure. But I know I can do things—important things—beyond Heartbreak Creek and these mountains."

His grip loosed, but she wouldn't let him go, clasping him tightly to keep him close as long as she could. "It's the same thing that calls you into the mountains," she said in a voice thick with tears. "A voice inside that can't be ignored."

Closing his eyes, he tipped his head forward to rest against hers. "And what does this voice tell you, *Eho'nehevehohtse*? What is so important that it takes you away from me?"

"That others need me more than you. That I must try to help them prepare for their new place in the white world. Neither the

Indians nor the Negroes will ever stand alone if they can't read or write. Or vote. Everyone should be able to vote."

He gave a bitter laugh. "Even me?"

"Especially you." When he didn't respond, she took one arm from around his neck and cupped his jaw, forcing him to look at her. Mist coated his cheeks. Or maybe it was tears. Her own flowed freely to drip from her chin, despite the resolve in her heart.

"I know you've been lied to and cheated and driven from your land, Thomas. But this is still your home. It may have changed from what you knew, but there's a place in it for you and all the tribes, as well as the whites, and Africans, and Chinese, and the countless others flooding this country. But it won't wait for you to claim it. You must put your stake in it and make your voice heard. I can help with that. But not from here. I have to go where the need is."

He was silent for a long time. Then in that flat, expressionless tone, "Will you ever come back?"

She felt as if her heart were breaking. "Of course I will, Thomas. This is my true home. These people—and you, especially you—are my family. I don't want to leave you, but I must."

"No one makes you do this. It is what you choose."

"Do you choose to go in the mountains when your spirit guides call? Or is it something you feel you must do?"

He had no answer, but she felt defeat in the slump in his shoulders.

"I need to do this, Thomas. Can you understand?"

Without answering, he carried her to the side of the pool and set her down on a warm flat rock jutting out just below the surface. Sitting beside her, he gently ran his hand over her breast and down her belly, as if imprinting the curves and hollows on his mind in preparation for the parting to come.

"The People have a saying," he said, watching his hand move over her beneath the water's surface. "'In an eagle there is all the wisdom in the world.' I named you *Eho'nehevehohtse*— One Who Walks in Wolf Tracks—because you are smart enough to fool men. But I was wrong." Tipping his head back, he looked into her face. "You are *Voaxaa'e*. The Eagle."

He leaned forward and pressed his mouth to hers in a tender, sweet kiss that spoke more of love than passion. Then he settled back, a sad smile playing at his lips. "Did you know that eagles have one mate for all of their lives, Prudence Lincoln? They might fly away for many months, but they always return to the same nest. The same mate." His hand stroked up her inner thigh. "Will you come back to me, *Voaxaa'e*?"

"I could love no other, Thomas."

"Then I will wait for you."

"I couldn't ask you to do that."

"I will wait for you," he said again in that solemn way of his.

"Then I'll come back to you whenever I can," she promised. "There will be no one but you in my life, Thomas. Ever."

"Do not stay away from me too long," he warned, his hand stroking higher as he pressed gentle kisses across her jaw and cheek and brow. "Or on some snowy night like this, or maybe in summer as you sleep to the song of the crickets, or when a storm awakens you with rolling thunder . . . you will open your eyes and I will be there."

She shifted. Opened her legs wider. "I would like that, Thomas."

"Maybe I will step out of the darkness and touch you here." He brushed his fingers against her, knowing exactly where to touch. "And you will fly away with me."

She gasped, her body arching in the water, her mind exploding into bright flashes of light. He continued to stroke her, murmuring words she didn't understand, until she sank, trembling, back to earth.

But the lights were still there, hanging in wavering bands of green and blue and yellow with streaks of red. The snow had stopped, the clouds had parted. And overhead, a sensuous, undulating ribbon of colored light bled across the black canvas of the sky. "Thomas, look," she said, pointing.

He turned to look up, and smiled. "It is the dance of the spirits, *Voaxaa'e*. A rare thing. They have come down from the top of the world to dance for us."

"It's so beautiful," she whispered, awed by the otherworldly sight.

"It is a blessing, I think."

"Yes." Pru wrapped her arms and her heart around the man

she would love for all of her life. And safe in his care in this sacred place, she watched through her tears as mist rose up to meet the ghostly lights that rippled and danced and arced across the wide Colorado sky.

A blessing, indeed.

Read on for a special preview of
the first book in Kaki's newest trilogy
set in Heartbreak Creek

BEHIND HIS BLUE EYES

Available August 2013 from Berkley Sensation

One

"Another letter came today."

Audra looked up, her mind still caught on whether to use *further* or *farther*—she always confused the two no matter how many times she consulted *Butler's English Usage Manual*. "From whom?"

"That dismal sounding place in Colorado Territory," Winnie said with disdain.

Audra checked that the letter had, indeed, come from Heartbreak Creek then dropped it, unopened, into the overflowing waste bin beside her desk. "Has Father eaten?"

"Had a good lunch. Hardly spilled a drop."

Motion drew Audra's eye and she looked out the front window to see a black closed carriage stop before the rented house she shared with her father, Winnie, and Winnie's husband, Curtis. Four figures stepped out. Men.

She jumped to her feet. *Why were they here? Had they found out what she had done?* Frantically, she gathered the notes piled on the desk and shoved them into the desk drawer.

"It's Father's colleagues!" Racing to the bookcase, she stuffed her papers into the lower cabinet, while Winnie crammed down the wads of paper in the waste bin and shoved it under the desk.

"Maybe they found out about Father." Audra slammed the cabinet door and looked around. Her heart pounded so hard she thought she might faint. "Where are Father and Curtis?"

"Last I saw, headed to the stable to pet the cats."

"Make sure they stay there."

They both flinched when the knocker on the front door sounded. With trembling fingers, Audra tucked a loose strand of brown hair into her bun, then faced the stout, dark-skinned woman old enough to be her mother, and who, since Audra's sixth birthday, had served as such. In the twenty years since, Winnie had added housekeeper, cook, nurse, and benevolent tyrant to her duties, ruling the household with sharp criticisms and gentle hugs. Audra was terrified of what might become of her and Curtis and Father if she went to jail. "How do I look?"

"Best remove those." Winnie pointed at the cloth shields tied around Audra's cuffs.

Quickly stripping off the protectors, Audra stuffed them into the cabinet with the papers and slammed the door shut again. "Anything else?"

"Spectacles."

Audra slipped those into her skirt pocket then smoothed her hair again. "Better?"

"You might at least try to look pleased. Not every day you get callers."

"Especially ones who have come to accuse me of fraud."

"Smile anyway. Wouldn't kill you and might fool them."

Audra pasted on a stiff smile. "How's that?"

"Make an undertaker proud."

Another wave of panic rolled over her. "Oh, Winnie, what if they—"

"Quit twisting your hands. I can hear your knuckles cracking from over here."

Audra struggled to breathe. Her throat was so tight she felt suffocated. Excuses and explanations and lies tumbled through her head. She could tell them she had always transcribed Father's papers and that when he became ill and she had found his notes in his desk, she had continued to do so. It was his research, not hers. She had just put it in readable form.

And forged his signature on the royalty checks then lied to anyone who asked about him.

Another knock almost buckled her knees.

She took a deep breath, let it out, and nodded. "You may let them in, Winnie. Then go tell Curtis under no account is he to allow Father to come into the house. Understand?"

Muttering, Winnie crossed the entry hall and flung open the front door. "Afternoon, gentlemens. What a fine day for visiting. I'll tell Miss Audra she got company."

"Actually," a deep voice said, "we've come to see the professor. Is he in?"

"No, sir. He off studying whatever it is he study. But Miss Audra here."

A moment later, they filed into the room. Scarcely daring to breathe, Audra studied their familiar faces, but saw nothing to increase her alarm. Richard even smiled at her.

Her father, Professor Percival Pearsall, had once been a revered member of the group these men represented. He had been the driving force behind the Baltimore Society of Learned Historians for so many years he had become the yardstick by which all other members were measured. It had been her father's exacting standards that had made the society and its annual competition the final word in historical analysis. Now all that was in jeopardy because of her.

Struggling to keep her voice steady, she nodded to Misters Uxley, Beamis, Collins, and her onetime suitor, Richard Villars. "May I offer refreshment, gentlemen?"

Hiram Uxley, the president of the group, shook his head. "We cannot stay long, Miss Pearsall. But it's imperative that we see the professor. Do you expect him soon?"

"I regret not, sir. He is still visiting the ancient pueblos in New Mexico Territory and will be gone for several more months." This was the third time she had put off her father's colleagues with that excuse. Had they finally seen through her lies?

"Several more months?" Uxley's muttonchops trembled in agitation. "He's already been gone over two years. What on earth could he have found?"

"I ca-cannot tell you, sir. He's been very secretive about it."

"This certainly puts a twist in our plans." With a huff, he turned to the other three gentlemen and engaged in a low-voiced conversation.

Audra watched them, terror pounding through her. A familiar

bark sounded, and she looked out the window behind her guests to see Winnie chasing after Curtis, who was chasing after her father, who was shuffling after Cleo, his little dog. Horrified, she glanced at the others to see if they had noticed, and found Richard also watching the drama by the buggy house.

She watched puzzlement come over his face. Then recognition. *Oh God. He knows.*

He turned to her and started to say something, but Uxley interrupted. "Well, there's no help for it. Richard, present the award to Miss Pearsall and she can hold it for her father."

Award? Her mind still trapped in fear, Audra watched Richard pull a folded paper from the inside pocket of his frock coat.

"As treasurer of the Baltimore Society of Learned Historians, I am pleased to present our Historian of Merit Award, as well as the Peabody Grant, to Professor Percival Pearsall for his excellent essay on 'The Development of Gas Artillery Capsules During the War of the Rebellion.'" With a bow, he offered the paper to Audra. "Please convey to your father my congratulations. His article was one of the most articulate and compelling I have ever read."

Audra stared at the paper in his hand, her mind slow to take it all in. They didn't know? They hadn't come to have her arrested? Looking up, she forced a smile. "T-Thank you." She took the folded paper in trembling fingers and slipped it into her pocket. "I-I wasn't aware he had entered it in the competition." She had certainly not done so, and had only transcribed her father's notes in hopes of gaining another small royalty to augment their meager income.

Mr. Uxley stepped forward. "That was my doing, Miss Pearsall. With so few entries of true merit, I thought it wise to put the society's best work forward. Reputation is all, you know."

Color flooded Richard's face, but he didn't respond.

"It's an excellent piece," Mr. Beamis offered.

"Hear, hear," Mr. Collins seconded. "Does us all proud."

Audra felt wretched. One of the reasons she hadn't entered the article in the contest—other than the fact it would have been even more dishonest than offering it for publication—was that she guessed Richard would be submitting his own paper on cave drawings in the southern Appalachians. He was so desperate to establish himself as a leading American historian it was almost painful to watch. Sadly, he was a much better researcher than writer.

Uxley waved the others toward the door. "We must be off. Our congratulations to your father." He glanced at Richard, who hadn't moved. "Are you coming, Villars?"

"I'll be along in a moment."

As the other men filed out, Richard frowned at the buggy house. Thankfully, neither Winnie, nor Curtis, nor Father was in sight. "Was that your father I saw, Audra?"

"My father? When?"

"Just now. Out back."

Audra pretended confusion as her mind raced for a plausible lie. Then she smiled and shook her head. "You must have seen Uncle Edward, Father's older brother. He took ill not long after my aunt died, and has been slow to recover. We've taken him in until Father returns."

"I could have sworn he was the professor."

"They do look very much alike, don't they? Although since his illness, Uncle Edward has become alarmingly frail. I'm not sure how much longer we can keep him here, although I would hate to put him in a home. I'm quite worried about him." She realized she was babbling but couldn't seem to stop herself. She was a horrid liar.

Richard's dark eyes bored into hers in that intense way she had always found intrusive. "Perhaps on my next visit I might meet him. The coming week, perhaps?"

Audra held her smile, the muscles in her face trembling with the effort. "That would be lovely. But do let us know when you plan to come so we can be sure he's up to a visit."

"Of course. Until then."

After the door closed behind him, Audra collapsed into the chair at the desk, tears further blurring her faulty vision. "Now what am I going to do?"

Winnie came in. "What happened?"

"Richard Villars saw Father. I told him it was my uncle Edward, but I don't think he believed me. He's invited himself back next week to meet him. What should I tell him?"

"The truth."

Audra pressed fingertips against her throbbing temple. "I fear it's gone too far, Winnie. If Richard tells Uxley, he'll feel honor bound to bring my deception to light. Father's reputation will be ruined and all his hard work will be forever shrouded in doubt. And if I go to jail for fraud, you and Curtis will be on the street, and Father will be shuffled off to one of those wretched institutions for mentally impaired indigents. I can't allow that to happen."

Winnie gave it some thought. "Mr. Villars cared enough to propose to you last year. Maybe he'll go along and not tell." She gave Audra a critical look. "'Specially if you fess up."

Audra doubted it. Richard didn't like being thwarted and had taken her refusal hard. But how could she have accepted him—even if she'd wanted to—without revealing Father's dementia? And if he now found out she'd been lying to him and had fraudulently cheated him out of a coveted award, no telling what he might do. He had more to gain by exposing her father than by covering up for her. And Richard had always been ambitious.

"Or you can leave."

"Leave? How? You know I have barely enough money to keep the four of us fed. And even if I could afford it, where could we go?"

Winnie dug through the wastebasket, then straightened, the sealed envelope Audra had thrown away earlier in her hand. "How about here?"

"Heartbreak Creek?"

"Why not? You say your daddy inherited a cabin there. Dismal-sounding town like that would be a fine place to hide. Doubt anybody there ever heard of your daddy, or would care that you wrote his papers for him." Tossing the letter on the desk, Winnie turned toward the door. "Your choice. The truth and marriage to Mr. Villars, or Heartbreak Creek. You pick. Though after thirty years married to that no-account Curtis, if I had the choice, I'd pick jail. Yes, ma'am, I think I would."

Audra pulled the society letter from her pocket. Richard had said something about a grant. If it was enough . . .

She unfolded the letter then gasped when she saw the amount. With that much money, they could cover a lot of miles . . . assuming Father was strong enough to make the trip, and the cabin was even habitable, and she was willing to leave everything she'd ever known.

A ghastly prospect, but what other option did she have?

Pulling out her pen and a fresh sheet of paper, she began to write.

> *Dear Richard, I know this comes as a surprise, but Father has asked us to join him in New Mexico. By the time this reaches you, we will already be gone, and I doubt we'll return in the near future . . .*

Two

MARCH 1871, COLORADO TERRITORY

He should offer assistance. That would be the neighborly thing to do.

Instead, Ethan Hardesty crossed his arms and his outstretched legs and settled back on the bench outside the depot. The woman was clearly out of her depth. Yet she kept at it. He'd give her marks for that, at least.

A gust of wind flipped up the hem of her skirt, giving him a fine view of narrow feet encased in delicate low-top shoes. City people. They never understood that in hard country like this, sturdy footwear was second only to a good jacket, no matter the season.

Hearing a ruckus toward the end of the idling train, he glanced back to see a drover lead a fractious bay down the ramp and hand the lead to an elderly African man who was clearly frightened of the animal. Sawing on the lead and stepping lively to keep his feet from beneath the prancing hooves, the man wrestled the horse over to where the woman was supervising the unloading of a closed four-wheel, single-horse buggy in the Amish style.

It wasn't going well.

In addition to getting in the way of the freight handlers, she was busy trying to calm the horse and the old man holding him, attend questions and complaints from a cantankerous Negro woman she called Winnie, keep an eye on a mumbling old man—probably her father—and hang on to a squirming badger-sized dog that barked continuously.

It was like watching a circus. A poorly run circus.

Ethan couldn't remember the last time he had been so entertained.

The man he assumed was her father made a shuffling escape, heading purposefully down the track toward the outskirts of town. Ethan kept him in sight, knowing there was nothing out that way but rough mountain country and waiting for the woman to do something.

She continued to harass the freight handlers.

Ten yards. Thirty. Was anyone watching the old fellow?

Hell. With a sigh, he rose from the bench and walked toward the woman. On the way, he stopped beside the dancing horse. Grabbing the lead just under the halter, he gave it a yank to get the animal's attention then looked him hard in the eye. "Stand," he said with calm authority.

The horse blinked at him, nostrils flared. After a brief staring match, the animal slowly let his head drop enough to ease the pull on the halter. And stood.

Ethan gave his neck a friendly pat and turned to the surprised Negro. "And your name would be . . . ?"

"Curtis. How'd you do that?"

"Hold him closer to the halter ring, Curtis." He had to raise his voice to be heard over the barking of the dog. "And stand by his head where he can see you. That way he'll know where you are and will be easier to control. And talk quietly to him. He's just afraid."

"Me, too," the old man muttered, but did as instructed.

Stepping around the African woman—Winnie—who looked to be near in age to Curtis—spouses, perhaps?—Ethan approached the circus ringleader.

She was surprisingly small to be generating such a fuss, yet was able to convince two hulking railroad workers to do her biding. Ethan realized why when he stopped beside her. Even with that furrow between her dark brown brows, she was uncommonly pretty . . . in a fine-boned, delicate, citified sort of way. Hardly the type of woman he normally found attractive.

"Would you like some help, ma'am?" he asked.

She gave him a distracted look. "What?"

Remarkable eyes, even with the squint. A greenish hazel that he suspected would look greener if she wore something other than that drab gray dress that did little to set off her gold-streaked hair. Although why he would notice such things was beyond him. He was more partial to breasts, himself. And she had a nice pair of those, too, he was pleased to note.

She noted him noting and narrowed her eyes even more.

Removing his Stetson, he gave a slight bow. "May I help you?"

"With what?"

He tipped his head toward the old man scurrying along the tracks. "Him?"

"Oh, Lord!" Almost crushing his hat, she shoved the yapper against his chest and she raced off, calling "Father," in a high, panicky voice.

Ethan looked down at the dog in his arms, which had thankfully paused for breath, realized by the cloudy eyes it was blind, and thrust it toward the Negro woman.

She backed off, pink palms upraised. "Not me, suh. I'd as soon throw it under the train, and that would upset Miss Audra, sure enough."

"Do you want the buggy unloaded, or not?"

She thought about it, then reluctantly took the dog.

By the time "Miss Audra" returned, leading the mumbling old man by the hand, the buggy was on solid ground, Ethan had almost finished harnessing the bay into the traces, and Curtis was tying valises and boxes to the back of the buggy under the barked supervision of both the badger-dog and the Negro woman.

A forceful pair, Winnie and Miss Audra.

Waving Ethan aside when he stepped forward to help, Miss Audra opened the door of the buggy and dropped down the mounting step. "There you are, Father," she said in a voice much gentler than the one she'd used on the freight handlers or Ethan.

The old man frowned at Ethan. "Come for the transcripts, have you, Mitchell? They're not yet ready. The girl has been dreadfully slow this time. You must talk to her, Mary," he added to the woman waiting for him to board.

Mary? Ethan thought her name was Audra.

"I will, Father. In you go."

Once she got him settled with a lap robe over his legs, she took the squirming dog from Winnie and set it in the old man's arms like she was presenting a precious newborn. "And here's Cleo."

The old man grinned. The dog shut up. And the show was over.

If Ethan had expected a "thank you," he didn't get it. But feeling ornery, he couldn't let the oversight pass unnoticed. "You're certainly welcome, Miss Audra. Or is it Mary?"

"Mary was my mother's name." She turned to squint up at him. "How do you know me, sir? Have we met?"

"Alas, no. And I admire your ability to disregard those pesky social courtesies and accept my help anyway. If you have no further use of me . . . ?"

She blinked, obviously befuddled. Confusion must run in the family.

"Then I bid you good day." Hiding a smile, he tipped the Stetson and walked back to the stock car. Renny had already been unloaded. As he tossed a coin to the hostler, he saw the buggy disappearing down the road at a rapid clip. Fleeing, would be more accurate. Much too fast in a lightweight buggy on a rocky country road. He could guess who was driving.

With a mental shrug, he put the woman and her amusing antics out of his mind and quickly saddled the big buckskin, securing his saddlebags behind the cantle with the fiddle case on top.

If he left now, he could make it to Heartbreak Creek in time for dinner. His meeting with Tait Rylander and his wife—the two principals in charge of the Pueblo Pacific bridge line through

Heartbreak Creek Canyon—wasn't until morning. Apparently there were issues with both the right-of-ways and the sluice bringing water from deeper in the canyon. The railroad had sent Ethan in to identify the problems, eliminate them, and get the surveyors back to work so the graders could get started.

He figured it was a two-week job.

A half hour later, he was on his way, Renny stepping out at a fast gait, obviously as happy as Ethan to be off the train. It was a beautiful afternoon with the clarity that only came in early spring before summer's dust hazed the sky. The mountains still wore caps of white, and the breeze was cool and heavy with the scent of wet earth and new grass. The freshness of it raised Ethan's spirits and helped dispel the melancholy that always plagued him after a restless, dream-filled night.

He had ridden no more than an hour when he saw a familiar black buggy stopped in the road ahead, the back tilted at an odd angle. As he drew nearer, he saw Miss Audra seated on the mounting step beside the open door, shoulders slumped, head drooping in her hands. A sad picture, indeed. The others were some distance away, enjoying a rest under a long-limbed fir. Even from thirty yards, he could clearly hear the badger barking.

"If it isn't Miss Audra," he called cheerily as he reined in beside the disabled buggy.

Dropping her hands, she squinted up at him through red-rimmed eyes.

She must require spectacles, he decided. No one would wear that expression without good reason.

"It's you," she said in a tone as welcoming as a stepmother's kiss.

For some perverse reason, he found that amusing. "It is. I see you've broken a wheel. How unfortunate."

She stiffened. "You find that amusing?"

"Not at all."

"Then why are you grinning?"

"Actually, I was trying for a smirk."

She gave a snort that ended in a sniffle. Then another. Horrified she was about to cry, Ethan softened his tone. "May I offer assistance? Again."

Shoving back a wad of hair that had slipped from her matronly topknot, she regarded him through eyes that were suspiciously wet. "Do you have a gun?"

Surprised, he nodded. "I do."

"Then shoot me, please. I have reached my limit. Not in the head or face, mind you. I wouldn't want to look a mess in the undertaker's picture. Here in the heart will be fine." She placed a hand over the bosom he'd so admired.

Leaning forward, he crossed his arms over the saddle horn. "Having a bad day, are we, Miss Audra?"

Her top lip curled in a sneer, marring an otherwise lovely mouth. "Armed *and* astute. A potent combination."

Potent? How gratifying that she had noticed.

"Well, get on with it." Closing her eyes, she hiked her chin in a martyr's pose. "I await your pleasure."

Even better. Several pleasurable scenarios came to mind, but he knew better than to voice them. "And the others? Shall I shoot them, too? I could start with the dog, if you'd like."

She actually seemed to consider it.

"Or I could simply replace the broken wheel."

Her eyes flew open. "You can do that?"

"I can. Assuming that's a spare wheel I see strapped to the bottom of the buggy and you don't mind untying the luggage on the back."

Hopping to her feet, she bent over to peer under the vehicle, this time hiking her skirts high enough to reveal trim ankles and rounded calves. "Good heavens! I had no idea that was under there."

"Nor I," he murmured, musing on what other delights might be hidden beneath that drab gray skirt.

"Excellent." She straightened, shoved the hair back again, and gave him a smile that lit up her face in an unexpectedly alluring way. "What can I do to help?"

Very little, it turned out, but that was due more to a lack of strength than a lack of enthusiasm. If the woman had been as strong physically as her personality was forceful, she could have held up the wagon with one hand while he replaced the wheel.

Instead, he used the biggest boulder he could carry, a sturdy three-foot log to brace under the axle, and a long, stout pole to lever the buggy off the ground—luckily Curtis had packed an axe. Once the buggy was unloaded and the wheels chalked, Ethan positioned the rock a foot behind the rear panel, slipped two feet of the long pole beneath the undercarriage and pushed down with all his strength on the part extending past the rock.

The buggy rose. Curtis slipped the brace under the axle, and from then on, it was simply a matter of exchanging the broken wheel for the spare. Thankfully the women hovered close by, poised to offer helpful tips in case he somehow lost the ability to reason or forgot what he was doing. God bless them.

Soon—even with their help—the new wheel was in place. While Winnie supervised Curtis in the reloading of the luggage, Ethan lashed the broken wheel beneath the buggy then rose, almost bumping into Miss Audra, who had bent down beside him to inspect his knots.

"You're sure it's tight enough?"

Ethan's gaze drifted down her bowed back to the round, pear-shaped bottom pointed his way. "I have no doubt of it."

"Excellent." She straightened. "For the second time, I owe you my thanks, Mr. . . ."

"Ethan Hardesty." He touched the brim of his hat. "And you're quite welcome, Miss Audra. Both times."

"Pearsall. My proper name is—oh, dear!"

Turning to see what had captured her attention, he saw her father dunking the dog in a puddle of stagnant water beside the road. Ethan refrained from applauding.

"Father, we're ready to go now," she called, rushing toward him.

Propping a hip against the rear wheel, Ethan crossed his arms over his chest and watched her tuck the dripping pooch under her arm then gently steer her father toward the coach. He admired her patience. The woman truly did have her hands full with this scatterbrained bunch, yet she hadn't once lost her composure . . . except with him, of course, but since that had been his intent, he didn't hold it against her.

"Where are you headed, Miss Pearsall?" he asked once she'd loaded her father into the buggy and placed the dog, wrapped in a robe, in his arms. He caught a whiff of swamp and was thankful to be riding outside.

"Not far." Backing out, she blew that errant lock of brownish gold hair out of her eyes and waved the two Africans to their places—Winnie in back with the old man, Curtis up front on the far side of the driver's box. "A town called Heartbreak Creek."

"Oh? What a coincidence."

"You're going there, too?" Surprised, she turned to face him.

He almost choked.

She was wet. From collar to waist. And cold, judging by the puckered nubs straining against the damp fabric that clung to every rounded curve.

He owed the dog an apology.

"I am," he said, tearing his gaze away before she caught him again.

"Excellent. Now we can travel together."

Not excellent. He didn't want to have to rescue her at every turn. Or feel responsible for her. Or wonder what catastrophe might befall her next. He didn't need a woman like Miss Audra Pearsall complicating his life.

But she was a beautiful woman.

And two years was a long time.

And he was weary of the night terrors, and awakening to the sound of breaking glass, and reaching for his gun to stop the screams echoing through his mind. It would be nice to feel something other than self-loathing for a change, to be near a woman and not hear those screams in his head.

Just for a while.

So he said nothing. Swinging up on Renny, he waved the woman to follow, and headed down the road to Heartbreak Creek, feeling better than he had since the walls at Rincon Point had shattered around him.